Friday Night Mistress

Jordan La............................nate takeover.

"Does it bother you," he asked roughly, "this secret of ours? This thing between us?"

Jordan was past reason. She wanted much more of "this thing" between them and she wanted it now.

With an effort almost too much to bear, she forced her mouth to open, to speak. "I know the score, Nick," she told him tightly. "I'm playing the game."

Sex.

Simple. Sensational. Secret.

THE ILLEGITIMATE KING

KING

BY

OLIVIA GATES

FRIDAY NIGHT

MISTRESS

BY

JAN COLLEY

🌹™ MILLS & BOON®

® and ™ are trademarks owned and used by the trademark owner and/or its licensee. Trademarks marked with ® are registered with the United Kingdom Patent Office and/or the Office for Harmonisation in the Internal Market and in other countries.

First published in Great Britain 2010
Harlequin Mills & Boon Limited,
Eton House, 18-24 Paradise Road, Richmond, Surrey TW9 1SR

The publisher acknowledges the copyright holders of the individual works as follows:

The Illegitimate King © Olivia Gates 2009
Friday Night Mistress © Jan Colley 2009

ISBN: 978 0 263 88171 4

51-0610

Harlequin Mills & Boon policy is to use papers that are natural, renewable and recyclable products and made from wood grown in sustainable forests. The logging and manufacturing processes conform to the legal environmental regulations of the country of origin.

Printed and bound in Spain
by Litografia Rosés S.A., Barcelona

THE ILLEGITIMATE KING

BY
OLIVIA GATES

Dear Reader,

As I wrote the last words in *The Illegitimate King*, the book that wraps up THE CASTALDINI CROWN trilogy, I found myself sighing in pleasure and regret. To have come to the satisfying end of a family saga that has been all I thought about for five months made me feel at once elated and wistful. I've fallen in love with each of my magnificent heroes. It was as wonderful to have known them as it was hard to leave them behind.

Then I remembered that I can always open the books and revisit them and that I can and will create more one-woman men who are everything a woman might dream of. Men who are powerful in character and passion as well as in sensitivity, who are towers of strength and tenderness at once.

The Illegitimate King's hero, Ferruccio Selvaggio, aka the Savage Iron Man, is such a man, but he surprised even me as I wrote his story. He was bent on revenge, but the side of him that longed for love and family overwhelmed his harsh intentions at every turn. I loved him that tiny bit more for having triumphed over unimaginable horrors and hardships to become the incredible man who would become Castaldini's king and the one man his heroine, Clarissa, could love.

I hope that reading their story will give you as much pleasure as writing it gave me.

I would love to hear from you at oliviagates@gmail.com. You can also visit me on the web at www.oliviagates.com.

Thank you for reading.

Olivia Gates

Olivia Gates has always pursued creative passions – painting, singing and many handicrafts. She still does, but only one of her passions grew gratifying enough, consuming enough, to become an ongoing career: writing.

She is most fulfilled when she is creating worlds and conflicts for her characters, then exploring and untangling them bit by bit, sharing her protagonists' every heart-wrenching heartache and hope, their every heart-pounding doubt and trial, until she leads them to an indisputably earned and gloriously satisfying happy ending.

When she's not writing, she is a doctor, a wife to her own alpha male and a mother to one brilliant girl and one demanding angora cat. Visit Olivia at www.oliviagates. com.

At the end of this trilogy, I again dedicate it to the two ladies who made it possible for me to write it.

My phenomenal editor, Natashya Wilson.

And Melissa Jeglinski, a wonderful lady and Desire's former senior editor.

Thanks, ladies. It's been a fantastic ride.

Prologue

Six years ago

"So gods *do* walk the earth!"

Clarissa D'Agostino frowned at her friend's breathless exclamation as she dabbed at the stain on the décolleté of her lavender chiffon gown.

She cursed herself for biting into that overripe plum. Way to go, making a fool of herself when she was supposed to be Castaldini's princess, all grown up and fit for court appearances at last. It seemed that four years in the States and graduating at the top of her class from Harvard Business School hadn't done a thing to improve her ability to handle public appearances.

She grimaced at the visible stain. "What are you going on about?"

"I'm all about that…*god* over there!"

Clarissa swung around. Not to search out the proclaimed deity, but to check her best friend for signs of intoxication.

She found Luci fanning herself. "And I thought his profile was hard-hitting. His full-frontal assault is devastating."

Clarissa gaped at her. Luciana Montgomery, whose feminist outlook and American side dominated her Castaldinian roots, was the last woman she knew who'd drool over a man. She'd never seen Luci react like this to anyone—not in the States, where they'd gone to college together and where hunks had regularly pursued the vivacious redhead, and not in Castaldini, which was crawling with gorgeous men. The only men Luci had ever even said were drool-worthy were Clarissa's brothers and a few of her cousins. And she hadn't reacted this way to any of them. It was weird, seeing her tongue almost lolling out.

The weirdness took a turn into the absurd when Luci grabbed her arm and squeaked in excitement, "He's looking our way!"

"I could have sworn you had only one glass of champagne, Luci." Clarissa turned to investigate the phenomenon who had made the most poised twenty-two-year-old woman she knew flutter like a giddy schoolgirl. "I'll have to see if someone's spiking the…"

The words backed up in her throat.

There were so many men in the ballroom whom Clarissa didn't recognize. She'd been away for so long and had never been active in court life, and she was the one member of the king's family who everyone almost forgot existed, just the way she wanted them to. But there could be only one man who warranted Luci's overreaction.

There was only one man who Clarissa could see.

He wasn't a god. He surpassed all depictions of gods she'd ever seen, with all the perfections worshippers' imaginations had lavished on them. No one could have imagined *him*. She certainly hadn't. She could barely believe he was real.

He was. And he *was* looking their way. *Her* way.

Her heart plunged into the pit of her stomach. Time ceased. Reality fell away. Existence converged onto one thing. His eyes. Stormy skies illuminated by lightning, all their focus and power targeting her. But what started tremors arcing through her was what she saw in them; a reflection of her own state, stunned free fall into the awareness that crackled between them.

Suddenly he blinked, turned his face away. Through the fugue encompassing her, she realized why he had severed their connection. Her father.

King Benedetto had appeared beside the man, a wide smile—one she couldn't remember seeing since she was a small child—spreading across his lips.

The man gazed at her father as if he didn't recognize him. Her father spoke, the man listened. She found herself moving, unaware of anything or anyone, just needing to be closer, to find out what had just happened. Suddenly the man turned back, snared her again in the bull's eye of his focus.

She stopped. Moving. Breathing. Her heart quivered inside her to a standstill. Shock splashed through her like ice water.

It was unmistakable, what she saw in his eyes now. Coldness. Hostility. Which meant one thing. She'd been wrong. It hadn't been a blast of attraction she'd seen in his eyes, felt radiating from him. That had all been on her side.

Before she could recoil from the rush of mortification and letdown, he turned and walked away from her father.

She stood there, feeling as if a knife had been thrust between her ribs, heard Luci's voice as if it were seeping in from another realm.

"Lord, what was *that?*"

Clarissa couldn't produce a thought, let alone an answer.

"*That* was the Savage Iron Man."

Clarissa swung around unsteadily toward the purring voice. Stella. She'd been making Clarissa's skin crawl ever since they were children. Thankfully, they were only third cousins, so she'd seen as little of Stella as possible. She would have liked to see far less. None.

Stella's words made as much sense now.

It was Luci who summed up Clarissa's thoughts: "Huh?"

"Ferruccio Selvaggio, shipping magnate extraordinaire, who, at thirty-two, is one of the richest men in the world. He's like a wrecking ball, rising so high so young, over the smashed remains of anyone who's dared stand in his way. Hence the nickname, which also happens to be the meaning of his aptly given names."

"That's according to you, of course." Luci smirked.

"That's according to common knowledge. He's a terror. But judging by our king's enthusiasm, it seems he's willing to overlook that fact—along with the other fact, that Ferruccio is a bastard, literally—if he'll only invest heavily enough in Castaldini."

"My, Stella, I hope nobody thinks you're the example of what royal blood does for a person," Luci said. "It would be so unfair if you gave us all a reputation for being stuck-up bitches."

Stella pouted. The perfect beauty was always putting on an act, oozing class and subtle sexuality, showing her true self only to other women, knowing men would think them jealous harpies if they criticized her. "Being a mongrel yourself, Luciana, you don't have to worry about that. But then, that makes you the perfect merchandise he's here to shop for. You have enough diluted blue blood that you might fit the bill in his bid to buy legitimacy. With what he has to offer in return, I say go for it."

As Luci continued to argue with Stella, Clarissa turned and walked away. Stella's vile words were like acid poured over the rawness of that incendiary moment. It didn't matter that it had all been in her mind. The damage was real.

She'd moved a good way through the crowd when something made her turn around.

He was heading toward where she'd been standing. Coming back for her? Had she been wrong about that second look? She began walking back.

Her feet gathered momentum as he zeroed in on Luciana and Stella. Would he ask them about her?

Then she was close enough to see the glazed look entering the women's eyes at being under his immediate influence, to hear the rumble of his deep voice, the predatory flirtation in it.

Something shriveled inside her, like a paper curling up as flames ate it to ashes. Her feet changed course again, quickened, until she was almost running as she exited the ballroom to the verandah. She breathed hard, snatching air into constricted lungs.

Stop it. You fool.

She'd imagined it all. The attraction *and* the antipathy. He'd been looking at Luciana all along. Or perhaps he looked at every woman the way she'd thought he'd looked at her.

Get ahold of yourself.

She slipped into the shadows, trying to do just that, to suppress tears she'd long thought had run dry.

She was a lousy excuse for a princess, but her father had asked her to take an active role in the court and in the kingdom, at his side, in her mother's place. It had been the first thing he'd asked of her in…ever. She was damned if she'd run out on him. Again.

She straightened her aching back, started to move—and walked into a wall of hot, hard muscle and maleness. *Him.*

She stumbled back, started to apologize, to sidestep him, air shearing into her lungs, chaos invading her synapses.

He blocked her escape route. He didn't touch her—he didn't need to. His very presence reached out and snared her in an inescapable embrace. And that was before her gaze streaked up to his, to find him looking down at her with that trance-inducing intensity.

The effect was the same as it had been during that first flash flood of recognition.

Her consciousness wavered. The world swirled around her as his eyes ate her up. Then his lips moved and she heard his voice, unobscured by the din of background chatter and music. Rich and fathomless, sweeping over her like a binding spell.

"I'm leaving. And you're not enjoying this reception any more than I am. Come with me."

She stared up at him. No one should be endowed with all

that. He was too…everything. He towered about ten inches above her five foot eight, his physique that of an Olympian, his face that of an avenging angel, planes and hollows and slashes of power and perfection, a being of bronze and gold and steel, who took her breath away and held it just out of reach.

Dangerous. And if he could do this to her with a look, he was beyond that. Lethal. But that wasn't just a look in his eyes. That was…unadulterated coveting. Pure possession.

It was what she'd imagined she'd seen before. But she hadn't imagined the cold way he'd looked at her afterward, or the way he'd gone straight to the other women who'd caught his eye.

What was he playing at? He must expect all women to lose their mental faculties at the sight of him, and fall to their knees at his approach. And after he'd conquered Luci and that scorpion Stella—who couldn't have been immune to him—he'd come after her. Why?

He took a tight step closer, practically vibrating with something vast and overwhelming. She could have sworn it was hunger, barely checked. And it would be unleashed at the slightest provocation—a gasp, a tremor.

She was incapable of any physical reaction, caught in stasis, waiting for his next words to reanimate her.

Suddenly, the spectacular wings of his eyebrows drew together. "You're uncertain whether you can trust me? Don't you know that you can?"

He was talking as if they knew each other. She would have found it the most natural thing in the world if this encounter had taken place immediately after that first glance. She had felt as if she'd known him, then.

When she remained staring up at him, mute, he exhaled. "I thought we didn't need formalities, that we could revel in this…" he made an eloquent gesture, from his heart to hers "…connection, without outside interference. Maybe I'm asking too much." He exhaled again. "Let's go inside. We'll find your father on the way out. He can vouch for me."

He knew who she was.

That was why he was out here rather than with the women who'd interested him for real. He wasn't here for her. He was here for Princess Clarissa D'Agostino, the king's daughter. Just like every other man who'd ever found out she was royalty.

Stella had said he wanted to add some blue-blooded legitimacy to his image. She might or might not be right. But Clarissa knew one thing. He didn't want *her*. And why should he?

Nobody had ever wanted her.

The hurt and humiliation finally forced an answer from her spastic lips. "That won't be necessary, *Signore* Selvaggio."

The heat and assurance in his gaze wavered. "You know me?"

"I know *of* you. Ferruccio Selvaggio, shipping magnate and potential investor in Castaldini."

His lips tugged, not into a smile, tension entering his gaze. "Right now I'm only the man who wants the pleasure of your company for the rest of the evening. Join me for dinner."

Not a request. A demand. One she would have stumbled over herself to accept if he hadn't bypassed her for her glamorous friend and relative, only to pursue her when he realized she better served whatever purpose he had in mind.

She tilted her face, as princesses were supposed to do to end unsavory situations, striving to project detached authority and nonnegotiable dismissal, for the first time managing to implement the teachings of two dozen etiquette instructors who'd begged to be relieved of the impossible duty of teaching her to act her part. "Thank you for the invitation, *Signore* Selvaggio. But my…situation doesn't allow me to…be with you. I'm sure you'll find someone else who can."

His whole body tensed and his nostrils flared as if he had braced himself against the force of a resounding slap. He understood. She wasn't talking about her situation tonight. She was giving him a taste of his own medicine. If he wanted her for who she was in society, she was letting him know she *didn't* want him for the same reason.

Heat seeped from his eyes, something almost scary flooding to fill the vacuum it left behind.

He finally shrugged. "Pity. But there may come a time when your…*situation* might not leave you any option but to…be with me." With a nod of his awesome head, he pivoted, took a couple of relaxed steps away before he tossed a glance over his daunting shoulder. Then he murmured softly, menacingly, "Until then."

One

The present

Finally.

The word reverberated in Ferruccio Selvaggio's head, spread in his blood along with the thick, bitter ooze of grim satisfaction.

He'd finally gotten Clarissa D'Agostino where he wanted her.

A supplicant coming to beg his favor. In—he flicked a glance at his Rolex—twenty minutes' time.

She couldn't be here soon enough. He'd been waiting too long for this moment. Six years. That was how long she'd evaded him. Snubbed him. The princess who thought his hard-won wealth and power not enough to raise him to the status of the men she deigned to mix with, men born with the right lineage. The blue blood who thought a bastard, no matter how rich and influential, not worthy of civility.

But despite all her haughty disdain, he had Princess High-and-Mighty coming to do his bidding. And if everything went according to plan—and he now possessed all the leverage to make sure it did—he'd have her doing his bidding far longer and in far more ways than she thought.

He'd have her, period.

He'd been fantasizing about having her ever since that first night he'd seen her. That first glance.

It had been his first time in the royal court. He'd been uncertain of his reception, of his reaction to being there. Most of the people there had been D'Agostinos. His so-called family.

But he didn't share their name. His parents hadn't had him the acceptable way, hadn't given the name to him. Others had given him the surname he used now. He'd been called by it so many times, it had stuck. So he'd made it legal.

The evidence that he was a D'Agostino had been presented to him long ago. At the time, he'd demanded public recognition. His parents had been willing to give him anything but that. He'd told them what to do with their love and offers of support. He'd survived so far without them. He'd make it on his own, make it to the top, the same way.

Finally he'd reached a height of success from which he thought it time to satisfy his curiosity. He wanted to see what it was like, the place that should have been his home. What they were like, the people who should have been his family. If he'd been missing anything. If he could make up for it if he had been; if he could grow the roots he'd never had.

He'd entered the king's court unannounced. By then, he'd had enough clout that he could walk in anywhere in the world and be welcomed. And the court had welcomed him. To this day, he remembered none of those who'd done so. Besides his meeting with the king, he remembered nothing before and nothing after he'd seen *her* across the teeming space.

She'd been wiping at something on the neckline of that ethereal violet dress. In profile, her face had been a study of concentration and consternation. He'd felt everything inside him prime, rev into awareness.

Stunned, not knowing what that upsurge meant, he'd needed to look her in the face, in the eyes. Then she'd turned, fulfilled his need. And something he'd always scoffed at had ripped through him. A bolt of attraction. More, of recognition. Of the one woman who translated his every fantasy into glorious reality.

Physically, she'd been the amalgam of all the endowments he'd never thought could be gathered in one being. Hair the color of Castaldini's beaches, streaked with rays of its sun, permeated by tones of the rich soil of its mountains. A body at once willowy and womanly, unconscious femininity screaming in its every line and curve. A face that embodied all his tastes and demands.

But it had been her eyes—which really had turned out to be violet, when he thought he'd imagined the color from that distance—and what he'd seen in them, that had snared him.

To think he'd thought they'd shown a reflection of his awareness, his discovery. He thought he'd seen more, too, a quality that had snapped the trap shut: Vulnerability.

Right. Clarissa D'Agostino was as vulnerable as an iceberg to the Titanic.

He still seethed to remember how he'd sought her, bared his need to have more of her, revealed his moronic belief in the existence of a connection between them that had transcended time and logic. He still burned at the memory of the moment he'd gotten what he deserved for such idiocy, when she'd stared at him as if he'd lost his mind, then told him to go find someone in a lesser…situation—who'd deem him good enough to…be with.

She'd told him that dozens of times since then. With every rejection of the invitations he'd never ceased to issue. Making them had become the masochistic lash he used every time he found his will to go on flagging, using the anger and frustration to keep on rising, keep on acquiring everything in his path. As he couldn't acquire her.

But now he finally would. One way or another.

He'd teach her a lesson. Many lessons. He'd take her down a few dozen pegs, and he'd revel in every one.

He braced his arms against the balustrade, cast his gaze into the distance. The sun's gold was starting to deepen as the star quickened its descent toward the endless expanse of liquid turquoise and emerald that was the southern Castaldinian Sea.

Another rush of bitter anticipation tumbled and sprayed through his system like the waves did on the shore. He wasn't here only for the spectacular vista the tower of his mansion afforded him. This was also the best vantage point from which to view the winding road over which she'd be brought to him….

Everything seemed to dim as the last three words replayed in his mind like a distorted old recording.

Brought to him. Not coming to him of her free will, unable to wait to see him, as she had in too many dreams to count.

What would he have felt if she'd been rushing here with hunger in her eyes, with longing on her lips?

If only…

His lips compressed as he tore his eyes away from the road and blindly roamed the view he could no longer see.

No. No *if onlys*. She'd made her choice that first night. Had reinforced it countless times throughout six interminable years.

Even if she changed her mind now, for whatever reason, it would be too late. Now only one thing mattered. That she had no choice. That there was no way she could reject him again. And he intended to savor every second of her downfall, starting—he snapped another look at his Rolex—ten minutes from now.

He pushed away from the balustrade, swung around.

Time to put the finishing touches to his plan.

"Until then."

The words, spoken like a pledge, a prophecy, in the lethal tone of a dangerous man, reverberated inside Clarissa's head.

They had done so for six years now.

Twenty-four hours ago, she'd found out that "then" had arrived.

Ferruccio Selvaggio had her cornered.

She exhaled and gazed through sunglasses and rioting hair

at the vista rushing by as the limo zoomed over the road that snaked parallel to the shore.

She knew the sun was turning flame orange and speeding on an intercept course with the sea, that the horizon would be changing into a thousand hues and the waters would be starting their transformation from aquamarine to royal blue.

She saw none of it. Her vision was turned inward, where there was nothing but gray chaos.

Calm down. Breathe.

She carefully drew in a stream of the fresh sea air that buffeted her face. Then again. And again.

And nothing. Taking one breath at a time wouldn't restore any measure of calm. It hadn't since yesterday. Since her father had made her cut short her first official mission to the States to give her the news. The shock of her life.

She thought she'd known the limit of her father's desperation to find himself a crown prince after his stroke. He'd proven her wrong.

The crown of Castaldini was by law not passed from father to son, but rather earned by merit. With the approval of the royal council, the current king would choose his successor from the royal D'Agonstino family—a man of impeccable reputation, sturdy health and no vices, solid lineage, a leader with character and charisma, and above all, a self-made success of the highest order.

She'd been the only one who hadn't been stunned when he'd announced his first candidate. Leandro, the prince whom eight years ago her father had declared renegade, stripped of his nationality and exiled. She'd thought Leandro the wisest choice of any candidate for the crown. It had been time to forget grievances and think of Castaldini's best interests. But when her father had wrestled the Council into making the offer, Leandro had done the unthinkable. He'd turned the power and responsibility down.

And her father had dropped another bomb. He had another

even more impossible candidate. Her oldest brother, Durante. And in an undreamed of precedent in Castaldinian history, he'd gotten the Council to amend the most fundamental part of the kingdom's constitution to make his son eligible for the crown.

She'd never been so excited. She'd always thought how unfairly absolute the laws of succession were, that while they protected Castaldini from unsuitable heirs, in Durante's case they were depriving it from having its best king ever. But the Council had voted, and the impossible had become possible.

Then Durante had come back with his bride-to-be, and Clarissa had even dared to hope that he and her father would work out their rift. Everything had looked like it would have a perfect happy ending for her family and for Castaldini.

Again the impossible had happened. They *had* sorted out their rift, but Durante had turned down the succession.

She'd tried to speak to him, but he hadn't been available for discussion as he'd prepared for his wedding and disappeared with his bride on an extended honeymoon. Clarissa had gone to the States, her father assuring her that he was working on securing the next candidate, the one he believed most suited to the job despite there being an even more insurmountable barrier to overcome to make the Council agree.

She hadn't been able to imagine who could possibly be better than Leandro or Durante. Then the king made her cut her mission short to drop the biggest bomb of all.

He'd gotten the Council to make an even more incredible amendment, allowing the king to extend another offer of the crown of Castaldini.

To Ferruccio Selvaggio.

She still didn't know how she hadn't collapsed in a heap of shock and confusion upon hearing that.

From what she'd heard in the media about Ferruccio, he was a man with no origins. All that was known about his parentage was that he'd been given up for adoption in Napoli when he was born.

But he'd never been adopted. By the time he was a difficult

six-year-old, he'd been placed in a foster home, the first of a dozen, until he ran away from the last one at age thirteen. He'd chosen to live the harshest of lives on the streets of Italian coastal cities and in Sicily and Sardinia rather than return to the system. Over the next two decades, he educated himself extensively and worked his way up to the highest echelons imaginable.

When his status had solidified, he'd come to Castaldini. Since then, he'd been a recurring figure in her father's court, and a constant one in her dreams and nightmares. Worse, his businesses in the kingdom now comprised almost one quarter of the national income.

When she'd told her father that that didn't make him king material, that Castaldini couldn't just waive the laws that had made it unique in the world for eight hundred years to have a king who only answered the financial criterion of the ancient laws of succession who wasn't a D'Agostino or even a Castaldinian, her father had dropped the biggest bomb yet.

Ferruccio *was* a D'Agostino.

The king had been entrusted with this fact before Ferruccio had first come to Castaldini. He'd told a select few, among them Durante and Paolo, her brothers; but knowing the delicate dynamics involved, he'd chosen not to divulge Ferruccio's parents' names so that the house he belonged to wouldn't suffer the repercussions of exhuming buried secrets.

After his stroke, he'd given the Council his word as proof of the fact. They'd argued that illegitimacy was by far the worst breach of the ancient laws that he'd asked them to commit in his quest to find the next king. They couldn't accept a bastard contender for the crown. But the king had made a solid case for Ferruccio otherwise.

Ferruccio was everything the king must be, he said, even more so than his first two choices. He was even more radically self-made, as his rise had been against what should have been insurmountable odds. He was a leader by nature, his shipping empire the largest in the world and his political powers far-reaching. At last the Council succumbed and made the offer.

Contrary to Durante and Leandro, Ferruccio had been instantly amenable to discussing that offer. But he'd refused to give a word of either consent or refusal. Before he would give either, he had terms to negotiate.

He would negotiate with only one Council member. Her.

Clarissa closed her eyes again on another eruption of fury. How *dare* that arrogant jerk!

Castaldini was not only acknowledging him, it was offering him the incalculable honor and privilege of becoming its future king, and he had *terms?* What more did he want? A binding contract adding the island to his real estate acquisitions?

Not that that was too far-fetched. Among her shocking discoveries, she found out that he'd long ago purchased a huge chunk of Castaldinian soil. Three hundred square miles of the six thousand that made up the island. It didn't matter that this was the south eastern area that was said to be unreclaimable for being too mountainous, it was still five percent of the whole damn kingdom.

And why negotiate with her? She was the most junior Council member. Wasn't really even that, yet. She'd been made a member the day before she embarked on her trip to the States, a training mission that had been cut short, too.

But she knew why.

Now that Ferruccio was in a position of unprecedented power, he wanted to lord it over the D'Agostinos, the royal family, maybe over the whole nation he felt had spurned him. He wanted to lord it over her, too, the only female, she believed, who hadn't fallen flat on her face at his approach, quaked at his every glance, melted when he beckoned.

Well, she had… But *he* didn't know that. She hadn't let him know, and she thanked God for that daily. She hated to think what would have happened if she hadn't been forewarned of his true nature and intentions and had succumbed to the dictates of her desires that first time he'd expressed interest.

His ruthless reputation proclaimed him to be an overendowed, overprivileged, overeverything boor who believed people's—especially women's—only use was to throw themselves at his feet, follow his orders and satisfy his appetites before being discarded. He'd lost no sleep over her rejection, as evidenced by the constant stream of interchangeable hotties who'd been flitting in and out of his bed ever since.

Not that he'd taken no for answer. Her dismissal seemed to have roused the conqueror in him, and he'd continued to approach her despite her consistent refusals.

After she dared to decline his first invitation, she'd seen him everywhere she went during the week he spent on Castaldini. She hadn't been able to breathe until he left. Then he'd come back within a month to issue another invitation and had continued to do so whenever he returned, and even more when he hadn't. He kept asking her to hop over to Milan, Monaco or Madrid, to join him for a meal, Hong Kong or Tokyo or Rio De Janeiro to join him for the weekend, among a party or alone.

She turned him down every time, with one excuse or another, struggling to observe formal politeness and neutrality, since he was such an important man to her father and Castaldini.

But he'd left her that first night with the augury that there would come a time when she'd have no option but to do his bidding.

That time was finally here.

She wondered how he'd justified his demand to her father. He must have said something convincing, or her father wouldn't have been so matter-of-fact about it.

So he'd finally have his laugh. That had to be his objective. If there'd been a shadow of a doubt that he'd been pursuing her to freshen his image with a coat of legitimacy, it had evaporated. He was a D'Agostino, would be proclaimed the future king of Castaldini. There was no higher status or recognition he could aspire to.

The limo slowed down, and with it her streaking thoughts.

That only made her anger gain momentum again. She'd been fuming since he'd sent his aides to summon her. She'd grudgingly let them escort her to his jet. She hadn't found him onboard as she'd expected, had been stunned to find the jet taking off, whisking her away to his private part of the island without so much as an explanation or request for her token agreement.

And here she was. Approaching the only man-made construction and landscaping she'd seen in the last twenty minutes since the jet had landed at what was clearly a private airport.

There were no fences anywhere. The limo passed through a gate made by an opening in a row of towering cypress trees.

As they cruised down the driveway she realized the estate must cover hundreds of acres and the mansion at its middle must be over thirty thousand square feet. It sprawled in many levels, crouching over the highest point in the landscape, surrounded by manicured, mature gardens that on one side gave way to a mile-deep, golden beach, on another to the terrain where the road ended, and on the remaining sides to densely verdant groves ripe with fruit.

It felt like she was forging deeper into a tranquil paradise as they passed acres of oranges and tangerines, the fresh, tangy scent filling her.

The moment they stopped at the beginning of a stone path, she disembarked, more than usual unable to bear the pomp of ceremony.

Her chauffeur hurried to lead her on the path flanked by magnificent palms and a plethora of other Mediterranean flora to the entrance of the mansion. Her eyes wandered over its neo-Gothic stone facade as they neared. It looked as if it had been built centuries ago and transported through time the moment the last touch had been applied. The most characteristic features were the arched motif to all its windows, passageways and doors and the central tower.

She squinted up at the elaborate coat of arms that decorated

the tower's top. She wondered what it was, if it had any signif-
icance, or if it was just something that had appealed to him. It
did bear resemblance to the D'Agostino family's crest. Had he
meant it that way, to express his affiliation, yet not wanted it
to be the same, as he considered himself an outsider?

Her futile conjectures came to an end when the chauffeur
opened the huge, arched antique oak door for her. She
preceded him inside, but rather than following her, he closed
the door behind her. She heard his steps receding quickly. Her
lips tightened.

He'd delivered his master's package and ran away as if he
were being pursued by some malevolent force. It seemed everyone who must populate this place, who took care of all the im-
maculateness she'd seen, had the same orders. She hadn't seen
a soul so far.

She waited for Ferruccio to appear, her heart thudding. She'd
never been totally alone with him. Even that first night when
he'd followed her out to the seclusion of the verandah, masses
of people had been within reach. She made sure he never found
her alone from then on. Here in his domain where he ruled
supreme, she felt cut off from the world. As she was sure he'd
meant her to be. Another wave of resentment crashed over her.

And the worst part? She couldn't act on her antipathy. More
than ever she had to observe the dictates of diplomacy. Her
position on the Council demanded that she strip her demeanor of
any personal reaction, save only what would serve her mission.

But with every second that he didn't appear, he was trans-
forming that task from difficult to impossible.

Her hearing sharpened until every heartbeat was amplified
to thunder in her ears. But she didn't hear approaching footsteps.
There was only the distant drone of the waves and the tranquility
of the internal courtyard in which she stood. It was at least two
thousand square feet, paved in lava stones, lit with the impending sunset's red-gold beams, which filtered from arched and
round windows inset in the walls just below its domed ceiling.

He wasn't coming. Not yet, at least. He must be letting her stew. She exhaled, moved. Might as well take a look around.

She strolled to the end of the courtyard, opened doors, her surprise rising as she found an olive press and wine-processing rooms. She wouldn't have thought he'd go to the trouble of making his own oil and wines.

Mulling over this discovery, she headed to the other side of the courtyard where a corridor of arched columns ended in five stone steps. These led down to an arrangement of expansive sitting rooms with a unique take on Roman décor, in a combination of stucco and stone walls, and strewn with luxurious couches and low tables.

She wondered if he entertained a lot, if one of his many unspecified-destination invitations had been to come join him here. She wondered how she would have reacted to this place if she'd come here ignorant of the truth of his intentions, breathless with anticipation, ready to be swept away by the spell of his domain, to sink into its sensory decadence.

Shaking her head at the pointlessness of her musings, at the stupidity of letting them depress her with what ifs, she crossed into an amazing dining room with a round bronze table and a circular stone platform for chairs, with pillow seating.

This section had a medieval feel, with wall torches and large white cushions abounding in every corner. The floors were layered in old Sicilian pottery tiles, the designs flowing into variations as she progressed through the rest of the ground floor. Huge stone fireplaces sprouted in strategic spots, though subtle evidence of state-of-the-art electric heating was also present.

But what really amazed her was some of the most ingeniously placed and painted trompe-l'oeil she'd ever seen in the walls and ceilings. The murals' optical illusions were almost indistinguishable from the three-dimensional imagery they depicted in depth and realism. They felt like portals into alternate realities.

She stopped in front of one, a tableau of a pigeon on a *fer forgé* windowsill, the glass behind it reflecting it and a distant sea and sky. It looked so real she almost thought the glass was there, did reflect that vista, that she could pet the gleaming feathers of the bird, that it would take flight if she tried.

Ferruccio must have spent untold millions here, from acquiring the land, to equipping it with a private airport and silk-smooth roads, to building that incredible edifice that must be maintained year-round so he'd find it in perfect condition whenever he hopped over, maybe a few days each season.

It was clear to her why he brought her here, and why he hadn't appeared yet. He was flaunting his wealth and power, giving her time for every detail to sink in, make its mark.

He'd picked the last woman on earth to be awed by affluence.

She lived in a palace, and she'd come to associate the grandeur that had surrounded her since birth with the anxiety and despair that had tainted her turbulent childhood. In fact, she'd been almost relieved that the opulence had long faded, with her father barely maintaining the parts of the palace that were national monuments. She sure wasn't about to swoon over pretentious extravagance.

But she grudgingly had to hand it to Ferruccio. This place wasn't pretentious. Or extravagant. It was a masterpiece of architecture and attention to detail but every article and line of design spoke of taste and discernment, everything so simple and unobtrusive it amalgamated into a retreat that promised enjoyment and ease to both mind and body.

Suddenly, ever fiber of her mind and body seemed to become a compass needle, obeying the magnetism that mushroomed at her back. She spun around.

And there he was. The man who'd ruled her every thought since the night she'd laid eyes on him, who'd manipulated her reactions and emotions with the slightest tug here, nudge there, just because he could.

He was standing at the mezzanine level gallery that overlooked the courtyard she'd wandered back to, looking down on her like a Roman deity would on a supplicant coming to beg his mercy.

She thought he'd stand there until she begged for real, for him to just come down and get this over with. Then, without a word, his eyes maintaining their lock on hers, he started moving toward the stone stairs. He descended soundlessly, effortlessly, his long legs turning the movement of taking each wide step into a performance of predatory grace.

Then he was striding toward her, his every step like an expanding shock wave, rattling her bones with reaction.

Was it possible that he had become more vigorous, more virile, that every time she saw him she'd find new things to marvel at, that his effect on her would keep intensifying? She'd thought him magnificent in the formal outfits she always saw him in. But in faded jeans and a partially unbuttoned denim shirt, he was…unfair.

She looked up at him, praying that her inner turmoil wouldn't be translated into an outward manifestation that he could read and exploit.

He stopped a breath away, took the rest of her breath away as his gaze sliced through her like a steel blade. Then his lips spread in the first smile he'd ever trained on her.

"*Principessa* Clarissa," he murmured, low and lethal, "It's such a delight to see your…situation has finally allowed you to…be with me."

Two

He remembered. What she'd said that first night.

Of *course* he did. And he was throwing it back in her face.

She bet the injury to his pride had been the prod that had kept him issuing those invitations, intent on breaking her resistance so that he could avenge what he must have considered a colossal insult—so that he'd keep his perfect score.

And he'd kept it. He'd made her bow to his will. She should have known he would. He'd gotten where he had by being inexorable.

She'd known that, yet thought there'd be no way he could prevail in this. She couldn't have imagined the developments that had led her here.

But even without them, she now believed he would have won eventually. Hadn't she studied his methods at length, both on her own and where they were taught in business school—to demonstrate the ultimate model of long-term, unrelenting, undetectable planning?

Even if she'd been dead wrong about her safety from his

octopoid reach, she'd been spot on about another thing: He *was* gloating. And there was not a thing she could do about it.

Not only that, but she had to be on her best behavior, answer with something unrelated, divert the dialogue away from personal hostilities. In short, she couldn't rise to his bait.

Then she opened her mouth. "What can I say? Life takes such…regrettable twists and turns. And downward spirals."

She almost groaned out loud. What was she *saying?* And in that long-suffering, condescending tone, too? He'd take it as provocation. And he'd be right. It was.

Sure enough, his lips tugged wider, the cool smile heating, the assessing, dispassionate eyes sparking. "Indeed. But I don't know about regrettable. I'm quite the fan of roller coasters."

She should keep her mouth shut, hope he'd take the conversation to safer areas. Even if he didn't and kept poking at her, she should nod and agree. Let him have his victory, let him rub her nose in it, shove its bitterness down her throat. She'd bet that was the "negotiations" he wanted to conduct—an extended session of having her here on his "terms," in a position where she couldn't say no or walk away. She should let him have his fill, get it over with.

Then she opened her mouth, and it seemed someone willful and inflammatory had hijacked her voice, which taunted in its husky tones, "You would be. It has taken a twisting, turning spiral upward with you. Apparently with no drop in sight."

His lips twitched as he pretended to suppress his mockery. "I should hope not. Can you imagine a fall from such heights?"

Dio, he was giving her more rope. She duly took it and secured it around her neck. Then she kicked the bucket. "Oh, how I can."

His mouth lost the fight with the sobriety he'd been forcing on it and spread wide, almost blinding her with a flash of white teeth and brutal charisma. "I see you've given it some serious thought. Seems you enjoyed the detailed visualization of such an event."

She gave up trying to rein in her responses, gave in, admitted her acrimony. "Enjoyment would be a mild term if such an event came to pass. It would be—how did you put it—such a delight."

She heard the fervent venom in her voice, knew he'd heard it, too. Everything stilled as he stared at her, probably unable to believe that anyone dared talk to him that way, princess or not.

Then suddenly, he threw his head back and guffawed.

It was her turn to stare, feeling as if one move now would snap the last tatters of tension holding her up.

She'd never seen him laugh. She hadn't known he was capable of such a human indulgence. She should have known he'd do it like he did everything else. Overridingly.

The sight and sound of his unbearably male amusement hit her between her eyes and forked a downward path through her heart and gut to lodge in her loins. The semiarousal that burned inside her just because he existed roared higher. Along with the blaze of her anger.

He was goading her into even more catastrophic antagonism, into giving him enough incriminating evidence to report back to her father and the Council that their newest addition was a disgrace to the body of power she represented and should be banned from public service forever.

And she didn't give a damn. Not anymore. He'd won. Six years of dangling himself before her, of pricking and prodding her periodically until she was inflamed and perpetually on the verge of an explosion, had taken their toll. She thought she'd been far from the breaking point. She was clearly way past it.

Ferruccio still chuckled, rich, dark reverberations from deep in his chest, annihilating what remained of her restraint. "Wouldn't your conscience prick you if you felt 'such a delight' in my downfall? Now that you know I'm a newfound family member?"

Clarissa rolled her eyes. "Don't remind me."

He hooted on another surge of amusement. "*Si. There* she is. I always knew that beneath all that impassive decorum you had the temper of a lioness. I kept wondering what could rile you enough to get you to unsheath your claws and slash away."

She harumphed, disgusted at her pathetic excuse for self-control, at his ability to peel it away. "Congratulations. You've succeeded in finding out. I hope you're enjoying your success."

"I've never enjoyed anything more. Ever."

"'Never' got the point across. Don't be redundant."

He laughed again. "What a cruel cousin you are."

"A *very* distant cousin."

His eyes seemed to turn to molten steel. "*Si*. In every way."

He was referring to her keeping him at an arm's to a continent's length all those years. As if he'd really cared.

"But you're not distant now, at least not in one sense." He took a step closer, his thigh almost touching her hip. She stumbled backward two steps. He lowered his gaze for a moment—as if debating closing the gap again—before raising his eyes. This time he almost did knock her off her feet. And that was before he added, deeply, smoothly, "See how easy it turned out to be?"

"What did? Being flown in to you like a package? One that you had dropped on your doorstep, to be left untended and un-acknowledged until you stirred from your beauty sleep and puttered down to reluctantly receive it? Yeah, that sure didn't involve any effort on my part."

"You think there was any reluctance involved in my…receiving you? After I've gone to the trouble of insulting all the senior Council members by refusing to negotiate with anyone but you?"

"That's my proof that you welcomed my arrival? Try another one, Signore Selvaggio. The only insult you hurled was at me. The others must be thinking you asked for me because I'm the only Council member who's a young woman, the demographic where you reign supreme, and you think me the pushover who'll promise you rights to every Castaldinian citizen's immortal soul in return for your acceptance."

He snorted. "Now those are rights that might be worth my

while to investigate acquiring." Before she gave in to the urge to smack him, he added, "But if anyone thinks you a pushover, they need to be declared mentally incompetent. Whatever else you think of me, you know my mental faculties aren't among my dodgy areas."

She huffed. "Then they'll think something even worse. That you're exploiting the situation for a personal purpose, which must again have something to do with my being a woman, devaluating my position within the Council even more."

As the word "position" left her mouth, his gaze traveled down her body. Her throat closed at what she saw there, in her own mind's eye. His gaze finally burned a path back up to her eyes, the hewn planes of his face simmering as they had that first night. When she thought she'd imagined it. She wasn't imagining it now.

"Your...*position* is quite safe, I assure you. You should know by now that no matter what the textbooks they stuffed your mind with in business school said, in the real world, the personal factor is what ends up making or breaking business deals. If the Council thinks I'm being personal about you being a woman, they'll think it only natural, even logical. After all, what kind of a businessman would I be if I didn't maximize on my opportunities? If I didn't use my stones to hit as many birds as possible?"

"I should have known you wouldn't even bother to deny it."

He gave her an enigmatic look. "I'm not admitting it, either. So it's all open to interpretation. And here's a third one: That I asked for you because I want to talk to someone close to my own age, rather than with men my absentee father's age or older."

Her chest suddenly felt as if it had caved in. It was that distress again, the one thing that had always stopped her from despising him completely. The knowledge that he'd grown up without a father, or any parents at all.

How many times had she imagined him as a young boy desperately in need of the firm and loving guidance and protection of a father figure, and knowing he'd never have that? How many times had she woken up with tears in her eyes imagining the fear and loneliness he must have suffered until he'd grown that impenetrable shell of capability and ruthlessness that had seen him through his meteoric rise? How hard had she struggled to separate her empathy with the tormented child he'd been from her antipathy toward the man he'd become?

When she made no answer, his lips twisted. "Here's a fourth one. That you're the easiest Council member on my eyes...on all my senses."

She was glad to hook onto something to drag her out of her turmoil. "Now *that* I can buy. Considering the alternatives."

His eyebrows rose in astonishment. She could swear it was genuine. "You think the I'd only pick you when the alternatives are sour-faced older men and their feminine counterparts?"

She bit her tongue to stop herself from blurting out that she didn't think it, she *knew* it. Hadn't he just said what amounted to that? Even if he hadn't, she knew that when there'd been more glamorous options, she hadn't featured as one at all. She'd made sure of that.

Pathetic wretch that she was, she'd sought Luci's version of what had happened that night, hoping she'd misinterpreted what she'd witnessed. Luci had only confirmed her worst suspicions.

Ferruccio had come on hot and heavy, expressed interest in both Luci and Stella. At the same time. Luci had said he'd been so overpowering that she'd found herself wondering whether she *could* share a man, and with the dreaded Stella, of all women, too. She'd said she thought Stella herself had been tempted. That was, for the fleeting moments before he suddenly moved on without a look back.

Throughout the years, Clarissa had seen him acting as if he'd never said a word in private to either woman, let alone propositioned them so outrageously. That had reaffirmed her belief that he went through life making sure all women were his for the taking, but not actually taking up with anyone whose connections might cause him trouble. *Her* only lure had been that she was the king's daughter, and later on that she was the only woman who'd told him no. And if she thought she'd seen something in his eyes every time he caught her gaze—something that told her what he'd do with her if he ever got her alone—she reminded herself of the facts, concluded that she'd been superimposing her fantasies on his expression. As she must be now.

"No more contentiousness, *Principessa?* Hmm, I think I know why." His gaze dropped to her lips, clung, until she felt his mouth was there, drawing hard on her flesh until it swelled, ached, until *she* ached for him to do it for real. "You're… hungry."

Alarm erupted, followed by a flood of mortification. He knew. Or was he guessing, based on universal female response to him?

Before she could say anything, he took her elbow in a phantom grip. "Come. Let me feed you, get you back in fighting form."

Food. He'd meant hungry for *food.*

She was so relieved she let him guide her without a word.

She lost all sense of direction as he led her through his mansion, until they reached another huge oak door. She followed him through it, her every movement feeling controlled by his will.

Minutes later, they came to an elevated, open-air deck overlooking a stunning, symmetrical landscaped scene. Its centerpiece was a gigantic rectangular pool with a semicircular protrusion at its near end, glittering pure aquamarine in the declining sun. Its lava stone and mosaic periphery segued at its far end into a cleared passage between olive groves that continued until it melted into the vegetation-covered mountain in the distance. To the left, the groves gave way to dunes of pure gold, leading down to the serpentine shore and the azure and emerald waters.

She stopped, paralyzed by the magnificence of the sight.

She'd been raised on this island, but she never knew it still had such pristine natural places. The contrast with such lavish human design was breathtaking. But it was the seclusion that intensified that otherworldly feel. She'd never been anywhere so totally devoid of people. It felt as if they were the only man and woman on Earth.

The side of her face felt as if it were burning. She tore her eyes away from the scene, blinked up at him. She found him brooding down at her, his eyes heavy with so much emotion she didn't understand. Didn't want to understand.

He reached out a hand as if he was going to cup her cheek. At the last moment, he swept a lock of her long hair from her flaming face, tucked it with extreme care behind her ear. "You like?"

She swallowed, her heart spiraling in a nosedive like a shot-down plane. "I'm alive, am I not? I have to like."

His lips twitched. His eyes didn't change expression, seemed bent on liquefying her. Then he reached for her hand.

She felt as if he'd electrocuted her as he strode ahead, had her almost running behind him. She gurgled something about his legs being longer than hers. He turned as he slowed down, his smile riddling her vision in spots of blindness.

He had them circumventing the pool before taking one of the passageways that ran parallel to the groves and ended up at the edge of the beach. He suddenly stopped.

She rocked on her heels as he dropped to his haunches. Before she could process his action, he took her hands, placed them on his shoulders. She gaped as he lifted her right foot off the ground. Breath deserted her as he so slowly, so gently slid off her high-heeled sandal strap. The sandal fell off her suddenly stinging foot into his hand. Her toes curled, a gasp tearing from her. He looked up, noted her distress. Then he closed his hand over her foot, raised it, his lips parting, filling with sensuality.

He was going to…to… She couldn't let him or she'd…she'd…

She lost her balance, forced him to let her regain her footing. She leaned heavily on his shoulders so she wouldn't keel over him, electricity roaring from where her fingertips clutched their daunting power to zap incapacitation through-out her nervous system. He pressed her hands harder to his shoulders before repeating the de-sandaling ritual on her other foot.

When she was sure she would faint, he let her foot down, rose, bent and took his own sneakers off, placed them at the sand's edge with her sandals and spread his arm, inviting her to walk on.

She stumbled forward a few steps before she gasped, stopped. The feeling of the powdered gold beneath her feet, its warmth and complex texture, its gritty softness, its resilient malleability heightened her sensory tumult.

He turned her toward him, his gaze solicitous. "Did you step on something? Are you hurt?"

Before she could answer he swooped down again, inspected one foot then the other, feeling for injuries or foreign bodies.

An uproar swept through her at his action, at the sight of his eyebrows drawn and his head bent in such concentration, the severely trimmed raven luxury of his mane gleaming copper in the sun as his perfectly formed fingers traced over her soles.

She was about to cry out that she was fine, when he heaved up to his feet, and in the same movement swept her up in his arms.

She went limp with shock.

He'd never touched her before. She hadn't even let him shake her hand. She thought she knew how dangerous it would be to have any physical contact with him. She'd known nothing. Feeling his flesh pressed on hers, his heat and scent invading her senses…it was too much.

She choked out, "Put me down—I'm OK."

He frowned. "Then why did you jerk to a stop like that? Why did you look so…distressed?"

"I was just…surprised. I—I've never felt anything like this."

His eyes narrowed. "You've never felt sand beneath your feet?"

She gulped, shook her head. "I…no."

"You've lived most of your life on a Mediterranean island

legendary for its sea and shores. How is it possible you never ran barefoot on the beach? Never swam in the sea?"

"I…uh…just didn't. The sea hasn't been part of my life."

"How was it even avoidable? Going to the beach is part of most people's childhoods, especially in seaside countries."

Her discomfort rose with every word. She wanted this conversation, and what it made her think of, what it could reveal, to be over. "I'm not 'most people.'"

"You mean because you're royal? That doesn't make sense. Durante and Paolo have both told me they spent much of their childhoods soaking in the sea and baking in the sun. And on Castaldini, royals aren't pursued and encroached on as they are in other countries. Even if you had been, your father could have provided a private beach for your use."

"I—I sunburn easily. I spent most of my childhood inside the palace. I'm almost always indoors, even now."

His gaze sluiced over her like silky, warm water, lingering on each inch of visible skin, making her want to moan with the pleasure of his visual caress. "Your skin is the finest and softest that I've ever seen. Or touched." His lids grew heavier as he smoothed the expanse of skin where her jacket and the form-fitting top beneath it had ridden up at her back. She stiffened with the blow of sensation. He gathered her more securely to him. "But it isn't the type prone to sunburning. In fact, I think you'd tan spectacularly."

His compliment went straight to her every hunger and vulnerability. Confusion over his motivation gave way to intense pleasure and self-consciousness. "I probably got badly burned once, when I was too young to remember. That and an over-protective mother kept me indoors from then on."

He gave her a long look, eloquent with disbelief. Out loud he said, "And you just agreed? You didn't want to rebel, seek all the freedoms and pleasures the sea has to offer? Doesn't sound like the Clarissa D'Agostino I know."

"Uh…you have a very rosy picture of the life of a princess."

"You mean I can't appreciate the impositions you had, and still have to put up with, as part and parcel of your status?" She braced herself for the frustration his next words would provoke. Everyone, especially men, had always said they understood how it had been for her, had tried to…console her for being such a poor, oppressed royal girl. His next words sent her preconceptions scattering. "No, I can't. I can only imagine some of them. But, since I never thought running on the beach and swimming in the sea were among the things you had to forgo, I must have imagined quite wrong. Even if I didn't, only you can speak of your experience."

She blinked back hot tears. He *had* understood. Something she'd never thought she'd ever feel toward him spread its balmy coolness inside her chest: thankfulness.

She bit her lip, nodded. "Whatever the reason, I never developed any fascination for the sea."

"You're fascinated now."

She tore her gaze away from his all-knowing one, cast it wide.

He was right. She'd never felt this thrill at witnessing what had always been there since she'd been born. She felt she was experiencing it all with new senses. With a few word of soul-searing insight, he'd made her realize the deprivation she'd suffered, of something so rich with pleasures, so available to anyone. Just being so close to him, his hands hugging her behind her knees and back, her palm still resting over his heart feeling it pumping steadily, as if he hadn't covered half a mile of beach with her in his arms, had made her… *Dio,* she was still in his arms!

She couldn't take one more second of this. She began to wriggle to free herself and he suddenly stopped, whispered, "Watch."

She jerked toward the point his eyes were fixed on. They were at the top of a dune where the shore extended to her vision's limit. She held her breath, felt him holding his as the red sun seemed to accelerate toward the darkening azure waters.

Then they touched, seemed to melt into one another, and he exhaled, molded her closer, as if to echo the celestial embrace.

A long moment passed as they shared the evocative display of sheer beauty, before she at last insisted he put her down.

He tightened his hold. "You're sure you're not uncomfortable walking barefoot on the sand?"

"It really was just a shock how good it felt."

A strange watchfulness descended on his face. Then he slowly released her, his eyes clinging to her face as if he wanted to record her reaction, memorize every nuance passing through her.

For the first time, she didn't want to hide her responses from him. She felt he had a right to witness them, in return for this gift he'd given her.

She moaned in pleasure as she again felt the sand flow between her toes, tickling her skin and massaging her soles.

The feeling was incredible, energizing. She gave in to it, to the unadulterated freedom and vitality it imbued her with.

She whooped, giggled, ran.

With every bound on the magical medium she'd lived her life looking at and never seeing, never experiencing, a burst of speed poured into her limbs. She heard his deep chuckles pursuing her. Unfettered laughter escaped her in response. And if a voice told her she must have plummeted into a parallel universe, to be running on a beach with Ferruccio Selvaggio chasing after her, it was silenced as soon as it spoke up. So what, if it felt this good?

Then she cleared another dune and saw it by the gently frothing waves. A huge circle of torch-topped, polished brass poles with a table set for two in its middle.

She turned to him in excitement, then sped ahead, the setup's details coming into focus. A lavender silk tablecloth draped the table, undulated like something alive in the gentle breeze. Gleaming black plates contrasted with its dreamy hue, while glittering silver utensils and crystal glasses added flashes of splendor. A buffet was set to the side.

She arrived at the table, swung around and grinned at him as he caught up with her, her breathing and heartbeat accelerating under the effect of his approach rather than from exertion.

His breathing was a bit quicker, but even, easy, his eyes gleaming silver with exhilaration. "Not only do you run like a lioness in that constrictive skirt, but you beat me, too. How fast would you be in something suitable?"

More heat rushed to her head, her cheeks. "It isn't that constrictive. And you weren't trying to outrun me."

He huffed a chuckle. "I gave it a good shot, believe me. I'm pretty fast. But you're much faster."

Her grin widened with pleasure at the ease with which he admitted she'd beaten him, his obvious enjoyment of the fact even. "I'll tell you my secret so you won't feel bad about it. I held my university's record in the indoor pentathlon for three consecutive years, and the regional one for two of those."

He looked genuinely impressed. Even though she got the feeling he already knew that. "And it's clear you've kept in shape ever since." His eyes again detailed how much said "shape" pleased them. "And now you'll add outdoor events to your repertoire. Including swimming in the sea. With me." She opened her mouth, closed it, the images his words had playing in her mind's eye turning her mute. Suddenly his smile's wattage spiked. "I bet you've crossed from hungry to starving after the unexpected exercise."

He tugged her to the buffet, exposed hot and cold serving plates, piled her plate with mouthwatering delicacies. She didn't protest. After going without more than a cup of tea since seeing her father yesterday, she *was* famished.

What followed was something she'd only dreamed of.

Even in fantasy, it had never been so easy, so natural. So unbelievable. They ate and exchanged anecdotes about their lives, opinions about almost everything, agreed, teased, laughed, and she found herself with the man she'd seen that first time—the one she'd felt connected to. Before everything had crashed around her ears and remained there in ruins for the past six years.

Now it was as if the years hadn't passed in tension and avoidance, as if this was the natural progression of that moment she'd thought so enchanted. And it did feel enchanted, yet more real than anything she'd ever experienced. *He* felt real. His real self, not the persona he projected when he moved through the ultra-formal settings where she'd made sure they always met with the buffer of her family around. Now that he was away from it all, he showed her sides of him she hadn't suspected existed, every glimpse enthralling her, embroiling her in the exhilaration of tangling with his wickedness and wit.

Sunset had morphed into the most breathtaking twilight she'd ever witnessed. The impossibly clear, totally unpolluted skies became a sweeping canvas of hues jeweled by strokes and patterns of clouds that had seemed to materialize just to reflect and prism the lingering light into ephemeral paintings that stunned the senses. Then it all gradually faded under the dominion of darkness until moonless, star-blazing night had taken over. She was dazzled by the spell of the ambiance, but more so by her companion.

He'd just served her fresh watermelon, grown on the land everyone had given up as irreclaimable, among many vital crops of which she'd seen oranges, tangerines, olives and grapes. As he sat down she commented on that before resuming her comments on one of his latest takeovers, and he leaned back in his chair, grinning.

"I always let my opponents fight me until they're exhausted, all the while showing them how sweet surrender would be. Then, when I judge they've had enough, I move in, and at that point they're ecstatic for me to take over."

Air escaped her lungs in a rush. She couldn't draw it back.

That could describe what he'd been doing to her.

It could, because it did.

Dio, what a fool she was. She should have known, when it

had all felt too good to be true, when he'd started lavishing praise and understanding on her.

He had done so to make her putty in his hands. And he'd succeeded. He'd made her forget what he was, the danger he posed to her, the reason she was here. He hadn't just overcome her antipathy and turned its tide into acceptance and eagerness, he'd negated reason and memory, silenced every caution. And he'd done it imperceptibly.

She had to surface from under his spell, run for her emotional and psychological survival. She had to get back on track, do what she'd come here to do. Quit playing the game by his rules, according to his agenda. Whatever that was.

Disillusionment became venom as it exited her lips. "That's interesting, how you get your conquests to become your willing thralls. Thanks for sharing that insider tidbit. Especially as it gives me the opening to get to the point of this…charming evening. Now that we've gotten the dinner you've been harping on for years out of the way, I hope you're satisfied and we can finally get down to discussing something important." His eyes drained of the warmth that had ignited them for the past hours. She braced against the moronic urge to soften her tone, to see his eyes fill with that fake intimacy again. "So…go ahead. Negotiate. I can't wait to hear your 'terms'. They should be…entertaining."

Ferruccio almost flinched. He felt as if she'd kicked him in the gut. And she had. Figuratively speaking.

After the first shock passed, rage crashed over him.

How had this happened? He'd set out to lull her, to overcome her resistance. Where had it all taken such a sharp detour, so that he'd been the one who'd been lulled, who hadn't seen this coming?

For the past hours he'd forgotten his harsh intentions. He'd gradually drowned in the pleasure of her nearness as she'd shown him a persona that combined the vulnerability he'd thought he'd seen that first night with a steel shield of will and wit, wrapped around a core of fun and warmth and passion.

And it had just been another of her masks.

How had she blindsided him again? He could still swear she'd finally taken off all her masks and shown him her true self. Which her own words now told him was premium self-delusion.

She'd taunted him with the memory of his rejected invitations, intimating she'd considered them the undignified and *unimportant* pursuit of an unacceptable suitor, and that this evening was her way of giving him what he'd been "harping" on, to humor him, because of the situation she'd been forced into. And would he now stop behaving irrationally?

Her sarcasm sent the beast inside him clawing out of his gut. Disappointment spilled from there to burn his insides.

She hadn't been enjoying herself, had been leading him on to equalize the balance of power so that she wouldn't be the beggar here. She was trying to set a record that, no matter what upper hand he held now, between them, he'd get nothing but the condescension he deserved. It was clear it didn't matter that he was a D'Agostino. He remained a bastard in her eyes.

She really had no idea who she was dealing with, how out of her depth she was. He might be cultured and suave on the surface, but he was a street fighter at heart. Playing against odds she couldn't begin to imagine in her wildest nightmares, to win at any cost was what he did. And it was time to do so.

It was time to make her regret her snobbery.

His bared his teeth in a smile he knew would chill her bones as it had so many, from politicians to tycoons to mafia dons. "You want to negotiate, *Principessa?* By all means. And since you're so enthusiastic to hear my terms, here they are. Or here *it* is. I have one term for taking the succession. That I take you with it."

Three

"You're insane."

Ferruccio leaned back in his chair, stuck his hands in his pockets and indolently surveyed Clarissa, savoring her shock and indignation as she choked on his declaration.

"Am I, now? Hmm. Literally all the financial world disagrees with your verdict."

"That's because you're so intelligent that you manage to hide your insanity. And it's possible to be a financial genius and a raving lunatic all at once."

He feigned boredom even as he cursed himself for letting her barbs prick him. "Maybe. But you've heard my term, Clarissa. And it should answer all your questions about why I asked for you, why I summoned you here. To pay you the courtesy of demanding it directly from you, rather than from your father and his Council."

Her mouth opened on a silent O. The lust that had been eating through him like slow acid all those years poured through his system in seething torrents. Imaginings of what devouring those dimpled lips would be like had ratcheted to a new dimension after watching them do so many things he'd never seen them do before—thin, curl, purse, tremble, quirk, spread in smiles and laughter, get bitten by those pearls she had for teeth, licked by that tantalizing-in-every-way tongue....

As for that vital body of hers, which had grown progressively more voluptuous as he'd burned for her from afar, he now knew how limited his fantasies of possessing it had been. Now that it had filled his arms, pressed against his flesh, trembled in his hold, buzzed with what he knew, against all her condescension and disdain, had been as unbridled a hunger as his own, he knew. Possessing it would be beyond anything he'd experienced or dreamed about.

Which meant one thing. Pulverizing her resistance had just turned from a resolution to a necessity.

At last, she seethed, "You think they would have even considered your crazy demand? What do you think this is, the Middle Ages?"

He reached out and calmly poured himself a glass of pomegranate juice, quirked an eyebrow at her over the rim after the first sip. "This juice shares so much with you. The richness of the complex flavors that make it up, the sour sweetness."

Her hands fisted on the table. "Spare me the false praise."

"I won't spare you anything." He watched his multifaceted threat invade her sculpted cheeks with a peach hue that burned bright, even in the dimness of the flickering firelight, made him struggle not to storm up and go devour it and her. "You really think I'd make such a demand if I had any doubt I'd obtain it? You claim to have studied my methods, Clarissa. Didn't your extensive studies and all those postgraduate degrees reveal that I don't make a move if I'm not one hundred percent certain of its success?"

She sank her teeth into her lower lip to control the tremor that took hold of it. His own twitched with a surge of intoxication. What could he say? It was such a delight to see her with her composure shattered, with anger, dread and arousal tearing at her.

Just as he thought she'd realized she was outclassed and overpowered, those uncanny eyes seemed to pulse purple with each flare of the flames. "My studies and degrees also revealed another thing, Signore Selvaggio. That sooner or later, even impervious, unstoppable business gods miscalculate. As you did this time. Big time. I'm not some commodity Castaldini can bestow on you as a side benefit. And I sure as hell am not volunteering myself as an incentive to sweeten the deal."

So. She wasn't cowed yet. *Bene.* In fact, it was great that she wasn't. He would have been seriously disappointed if he'd won that easily. He hated easy victory. And when it came to her, after all the years of frustration she'd put him through, he wanted—no, *needed*—her surrender to be a struggle. That way, the pleasure of her capitulation, when it came, would be all the more intense.

He was going to revel in this. Big time, like she'd said.

Time to play hardball.

The exhilaration of taking the skirmish to the next level danced on his lips. "Let me share a fact of life, *Principessa.* One from real life, not the sterilized, rarefied version it seems you've lived for all of yours. I don't need the crown. It's the crown that needs me. Desperately. That's why you're here. That's why you have no option but to abide by my terms and demands, to do everything I tell you to." He knew he had that serene look on his face that lions had on theirs as they took down their kill. He savored stressing his point. "Everything."

Clarissa's heart stopped for what must be the hundredth time today.

After a couple of dropped beats, it burst into another stumbling gallop that pushed no blood to her head, that left her feeling she was teetering on the verge of oblivion.

This wasn't happening. This *couldn't* be happening. He couldn't have said all he'd said. This *was* insane.

And he was watching her with the same coldness with which

he'd once looked at her across the ballroom on that first night. Which made it all crazier. Why was he even demanding this, her, if that was what he really felt toward her?

She struggled to keep hysteria from tingeing her voice and features. "I said that should be entertaining. And it is. You think you're irreplaceable, don't you? Well, you're not. My father is just going through his list of candidates. In case you didn't know already, you—in spite of your belief in your own indispensability—didn't rank first there. You merely happened to be third."

He took another sip of his juice, savored it slowly, made her imagine what he no doubt meant her to, those lips on her every secret, savoring *her,* before he murmured languidly, "Third *and* last."

"You really have an inflated sense of your own importance, don't you? Figures. Too many billions can do that to a man."

"When they're not inherited, and have been gained through legal venues, it's safe to say they do indicate indisputable personal value."

"Legal? Are you absolutely certain about that?" The look he gave her sent shivers of alarm, almost fear, zigzagging through her. She'd crossed a line.

She didn't give an ant's leg. Just as he didn't, about her or how she felt. "May you live happily ever after with your indisputable personal value, Signore Selvaggio. We'll find someone else. Someone who won't play cheap games when he's offered something as incalculable as the honor and privilege of the crown of Castaldini."

The danger in his eyes switched off, but the benevolence in the smile he bestowed on her was far worse. She felt her blood freezing in her arteries. "Good luck with that."

She stilled, the ice spreading. "What do you mean? And quit being cryptic. If you have something to say, then say it."

He gave a lazy shrug. "I don't have anything more to say. You know the rest, even though you're pretending not to. Contrary to what you accused me of, and unlike you, I don't play games."

"What are you *talking* about? What's that 'rest' I'm supposed to know?" she snapped.

His gaze sharpened, the steel luminosity of his irises flaring and subsiding with the flames of the torches until it seemed that the shifting shadows and golden lights they cast over his face would expose some supernatural entity that his magnificent body housed—one who examined her with brooding, malignant amusement.

Suddenly he threw his head back and laughed—a harsh, ugly sound so unlike his laughter during the past hours. Despite everything, this confirmation of the loss of the illusion of harmony and affinity they'd shared sent regret skewering through her.

"*Dio santo, sei serio.* You're serious. You know nothing. They left you in the dark, the old jackals. That explains everything. Why you think you can be your usual scathing self with me. They didn't warn that you they can't afford for you to alienate their last option. How remiss of them."

"That isn't true. It can't be. Someone else w—"

He cut her trembling protest short "—would bring about the end of Castaldini as we know it. No other man of Castaldinian origins or with the prerequisite D'Agostino blood—whether obtained on the right side of the sheets or not—possesses enough power to drive away the kingdom's external enemies and to defuse the internal conflicts. But I have my own empire, to which I owe my allegiance. On the other hand, even you can work out that I don't owe Castaldini or its people any measure of that. So don't play the honor and privilege card with me. I'm not in any way duty or honor bound to take on the responsibility of safeguarding Castaldini's crown and future. If I'm to accept doing your kingdom that 'incalculable' favor, I demand an 'incentive to sweeten the deal,' as you put it. And you're it."

She stared at him, at the face of his serene cruelty, his

absolute certainty, the tremors she'd been struggling to hold back breaking free, starting to rattle her bones.

He went on as if he was auguring something as trivial as a soccer game's outcome. "If you refuse, you can go back to your precious father and Council with my refusal, and let them pick someone else from the inadequate choices they've already rejected for the best of reasons, and let Castaldini go to hell."

He couldn't be lying about all this, could he? But maybe he didn't consider it lying, just maneuvering her by any means necessary to corner her. He was a master manipulator, after all.

And he wasn't even finished. He went on, and she discovered he'd saved the worst for last. "And when Castaldini is in ruins, maybe becomes some second-rate, exploited annex to one of the surrounding nations panting to drain its riches into their resource-poor, overpopulated, debt-ridden bellies, I'll still come after you. And I will have you. The crown will be lost, but you'll be mine in the end, Clarissa."

She was panting by the time he finished. Quaking. Then it all blurted out of her, all the indignation and distress he'd so expertly inflamed beyond the danger zone. "You're the one who can get lost, or can go to hell, Ferruccio Selvaggio—or D'Agostino, or whatever your name is. Be sure to take your toxic conceit and cruelty with you. Castaldini will survive without your oh-so-vital intervention, and you're not coming near me…."

Her tirade choked off into panting silence. It wasn't because he'd made any threatening move. It was his very tranquility, as he leaned forward, placed his glass on the table then heaved up to his feet, that made her every cell scream with alarm. Each movement was the measured advance of a predator with all the time in the world to pounce on his prey. Then he did.

He stopped by her, leaned down, took her hand and pulled her out of her chair and onto her feet.

"Wh-what are you doing?" she sputtered.

"What I should have done years ago."

He gave her a firm tug, slammed her against his body. Before she could draw another breath, one of his hands slipped into the hair at her nape, twisted there, immobilizing her head, tilting her face upward, the other trailing a heavy path of possession down to her buttocks. Then, as he held her prisoner, exerting no force but that of his will, he let her see it—the beast he kept hidden under the civilized veneer, its cunning savagery having assured his survival in hell, conquering of it, before being unleashed on this realm. The beast was hungry—and she was the meal it craved.

Holding her stunned gaze, his own crackling with the first unchecked emotions he'd let her see there, he lowered his head.

She felt as if she were in the path of a comet, that she'd disintegrate at impact. At the last moment before his lips took hers, she averted her face in an act of pure survival.

His lips landed on her cheek, at the corner of her mouth, with a chain reaction of insistent, escalating voracity. The feel of his lips on her flesh, the gust of his breath filling her with his scent and virility, left her suffering a widespread synaptic disruption. It was as bad as being a few feet from ground zero. Then he took his destruction to another level.

The hand on her lower back pressed her into him. Before she could deal with the blow of sensations at feeling his arousal against her belly, he relinquished his hold on her head, combed his fingers through her hair, over and over, sending pleasure cascading from every hair root, before that hand caressed her back, on its way to delving beneath her jacket and top.

She moaned a sound she'd never before produced, as the hard heat of his fingers splayed against her back, a part of her she'd never thought sensitive. Every inch of skin he imprinted felt moments away from the spontaneous generation of fire. She jerked away to escape, then pressed back for more. And he took his onslaught to the next level.

His other hand yanked up her skirt, cupped her buttocks through her panties and hauled her up against him. She gasped as she experienced weightlessness for the first time, then gasped louder as he ground the steel of his erection against her melting core. Something scalding rumbled from his depths as he tugged at one thigh, opened her around his hips for better access, splaying her for his thrusts. The hand at her back plastered her heaving chest against his, then he started rubbing against her. Her breasts swelled until they felt they'd burst, until the abrasion of her clothes, his shirt and the power it housed turned her nipples into pinpoints of agony.

She writhed in his hold, whimpered as he ravaged her neck in suckles that would leave their mark, that sent pleasure hurtling through her blood with each savage pull.

All existence converged on him, became him, his body and breath, his hands and mouth, as he tested her flesh and responses, tasted them, took over her will. She was no longer herself, but a mass of needs wrapped around him, open to him, his to exploit and plunder. There was nothing more to hear but his voracious growls and her distressed moans, their thundering blood and strident breathing as he raised her and slid her down his body in leisurely excursions, had her riding his erection through their clothing. Her top had somehow been peeled up and he dipped his head and took her nipples, one after the other, through her bra in massaging nips, sending ecstasy corkscrewing through her.

Her fingers buzzed as if they'd turned to live wires, and only digging them into his flesh could ground the excess charge. Her moans became a drone interrupted by sharp intakes of breath. The flowing throb between her legs escalated into pounding, needing something, anything, *everything,* to assuage it. When it tipped from discomfort into pain, she cried out his name, begged, she didn't know for what. He shuddered beneath her as he snapped his head up, crashed his lips on her wide-open mouth in a hot, moist vice, and thrust deep.

She plunged into his taste, rode rapids of delight as his tongue invaded her, taught hers to rub and duel and drink deeper of the fount of endless sensation, as his lips and teeth mastered her, gave her and took her and finished her.

This was nothing like the slow seduction she'd fantasized about. This was an invasion, a ravaging, and it catapulted her into a frenzy of need, an inferno of hunger. She wanted... wanted him to never stop, to do anything and everything to her, to take more, all.

She'd dreaded him and dreamed of him for too damned long. In her dreams, he'd always told her how much he wanted her, couldn't wait for her, but still lavished care and tenderness on her, in the only way she'd thought she could feel pleasure. Now he'd given her this. Overwhelming, no preliminaries, no boundaries, just raw need, unbridled ecstasy. Light years better, hotter than what she'd tormented herself with all these years, the insipid fantasies she'd thought the height of eroticism. She should have known he'd pulverize her expectations, as he took her and soared far beyond anything she could have imagined.

And if not for the debate that had finally pushed him to override her resistance, to no longer give her a choice...

Something cold and ugly seeped through her delirium. A memory. A realization. How this had started. As a measure to end that debate.

He'd gauged perfectly, as he always did, that this was the way to decimate her resistance, to take her over, mind and body.

And he'd been right. She'd succumbed to the hunger she'd been struggling against during all those years she spent escaping him.

He'd made her forget again why she had, how angry she'd been. At him, for pulling her strings when he didn't see her as a human being, just an asset, and at herself for knowing that and *still* yearning for him.

But her resistance was about far more than refusing to be another notch on his mile-long bedpost. It wasn't about pride. It was about bone-deep terror. She knew where surrender to him would lead. To a repetition of her parents' dismal pattern.

She'd grown up witnessing what misery could be wrought when involvement in a relationship was one-sided. Her mother's unrequited emotions toward her father had destroyed her mind, had led her—as Clarissa and her siblings believed—to end her life.

Not that she blamed her father. He'd done what he had to rule a kingdom. It had been her mother who'd been unable to understand the nature of their political marriage or accept it, who'd wanted to turn it into a love match and had only managed to drive her distant husband further away. Ferruccio was everything her father was—including whatever had driven her mother to destruction—a thousand times over.

The memory of her mother's life scared her enough to douse the insanity.

She started struggling in his arms, as if fighting for her life.

He stiffened for a long moment, unable to make up his mind whether her struggle was an attempt to get closer or away.

He finally grunted something and tore his lips away from hers, put her down.

Panting, every muscle spasming with the slow poison of the need he'd infected her with—a need that would eat through her if it went unappeased—she stumbled away, searching desperately for her equilibrium.

For a few seconds, the flames blazing on the poles surrounding her made her feel like an animal trapped within a circle of fire. As her mind rebooted, she realized how apt that fear was. She might not be physically trapped or in danger, but she was in every other way.

And her trapper—her hunter—was closing in on her again.

She squeezed her eyes shut, bit down on her lip, hard, to stop herself from turning around and throwing herself into his arms and letting him finish what he'd started.

His hands descended on her shoulders, pulled her back against him. She couldn't even tremble, could only lean back limply, exposing her neck for him to nuzzle. He took this as consent, again cupping her breast, her sex, rocking her against his arousal as he suckled her earlobe, whispered in her ear, "I didn't intend to go this far. But I touched you, and you responded and…"

She pushed out of his arms. This time he let her go at once. She finished rearranging her clothes, gave him a sullen look. "Sure, it's my fault, because I 'responded.'"

He shoved his hands into his pockets, drawing her eyes to the huge bulge in his pants. Her insides clenched. She swallowed. *Dio,* she was literally drooling over him.

"I'm not saying it's your fault. I'm saying I'm not proud that I set out to kiss you and almost ended up taking you. I never lose control like that, never surrender to the heat of the moment."

"No? Excuse me if I don't believe that, what with you being oversexed and overendowed, as well as overeverything else."

He looked incredulous. "You think I would have gotten where I am today if my libido had any say in my actions and decisions?"

"You're a man, aren't you? I'd say libido is the *only* thing that has a say in your decisions where women are concerned."

"Then you don't know much about men. Real ones, anyway. A man steered by his libido 'where women are concerned' is an immature dolt who ends up destroying what he achieves by making the wrong decisions at the wrong times for the wrong reasons."

"I happen to agree. So you're saying I made you lose your legendary control? Good one. Especially since you don't want me at all. This is just a hostile takeover for you."

He gave her a sweeping, lustful glance, huffed a short laugh. "You clearly have no concept of what *hostile* is. Or an inkling about what I'm like when I am. And if you think almost taking you standing up and becoming rock-hard whenever I so much as think of you isn't wanting you, I wonder if you even know the basics of the male sexual response."

"You're just aroused by the game you've been playing. You know, the one where you get to enforce your will on the only woman, it seems, who has ever said no to you."

A merciless gleam entered his eyes as his lips curled. "Your resistance always did infuriate me, when I sensed your answering desire. And now that I've felt how incendiary that desire is, and how it sets me on fire, if I wanted you to the factor of a thousand before, I now want you to that of a million. But even if it did get out of control, this explosive episode proved one thing. When I take you, Clarissa, it will be because you're begging me to."

She glared at him, hating him more for being so right about the magnitude of her desire. She had to vanquish it if she wanted to survive. "I wonder what level your arrogance can reach before you overdose on it. That would be a well-deserved end, not to mention an effective and fair solution to this mess. And before you gloat some more about how much I want you, that doesn't mean I'll act on it. I want to eat chocolate fudge day and night, but you won't see me giving in to the temptation any time in this life."

"But bingeing on me won't make you fat and sick. Giving in to the temptation of falling into my arms and bed will provide rigorous workouts that will keep you in perfect shape and health, and the calorie-free pleasure I'll saturate you with will make you realize you've been starving, make you wonder how you've lived so long with such deprivation."

She felt as if the whole world had become a tiny room, with its walls closing in on her. He was just too much, too powerful. Unstoppable. And when he turned coaxing, seductive, he was devastating. She couldn't resist him. And she had to.

There was only one way she could think of to stop him. Make him angry.

"Why don't you just drop the act? You only want me because I'm the king's daughter. That has always been my attraction, hasn't it? You've acquired everything else—God only knows how—but now the world has gone so crazy, *you* can become Castaldini's future king—and you still want to acquire me as the most suitable accessory to your impending royal status."

* * *

Ferruccio felt his heart turn to stone inside his chest.

He'd long believed she looked down on him because of the circumstances of his birth.

But not only had she now intimated that she believed he'd attained his wealth and power through criminal methods and that she still cringed at the idea of giving in to the desire that seethed like a bound beast between them, not only had she just confirmed his worst suspicions why, but she'd revealed that the situation was worse than he'd thought.

She thought he'd been pursuing her to acquire her lineage by association, still wanted it even now, to paint himself with her legitimacy. She didn't just think him a lowborn bastard but a sleazy social climber.

And she called *him* arrogant.

If he thought he'd enjoy punishing her for her arrogance before, he would now outright relish it. In every way imaginable.

He looked at her. Silky hair billowed around her shoulders like a caramel gold shroud of mystery in the night breeze. That body he'd almost lost his mind over was tense. He felt it emitting that tractor beam of attraction that had always drawn him inexorably. He'd always thought it had been the real her inside the body that had so attracted him. But no matter what he'd felt during the past few hours—that his belief had been more than validated—he'd been wrong.

Yet, he could still feel that body reverberating with the unassuaged need he'd sent storming through her. *That* he relished. If not as much as he did seeing that face of pure temptation pinched with worry. She must be wondering if she'd just made an irreversible mistake by baring her true opinion of him so blatantly.

She had no idea how right she was.

"As interesting as your opinions of my intentions are…" he gave her a smile that had had grown men sweating "…this… meeting is over, Clarissa. Now run along and go throw yourself in your father's loving arms and sob to him over your ordeal at the hands of the conceited, cruel man he threw you to like a human sacrifice. Let him soothe you and tell you exactly why you have to come back to me and beg me to take you."

Four

Clarissa went back to her father.

She was delivered back to him, more precisely. Just as Ferruccio had had her picked up like a package, he'd had her dropped back like one. His men had been implacable about carrying out his orders to the letter. He'd said to take her back to the king, and no matter how much she frothed with rage, they took her back to his very door. She'd barely managed to stop them from taking her to his bedside and have him sign a receipt for her.

She entered her father's apartments, shaking with chagrin, with the ever-expanding shock waves from every second she'd spent with Ferruccio, desperately hoping that everything he had told her had not been because he'd been certain of every word he'd said and of his damned hundred percent success rate.

She closed the door behind her, leaned on it and closed her eyes.

Finally. Some alone time. She needed to inject some semblance of calm and control into her thoughts, and hopefully in her expression and words, before entering her father's bedroom.

"Rissa, *mia cara figlia,* where have you been all night?"

She almost jumped out of her skin. Her father, who was so rarely out of bed these days, materialized at the passageway by the door she'd entered through.

Her frayed nerves snapped. "As if you don't know."

Pain stabbed dead center in her chest at her father's grimace of hurt surprise. She cursed Ferruccio with a new fervor. She'd never dreamed the day would come when she'd snap at her father like that. What made it even worse was that what once would have been a mere blink and tightening of lips had become a grotesque, one-sided distortion with the aftereffect of his stroke.

Her heart broke all over again at seeing the evidence of her once all-powerful father's incapacitation. For her to be the reason behind even a moment of his pain was unbearable.

Her heart thudded as she watched him drag his weakened leg, leaning heavily on his walking stick as he limped to the first chair in his reception area and collapsed heavily onto it.

He sat for a moment, not meeting her eyes, recovering from the few steps' effort, his breathing erratic. Then he finally rasped, "I knew only that you were meeting with Ferruccio earlier today."

"The meeting took longer than expected." She struggled not to let anger and bitterness taint her tone. She shouldn't let Ferruccio's words poison her against her father. She needed to hear how things stood from him before she made up her mind who to blame. "Do you know why he asked for me to be the one to negotiate with him?"

Her father exhaled. "If you've learned anything about Ferruccio, Rissa, you must know he never declares his reasons to anyone. But I had theories."

She tensed. "And those were?"

"He's…interested in you. He always has been."

All tension drained out of her as if with a punch to the gut. "And yet you sent me to him."

"Why are you so angry, Rissa?" Alarm suddenly entered her father's steel-blue eyes. "Did he…upset you?"

"That would be the understatement of the year."

Alarm was swept aside on a tide of fury. For a moment, Clarissa could see once again the formidable man and king who'd ruled for forty years, who'd made Castaldini a piece of heaven on earth for almost thirty of those. "What did he do? Tell me."

As if she would. She waved it away. "What's important here is that you knew he wasn't interested in my professional acumen. Why did you send me to him when you knew he had a personal agenda?"

"Why would you be so against that?" Typical. He never answered questions, always volleyed one back. "I never understood why you were so…reticent with him. I thought it might be a good time to settle this. He'll become my crown prince and your future king. And I wasn't against the possibility of him becoming even more."

As in her groom. Her skull suddenly felt too small for her brain. "So you thought the opportunity to indulge in some matchmaking had presented itself?"

"What father doesn't take every opportunity to try to see to his daughter's happiness?"

"And you thought Ferruccio, of all people, was the way to mine?"

"Who else could be, but someone like him?"

"There's *no one* like him."

"My point precisely."

"Dio, Padre…" The lament of how deluded his belief was recoiled in her chest as a terrible suspicion descended on her.

What if this was some side effect of his illness? He'd told her he'd been forgetting things, had been unable to focus. What if this skewed thought he'd formed of Ferruccio as her Prince Charming was a delusion he was suffering from? Brought on by his brush with mortality, his current condition? What if he was scared to die and leave her alone, and he'd latched onto Ferruccio as guardian-angel material based on his power and affluence? Maybe fueled by Ferruccio's expression of interest in her? Or maybe he'd gotten wind of Ferruccio's pursuit of her and built this imaginary scenario around it?

If that was the case, she should let it go. How could she possibly berate him for wanting the best for her, blame him for trying to see to it the best way he thought he could?

It didn't matter, anyway. What mattered was the real catastrophe Ferruccio had so coldly informed her was in progress.

She inhaled. "Is it true? Is Castaldini in danger?"

Her father blinked. "Ferruccio told you that?"

"Please tell me he was at least exaggerating."

"I don't know what he told you." He averted his gaze as he said that. And she knew that every word Ferruccio had told her was true. "But maybe it's time for me to tell you the truth."

"Maybe? *Dio Santo,* why did you even think you should hide it from me at all? *Padre,* I'm a grown-up, PhD-holding professional, I've been elected a Council member by the people. How could you possibly keep something of this magnitude from me? How did you even manage it, when it seems everyone else knows?"

His lips twisted. His condition leant the grimace even more irony. "I may not be the king I once was, but my word still carries some weight. I demanded that no one tell you."

She'd start tearing her hair out any second now. *"Why?"*

"Because no matter how much you've grown, how strong you've become, you're still my little girl, Rissa. Because all of Castaldini's troubles are my fault, and I couldn't bring myself to tell you how big a mess your father has made of everything. I hoped I could fix it, and never have to admit it to you and see disillusion or disappointment in your eyes."

Her tears gushed. She threw herself at his feet and hugged him around his waist with all her strength, sobs tearing out of her as she burrowed her face in his chest the way she had countless times during her tumultuous childhood, when he'd been the impenetrable fortress she'd taken refuge in. "You'll never see either in my eyes, *Padre.* You'll always be my hero."

He tried to hug her back, managing to apply real pressure

only with his healthy arm, the other one barely capable of smoothing her hair a couple of times before the tremors of weakness made him drop it to his side.

They remained like that, locked in the cocoon of their soul-deep connection, the king kissing the top of her head and crooning to her the soothing endearments and the unconditional love that had once been the sole thing that had made her safe enough to sleep, brave enough to live.

Then he began to talk. "It began about ten years ago. I started to lose my perspective in external affairs, to slack off in internal ones. I made many enemies within Castaldini, making it easy for outside enemies to find openings through which to infiltrate our land, take a foothold. I am guilty of glossing over too much, hiding it from all but the highest ranks of Council members. Then I had my stroke. To the world, to the people of Castaldini, the only serious thing seemed to be the market crash, but that is only the tip of the iceberg of problems. I know what you'll say, that Leandro and Durante are dealing with the financial situation, that things seem stable now.

"But it's the calm before the storm. With Leandro and Durante regents only, with me still the king, a crisis is inevitable. Without a formidable crown prince and future king, it's a matter of time before the internal decay weakens the kingdom, until it collapses under the pressures applied by the nations vying to assimilate our resources to feed their expanding needs. Only Leandro and Durante have enough power to stop that temporarily, but they both declined the crown. For the best of reasons, I admit. In their positions now, they'd stave off many immediate dangers, but only a king can have the long-term influence to do it permanently. Ferruccio is the only one left who has the power needed, both financially and politically, to maintain Castaldini's sovereignty."

Clarissa lay on her bed staring at the ceiling, waiting for the wave to crash.

Next second, like clockwork, it did.

She shook with it, the fury that had been wreaking havoc on her since she'd left her father's apartments last night.

She hadn't slept a wink, had risen from her bed as dawn stretched its first fingers across the sky and paced her room for hours. It was 10:00 a.m. now, and she felt exhausted, beaten.

Castaldini *was* in clear and present danger.

When she'd realized in how much danger the kingdom was in, she'd raved and ranted that her father should draft either Leandro or Durante to the duty, that they weren't entitled to refuse when stakes were that catastrophic. But he'd told her why either Leandro or Durante would still end Castaldini as they knew it—Leandro by his incompatible political views, and Durante by bringing an end to the very law around which Castaldini had been built.

She'd struggled to enumerate the measures that could be installed so that either man's reign wouldn't do the predicted damage, but her father had countered every one with an undeniable projection of how it would fail. He'd told her that, before she'd become part of it, the Council had discussed everything in dozens of raging closed sessions, until they had admitted there was no other way out. Did she think anything less could have made them reach the decision to make the offer to Ferruccio?

So this was it. It *was* down to Ferruccio. It was up to him to save Castaldini. He was, in every way, the only one who could.

And that *bastard*—and the epithet had absolutely nothing to do with his birth, but with his character, his behavior—cared nothing about it. He cared only about getting his way. He wanted his "incentive." *Her.*

She'd once thought him a god. He lived up to the belief in many ways. He now did in the most maddening way of all. To save king and country, she had to offer herself at the altar of the vicious deity he'd turned out to be.

She twisted around in bed, reached across to her nightstand, picked up her cell phone.

Time to discuss the terms of her sacrifice.

She pushed the buttons. The private number he said only a handful were privileged enough to have. She'd never called it before. She'd memorized it the first time he'd given it to her, with the second invitation she refused. She was in no position to refuse him...anything...anymore. As he'd said she would be.

The line clicked open before the first ring ended.

He'd been waiting for her. Figured.

She waited for him to speak. To gloat. But there was only a protracted moment of absolute silence on the other end.

He was waiting for her to initiate the second and final round.

Good luck with that, as he'd said. She was holding her breath as she did to get rid of hiccups. She had this ridiculous conviction that if she held it long enough, she'd get rid of this whole nightmare. Yeah, right. By passing out, maybe.

At last *he* breathed, the sound of his inhalation, then slow exhalation pooling warm moistness at the juncture of her legs. And that was before he murmured darkly, intimately, "Clarissa."

She covered the mouthpiece with her hand and almost coughed out the air that would have ruptured her lungs if she'd held it in another second. *Just get it over with.*

She drew in a hasty breath then blurted it out along with the question that had been eating at her. "What did you mean by 'taking' me with the crown? You want to marry me, right?"

A bark of cruelly masculine laughter ricocheted inside her skull. "*Marry* you? Without a long, hard test drive?"

She shut her eyes. How did he do it? How did every word he uttered blind her with arousal even as it also did with anger?

"So you want to have an affair first?" she seethed.

A shorter laugh revved through the ether to buzz through her every bone. "It might be an affair *only*. You might dissatisfy me, and it would end there."

She counted to ten. "If you'll be satisfied with an affair, considering the situation, as you've so...kindly said, I have no option but to accept. But I need to set parameters up-front."

He tsked. "Parameters? How businesslike of you. Highly inappropriate, when you're discussing the plunge into sensual decadence I had planned."

She jerked onto her back, tremors coalescing into one violent shudder before she went still and tense all over. "Had? Does that mean you've changed your mind?"

He let her reach screaming pitch before he said, "I have."

She almost felt her components scatter apart with the sudden loss of the tension that had been holding her together. The cacophony of emotion that rushed to fill the void was a deafening mixture.

Relief yelled loudest. Thankfulness mumbled its grudging concession. But to her disbelieving chagrin, it was disappointment that somehow made its whimpers heard over everything else.

It seemed he'd paused, knowing that these reactions would prey on her. His next words made that clear—made them all redundant. "I've changed my mind about what you deserve."

She gritted her teeth. "Meaning?"

"Meaning that for six years, you must remember with crystal clarity, I've given you the courtesy of being the pursued. But I've decided that you've forfeited your right to such consideration."

"And in your infinite wisdom, what did you decide I deserve?"

"That you must get down from your high tower and do all the running from now on. After all, you're a record-holding champion at it."

"If that means you'll be running ahead, there's nothing I'd love more than to run after you until you drop."

She knew his smile turned to its most wicked. The illicit excitement that thrummed through her told her so. "No danger of that. I'm not as fast as you are, but my stamina is legendary."

And the terrible thing was that she knew he was stating facts. He wasn't a self-deceiving braggart like so many men she'd heard making such pompous claims. He was a man who knew his worth, his powers, and made no pretense at false modesty. A man who'd survived and triumphed over obstacles and dangers, over horrors she couldn't begin to imagine. He also had the most glamorous women in the world fighting for a place on his one-night-stand waiting list. She'd bet he had stamina by the freight-load.

She harumphed. "So you'll employ that Herculean stamina to stay one step ahead as I play 'pursuer' this time around. Any rules to this game I should be aware of? Any points to be scored? Any ultimate goal? Or is this going to be a wild swine chase?"

His chuckles rose at her insult. He loved it when she played rough, didn't he? Who knew he had a masochistic streak. But then, it made sense. A steady diet of simpering obedience and syrupy adulation must make him sick to his stomach. What better than the corrosive sourness of her irreverence to equalize the queasiness?

If that was the case, he'd be happy to know she had verbal abuse by the truckload to pour over his arrogant head.

Meanwhile, *he* poured the black magic of his amusement directly into her brain. "As long as you keep the wild part of that chase going, this…swine will let you get as creative as you like about the rules. Points are scored at my discretion, of course. As for the ultimate goal, it's changing my mind. You see, I'm no longer convinced you're a…good enough incentive. Your mission, should you choose to accept it, is to convince me otherwise."

"Any tips about how I'm supposed to achieve mission impossible?" She injected as much poison as she could into the sweetness of her tone.

His voice deepened. "If you succeed in making me spontaneously combust, that would be a good start."

"And a fitting end."

He hooted with laughter. She shuddered, pressed her thighs together, trying to ameliorate the throbbing ache deep between them. "Go ahead, give me your best shot."

"I'd rather do my worst. Pity you're dozens of miles away."

"Are you alone?"

His sudden question aborted the flow of her venom, yanked sexual awareness to the forefront. "Y-yes...."

"Where?"

"I-in my bedroom."

"Describe it for me."

She tossed a frantic look around. "Uh...it's big. Huge."

"Details, woman."

"You've been inside the palace. You know the dimensions and the general style of an average room here."

"Your bedroom isn't an average room. And I haven't been...inside it. Yet."

She latched on the first part of his statement, skirted the provocative part like she would a land mine. "Actually, it's way below average."

"Explain." She cursed herself for getting into that, fell silent. He growled, "*Bene.* Be prepared for an inspection visit."

"I thought I was supposed to pursue you now."

"My visit will be in pursuit of answers, not your delectable body."

"My room is a mess, okay?" she blurted out.

"You're untidy?" She heard his surprise, then his disbelief. "Even if you are, you have a dozen ladies-in-waiting cleaning up after you."

"I'm not a paragon of personal organization," she hissed. "But if you think I'm allowed to be 'untidy,' just because I'm a princess, maybe you haven't met Antonia, my *bambinàia.*"

"I have. A formidable woman. Is she still your nanny?"

"I call her nanny, but don't you think I've outgrown the need for one? She's my so-called lady-in-waiting now, but she's more like a mother to me. And not only hasn't her job description as my nanny ever included picking up after me, but her method of turning little girls into princesses was something close to what the U.S. Special Forces use in training Navy SEALs."

Silence expanded after her words died away. Then he inhaled. "So you haven't been pampered and coddled, *mia bella unica?*"

She swallowed past the sudden barbed tightness in her throat.

That kindness. When she'd thought it an impossibility. It was probably her imagination. Maybe a glitch in the line.

But she hadn't imagined him calling her his unique beauty. "Your view of my life isn't just rosy, it's fluorescent fuchsia."

She expected him to laugh his hardest this time. And again, he did the last thing she expected him to do.

His tone became a gentle stroke, smoothing her frayed nerves, soothing her rawness. "I stand corrected. But your parents have a lot to answer for. You were born for pampering and coddling."

She almost snorted. "No, thank you. I'm glad they didn't agree with you. I would have grown up a thoughtless, useless brat."

"Pampering and coddling don't have to mean spoiling. Used right, by firm, loving parents, they can be fortifying, nurturing, stabilizing. There's nothing better to contribute to the development of a balanced character and the maintenance of a healthy psyche."

She almost blurted out *And what would you know about that?*

She burrowed back into the mattress with relief that the words hadn't exited her lips. He would have taken them in the worst way possible, and she would have felt even worse.

She meant only to marvel at his insight into something he hadn't experienced. But then again, she shouldn't wonder. His uncanny knowledge of the mechanisms that made humans tick was behind his almost frightening success.

He was going on. "But your parents decided it the best course of action to be tough on you, so instead of a thoughtless, useless brat, you've grown up a merciless, shameless siren."

After another silent beat, she sat up. "Hello? Are you taking another call? Shall I wait on the line until you finish talking to whomever it is you just called all those far-fetched things?"

"You see? Shameless." Before she could answer, he went on. "But since you're not untidy, why is your room a mess?"

Dio, the man forgot nothing, couldn't be distracted. Figured.

She gave in. "Because it hasn't seen a coat of paint in over fifteen years. Name any sign you can imagine of long neglect in such an old building, and it's here. Distintegrating wood paneling, leaking ceiling and peeling paint, just to mention the surface stuff."

An edge entered his voice. "The rest of the palace is in good condition. How is it possible your living quarters haven't been given priority in maintenance and renovations?"

"My living quarters aren't part of the national monument area of the palace."

"You're the princess of Castaldini." He sounded indignant.

"You should see the king's quarters."

The silence lengthened beyond her ability to bear it this time. Especially when she could almost hear that warp-speed mind of his streaking to conclusions. It was another thing to prove how much Castaldini needed him.

At last he inhaled. Then, after a long pause, slowly exhaled. The nuances of the sounds didn't transmit male awareness and triumph this time, but contemplation, deliberation, and if she could possibly believe it, thoughtfulness, consideration. It seemed her sensory capacity had converged on her sense of hearing. She was picking up more through his breathing and tones than from his words. And whether she was picking up right or wrong, it moved her, messed up her insides. Then—of course—he made it far worse.

"What are you wearing, Clarissa?"

His whisper, the total unexpectedness of the question, made her heart skip over a few beats like a little girl would over squares in hopscotch. She wet her aching, parched lips. "Clothes."

"Really? Whatever happened to fig leaves?" Her lips twitched. How did he engage her sense of humor, when she wanted to murder him? "What do you sleep in?"

"What *do* people sleep in? But I'm no longer in my pajamas."

"You're not 'people.' And if I become the future king of Castaldini, I'll issue a royal decree prohibiting you from wearing pajamas. A body like yours shouldn't be encased in anything but drapes of chiffon, wraps of tulle, veils of gauze. Or just jewelry."

"Sure. Just the things to attend Council meetings in," she scoffed. "Fig leaves would be preferable."

"You haven't answered my question again, Clarissa."

She sighed. "In the interest of preventing an inspection visit—I'm wearing another nondescript skirt suit."

"Nothing you put on your body remains nondescript. After last night, skirt suits have entered the realm of highly erotic garments. Following the same rationalization, pajamas on you are probably the height of sexiness." If he thought she had anything to say to that, he could think again. She was busy dealing with the impending heart attack he'd so casually caused. But he didn't wait for her commentary. "What are you wearing beneath the jacket? Is your top buttoned, or pulled on, like the one you had on yesterday?"

"I don't see—"

"It's I who wants to see. In my mind's eye. Now, do as I tell you. Take off your jacket. Slowly."

His whispers, hypnotic, incendiary, were dragging her down into an endless well of mindlessness, incinerating rules and logic and memory. She still struggled. "Ferruccio, I don't think—"

"Don't think. Do it. This is where you start convincing me again. The jacket, Clarissa. Off."

She took the phone away from her ear, stared at it, wondering if it had turned into a device that was whispering delusions. She put it back on, gritted, "It's off."

His whisper grew hotter, darker. "Liar."

"How do you know if I'm lying or not?" She struggled not to pant. "Do you have my room bugged? Am I on camera now?"

"I can tell from your tone, from your breathing. From every cell in my body that's telling me you're still covered in layers of clothes. And you haven't answered me. Buttons or pulled-on?"

"B-buttons…" she stammered.

"Leave the jacket on then. For now. Unbutton your blouse for me, Clarissa. Start at the top." This time her hands trembled to obey him, as if powered by his will, his impatience. "Stop at the button just below your breasts." She did. "Turn your phone to speaker mode. I want both your hands free." She did that, too. "Now cross your hands inside your blouse, *bellissima*. Knead your breasts, then flick your nails over your nipples through your bra." She fell back on the bed again, did as he instructed. "They're hard now. Aching. Begging for my fingers, my lips and tongue and teeth." And they were. How they were. "Do you remember the pressure I applied when I nipped them? Pinch them as hard." She did, gasped, arched off the bed. "Again." And again she did it, and every time he prodded her.

Fire raged through her. Her brain was sizzling, her chest, her eyes steaming, the heat in her gut converging to pour between her thighs, the pounding there beating to the frantic rhythm of her heart. She felt as if he'd taken over her body, was using her own hands as extensions of his lust, as if he was the one doing these things to her again. As he was. Whoever said the mind was the most powerful sex organ had been right. And he'd taken over hers.

"Pull your skirt up, touch your buttocks as I did, squeeze them." She obeyed, unable to suppress her whimpers anymore. "It's me doing it, pulling you against my erection, grinding into you. Spread your legs, Clarissa, let me have better access, open yourself and take more of me."

She opened herself, could swear she felt him bearing down on her, the throbbing where he said he was, but wasn't, becoming erratic with her heart's short-circuiting rhythm.

"Now, do what you wanted me to do—what I would have done if you didn't stop me. Cup yourself, Clarissa, tight. You're burning now." She was. And she couldn't bear it. "Slip your hand inside your panties, spread your lips open. Now slide your fingers through your flowing nectar." She did, keened, trembling on the edge now. His voice thickened, became harsh as gravel. "You're melting, empty, losing your mind, unable to breathe with the hunger. I can see you, Clarissa, quaking on the edge of release. I can scent your need. I can feel your heart stampeding, your body tautening, your core demanding me."

He stopped, drew in a shuddering breath.

Her lips trembled on a smile. He was as affected as she was, as distressed. His breath, when it rushed out, felt as if it filled her, the stimulus that almost tipped her over. She waited, needing it to be his words that did.

"But this stops here, *mia magnifica*. Anything more, you'll have to come get it."

Everything stilled, froze. The world. Her body. Her heart.

"I'm flying back to Castaldini as we speak." His voice was crisp and distant all of a sudden, all intensity and intimacy evaporated. "I had to tend to some business, but I'll be back in my mansion within the hour. You've gone a long way toward convincing me. I expect you to continue your...persuasion, then."

Five

It was hours before Clarissa made herself leave her bed.

The first hour, she could barely move, think, breathe.

The frustration, the humiliation, had been paralyzing, suffocating. She'd tried to escape into oblivion. And to her enormous surprise, she succeeded. It seemed her nervous system had taken all it could, had done the one thing that would spare her real and lasting damage—shut down.

She woke up disoriented, sobbing.

More hours passed while she tried to regain semblance of equilibrium. She'd stood beneath scalding water and tried to let it wash away her confusion and anger—and most of all, the insidious craving Ferruccio had infused in her blood, the memory of those moments when he'd remote-controlled her, driven her to the brink of insanity, before withdrawing and leaving her feeling like she'd never stop falling. The next hour was spent going through the motions of drying her hair and getting dressed—and not in a skirt suit. Then she'd sat down at her computer table and finally let herself think. Let the one thought that now filled her being take the form of words.

She didn't want to see or hear of Ferruccio ever again.

But she had to.

He'd demanded that she report to his mansion.

And she'd made her decision.

This ended tonight.

She'd tell him where he could stick his demands and terms. She was done being more fuel for his planetary-size ego. If he wanted to to punish her, and appease said ego, she'd assure him, he'd dealt her a blow that should satisfy him for the rest of his unnatural life. Then she would show him why he couldn't refuse to be Castaldini's crown prince, what was in it for him. So many things that didn't include her. She'd *persuade* him, all right. To leave her out of the bargain and still go ahead with it.

With that fortifying hope powering her, she sprang into action.

The moment she left her apartments, Antonia descended on her like a disapproving mother eagle.

"Clarissa, can you tell me what exactly you're trying to do here? Signore Selvaggio's envoys arrived *ten hours ago,* saying you have an appointment with him!"

"And you didn't swoop down on me the minute they arrived? That must be the minute hell froze over."

"I did swoop down, many times. You were dead to the world. In your clothes. I gave up hours ago."

"Take heart. It must have been that final trial that succeeded in yanking me out of my stupor."

"What's wrong with you, Clarissa? You sound...intoxicated."

Clarissa barked a mirthless laugh. "You know what? I think you're absolutely right, since intoxication happens when something rises in the blood to the level of toxicity."

The woman looked as if she'd said the sun was checkered purple and blue. "You're saying you've been consuming alcohol...or something even worse?"

Clarissa smirked. "I'd say arrogance and testosterone are definitely worse."

Antonia looked to be at a total loss. "I've never seen you in this condition, Clarissa. Are you really sick? Or are you just trying to gloss over the fact that you disregarded an appointment with a man of Signore Selvaggio's importance?"

Clarissa gave her a serene look. "Hey, I'm just fashionably late. That's a woman's prerogative, isn't it?"

The raven-haired, green-eyed battleship of a woman, whom Clarissa loved dearly, dragon ferocity and military discipline and all, tutted. "You're inexcusably, *obscenely* late. And you're not 'a woman,' You're a princess."

"Believe me, *bambinàia,* right now I wish I wasn't either. I'm in this damned situation because of those damned double X chromosomes and that damned accident of birth."

"What 'damned situation' is that? I hope you don't mean having someone of Signore Selvaggio's caliber interested in you."

"First my father, now you. And no doubt I'll find out everyone knows of his so-called interest in me. And it seems you're all thrilled about it. I wonder why none of you ever told me that?"

"I've spent six years wondering how you could possibly be not falling all over yourself to return his interest."

"And you didn't try to bulldoze me into seeing the error of my ways? Shock and awe!"

"That's the one thing I took it upon myself never to try to influence you in, Clarissa." Clarissa met her nanny's shrewd eyes, saw the sadness there. She was talking about Clarissa's mother, to whom Antonia had been lady-in-waiting since she was eighteen, twelve years before she'd become Clarissa's nanny. Antonia was the one who'd witnessed how Angelica, Clarissa's mother, had been influenced to marry her father for business and political reasons, how the wrong reasons for marriage had never amounted to a healthy relationship and had ended up destroying the queen. Antonia finally sighed. "And then, it's been a long time since you've needed my guidance in anything."

A surge of love and emotion welled up in Clarissa. She hugged Antonia, needing the assuagement of her sturdy body and spirit, the impenetrable haven of her embrace. "As if that ever stopped you, *bambinàia.*"

After a moment of hugging her back, Antonia pushed her away. "You're right. I'll always be an overbearing, interfering woman where it comes to you, the jewel I spent a good chunk of my life polishing and protecting, the daughter I didn't bear, who is now the one thing that brings joy to my heart after I lost my Benito. So here's some more unsolicited guidance. This Selvaggio man is the one for whom I will break my rule of non-interference in your future choices where men are concerned. Stop being a fool, girl. Snatch him up."

"Ah, *bambinàia,* you really have no idea who he is, do you?"

"If you mean that he's an illegitimate D'Agostino, yes, I do."

Clarissa coughed an incredulous laugh. "Seems I was the last to know that, too. But that's not what I meant. I meant his character, his nature."

"He's the most complex man I've ever met. And that's what makes him the right one for you."

"If you mean that because I'm such a multifaceted character myself, thanks for the implied praise. I think. But the problem with such a labyrinthine man is that, among the qualities you admire, you find others to abhor. He might be godlike in looks and personal influence, in success and power, but he's also arrogant, driven and cruelly ambitious."

Antonia gave her a considering look. "Hmm. Arrogant, you say? I've seen only evidence to the contrary. All those exquisite invitations he sent you that I found in the bin, torn apart as if they had tainted your hands. Besides being confounded by your reaction, I know that an arrogant man would have taken one such rejection and never again given you the time of day."

Clarissa's lips twisted. "That's where 'driven' and 'cruelly ambitious' come into play. Ferruccio Selvaggio pursues his target until it drops of exhaustion in his lap."

"So that's your evasive maneuver? Going to him, not when he demanded, but when you deem to, half a day later?" Antonia scowled. "You were free to act as you wished when it was a personal matter, Clarissa, but this meeting is official business. After the way you treated him in the past, any other man would have called the king and Council and filed a formal complaint against you. Frankly, that he hasn't, makes me admire him more."

"So why don't *you* go to him?" Clarissa snapped, and immediately burned in embarrassment at the look that devolved her into a ten-year-old. She shook it off, went on determinedly. "He should be thankful I'm going at all. If this meeting didn't have 'official business' squished in between his personal agenda, he would have never gotten the chance to be in the same square mile I'm in. And if any woman can be late, surely a princess can get away with being inexcusably, obscenely late."

Antonia raised one eyebrow at her. "When did you get a personality transplant?"

Clarissa shrugged. "It's a personality that sprouts up at the mere mention of Ferruccio Selvaggio-slash-D'Agostino."

Antonia gave her suspicious look. "You're playing the spoilt princess, trying to drive him away, aren't you?" She stopped, her eyes rounding, as if she'd just realized the secret of the universe. "*Dio Santo!* How didn't I see this before? You're not *interested* in him, you're *crazy* about him!"

There was no use trying to pull the wool over the eyes of the woman who'd practically raised her. It *was* astounding that Antonia hadn't realized the true nature of her feelings for Ferruccio till now. Seemed she was a better actress than she'd thought. "And I'd be crazier if I did 'snatch him up.'"

For the first time in twenty-eight-years' worth of memory, Clarissa witnessed the sight of Antonia dumbstruck. After a long moment of gaping at her open-mouthed, Antonia shook her head. "*Si,* it's true. I have absolutely nothing to say at the moment. I'm speechless. I'll probably overcompensate later, but for now, go ahead. Either apologize to his envoys and reschedule, or go to the meeting and try to explain the hefty *oops* of a ten-hour delay. Or just do him the courtesy you've been doing for six years. Turn him down and be done with it. You've had plenty of practice after all. Or…no, scratch that. I have no clue. This situation isn't complex, it's incomprehensible."

Clarissa gave a sarcastic huff. "Even when you don't get something, you always end up summing it up perfectly."

Antonia turned and walked away, still shaking her head. Clarissa duly went to Ferruccio's envoys.

They again escorted her to the royal airport to board the jet he'd sent to collect her. During the twenty-minute flight and the drive on landing, she was accompanied by the man who'd met her last night at the airport and had driven her to Ferruccio's mansion. From the few words she managed to extract from him she found out he was Alfredo, Ferruccio's valet and personal assistant.

She got the distinct feeling that this thin, tall, hawkeyed man hated her.

Upon arriving at the mansion, he again walked her to the door and let her in. As he retreated, she detained him.

"Would you please tell him I'm here? I have to see him right away. This shouldn't take long, and then you can drive me back to the jet."

The man looked pointedly at the hand grasping his forearm, cleared his throat. "I'm sorry, *Principessa,* but I am under strict orders. Signore Selvaggio specifically said that whenever you arrive, you are to be let in and that everyone should retreat to their quarters off the estate until he orders us back."

Just as she'd thought yesterday. How convenient. To get her alone, to be free to do whatever he liked without worrying about witnesses. The only wagging tongues this would provoke would be those lashing at her, his latest conquest.

"If he's forbidden you to be on the premises with me here, please call him." He gave her an impassive look. She summoned every iota of control and princesslike graciousness she'd ever have drummed into her, let out a calming exhalation. "I couldn't tell him I was on my way, since his phone was turned off. But you must know how to contact him."

"Signore Selvaggio contacts me. I never intrude on him."

"This is no intrusion. He's expecting me."

"He *was* expecting you. Twelve hours ago."

So that was it. The man who seemed to despise her with a passion, was punishing her for daring to stand up his god!

"Well, I'm here now. How will he know that I am? How do I know he's even here anymore? He could be out doing one of those night sports he told me about."

"I have no idea, *Principessa*. He didn't inform me of his movements tonight. I regret that I can't help you. It's really up to you, what you do now. You can wait until he turns on his phone and you can inform him of your presence. Or he might come in if he's outside, or come downstairs if he's in the mansion. Or if you wish, I can escort you back to the jet and you can reschedule and return some other time."

All graciousness evaporated on a spike of frustration. "It isn't as if you're selling top-secret info to his rivals. *Dio!* So he gave you an order to let me in and leave. That applies only if he's waiting for me. But, because of my…tardiness…he's no longer doing so. So he won't consider you locating him to inform him of my presence a breach of his orders." Alfredo just looked back at her stonily. Clearly, he'd said his last word. And had driven her to the very tip of her wits' end. "Is he so indiscriminating in what he considers insubordination and so unreasonable in meting out punishment that he has you cowering in terror? If he is, then my father and the Council have it all wrong in thinking such a despot can possibly be king material."

The man seemed to expand with affront. "It is Your Highness who has it all wrong. It isn't fear that motivates anyone who works for Signore Selvaggio. It's allegiance. We strive to live up to his expectations, as he always surpasses ours."

Clarissa gaped at the man.

Whoa. Now that was an impassioned little speech. And no doubt the man had meant every word.

Figured. Hadn't Ferruccio himself told her how he manipulated people, had them writhing in contentment under his influence? If his conquests were ecstatic to be conquered by him, as she'd proved to be herself, what would his aides and employees feel? They must believe they were blessed to be chosen to serve in his pantheon, smiled upon by his approval. Just great.

She let the man go, watched him close the door behind him, feeling a cloud of resignation settle over her shoulders.

Which didn't serve any purpose. Alfredo was probably right. Ferruccio was bound to come back. Or down. Or something.

Or nothing. That was what had happened for the next hour.

Ferruccio hadn't appeared. And now she was certain he wouldn't. He was punishing her for being late. The bastard.

She could excuse his right-hand man for being disdainful of her actions, since he didn't know the particulars. But for Ferruccio to dare think she would have rushed over here, after what he'd done to her! And he'd fooled even Antonia, the woman with the character-fathoming X-ray powers, into thinking he was such an outstanding and worthy man. Not that it mattered now. She had to sort through her options about how to deal with this situation.

Alfredo had given her only two options. Wait. Or leave.

Waiting was clearly a futile endeavor. Ferruccio would probably leave her stewing till morning, would maybe even leave the island without letting her see him. Leaving wasn't an option, either. It would draw this out to one, or many more, rounds.

She needed this to be over tonight.

Which brought her to a third option. Go looking for him.

She'd start by combing the upper floors. He was probably sitting in some office upstairs, watching her chase her tail on hidden surveillance cameras.

According to her exploration of the ground floor, there were three staircases leading to different places of the complexly designed mansion. One led to the tower, another to what comprised the eastern facade, the last to the western one.

Without stopping to consider where to start, she found her feet moving. Only after the compulsion had her scaling the stairs did she recall something he told her last night, during those magical hours by the sea. He said he'd insisted on changing the orientation of this place before building commenced. He'd said he was at his clearest, at his most tranquil and powerful, when he slept and worked facing west. That was where she was heading. That was where he was.

With every step up the stairs, her breath shortened. She was far from winded, but that premonition that had told her where she'd find him also told her she was walking into a new plane of existence. One she'd never exit the same, if at all.

She reached the mezzanine-level gallery where he'd stood looking down at her yesterday. From there, the western wing converged into two areas. She didn't hesitate, took the left passageway into a wide corridor of arched columnns.

At regular intervals between the arches about a foot above her head, triangular, bronze sconces, with their apex down and their bases up and open, radiated muted, golden lights across the stone walls, deepening the textures and casting shadows on every structure, boosting the impression that this was an ancient place that had been transported, intact, through time.

At the blind end of the corridor, a smaller replica of the mansion's main door was centered in a thirty-foot wall.

As she approached it, her upheaval rose until it shook her, deafened her.

She stumbled on the last step, ended up with the side of her face plastered to the cool oak. And then she heard them.

Rumbles. Dark, deep.

Agonized.

She froze, held her breath, attempted to silence her heart, strained to catch every nuance, fathom it.

Dio, why was he groaning like that? The terrible sounds quaked through her as explanations streaked through her mind. Suddenly one screeched to a halt, freezing her tremors with horror.

He could be with a woman. Or more than one. She could be hearing the sounds of him in the throes of passion.

The suspicion lasted seconds before conviction vaporized it.

No. He sounded like he was in *pain*.

Suddenly he went silent.

She barged into the room, her heart pounding.

The expansive room was dimly illuminated by sconces similar to those in the corridor. She'd taken two dozen leaps before her momentum died on the beige-marble floor. She came to a stumbling halt a few feet from what must have been a nine-by-nine bed, draped in darkness at the far end of the room.

And there he was, in its middle, spread out on his back. One muscled arm was thrown over his head, the other stretched at a right angle to his body. His formidable chest was bare, his hips and part of his slightly parted, endless legs twisted in dark sheets the color of which she couldn't fathom. His head was tipped back, his face turned toward an arched verandah door framed by white, translucent curtains that billowed in the balmy night breeze.

He looked like a decadent god in the depths of slumber.

But he was totally still. He didn't seem to be breathing.

Panic wrenched through her, propelled her to his side, breath and heartbeats shattering inside her chest.

Before she crashed beside him on the bed, ready to grab and shake him and sob for him to wake up, to be all right, he stirred.

She almost fell to the floor on her knees under the weight of overwhelming relief. *Dio, Dio, grazie, grazie* filled her head. He was…he was…just sleeping.

But he wasn't just sleeping.

Horror seeped back into her blood as she watched his face contort, jerked with the sound his teeth made as they gnashed into a silent snarl, as his whole body tensed.

His every muscle bulged as he arched up from the bed. His

veins, distended as if under a high-pressure surge, stood out like thick ropes running across his sweaty, sculpted flesh. Even in the dim light she could see his golden bronze color become livid with the rush of blood. His breathing turned explosive, erratic. The bed started to shake with the terrible tension arcing through him.

It was as if he were having a seizure. No, worse. It was as if he were struggling to escape a weight that was dragging him under, or crushing him. As if he were bracing for unendurable torture, suppressing agony so that it wouldn't escape his lips in vocal suffering. Then it did.

The rumbles seemed to originate from the deepest reaches of his soul before seeping through his body, guttural snarls filled with fury and ferocity, with dread and desperation, before they burst from his throat in growls of pure torment.

He was in the grips of an inescapable nightmare. Like the ones that still haunted her. The ones she'd assured everyone she no longer had. She'd learned to live with her chronic sleep invaders, trained herself to recognize their advent, to ward off their damage, to escape their talons. At least after she'd woken up. They came far and few between now, but seemed to have gained in power for being less frequent, as if each one slowly built to a crescendo before being unleashed on her unguarded psyche.

She recognized the same anguish radiating from him now, a frequency of distress that resonated with her own.

Was this a one-time occurrence, or was it recurring?

It *was* recurring. She recognized the signs. So, what pain and horror did he relive every time he closed his eyes, surrendered to the supposedly healing embrace of sleep?

The unending possibilities seared her imagination, all the things that could have scarred him body and soul as he grew up, things of which she knew she'd never have anywhere near an accurate picture of their damage and cruelty.

She thought he'd survived them all unscathed. She'd thought him invulnerable.

He wasn't. And here was the proof. This was a man writhing

in torment so deep, suffering from wounds so indelible, they made anything she'd ever endured laughable.

Empathy flooded through her, drove her to her knees beside him on the bed. Her heart would burst if she didn't reach out to him, try to save him from the fangs of the darkness festering inside him, preying on him. She'd do anything to tear him away from its ugliness, absorb all she could into herself. And if some distant voice said this was her nemesis, her tormentor, she willfully ignored its insidious warnings.

This was the only man who'd ever aroused her emotions and passions. Now he aroused every compassionate, protective fiber within her. She couldn't bear the thought of his pain. Not him. Not her conquering, indomitable Ferruccio.

She leaned forward, touched her lips to his clenched eyelids, one after the other, placed her shaking palms on his chest, exerted as gentle a pressure as she could to defuse the excess electricity of upheaval, to persuade his body to relinquish its tension, to subside, let go, be at peace.

His eyes snapped open. In the same split second, her world blurred by then somersaulted in a burst of vertigo and friction, before colliding to a standstill with a lung-emptying slam.

She found herself flat on her back, her hands held above her head in a merciless vise, her throat pressed closed, with two hundred-plus pounds of granitelike manhood and a ton of premium male aggression pinning her to the bed.

She blinked up in shock, saw him looming over her, his face a mask of ferocity, a huge, sleek feline in killing mode, immobilizing his prey before he gouged out its neck.

He blinked, too, then again, dazed, fazed as he removed the hand that had almost choked her. "Clarissa…"

She coughed, realized he'd thought her an attacker.

How many times had he been assaulted, hurt, to develop such an ingrained, lightning-speed reflex in response to a threat?

Hot needles sprouted behind her eyes, the tears seeping from them seeming to originate from her heart.

She felt all his aggression and tension melt away just as his manhood hardened, expanded against her in acute response to feeling her beneath him, so completely accommodating.

Suddenly he let her hands go, rolled off of her and onto his back once more. This time he threw his arm over his eyes.

"*Perdonami… Dio,* Clarissa, I thought you were…were…"

She shakily dragged herself up to her elbows. "What?"

He muttered something indistinct then exhaled. "Nothing. Just what the hell are you doing here anyway, Clarissa?"

She leaned over him, feeling strain still clutching his every muscle. She needed to alleviate it, had to let him know he wasn't alone in dealing with demons that wouldn't let go. "I came looking for you. Then I…heard you. I had to come in, Ferruccio. You were having a nightmare, and I…I wanted to help." Her hands trembled as she grasped his arm, pulled it away from his eyes. "I still do."

Suspicion flared in his gaze before it dissipated and something else took over. Something that, before the past fraught minutes since she'd walked in on him, she hadn't believed him capable of feeling, let alone exhibiting. Naked emotions. Intense, permeating, sincere. She could read them all as if they were being generated inside her, were hers to experience, to revel in, to share. Relief, gratitude, need—or solace, for closeness.

He grabbed one of her hands, pressed it to his chest as his other one trembled its way to her throat. He let out a shuddering breath, as if venting the scare of his life. "*Dio Santo,* Clarissa…I could have hurt you."

She couldn't bear his guilt. She reached out with her free hand, smoothed his forehead. She cursed herself when her lips trembled and lost their grip on her smile, let it slip off. "You didn't. It was like a new kind of roller coaster. You have this flattering way of making me feel like I weigh five pounds instead of a hundred and fifty."

Those painstakingly sculpted lips of his, which had been

pressed into an austere line since he'd jerked awake, relaxed a bit, filled with a measure of his humor and sensuality. "I'm just sorry you got in the way when I was still fighting with whatever it was that invaded my dreams. For a moment there, I couldn't tell that I was awake, that it wasn't happening…anymore."

She sat up, tucked her legs beneath her, used the movement, the moment, to steady herself after that last "anymore" played havoc with her imagination, her heartbeats. "You're not talking about what you've experienced during this nightmare alone."

His eyes escaped hers. Then he seemed to decide not to evade the issue, nodded. "There've been some…bad times. They come back from time to time. I'm not sure why. It's been a very long time since I was a kid on the street fending for my life. The memories have dulled to a distant echo."

"Have they?" She didn't buy that for a second. He didn't know he was talking to an expert in childhood trauma here. "Some memories remain as clear as ever. They even take on sharper clarity with time, become augmented, having been experienced through and recorded by the impressionability and exaggeration of a child's psyche."

His eyes snapped back to hers, amazement glinting in their silver steel depths. She could almost hear him wondering where she got such insight, debating whether to broach the subject. She steeled herself for his questions, preparing evasions, but he seemed to let it go, as she'd fervently hoped, steering away from the land mine of going into her personal history, focusing on his revisited trauma. "I wasn't exactly a child when I ran away from my last foster home."

"You were before you ran away. The reasons you left must have been as…unerasable. And then, thirteen isn't that grown-up. I can't even imagine spending one day on the streets *now,* let alone when I was that age. To be that young and know I have no one to run to, no one to think of me or protect me, to even shelter me and give me a bite to eat when I'm starving…how did you do it, Ferruccio? How did you survive all that?"

His gaze wavered. His voice grew thick, impeded. "Millions of kids survive that and worse every day, all over the world."

"None have become what you've become. There's only one explanation for that. You're a miracle, Ferruccio Selvaggio."

He looked completely taken aback. Flabbergasted. He looked at her as if he thought he was still dreaming, or wading through the aftereffects of a mind-tampering drug.

He must be trying to understand what had brought on her change in attitude. To tell him that, she'd have to tell him things she never wanted to reveal. To him of all people.

Apart from the shock of hearing her admitting her admiration, her awe of him, she could see he was nowhere near back to his steely controlled self. Judging by the redness creeping beneath his razor-sharp cheekbones, he was embarrassed by her praise!

Before she could tell him it wasn't praise, just statement of fact, he shook his head. "I don't think there's any miracle involved in what I achieved. I've had as many good breaks as I've had bad ones. I haven't only been exposed to monsters who live to prey on the vulnerable just because they can, I've been gifted with finding angels who help and guide, also just because they can. I dream of them, too, even if their guest appearances don't elicit such a…dramatic response. When all is said and done, I have more to be thankful for than any man I know. And if the occasional nightmare pops up every now and then as a sort of a 'thou art mortal' reminder, it all comes with the territory."

Her lips twitched at his attempt at levity. But not with humor. With aching. She'd so recently likened him to a drunk-on-power, malicious god. His reference now to what kept him human made her realize more than ever how indescribable his ordeals had been, that he still struggled, that his imperviousness was only a perfected act.

And she realized another vital thing. The likely reason behind his reputation as a heartless womanizer who didn't let women stay the night after he'd had his pleasure. He'd wouldn't want to expose what she'd just witnessed, what he must consider a weakness, to another human being. He probably never thought of seeking solace.

Though he hadn't *chosen* to expose that Achilles' heel to her, he'd easily accepted the fact that she witnessed it and had bared more of his inner self willingly, almost eagerly.

"Grazie molto, mia bella unica."

She stared at him, truly at a loss. "For what?"

He cupped her cheek in his large, warm hand, stroked a gentle finger across the arch of her eyebrow, down her nose to the slightly parted lines of her lips. "For going up against the monsters that go bump inside my head."

The suddenness with which communion, emotional and sublime, switched to awareness, carnal and greedy, was dizzying.

Her eyes had adjusted to the subdued lights, which seemed to have been calibrated to highlight every chiseled plane of his body, every honed groove, every gleaming, silky hair accentuating each line and bulge of power. He'd already been beyond unfair when clothed. Almost naked like this…the injustice was unspeakable.

"You like?"

He'd asked her that her yesterday. Then, he'd meant the masterpiece nature and his domain combined had painted.

He was asking about another work of divine art and human perseverance here. Himself.

She swallowed, gave him the same answer. It still applied, after all. "I'm alive, am I not? I have to like."

His lips spread even as he fully did. "Then…help yourself."

Six

Clarissa didn't know where to start helping herself.

At the jut of his cheekbones, the slope of his forehead, the power of his jaw? Or should she start at the command of his brow, work down the slash of his nose to the hypnosis of that mouth that turned her inside out no matter what it said or did?

Maybe she should bypass his face for now. Take the unprecedented chance to explore his exposed perfection.

But there her choices were even more abundant. Should she start at his shoulders? Which part would she start with? That sculpted clavicle or those ripped deltoids? At his chest? At the daunting expanse of his pectorals where they tapered into the effortless strength-producing bulges of his biceps, or where they were sharply demarcated from his marble-hard six-pack? Or should she start with the raven silk hair that had the exact formation and density to emphasize each muscular mass? There was nothing but more to marvel at along every inch of the taut, polished skin encasing him in an amalgam of living, golden bronze.

And that was just the part that was exposed. The sheets hid

more. She felt almost sorry she hadn't been in any condition to stop and take stock of his below-waistline assets before.

"Let me help you help yourself," he whispered.

Still on his back, seemingly relaxed now, he reached out languidly, took both her hands, brought them to his body.

She moaned at the spike of sensation as he flattened one of her palms against his chest, over his heart, the other low on his abdomen, an inch above the sheets heaped around his hips and thighs.

"Feel that?" She knew he meant the high-voltage current it seemed his flesh was generating. She felt electrocuted and supercharged at once. She nodded. "Your touch paralyzes me with too much sensation, yet makes me feel I can leap buildings."

Just what she felt! She nodded again, more eager. His eyes were slits of passion as he started moving her hands over him, as if he were a master artist, painting an impressionist creation with broad strokes at times, with short flicks and tantalizing dabs at others. Then he brought one of her hands to his face, held it there with both of his, relinquishing the other. He showed her what to do before taking it to his mouth. He alternated between massaging its fleshy parts with nibbles to burying kisses along her palm's lines, to flicking his tongue at the junctures of her fingers, to sucking on each one as his eyes showed her he'd do all that to her everywhere else. Sensations and imaginings sent a current of arousal flowing through her, lodging in her womb.

When her hands resisted him, started to linger where they pleased, to absorb the details she'd longed to touch, he took his hands away, lay back, surrendering to her impending exploration.

Her first totally voluntary action was to cup his face, as she'd dreamed of doing for so long. As long as she could remember, it seemed. She met his eyes as she feathered her thumbs in the hollows beneath the arch of his cheekbones, glided to and fro across the sculpture of his lips, smoothing the wings of his eyebrows before caressing his heavy-with-desire lids shut.

She put her lips to each, felt him tense with every tickle of hot breath. "I did that before, to make you open your eyes, to take you away from the nightmare. Now I want you to savor this, keep your eyes closed, relax." His eyes snapped open instead, all intention of letting her explore him evaporating as he took her by the waist, by the head, tried to bring her lips to his. She resisted, burying her lips at the corner of his mouth as he'd done to her last night. "Let me, Ferruccio. I've wanted to touch you for so long."

He let her go, spread himself for her to take of him what she would. "*Si,* do everything to me, everything you want or have ever fantasized about. There are no limits, just freedom, pleasure."

She knew what her real problem was. Not that she didn't know how to help herself. But that she *couldn't* help herself.

She rubbed her aching breasts against the malleable steel of his chest, on her way to his lips. She paused to study how their chiseled planes were severe and uncompromising, how the bottom one filled into the essence of sensuality. She took it in both of hers, closing her eyes to focus on the tactile exploration, marveling at its strength and softness, its heat and moistness, that magnificent taste that was him.

His body buzzed with tension as her teeth trod her lips' path, as she nudged his lips apart with her tongue and plunged inside in search of more of that addictive taste. She felt him struggle not to grab her head and crash her mouth on his and take over. She almost wanted him to. Almost. She wanted to explore him more.

And she did. All the treasures she'd counted, she touched and tested and tasted. They were even more incredible when feasted on with all the senses.

She was running the tip of her tongue along the grooves separating his six-pack, wondering how was it possible for flesh to be so hard, so hot, to vibrate like that, when he groaned.

"Now do what you want to do most."

She obeyed, took hold of his sheet, and with heart-thudding slowness, pulled it off him. And stared.

The sheet hadn't been heaped. That height had been him. And then there was his girth, his shape.

She'd felt him last night, through their clothes, had thought he was as unique there as everywhere else. Again imagination fell way short of reality. Her mouth watered, her hands stung.

"Feel me, Clarissa," he urged, his eyes as glazed as hers. "Enjoy me, own me. Show me how good it feels to touch me, how alive it makes you feel to know you do this to me."

She was melting with need. But the enormity of what she wanted to do, what he was coaxing and commanding her to do, still overwhelmed her. She felt too inexperienced to live. Sure, she knew the mechanics. But only theoretically. She'd never touched a man. Not like this, not in any other way.

She'd been a recluse her first eighteen years, and the next four hadn't been much better as she poured all her focus and energy into her studies and sports. She'd rebuffed approaches, not only because they targeted her to exploit her status, to "score with a princess," but because she hadn't been interested in anyone.

Then she met *him*. And she knew. It was him or no one. And since she'd believed it would never be him, she believed she'd never know a man's touch. Now she knew it—*his* touch. Now she could touch and see and feel and exult—in him. Only him.

Her hand tried to close around him, couldn't. She swallowed as he throbbed in her grasp, as her skin absorbed the fusion of softness and hardness, the heat coursing in his shaft. He echoed her moan with a long groan as she stroked him. She watched pleasure slash across his hewn face, his muscled hips flexing as he thrust to her rhythm and watched her with mounting hunger. She worshipped him, brought her face down to his power and scent, all him, all male. She couldn't help herself again.

She flicked her tongue across his erection's crown, almost passed out at feeling the slick satin of his flesh against her tongue, his tangy taste against her taste buds. She inhaled deep to draw oxygen to her brain and only drew his scent into her lungs. With a cry of urgency, she opened her mouth to take in all she could of him.

His hand twisted in her hair, stopped her.

She whimpered. "I want to taste your pleasure."

"You will. As I will taste yours, over and over. But I want our first pleasure together to be flesh in flesh."

She wanted that, too. She was dying for that. But then, she was dying for everything. All at once. But he wanted that first. She was dying to give him everything he wanted.

She felt clumsy after the abandon of feasting on him, didn't know what to do now. Her gaze wavered to his face as he sat up.

His eyes burned a path down her short-sleeved, form-fitting top and its matching stretch pants. "Not a skirt suit, and yet another outfit that will forever feature in my most erotic fantasies. I want it off you. Now, Clarissa."

Without a word or thought, thankful for the instruction, she crossed her hands at the hem of her top and pulled it over her head. She wanted it off, too. Couldn't bear the friction of cloth on her burning skin, the imprisonment of her swollen flesh.

He growled something predatory at the sight of her breasts, fuller with arousal in the confines of her bra, deepening her cleavage. She fell back on the bed with the blow of arousal that slammed into her at the sound, the intention behind it.

He rose to his knees above her. "More, Clarissa. Show me the rest of you. Bare yourself fully to me. Drive me totally crazy."

Her hands felt unmatched as she struggled with the button and zip of her pants. She shuddered all over as she tried to wriggle out of them. He watched her writhe before him, the ferocity in his eyes mounting. Then he exploded to his feet on top of the bed, bent and picked up her legs, raised her by them until only her shoulders and head touched the bed. He stared down at her, their harsh pants of stimulation filling the air.

She knew how she must look to him, held in his power upside down like that, half-fainting, wanting and inviting anything he'd do to her, lying in a pool of her hair, her breasts almost spilling from her bra under the pull of gravity, her stretch pants bunched midway down her thighs, her light purple panties stained by the darkness of her desire for him, the legs he held trying as hard as they could to pull him down, bring him between them.

Then in one swipe, like a magician, he had her stretch pants off.

He lowered her legs to the bed, stood above her, eating her alive with his eyes before he came down, prowled on all fours over her, until his powerful limbs became a prison of muscle and maleness all around her. "*Mia bella unica.* You are the miracle. And you were right. I'm very good at hiding my insanity. For six years, I've been insane." His hands dipped beneath her and she arched up, helping him as he undid her bra. He peeled it off and her swollen breasts fell into his palms. She cried out as he pressed them together, mitigating the ache, increasing the need. He bent and showed her there was more suffering, more pleasure. Between long, hard pulls on her nipples, he swirled them with his tongue, grazed them with his teeth, blew the stimulation of his confessions on them. "You made me lose my mind with a look, a word. And that was before I touched you. Last night, early this morning, every gasp and moan, your pleasure and desire, whether I see them or feel them or imagine them, make me go mad. You were born to drive me to distraction."

"Ferruccio, please…" This time she knew what she was begging for. "Don't wait…I can't…I can't…"

His hands clamped her buttocks, squeezed and fondled, before he rid them of that last barrier in another magical move. "There will be no more waiting. Never again, do you hear?"

"Yes, yes…please." Her quaking thighs opened for him, unashamedly offering, hurrying, begging.

He took his erection in his hand, but instead of driving into her, filling the emptiness gnawing at her, he glided the scorching head, flowing with his own arousal, through the engorged lips of her sex until he reached her slit. Her flesh fluttered around what it could reach of his hardness, as if trying to grab onto him, drag him inside her.

"Do you see how wet and hot and ready for me you are?" He glided up, nudged her most sensitive knot of flesh. She rose off the bed with a shrill cry of surprise and ecstasy. "When you were touching yourself for me, what were you imagining, Clarissa? Was it my fingers fondling you, my tongue licking you…or this?"

He glided down then up again, circled her swollen knot until she writhed, everything in the world, all reason and meaning focusing where his flesh tormented hers.

She keened her confession. "This…I saw you, felt you doing this…I was dying for you to do it for real. But this is a thousand times better…I never knew…*anything*…could feel this good."

"Neither did I. And it'll only get better." He slid down a second before she came apart, then he thrust into her slit in compulsive strokes, shallow, fast, almost uncoordinated, his face driven.

Even as coherence seeped out of her, she realized he wasn't in control of himself. His actions weren't premeditated. He was as lost as she. And she knew something else. No one else had ever seen his vulnerability, provoked his uncontrollable need. Only her.

The conviction spread through her like a rush of lifesaving water after she'd been parched and withering.

She hooked her legs around him, tried to pull him, bring him inside her. She knew it would hurt. She wanted it to. She wanted him to brand her this first time.

Then he did. He lunged, tearing through her barrier, then plunging past into the depths that yielded for him, feeling like a sword just out of the fire. She screamed, writhed with the pain, with its excruciating pleasure, with the carnality, the completion of Ferruccio dominating her and surrendering to her captivation.

"*Dio, Dio santo*…so tight, so hot. Clarissa, *amore*…you're burning me." Her face was clenched in what looked like suffering as he withdrew then plunged deeper, again, and again, forging farther inside her, feeling as if he'd never bottom out. "Burn me, *cuore mio,* consume me as I invade you, take all of me, all the way inside you, all the way to the heart of you."

He did feel he was all the way inside her. For a moment she thought he'd reached her heart for real. And he had—the heart of her femininity, her womb. That intimate nudge was beyond anything she'd dreamed of. Beyond endurance. Just the concept of it, the reality! All her life, everything she'd ever felt for him, every spark of sensation gathered into one pinpoint of absolute being, of experiencing everything at once. Then it exploded.

She convulsed, shattered, then reformed for the next wave. She heard screams accompanying the rending ecstasy razing through her. Then she heard his roar, felt him stiffen in her clutching arms, ramming her deeper than ever before, breaching her completely as jet after jet of warmth flooded her. His release. His seed, filling her. Her first intimacy, her only man, taking his pleasure inside her as he gave her more than pleasure.

She shook, writhed, wept. Then... Nothing.

Ferruccio felt Clarissa slump beneath him, her satin limbs sliding off him like the shedded petals of a rose.

Panic mushroomed in his chest as he took his weight off her inert body on shaking arms. He groaned as he withdrew from the depths that still clutched him, a prisoner to her possession.

He frantically examined her. Her face, streaked in tears, her lips, shining and plum red, parted...and gusting tranquil breaths.

He collapsed beside her. *Dio*...for a moment there he'd thought...

He shook his head in self-deprecation. Had he started to believe his own reputation as a lady-killer?

He rose again and looked down at her, all of her, all the treasures he hadn't been in any condition to slow down and savor, when his first exposure to them had driven him into a frenzy.

Which wasn't an excuse for pouncing on her like he had.

For six years he'd promised himself that the first time he got her in his bed, he'd pamper and service her until he had her weeping with satisfaction before taking his.

He'd achieved that, had her in such acute pleasure, she'd wept. In an agony of release she came so hard that she fainted. But that wasn't the refined, protracted seduction he'd planned on. He'd lost control.

He'd never before come within miles of losing control.

But he'd touched her, and he'd become a mindless predator bound on branding his mark on his mate.

And how he had. He was shaken at the enormity of the experience. Branding her as his had been the first surrender of his life, his first real and total pleasure. But she'd branded him as hers, too. As he'd known she would when he'd first seen her and those intense feelings of possession, of belonging, had come over him. Before her rejection had swathed his feelings in harshness of bitterness, resentment and anger...

He ran a hand heavy with possession over her. His. At last.

He gathered her cooling body to him, took her into his still shaking arms...and froze. Beneath her. A tiny pool of blood.

Panic surged again. It subsided within a moment. The location and amount of the blood said it all; he'd been her first.

The discovery shook him. Elated him. Made him want to pound his chest and do backflips. She *had* been his all along.

But...if she had been, why had she put him—and herself—through all this? Why had it taken him going all caveman on her to make her give them this at last?

He looked down at the face etched by satiation, transformed by the experience. The image of all his dreams and fantasies, and far beyond both. And his rage crept back.

Why was he even wondering? He'd always known why.

He'd always felt her answering craving, felt her holding it on a tight leash, evading him so she wouldn't succumb to the temptation. Because it had been abhorrent to her. *He* had been. She might have decided to give in to her hunger now, since he'd made it in her best interest to do so.

He'd told her to persuade him, but she'd come here not bent on persuasion but on conquering. And when she'd gone up in flames in his arms, she *had* conquered him. If she could do this to him without experience, he failed to imagine what kind of hold she'd have on him when she gained sexual confidence. Now that he'd tasted her, he was already addicted. He had to have more—all of her.

Disappointment twisted inside him, damaging things he hadn't known existed there. Hope, need, dependency. All the things she'd unearthed in him since he'd first seen her, things she brought into the open when she'd seen him without his shields. She'd offered him a haven of her very self, given him a purity he'd never experienced, of appreciation, of empathy and eagerness to defuse his turmoil, to defend him against the shadows of his past.

And all along she'd remained the woman who despised him in her heart. There was no other explanation for the past years or her recent resistance. He should stop fooling himself, stop looking for excuses to exonerate her.

Not that that made any difference now. Now, she was his. And she'd remain his. As he'd remain hers.

Not that he was handing her power over him. Ever. He was getting what he wanted from her, and giving back only what would keep her in his power, in every way.

A wisp of gossamer slid down her face, her neck, her breast, the soothing contentment of it flowed until it suddenly turned into an electric current that zapped to her head, forked to her toes, turned to another pulse of heavy need between her legs.

Her eyes snapped open. He filled her vision in the now candlelit darkness.

Ferruccio. The man she'd been running from for what felt like her whole life. Spread out on his side beside her, propped on one elbow, running his hands in appreciation up and down the body he'd possessed, awakened, ravaged, satisfied, all to the point that she'd lost consciousness for the first time in her life.

This, him, was what she'd waited for for six years. And for all her life before she'd ever seen him, when she must have known on some level that he existed. Finding him had been like finding the answer to the incompleteness she'd suffered. Losing him, the hope and endless possibilities of him, had been a loss she dedicated herself to recovering from, to living with.

She'd been deluded. She'd thought what he made her feel yesterday and this morning was all she could feel. Now she knew what he could do to her every time his hands glided over her, his lips and teeth owned her, his potency filled and rode her. She knew the meaning of yearning.

It went far beyond the physical. After what they'd shared before they made love, then the way he let her have him before he had her, it spanned everything she was capable of feeling.

She'd long escaped admitting it. She could run no more.

She loved him.

How she loved him. With everything in her.

And it changed nothing. She was just a convenience for him. Or was she? The things he'd said, the way he'd treated her, taken her...could he possibly feel more for her than she believed?

"That was some persuasion." Her heart lurched at the tone of his voice. The passion and sincerity were gone. He rose above her, and his eyes were filled with lust untouched by anything softer or higher. "But I already feel the need to be persuaded some more. I'll need constant persuasion from now on."

She plummeted from heaven to crash into cold reality. His.

Here was her answer. She was another victory. A strategic one, guaranteed to put so many pieces of his plan into place.

He found her secrets, her triggers, disintegrating her body into pleasure even as he smashed her heart into smaller pieces. And she did the only thing she could to ward off the pain. She matched his nonchalance, his coldness.

"I assume you're satisfied with my test drive? You must be extra pleased to find me in brand-new condition."

He gave a cruel chuckle. "You have no idea. Let me demonstrate the level of my pleasure on your own made-for-pleasure body."

He rose from the bed and carried her to his bathroom, where he'd prepared a bubbling bath. He took her into the soothing waters, bathed her and healed her. His hands glided over her, possessing her, possessing the ability to dissolve her shackles, release her potential. He made her feel both vulnerable and all-powerful. Savored and devoured. He had her writhing, pleading. He made her watch his hand delve between her thighs. His fingers knew just where and how hard or gentle or fast to touch, plunging and withdrawing, stroking, stoking until he had her heaving with a screeching orgasm.

His mouth milked hers for each last shriek as his fingers changed rhythm, desensitizing her, infusing her with renewed desperation. He growled satisfaction at her resurrected hunger, as he raised her onto the marble platform by the tub, laid her there on her back, her legs parted and bent at its edge. He tormented his way down her heaving body, took her legs over his shoulders, came to lie where it all converged. "Open for me, *amore*. I'm hungry."

Incoherent under the pressure mushrooming in her loins, she opened wide for him. Legs and heart and abandon.

He bent to her quivering flesh, swept her in a long lick that knocked her internal lights out before he fused his tongue and teeth there and suckled and flicked until she thought something inside her was charring, until her body gushed molten agony, trembled with detonation after detonation of satisfaction. He sucked every spasm out of her in a tongue-thrusting kiss that went on until he again had her climbing, clawing, crazed. Ready for him again.

Her eyes clung to his as he lifted her from the platform where she lay in a pool of sweat, bathwater and condensed steam, dried her, carried her back to the bedroom and laid her down on the bed. Candlelight and moonlight cast flickering gold and steady silver over his rugged planes as he came over her, intersecting at arcane shadows. He bore down on her, opened her around his hips, raised hers and held them in one hand, the other supporting him as he rose halfway on both knees. Then he plunged.

He knew. Knew that she was suffocating to have his flesh in hers, the razing friction, the beyond-her-limits expansion. And he gave it all to her. Impaled her to her womb, her gut, her heart.

He slammed into her and she screamed for more. Then the tidal wave was cresting again. She pleaded his name, begging him to join her in oblivion. He did, in jets of completion, roars of surrender.

He came down beside her, tenderness back in his eyes, his hands, the coldness burned away in the inferno of what they'd shared.

And through the night, though he wouldn't take her again, said he shouldn't have taken her again so soon, he pleasured her in so many ways. And in every touch, every word, he confessed his pleasure, his inability to get enough. As did she.

Midday sun poured through the open windows when she next woke up. She was alone in bed.

She jerked up, looking for Ferruccio.

He found him standing on the other side of the bed, fully dressed, hands in pockets, looking down at her broodingly.

Her heart sank. In this insanity-inducing game of hot and cold that he played, were they back to cold?

His eyes said they were. Then his words completed the frost. "Now that your 'test drive' has proved so mutually and mind-blowingly pleasurable, I'm moving to the next logical step. Marriage."

Seven

Clarissa rose cautiously.

The soreness between her legs forced the carefulness. That, plus feeling as if she'd frozen and might shatter at any sudden move. She scooped up her clothes without looking at him, went to the bathroom.

She remained there for an hour, trying to regain some composure.

She came out to find him at the far end of the room, at his reading table. She walked over to him, running the words she'd decided to say through her head one more time.

She stopped before him, recited them. "I want to thank you for the tremendous initiation, but now I demand that you keep up your end of the deal, become crown prince and leave me alone."

Ferruccio gave her a bored smile. "This is getting old. When will you think before you talk? You now, more than ever, have no option but to fall in with my plans. I have no option but to marry you, either. That you were in 'brand-new-condition' is exactly why neither of us has another option."

"Taking my virginity doesn't mean we have to get married."

"Taking *you* twice, without protection, does," he retorted. "You could already be pregnant."

Everything stilled as the blow registered. A quick calculation told her he could be right. She felt she was falling into an abyss. "Even if I am, it isn't your responsibility. I'm way over the age of consent, and I consented to everything that happened. If I'm pregnant, I'll handle it on my own."

His benign boredom evaporated in a tide of aggression as he rose, neared her. "*Handle* it? As in an abortion? Or maybe have the baby then put it up for adoption?"

His most sensitive issue.

How dared he think her capable of either course of action!

"If I'm pregnant," she seethed. "I'll have the baby and love it for the rest of my life. You needn't concern yourself."

His scowl was spectacular. "You know nothing about me, do you? No child of mine is growing up a bastard."

"That's an antiquated view!" she cried out. "Millions of single moms raise children alone."

His lips curled. "Save your opinion about the advantages of single motherhood until you've been one. And then you shouldn't speak for your child. Would you, who had the benefit of two loving parents, deprive your child of the same security? Would you, a princess in a conservative kingdom steeped in family values, brave being an unmarried mother? Or would you leave Castaldini to be one, all so that you can have the last word? So you won't have to submit to me? So you can spite me?"

She flinched as his voice rose on the last words, his sudden move bringing her arm up in an instinctive blocking gesture.

She lowered it at once, praying he hadn't noticed her action.

But he noticed everything.

He looked at her as if *she* had dealt *him* a crippling blow.

He at last rasped, "*Dio santo,* you thought…you thought I was going to…*hit* you?" She looked determinedly away. "Clarissa! Look at me. Did you think I would? Don't you know that I'd sooner cut off both my arms than lay a hand on you in anything but passion?"

"Anger is a passion," she mumbled.

"No, anger is a weakness," he snapped. "Venting it in physical abuse is a *crime.* I never give in to the first, will never be guilty of the second. But I'm certain someone's hit you before. Who was it? I demand to know who the sick wretch is."

She escaped his seeking hands. "Leave me alone, Ferruccio."

He caught her back. "I will never leave you alone. And you will tell me who scarred you to the point that you cringed at my sudden move, expecting a blow. This hasn't happened once before, it has happened repeatedly. You've come to expect violence to be the only way someone would express their displeasure."

"Let me go, damn you."

"I won't let you go until you tell me who did this to you."

"So you're physically restraining me to make me bow to your will? And you think you're any better than the person who hit me? Both of you use physical force to vent your frustrations and impose your warped will."

He let her go abruptly, and she felt as if she'd lost all anchors. His grip hadn't even been uncomfortable. It had been possessive but not coercive, filled with a power that had told her it would be used on her behalf, would never be turned against her.

"Fine, don't tell me," he gritted. "It's easy for me to figure out who it is. You haven't had any relationships with men, so it couldn't have been a stranger. It has to be a family member. And it could only be one. Your father."

"*No.*"

"Yes. Who else could get away with abusing you? Your brothers wouldn't have. I *know* them. I'm going to take him apart."

"Ferruccio, stop it. You're not coming near him."

"Don't worry, I won't give him a taste of his own medicine,

even if compared to me he's as helpless as the child you were when he abused you. I can deliver hits that will hurt far more than kicks and blows. I will dethrone that twisted bastard and exile him. He'll never have the privilege of coming near you again!"

"You're wrong, he…didn't…" She felt she'd faint again.

"Don't defend him, Clarissa, or my punishment of him will only be harsher, last far longer."

"You just want to punish him, but not for me, for yourself."

He went still. "What do you mean by that?"

"You think he's the reason you remained unacknowledged by your family, and you're using me as an excuse to hurt him as you imagine he's hurt you."

He cracked a harsh laugh. "I couldn't care less about the acknowledgement of my so-called family. The two D'Agostinos who've become a part of my life haven't done so through the ties of blood—which I think are grossly overrated—but through mutual respect, through clicking on fundamental levels, through being able to like and count on one another. As for the rest of the extensive D'Agostino clan, I care nothing for their opinion of me, or their existence in this world one way or another. In fact, I think if those people had had any presence in my life, they would have only hindered me. I believe that by hiding me from them, your father has actually protected me from their interference and negative influences. So not having the 'acknowledgement of my family' certainly won't be why I'll punish him. I'll punish him for you, and only for you."

She grabbed his arm, shook him. "You won't come near him, do you hear? Or…or you'll never come near me again!"

He bared his teeth. "He abused you—"

"He *didn't!* He *protected* me!"

"From *whom?* Who could have had such access to you, a princess, that your father, the king, had to protect you from them?"

And she wailed, *"It was my mother."*

This shocked him so much she felt his whole body stiffen

as if against a brutal blow, saw his face seize with horror and confusion. "How? *Dio*...why?"

She shook her head dejectedly. "Just leave it be, Ferruccio."

"You didn't 'leave it be' when you woke me from my nightmare. You wanted to know, to help. You think I can do anything less?"

"As you said, it's in the past. It has been for twenty years."

"And it's clearer than ever in your memory. Having been 'experienced through the impressionability and exaggeration of a child's psyche.'"

She grimaced. "You have total recall, don't you?"

His lips compressed. "You should know by now that I can't be distracted when I'm bent on something. *Tell* me."

"You didn't really tell me anything. Why should I tell you?"

"I'll tell you everything down to the last detail you can possibly stomach. All you have to do is ask. Now start talking."

She knew he'd get it out of her one way or another. She gave in, shrugged. "She was having marital troubles with my father..."

"And she took it out on you?"

"She had a psychiatric disorder, I guess."

"You guess? She wasn't diagnosed? Treated?"

"She never admitted there was anything wrong with her. Lack of insight supports the opinion that she was deeply disturbed. You see, my mother was very beautiful and she'd been pursued since she was a teenager. Her father, a very rich and influential man, believed all her pursuers were fortune hunters. He drove them away then turned on her to 'discipline' her. Especially when she got attached to one of them for a while."

"He hit her when she was old enough to get married?"

"Do you want me to talk, or do you want to play commentator and analyst?" He raised an eyebrow, made a mock-contrite gesture for her to go on. "My grandfather then arranged her marriage to my father, a self-made billionaire and the new king of Castaldini, someone he thought worthy of his only heiress. Everything went like a fairy tale, and they had two male heirs to their lineage and combined fortunes, if not to the crown. But in truth, things went from bad to worse between her and my father. It seems they conceived me during one of their last attempts at being a couple. An attempt that failed. After I was born, they were unofficially separated and my mother focused on me to a pathological level."

"She wouldn't let you out in the sun, to play in the sea like all children should. She told you it was for your own good when she was using you to anesthetize her pain. She made you her life's project so she could have an excuse to suffocate you, used her innocent little girl as an antidote to her failure to earn the dependence of someone who had a choice. And when it didn't stop her pangs, she punished you for it."

She gave a mocking sigh. "Okay, I'm shutting up now. You're ready to write a book analyzing my mother's character, motivations and every last action."

"I became who I am by reading people accurately from a single word or action."

He was so outrageously sure of himself. And so right to be. She sighed again. "Yeah. You're so good, sometimes I think you read minds. So…now you know. How about we drop this?"

"And continue the other eagerly anticipated subject we were discussing before we diverged into that delightful revelation, you mean? All in due course. You haven't finished this story. Tell me how this ended, your father's role in this mess. Where was he when your mother was suffocating you and systemati- cally abusing you?"

"Listen, don't try to swing this back into my father's corner. I won't let you. He was the king and he had a job to do, a very complex job as you'll discover, if it becomes yours one day. My mother kept me in her apartments, and he had no reason to think anything was wrong. Apart from dogging my every step and controlling my every breath until I was about five, she was sort of okay. But I admit, I was a handful. Hyperactive and rebellious, never responding until she yelled at me or shook me, never obeying any order until threatened and punished."

"Good for you."

She hugged herself. "Not really. I think I drove her over the edge."

"She told you that, didn't she?" he snarled.

"When she started hitting me for real? Yeah, she said I made her do it, being so naughty."

"Every abuser's excuse. That their victim made them do it."

"I guess so. She…she also kept saying she hated me for being so like my father, that she hated him because he stopped loving her." She paused to gulp a breath and to brace herself against the terrible sound his teeth made gritting against each other. "Then it was over, just like that. A few days after my eighth birthday, Durante walked in unannounced and found her…found her…"

"Hitting you. How did she hit you, Clarissa?"

"How do people hit? The usual way."

"I've hit many people in my life. Bullies bigger than me or equals who attacked me first. But since I hit to end an aggression, I hit hard, go for the face. She didn't touch your face, did she? That was how she got away with it, leaving no marks on you. She covered you from head to toe in clothes and said you sunburn easily when she was covering the bruises she inflicted on you. She wasn't so crazy after all, was she, if she gave covering her crime that much care and premeditation?" Clarissa could no longer find air to breathe. He'd sucked it all out of her world with his insight, the way he'd framed what she'd always shied away from seeing, realizing. "How was she hitting you when Durante walked in?"

"She—she was kicking me. In the stomach."

There was that terrible grinding sound again, accompanied by the marrow-chilling purr of an enraged lion. "Did he hit her?"

"Would you have hit your mother in the same situation?"

He bared his teeth. "*Maledizione, si*…hell, yes."

"Well, Durante isn't you. He isn't used to violence or so quick to use his fists. And he'd had years with her when she was whole, when he adored her. He'd been torn over her deterioration for a long time, and he was so shocked to witness what he did. He had believed that I was her world, all that she lived for anymore. He restrained her, took her kicks and spitting and ranting that she hated him, too, for being so like our father. Then he took me away, gave me to Antonia, then went to our father and demanded that I be removed from my mother's apartments and care, forever. And I was. My father took me to his apartments and I've been safe ever since."

"What happened to your mother?"

"She seemed to…give up. On everything."

"Only abusing you gave her the will to go on, eh?"

"Please, Ferruccio. She's still my mother."

"She forfeited her right to be your mother the first time she hit you to vent her self-absorbed anger and petty frustrations."

She tried to huff a laugh. It came out a distressed rasp. "If that was universally applied, no one would have mothers or fathers anymore."

His scowl deepened. "You know what I mean. She injured you, repeatedly, systematically, got more vicious as time went by. She could have killed you."

"I don't think it would have gone that far. And after a few years, I—I became sort of her keeper, until I went to college. She wasn't the same woman who abused me anymore…and I— I loved her."

"How could you love someone who scarred you like that?"

She cast her filled eyes downward. "You wouldn't understand."

"Because I didn't have a loving mother who made all my nightmares come true, you mean? Now I'm really thankful I didn't. At least my nightmares were inflicted by strangers."

"I know it's inexplicable, the unbreakable bond a child forms with the first one who holds and cares for her. And she *did* care for me, in her way. There were good times, like you said, before and after the abusive period. And on the whole, I am far luckier than most women I know, too. I have amazing brothers, I'm healthy, I achieve good things, I live in a fairy-tale palace and I'm the daughter of the best king and father in the world. I bet any woman on earth would switch places with me in a second."

He caught his lip in vicious, white teeth, as if holding back something even he thought he shouldn't say. Then he said, "What I don't get is, after they found out your mother had been abusing you, how did they still turn you over to that Antonia battle-axe?"

A laugh burst out of her. His lips thinned. He thought she was going to make light of it, wasn't allowing it. "Sorry. It's just I always mentally, and very fondly, refer to her as a battleship! And here you are, coming up with something very close. But let me tell you, between my father's gentleness, Durante's protectiveness, Paolo's companionship and Antonia's discipline—which was as invaluable as her name proclaims her to be, and which was never in any way excessive and nothing but constructive— they probably saved my sanity. I think I turned out okay."

"As I said before, you turned out far beyond okay."

"Yeah, yeah, a merciless, shameless siren."

"As accurate an assessment as I ever made. One I can't be more thankful for. In case you're thinking of contesting my verdict, remember what you did to me all through the night. When you were fresh out of your box, too." He tugged on her, plastered her against him, showing her what she was doing to him now. "Which brings us back to our original discussion. Say yes, Clarissa."

How could she? And how could she tell him that the discussion they'd just had was why she was resisting?

She'd been running scared because she knew she'd fall for him all the way to no return. She'd been right. She now felt him mixed with her very blood and breath. He was more than she ever thought could be found in one man.

But he was incapable of intimacy. He had friends, allies, employees who worshipped the ground he walked on, but so did her father. Her father loved his children, his people, but hadn't been able to love the woman who'd literally lost her mind over him. Her mother had accused him of loving another, but Clarissa believed she'd been looking for reasons that he hadn't been able to love *her*. Her father and Ferruccio both seemed to have a glitch in their makeup. They were great men, but when it came to women it seemed they were incapable of loving one, or really loving any.

And just as her father was into leading, inspiring, Ferruccio was into vanquishing, acquiring. Sure, he made his acquisitions eternally grateful to be his. As he'd made her. But could she live with it, if that was all he could give her?

He was choosing her, using the same cerebral premeditation with which her father had chosen her mother. But it was even worse in their situation. Her mother didn't start out loving her father, and she was almost certain her father didn't set out to enslave her mother physically, like Ferruccio was doing to her.

Which meant it would be even worse for her.

But he was right, as he invariably was. If she was pregnant, her own life and emotions had to give way to her baby's. Just like her mother again. Not that she was like her mother in that she would follow the same path of psychological degeneration. Even if her heart was destroyed, she'd never take it out on her child. She'd do all she could to be the best mother she could be.

But she still had to try one final attempt to save herself.

She pushed out of his arms. "If I become pregnant, I'll marry you. If not, you become crown prince without me in the equation."

Would he *ever* learn?

Ferruccio wrestled with the tsunami of fury and offense that threatened to burst his arteries.

She made marrying him sound like an amputation, a drastic

measure to be resorted to only if all efforts to save the limb—in this case her life, from his infection—failed.

He struggled to summon the unfathomable facade that had been one of his major weapons as he considered her conditions.

If he agreed to them, she'd either end up married to him for the baby, or he'd find himself king of Castaldini without her by his side. Neither situation was acceptable.

So he countered her bargain. "We'll marry, *now*. I will wait until we're married to take you again. Give you time to heal." He gave her a taunting smile. "And to…miss me so much the wedding night will make last night pale into nothing." He saw her nipples jut against her top, conquer the thickness of both bra and top, knew her body was readying itself for his, needing him to ride it, pound it, satisfy it. But he wouldn't take her again until she begged. Again. And he would make her reach the begging point. "If you wish, I'll use protection, or you can protect yourself. If you are already pregnant, our immediate marriage will prevent speculation about the timing of our baby's conception. If you aren't, and in say, six months' time, we consider marriage between us not a viable endeavor, I'll let you leave my bed and we'll quietly separate. We can go on living in the palace without ever crossing each other's path. And if, one day, either of us wants an end to the marriage, to marry another perhaps, we'll work out something civil."

As she gaped at him, he congratulated himself for making it sound as if he wasn't desperate for her to say yes, as if she had a way out, if she wanted it, along the road, so she wouldn't panic and still say no.

But he would *make* her say yes. And keep on saying it. Forever.

This was his life's main objective now.

And he always got what he set his mind on.

Eight

"So now we know the exact time the world will come to an end."

Clarissa winced. Her friend's taunt, combined with looking at Ferruccio across the ballroom, made her feel as if she was wading in déjà vu.

Which was a misleading sensation. Apart from the same setting and faces, this occasion was poles apart from that first one.

Then, he'd been a stranger to her father's court. Now he resided over what would be his own.

Another major difference was that she'd escaped him then. Now she found no escape from his logic. Or her own weakness, which kept whispering that in six-months' time, she could become more than his convenient bride. With that hope prodding her and her love igniting its flame into an inferno, she'd capitulated.

The moment she had, yesterday, he'd taken her back to meet with her father and the Council to announce his acceptance and their decision to get married. Immediately.

They'd been in the general assembly chamber, and Ferruccio had just estimated that, to prepare the wedding befitting his princess and future queen, he needed six days. She'd been wondering if he was playing up the god connection when her father had dropped his biggest bomb yet. He was abdicating.

She vaguely remembered hearing him say he was no use as king anymore, that he wanted Ferruccio to have the full range of authority to turn around Castaldini's situation right away, that he wanted Ferruccio to be crowned king during his lifetime, *and* on the same day he married Clarissa.

"So, do you think five days is enough time for us all to make peace with each other, to say good-bye to this life and prepare for the next? Can't you convince your groom-to-be to give us more time? I'd say this mean feat needs at least a couple of weeks."

Clarissa rounded on her friend. "Oh, Luci, shut up."

Luci's eyes gleamed unrepentantly. "You know the price of my silence. Spill."

"What's to spill? You know everything."

Luci narrowed her eyes. "I was born a good bit before yesterday, you know. You're telling me, or I'm walking up to your godly hunk and asking him for his version of the developments. I bet he'd be willing to share..." She stopped, groaned. "I didn't mean it *that* way." Clarissa's lips twisted. Luci's embarrassment evaporated. "But you know that. So?"

Clarissa shrugged. "He asked me to marry him, and I agreed."

"Okay, our king, in five days' time, seems about to have an opening in the queue waiting to suck up to him. I'm running to take that spot in three...two..."

Clarissa rolled her eyes. "Okay, okay. What do you want to know?"

"You slept with him, didn't you?" Clarissa gaped at her friend. She knew Luci was straightforward, but she still hadn't imagined that would be her first question out of the gate. "Don't answer that. I know you did. You're radiating it."

Clarissa held her hand up, turned it back and forth. "I am?"

Luci snickered. "Cute. And you are. And he is, too. Remember that first night when you turned to look at him across the ballroom? It was as if you generated a field of attraction between you. That was why I was so stunned when he approached me and Stella, and then when you tried to pretend he didn't exist from then on. It was weirder when I sensed that he was always on your mind."

"Everyone's a psychic nowadays."

"Not me." Clarissa closed her eyes at the sound of the new voice. Antonia. Just what she needed. To be sandwiched between the two and only busybodies in her life, now of all times. "I certainly didn't see this coming. Not this fast, anyway. When I told you to go snatch him up, you took it to heart, didn't you, *ragazza impertinenta?*"

"She's not only a naughty girl," Luci complained. "She's downright wicked. She won't tell me details!"

Clarissa wondered if the earth had ever truly swallowed anyone. Now would be a good time. She was so ready to disappear.

Antonia looked at Clarissa shrewdly, her fighter jet–fast mind working it out. "*Si,* do tell us details. You were gone for a night and you returned with him on your arm, in an obscene hurry to get married and unable to tear his eyes off you. It must have been one hell of a night, to land you a man like Ferruccio Selvaggio."

Clarissa choked on shock. "And to think I lived all these years thinking you were a conservative pain, *bambinàia.*"

"Me? Conservative? By the time I was your age I'd had three lovers, and I've since had two husbands, God rest their souls."

"Donna Antonia conservative? She's a regular black widow!"

Antonia and Luci had overlapped. They looked at each other, Luci in impish challenge, Antonia in I'll-get-you-later threat.

Then Antonia sighed. "You were every nanny's dream charge as you grew up, one guaranteed to never get herself in trouble. But then you passed the age of consent...."

"About a century ago!" Luci put it.

Antonia glared at her, yet nodded. "What she said. And it got really old, this puritanical existence you led. I'd look at you and seethe with the waste of all that vital womanhood, especially with the epitome of manhood hanging around, courting you and getting rebuffed for his trouble. Now I'm wondering if you've just been devilishly clever all along."

"You mean, have I been sexually active and pulling the wool over your eyes?" Antonia's eyes wavered in surprise. "Hey, you can say intrusive stuff, and I can't say things like that?"

Antonia glowered. "If you were, and it wasn't with him, then you were a colossal fool."

"Then you'll be happy to know I wasn't a fool, colossal or otherwise, with him or with anyone else."

Luci poked her in the chest. "Till two days ago. I'm sure of it. You looked like another person then. Now you've…"

"Turned into some sort of radiator." Clarissa smirked at Antonia's confusion. "Previous bit of conversation before you barged in, *bambinàia*."

Antonia gave Luci a sideways glance. "And you, too, are a colossal fool, *ragazza delinquente,* that you haven't found yourself a man till now. And I mean a permanent one."

"Who knew my abstinence method would work better in the end?" Clarissa poked her friend back, taunting *her* for a change.

Luci poked back. "Hey. All I had were a couple of nonstarters. But I have to face it—not every woman is going to find herself a Ferruccio. Or a Durante. Or a Leandro. Or even a finger's worth of them. You're just plain lucky." Luci's eyes glowed with mischief, assuring Clarissa there wasn't the least tinge of envy in her friend's heart. "So…just *how* lucky were you? On a scale from one to a hundred?"

Clarissa's gaze panned to where Ferruccio stood. His eyes clung to her even as he talked to Castaldini's ambassador to France and his whole family. She turned to the two looking expectantly at her, let out a ragged exhalation. "A billion."

Both women gaped. Then Antonia burst out guffawing, "I knew it!" while Luci fanned herself furiously.

Suddenly Luci exclaimed, *"Citi che il gatto e lui viene salando."*

Clarissa had felt Ferruccio's decision to seek her out before she realized what Luci meant. The Castaldinian proverb "mention the tomcat and he comes bounding."

Every cell went into hyperdrive at his approach. She saw the other two women's faces light up in admiration, in anticipation of what they'd witness. The sound level in the buzzing ballroom dropped. It seemed everyone wanted to watch the interaction between their impending king and queen, now that the formal part of the evening was over.

Then he was behind her. She held her breath. What would he do?

The last thing she expected him to, of course.

He wrapped her in his arms, buried his scalding lips into her neck in open-mouthed kisses up to her ear. *"Ti manco?"*

Miss him? She'd spent last night tossing in her bed as if she were in the clutches of an unremitting fever. As she had been. And she'd bet he'd known that would be her condition. She considered her answer.

Nonchalant pretense? *Not really.* Sullen challenge? *Why should I?* Truthful fury? *You know I did, damn you into infinity!*

Then she decided her best answer.

She turned around in his arms, snaked hers around his neck, failed to bury her fingers in the too-short, thick silk at his nape, dragged his head down and brought his lips to hers.

After a second of stiffening surprise, his growl filled her as he his tongue did, took her over, thrust deep.

Even as she disintegrated in the pleasure of him again, the relief and freedom of letting what she felt show, a burst of noise impinged on her fogged awareness. She thought she heard claps and hoots among the uproar.

When Ferruccio let her up for air, looking down at her as if he'd haul her over his shoulder and storm off to his bed—or drag her down to the floor—she dazedly turned to her companions.

Antonia had joined Luci in fanning herself as she exclaimed, "Now I *know* Castaldini will never be the same!"

"I could have told you that, without that historical kiss."

The four of them swung around to see Durante walking toward them, clapping, with a gigantic smile lighting up his impossibly handsome face. Leandro was a step behind, looking just as amused.

The two men immediately started ribbing Ferruccio mercilessly. He deflected their satire effortlessly, and the three men had her and the other two women laughing helplessly.

Clarissa marveled at how close those three were, how much in common they had. She knew he'd become Durante's friend, but had had no inkling how close they'd become. His closeness to Leandro was more puzzling. Her father had said he'd told a select few about Ferruccio's parentage when Ferrucio had first appeared in Castaldini. She doubted Leandro, who'd been exiled then, had been among them. Both of them were businessmen who played on the same level, so they might have known each other for years. But with everything she'd found out about Ferruccio in the past few days, she was convinced it had been he who'd sought out his relative. He'd wanted those of his family he liked and respected to be part of his life.

A surge of almost unbearable warmth and love welled inside her. He made it worse, as usual, gathering her to his side with such gentleness, breathing in the scent of her hair before planting a kiss on the top of her head. His action affected her far more when she realized he'd done it absently while totally involved in his verbal skirmish with her brother and cousin. It was as if he needed to touch her, to feel her close.

He gave her a squeeze before he let her go and turned to Luci.

Luci blinked up at him. Clarissa knew just what the poor girl was suffering from. Any female, no matter how loyal or how happy she was for her friend, would quiver at his merest look.

"Signorina Montgomery," Ferruccio said, looking serious all of a sudden. "Since all the people who matter to me are present, it's time to offer you my sincerest apologies for the inappropriateness I insulted you with on first meeting you."

Luci looked flustered for a second, then her face blazed with delight and deviltry. "Whoo boy, you remember?"

Clarissa groaned. "He forgets nothing, trust me."

"What's that all about?" Leandro asked.

"On his first appearance in the royal court," Luci revealed, imps of enjoyment dancing in her beautiful eyes, "he propositioned me *and* Stella before he even said hello or knew who we were. At the same time, if you get my drift."

Durante gaped at Ferruccio. "What? If anyone but both of you said this, I would have sworn on my right arm it was a lie. Were you under the influence of something foul that night or what?"

Ferruccio's gaze settled on Clarissa, becoming heavier by the second. "The most foul thing imaginable. I apologize to…all concerned."

Clarissa quivered inwardly. Was he apologizing to her, too? But Durante seemed convinced it was something ridiculously out of character for Ferruccio. So why had he done it? What was the "foul thing" that had made him act that way?

Before she could think further, Luci challenged, "All concerned? To Stella, too?"

He flicked a glance at the woman in question. She'd learned to keep her distance after Leandro had come down on her like a demolished building for daring to try to come between him and Phoebe. "I apologize only to human beings, not vipers."

Leandro burst out laughing. "You've found her out far faster than both me and Durante."

Ferruccio gave him a sage nod. "Compared to me, you've both led very sheltered lives."

Durante raised a formidable eyebrow. "Who're you calling sheltered?"

Ferruccio gave him a serene look. "Both of you, that's who."

Durante poked him in the chest. "Just for that, you're going to have to grovel a bit to get us to take the positions of your guardian angels on your new Council."

Leandro's grin turned evil. "Make that grovel *a lot.*"

Ferruccio maintained the same assurance. "I don't grovel. I'll just draft you into my service."

Leandro smirked. "Dream on, pal."

"And may they be happy dreams," Durante put in sarcastically. "Just for Clarissa's sake."

As they laughed, Gabrielle, Durante's new wife, glided up in the background like a butterfly, homing in on her husband, her face ablaze with pleasure as she watched him enjoying himself.

Clarissa had met her a couple of times before her and Durante's wedding, which had taken place before Clarissa had gone to the States for her mission.

She was the only one who'd noticed Gabrielle yet. And even though Gabrielle had eyes only for Durante, Clarissa started to smile. During their short meetings, she'd really liked the woman. She had great hopes that Gabrielle would turn out to be another great friend like Phoebe, her brother Paolo's sister-in-law, who was now Leandro's wife. And then, all Clarissa needed to love her was to see how happy Gabrielle made Durante.

Then she saw Gabrielle's eyes fall on Ferruccio.

Clarissa's heart faltered as Gabrielle's smile and steps did. It froze as she felt Ferruccio stiffen and turn his gaze to Gabrielle, as if he'd felt her approach, her reaction at seeing him. The same reaction filled his eyes.

Clarissa didn't know what it was. She only knew it was intense and instant. And it affected them both.

But it *didn't* feel like attraction.

Could she believe that, because it didn't feel like that to her? Or was she just deluding herself?

Confusion descended on her like a boulder as Gabrielle plastered her smile back on and hooked an arm through her husband's, rubbing against him like a delighted feline. With a rumble of welcome Durante caught her, shared as demonstrative a kiss with her as the one Clarissa and Ferruccio had just had.

Introductions to the new king-to-be ensued. The king-to-be whose eyes were still filled with something she hadn't suspected he was capable of as they surveyed her sister-in-law. Tenderness.

That shook her more than if she'd seen lust there.

Dio, what was this all about?

Soon the gathering disbanded, and he took her out to the verandah where they'd had their first fateful conversation.

She decided to get it out in the open. Before her head split open. She turned on him. "You liked Gabrielle, didn't you?"

He looked taken aback for a moment. Didn't think she'd notice, did he? Then he shrugged. "She's very nice." Then a slow, triumphant smile stretched his lips. "And you're very hot—even more arousing than usual if that's possible—when you're jealous."

"Are you trying to distract me?" she fumed.

"Only because you're barking up a light pole, not even the wrong tree. And I'd rather spend our time together doing something useful. Like discussing your wedding night lingerie."

"So I'm wrong?"

"Do you think you're right?" he countered. "Do you think I was hit by a bolt of attraction to your sister-in-law?"

"N-no," she admitted. "It didn't seem like attraction."

"Because it wasn't. You know firsthand what I'm like when I'm attracted—and with every other inch of your body. Gabrielle is lovely and it was as lovely to see how much she loves Durante, how much happiness they share."

The happiness we'll never share? she wanted to cry out. *Or is there hope for us? Your raging desire means something, doesn't it?*

Out loud she said, "So you were inspecting your friend's wife to see if she'd pass your specs?"

"She passed his specs. And then some. Like you do mine."

"D-do I? Do you really want this, Ferruccio?"

"I can show you right now what kind of…provisions I'm suffering beneath my tux so I won't walk around showing the world how much I *want* this, *mia bella unica*." She gurgled as her eyes clung to the bulge that had conquered all his…provisions. "If you want…solid proof, I can waive my decree to wait until we're husband and wife, and unleash all the proof you need on your sanity-annihilating, potency-jeopardizing body. In fact, speaking of potency, maybe I'd better. Mine is in grave danger. Especially after that trick you pulled back there."

"You started it!"

"And I'm glad I did. You'll never cease to surprise me."

"Look who's talking!"

"I'm looking, and my insanity meter is nearing the red zone. So if you don't want the whole palace to stay awake all night hearing you scream with one orgasm after another— since the sound-proofing I'm installing in our apartments isn't yet complete—you should turn around and walk away now. And if you don't want me to pounce on you wherever I find you during the coming five days, you'd better stay out of my hunting grounds."

She gasped, turned around before *she* pounced on *him* and dragged him on top of her here and now.

He pulled her back. "Do you remember our first time out here?" She nodded, her head rolling against his muscle-padded shoulder. "I swore that one day I would make love to you in the exact spot where you stood and turned me down. And I will." He let her go so suddenly that she swayed. "Just not tonight. Now run, before my mind gives out and we end up giving the attendees of my first official reception something far more historically shocking than the most passionate kiss they ever saw."

She ran this time, her high heels clicking on the marble floor like the frantic heartbeats of an alien creature.

Before she could enter a quiet hall of the palace through an open French window, he called after her.

"For the wedding…layer on as much clothing as you can."

She turned around slowly. "Why? It's hot."

"It will be—as hot as you can survive." As she got his meaning, he was the one who turned around and walked away, like that first time, throwing over his shoulder, "Be as creative as you can be in the lingerie department. And most important of all, rest up, *mia bella unica.* You'll need all the stamina you can get from now on, now that you'll always be with me."

Defiance shot through her. She might have been only test driven, but she was now revving and raring to go. He shouldn't be the only one dealing out hormone-messing torment.

"Thanks for the instructions, my future liege," she chirped, pseudo-swooningly. She waited until he stopped, turned to face her, challenge rolling off him in waves. Then she let her voice heat, deepen, thicken. "Here are your future queen's instructions. No cologne or aftershave. I want to smell you. No…provisions. I want to feel your…proof. And though it won't make much of a difference in five days, don't get a haircut. Ever again. Until I tell you to. I want to feel my hands convulsing in a long, luxurious mane as you pleasure me."

Challenge became a shockwave of testosterone.

She turned and ran inside before it hit her, receded into the depths of the palace to the sound of his stunned, aroused, unbridled laughter.

Nine

"You do look like a queen!"

Clarissa stared at her reflection in the gilded, Rococco-style, antique full-length mirror. She had to admit that Antonia was right.

She felt like a new person, a real woman, a royal one, in this dress. It fit her like her skin did. No wonder. She'd stood for endless hours while a dozen designers had molded it around her.

But during the stages of its creation, she hadn't imagined how the finished product would look. Last she'd seen it, it had yet to be put together and embroidered. The result was… amazing.

Its second-skin bodice, with an off-shoulder neckline, accentuated curves she'd never noticed she possessed, nipped her waist to a sparseness she hadn't believed humanly possible—which remarkably wasn't achieved by a breath-depleting corset or contrast with a mushrooming skirt. The lack of the latter was Ferruccio's doing. "No parachutes," he'd decreed.

She'd fought against the "parachute" they'd planned for her to wear, until he'd ended the debate. Thankfully. Infuriatingly.

At least she now had what she'd petitioned for—a skirt that molded to her hips before flaring gently in layers made of the extra-light, bulk-free cloths Ferruccio had said should be allowed to touch her body. Chiffon, tulle, lace and, for public exposure purposes, a base of opaque silk. The whole dress was made up of these materials and was extensively adorned in pearls and transparent, rainbow-reflecting sequins. Those coalesced in the middle of her trimmed, scalloped skirt to form the crest of Castaldini.

She looked over her shoulder as Luci and Gabrielle hooked her twenty-foot train where it connected undetectably to the skirt. Also Ferruccio's doing. He'd demanded it be removable. Not that she had anywhere near enough layers to satisfy his expectations.

Well, he couldn't give her the mane she'd demanded, either. Not in just five days.

The ladies finished the tricky job and stood back, exclaiming over the beauty of the train. The heavily pregnant Phoebe applauded their efforts from a nearby sofa. Antonia came forward to add the final touch, the crown tiara of Castaldini.

Clarissa caught Antonia's tearful gaze in the mirror as she secured the tiara on top of her head. The heavily layered tulle veil flowed from the back of her chignon.

Clarissa knew that Antonia felt like the mother of the bride. Clarissa felt that she really was, too. But there was more to Antonia's distress than that. Not only was she seeing the daughter she'd hadn't given birth to getting married and crowned queen all at once, but she must be remembering the tragedy that had been Clarissa's mother's life, how different it could have been, how badly it had ended.

Her mother had worn this tiara, till she stopped appearing in public, around the time she'd gotten pregnant with Clarissa. Durante had insisted that Clarissa have it, had said that, when a new queen was crowned, he'd commission a replica to be made.

She'd told him she didn't want keepsakes, but he'd been adamant. She deserved to have something beautiful of their mother, a reminder of better times, when she'd been whole and had worn the crown with pride and grace.

She couldn't rebuff his thoughtfulness, misguided or not, and had taken the boxes containing this crown along with the rest of their mother's jewelry and personal treasures. She hadn't even opened them. She didn't ask who had, to get the crown out.

Now she was going to be the queen, and the crown was no longer just a keepsake. It was officially hers to wear.

Would her mother's misfortune go along with it?

Antonia placed her hands on her shoulders, squeezed, her breath uneven, her voice shaky. "Ah, *cara mia,* you are a vision."

Clarissa smirked at her in the reflection, so that her pillar-of-power nanny's poignancy wouldn't wreck her own fragile composure. "Clothes do make the woman, don't they? To your immense relief, I'm sure. You finally got me to look the part."

Antonia scowled, indignation palpable. "You *always* did. You always were the most beautiful, refined princess in the world."

"You tell her, Donna Antonia," Luci piped in, resplendent in her pale-gold gown with its corset-like bodice and full-bodied skirt. Yes, bridesmaids were allowed to wear parachutes. "I always said she was a true princess, unlike those affected, artificial types. But she never believed it. She has serious self-image issues, our girl. Where they originated from, I'll never understand."

Gabrielle sighed. "Ah, self-doubts. You never know what might form them. One thing is certain—every person you know has more to them that they let on or that you'll ever understand."

Wise woman, Clarissa thought. She'd never told Luci of the events of her childhood, so Luci had always been puzzled by what seemed inexplicable traits in Clarissa's character. Some had been as incomprehensible to Clarissa herself. She found the explanation to one now, as she gazed at herself in the mirror.

She'd thought pristine white would make her paleness look

sickly. Thinking that, she'd never worn white. In fact, she'd never given her looks much attention at all, believing there wasn't much to pay attention *to*. She now realized she'd been suffering from the sense of unworthiness that all who'd been abused as children suffer. It had made her unable to see her own assets.

She did now. She now noticed a golden tinge to her complexion, reflecting the hundred shades of her hair, and thought the white made her glow with vitality.

And she realized something more. It wasn't the effect of the dress. Ten days ago, its opulence and glamor would have only deepened her sense of gawkiness.

This new self-acceptance and assurance was all the magic of Ferruccio. The memory of his eyes and body worshipping every part of her. She now saw herself through his hunger and appreciation.

Suddenly a burst of sound shook the whole chamber.

It was the royal brass orchestra playing the royal anthem, heralding the beginning of the ceremonies. The coronation would start in twenty minutes. The wedding would follow immediately.

She turned around in panic. "Ladies, thank you for all your help. But can I please have a few minutes alone?"

"Our queen has spoken! Let's mosey on, folks." Luci winked at her as she and Gabrielle helped Phoebe up from the sofa. "You better not run away the moment our backs are turned, hear?"

Clarissa stuck out her tongue. But the moment the door closed behind them, she let her smile and shoulders droop.

Luci hadn't been completely joking. She felt Clarissa's turmoil, had assumed it was cold feet. If only Luci knew how hot her feet were. She wanted Ferruccio, wanted to be with him for as long as she lived with a ferocity that terrified her. Like he'd once said, she couldn't imagine a fall from this height.

She inhaled a steadying breath, neared the mirror.

She saw the difference in her that Luci had spoken of. The last of her naïveté and unawareness had been erased. There were no longer a girl's fears and uncertainties and suspicions in her eyes, but the openness of possibilities that limitless passion bestowed. The brand of a powerful male's possession showed in the intensity of her glance, the hunger in her lips. There was also a far deeper dread etched in her expression.

She did look different. She looked like a woman who had finally felt the range of emotions a woman could feel. A woman lost in love and fearing that love might remain lost to her forever.

She dropped her gaze to the necklace that lay heavy around her throat and chest, the centerpiece of the set Ferruccio had sent her, one of his wedding gifts.

In his note, he said he'd commissioned its creation for her from the top goldsmiths in Castaldini, who'd collaborated day and night to produce it in the past days.

The intricate design was a triumph of craftsmanship, a true resurrection of the ancient tradition of working in pure gold. The incredible luster, color and beauty of twenty-four carat gold made the piece even more incredible. She wondered how he'd gotten them to design it so that it would match the crown she'd wear, yet still have an individual look. And perfectly match her eyes.

Its foliate garlands were decorated with five hexagonal amethysts set within circular wreaths, alternating with pear-shaped scrolls. Everything was set with diamonds. According to the hefty certificate that had accompanied the set, the necklace alone had thirteen diamonds weighing seventy-five carats, sixty-nine smaller diamonds weighing fifty carats and numerous smaller rose-cut diamonds weighing twenty carats. The other pieces were earrings, a bracelet and a ring.

She couldn't even estimate how much they had cost. But a relative had once bragged that her five-carat diamond ring cost two hundred thousand U.S. dollars, so what she was wearing would probably plug Castaldini's financial deficit.

But cost was no issue to Ferruccio. What moved her was the thought he'd put into choosing the design, that he'd known how perfectly it would enhance her eyes and complexion and hair.

She had to believe that a man who'd given her that much pleasure, in so many ways, wouldn't end up destroying her.

And then, she wasn't a helpless bystander. Ferruccio had said her mother's expectations and actions had been at the root of her problems, that her attitude and surrender to her bitterness had exacerbated them. But Clarissa wasn't her mother. And she would love him as he deserved to be loved. He wanted her now—one day she might make him love her, too.

With that resolution bolstering her, she walked to the door, opened it. Her bridal party spilled in.

She laughed. "Oh, Luci! You really made them think I'd tear off my wedding gown, pull on black spandex and escape from the balcony using knotted sheets, didn't you?"

"The new you?" Luci snickered as she tidied Clarissa's veil. "I wouldn't put anything past you."

"Ladies, how about you get a move on?" Phoebe groaned. "If you keep me on my feet much longer, I'll have to watch both the coronation and the wedding from a TV in some maternity ward!"

"It's going to be a long day, Phoebe," Clarissa scolded, alarmed. "Quit being pigheaded and sit in the wheelchair!"

Grumbling that she wished them all to be in her condition soon, Phoebe complied.

Everyone laughed and rushed toward the throne room.

With every step, Clarissa felt that she was rushing toward her future. A future that for the first time she could visualize.

Lightheartedness and optimism suddenly flooded her.

She broke into a run.

Everyone burst out in excitement and ran after her.

The throne room was in fact a cathedral-size chamber that was a triumph of architecture. Its gigantic structure and one-hundred-foot-high domed ceiling seemed to have been built without pillars. The design married Moorish, Gothic and Baroque influences in perfect symbiosis and it boasted an extensive array of original Renaissance artwork by masters of the caliber of Raphael.

Clarissa thought the grandeur of the place was nothing, compared to that of the man who would today become its ruler.

She walked the twenty feet of her train ahead of her bridal procession, no bouquet in hand. She'd sent Ferruccio a note saying there wouldn't be one, and not to bother decreeing it. She wanted her hands free. He'd sent one back saying so did he.

She walked down the aisle among the hundreds of people congregated to witness the coronation, mostly nobles and members of the extensive D'Agostino royal family. She had to sit at the front row. After the king was crowned, it was Castaldinian custom that his queen be summoned to sit beside him on the throne.

For long years, while her mother lived, her seat had remained empty. It had been removed altogether when she died five years ago. It had been a year after Clarissa had finished college. But with Ferruccio in the picture then, and her escaping regularly back to the States on the pretext of starting postgraduate studies, she'd always wondered if her absence, both real and emotional, had been what had finally driven her mother over the edge.

She shook herself as she reached the front row. Today belonged to the present, to the future. No more dwelling on the past.

Her party hurried to sit down as trumpets blared again, heralding Ferruccio's arrival. From the corner of her eye she saw Leandro rushing over to scoop Phoebe from the wheelchair, taking her to the back of the pews where she could stretch out.

Then everything disappeared. Only he was left. Ferruccio.

The man she loved, had loved since she'd first seen him.

He entered the chamber from its northern end, walked in long, powerful strides toward the platform housing the thrones.

She'd seen the traditional black-with-gold-trim coronation costume, with its Roman-Moorish design and embroidery, its crimson sash and hanging sword in dozens of paintings on dozens of kings, her father among them. On Ferruccio it was different.

The clothes didn't make the man, after all. In his case, it was the other way around. If he'd looked like a god before, he now looked like a superhero god.

The eleven o'clock sunlight poured over him from the stained-glass windows high on the walls, making his skin glow, his raven hair glint, every thread of gold on his costume gleam with sparkles of magic. Deepening the impression was the crimson cape of kingship, with Castaldini's crest emblazoned in gold, that hung from his shoulders and flowed down his back. He looked daunting, majestic, a man born to be lord of all he surveyed.

As he approached, a movement to the side caught her eye.

Durante and Paolo were helping their father to his feet. He'd now perform another first in Castaldinian history. An abdication.

No new king had ever been crowned while the old one lived.

The head of the Council headed toward the king's throne to perform the transfer of power and the coronation rituals.

Her breath caught in her lungs as all the players converged toward the momentous event.

Then Ferruccio diverged from the path.

He left them all staring after him in total loss.

She sat there, her every muscle slack as he approached her with those inexorable steps.

He stopped right above her. Her breathing stopped, as well.

He bent, took her clammy hands, bowed deeply, planted a kiss on the back of each hand, then into her palms. She was quaking by the time he straightened. "Shall we, *regina mia?*"

His queen! "B-but you have to be crowned first."

"I'm going to be king in minutes. I say what happens first. First you sit were you belong, on the throne. Then I join you."

He was talking quietly, intensely. But she knew everyone around her had heard him. Judging by the buzz that swept the chamber like a gigantic swarm of bees, everyone had. Luci was suppressing giggles and fanning herself with exaggerated speed.

Ferruccio seemed unaware of anything or anyone but her, his eyes on her like a tractor beam, making her float beside him to the platform. He led her up the five marble steps that were covered in a crimson carpet printed with Castaldini's crest.

At the queen's throne, he stopped, the intensity in his eyes rising as he pressed her hands. "This is your throne, Clarissa. This is your crown, too. Yours alone."

She didn't get it for a moment. Then comprehension exploded.

It was...too much to believe. He *couldn't* have. Could he? How? When? Why? And she choked out, "You mean...?"

He pressed her hands harder. "I had them made for you. Everything is yours, Clarissa, no one else's."

This wasn't the throne her mother had sat on. This wasn't the crown she'd worn. He'd known. He'd understood. How she'd feel that they were tainted by turmoil and unhappiness. And he'd made her new ones, free of the blot of the past.

She collapsed onto her throne. Her king's gift. Of a pure and new beginning, of a future all her own to write.

It was too much. What he was. What he kept giving her.

Surely this meant she wasn't just his convenient bride, if he'd gone to these lengths to anticipate her desires, to circumvent and negate her anxieties and discomforts?

He bent and kissed her eyelids as she had his that night he'd claimed her, driving her nightmares away as she had his.

He crooked her a smile. "The sooner I get the formalities out of the way, the sooner you can show me how creative you've been."

A smile trembled on her lips as he walked away. Tears filled her down to the roots of her being, with gratitude so fierce it was exquisite agony. They flowed down her cheeks throughout the magical moments, as she watched the men who were the pillars of her life secure the future of her beloved Castaldini, as her father, passed the power and the responsibility to the man who most deserved it. Her lover. Her king. And within this day, her husband.

"*Dio,* who are all these people?" Clarissa squinted up into the extensive, packed, semicircular Roman theatre.

It was built into the hillside overlooking the royal palace, had stood there neglected for as long as she'd lived. Now it looked as good as new, bursting with lavish Roman-Moorish decorations, with thousands of guests milling around the sloping, steplike seats. Not to mention countless scurrying photographers from media agencies from around the world, and cameramen transmitting the wedding on global live feed.

Every detail had been brought into existence by Ferruccio's vision and orchestration, in the six days he'd specified.

He turned to her with a smile rivaling the summer afternoon's sun. "Those are your relatives and subjects, *regina mia*."

"The relatives are yours now, too. And the subjects are yours *first*, mine only by association. They're here because you invited them. You see those six ladies over there?" She pointed to her friends, who burst to their feet waving and hooting. She waved as enthusiastically back. "They are my contribution to the crowds."

"I know. Your friends from your college and postgraduate years." She blinked at him. He knew? No, he *more* than knew.

"You did something, didn't you?"

He waved to the ladies, who swooned down to their seats. "I took the liberty of returning the plane tickets you bought them, sent them my jet instead."

Her mouth fell open. "*Dio*, Ferruccio. The things you keep doing. I don't know whether to be delighted or alarmed."

"Be delighted. I'll never suffocate you or railroad you."

"Really? Strange. I remember you doing some of the first and a lot of the second in very recent memory."

His smile froze. She wanted to kick herself in the teeth.

Why had she said that? Those had been the sentiments she'd hidden behind until she faced the truth.

The truth was that she would have never agreed to marry him if she hadn't been dying to anyway. More important, she believed he would have never coerced her, would have let her go.

And if a voice taunted her that he still might some day, she couldn't and wouldn't listen to it.

"I thought we were past the hostilities, that you've accepted our situation, saw the good in it." He waited for her answer, but protests and explanations clogged in her throat. He seemed to misunderstand her frustrated stare. His voice thickened. "I wanted to make the best of it, to do things for you that only I can."

That was what he was doing? Making the best of the situation?

Suddenly the euphoria and optimism that had fueled her for the past hours drained out of her system, left her feeling helpless, hopeless. "And you can do anything, can't you?"

His eyes grew darker as they roamed her. "Not everything, no."

After that, they sat in silence on the thrones he'd transported there, until the royal guards converged at the back of the stage, heralding the arrival of Castaldini's cardinal.

Suddenly Ferruccio broke their silence, giving her a look soaked in challenge. "How appropriate it is to marry you here, Clarissa. Where else would a man marry a lioness but in a place where in ancient times gladiators fought lions for their lives?"

Her heart fluttered as she pounced on the opening, prayed her teasing tone and smile would show him there was no rancor left in her. "It was also in such places that sacrifices were tossed to predators like you to devour."

His answering smile told her he'd read her meaning, her mood, was delighted by both. "So, my sacrifice, which part of you would your recommend I devour first?"

She filed her nails against her bodice. "So, my gladiator, which part of you would you like me to shred to ribbons first?"

He laughed, heaved up to his feet, swooped down on her and dragged her to hers. "Come, *leonessa mia,* let the duel begin."

The cardinal came to stand before them, turning his back to the crowd so that they faced their subjects-to-be.

With everyone silent and with the acoustic structure of the theater, as soon as the cardinal raised his voice to recite the Castaldinian wedding vows, it was as if he was speaking into a sound-amplifying system.

He paused, waiting for Ferruccio to repeat the words after him. Ferruccio just gestured for him to go on.

Looking shocked, but not about to argue with his new king on global live feed, the man went on. But when he came to the part where he had to ask the questions answered by "I do"s, Ferruccio stopped him. Clarissa was as much at a loss as the poor man.

Ferruccio turned to her. "I've parroted enough pledges today. But this is one pledge I'm making on my own." Then he raised his voice. "Do you Clarissa D'Agostino, my lioness, my queen, my savior from the darkness, want me to be your defense and harbor, your support and succor, your ally and lover?"

She stared at him. *Too much* rang in her mind in a loop.

She had one answer.

She surged into him, hugged him with all her strength.

He hugged her back, exhaled as if he'd been bating his breath, whispered to her only, "Then take all of me, *mia bella unica.*"

The crowd treated them to a standing ovation.

After the tumult his unorthodox wedding vows had caused had died down, and they were again sitting in their thrones with her trembling so hard that she could barely sit up, she saw Ferruccio staring sideways. She followed his gaze.

Her heart twitched when she found it settled on Gabrielle. Gabrielle looked back at him and he gave her a conspiratorial wink.

Before Clarissa's heart could thud with alarm, Gabrielle turned and clung to Durante, seemed to be pleading with him. Durante kept shaking his head until she pouted. He sighed in what looked like defeat, stood up, mock-scowled down on her, then turned and walked toward the stage. Gabrielle gave Ferruccio a bursting-with-excitement smile. He gave her the thumbs-up.

Clarissa had never been so confused.

Durante climbed onto the stage, growled for their ears only, "You're paying for this, Ferruccio. Big time."

She grabbed Ferruccio's arm. "What's going on?"

He smiled. "Watch. Or more accurately, listen."

Durante faced the crowds. "This is for my sister and queen, Clarissa." He tossed a 'take that' look back at Ferruccio. Ferruccio retaliated with one bedeviling eyebrow wiggle. Durante narrowed his eyes then turned around.

And started to sing.

Sing? Durante? Had the world tilted on its axis?

Clarissa didn't realize her mouth was hanging wide open until Ferruccio's gentle caress closed it for her.

She looked back at him, flabbergasted. He'd known Durante could sing, had set it up with Gabrielle to give her this, the gift of hearing her brother singing for the first time in her life. And boy, could Durante sing! He was *incredible*.

By the time Durante finished the aria "Nessun Dorma"—none shall sleep tonight—from the opera *Turandot* by Puccini, and bowed to a storming-with-applause crowd, Clarissa was bawling.

She burst to her feet, zoomed across the stage and grabbed Durante in a rib-crushing hug. As he hugged her back, Clarissa saw their father, openly in a wheelchair now, watching them with his cheeks wet. The crowd roared, demanding an encore, with Paolo and Julia leading the petitions.

As Durante succumbed and sang something more light-hearted from *Le Nozze di Figaro,* by Mozart, Ferruccio came behind her, took her leaning back into him, as they listened along with the rapt crowd.

She was still weeping her joy as Durante finished his second aria and wouldn't be prevailed upon for more curtain calls.

Her brother turned to her, kissed her. Then, as he shook Ferruccio's hand, he grabbed him nearer, gave him a lethal smile. "King or no king, best friend or not, Ferruccio, if I don't see my sister bouncing with happiness, you're a dead man."

Ferruccio gave him an inexplicable smile before turning his eyes to Clarissa. "My life depends on you now."

She wanted to say, if it were up to her, he'd live forever.

She didn't, and after Durante went back to his wife and Ferruccio took her back to their thrones, she could only sit there, reverberating with the enormities that Ferruccio had put her through throughout the day.

He leaned close, took her trembling hand. "I wish I could have been the one to sing for you, but if you're looking for things I can't do, singing tops the list."

She wanted to tell him he'd given her far more than she could ever express. She knew if she did, she'd burst into tears again and this time wouldn't stop.

She gave him a tremulous smile instead. "It's okay. Lions aren't known for their singing ability. You roar and rumble and purr pretty good, though."

His eyes ignited as he got to his feet, sweeping her up with him. "Time to haul you to my lair, *leonessa mia*."

Ten

On the short "haul" to Ferruccio's "lair," he drowned her in exhilaration and arousal, every second solidifying the spell he'd woven around her with that first glance.

He took her inside the mansion, kissed her deeply as he took off her veil, shook down her hair, but kept her crown on. Then he almost drove her out of her mind taking off her train.

She was wondering if he'd take her right there in the lounge, when he straightened, kissed her on the nape, then walked away.

After ten minutes, she called out to him. He didn't answer.

Confusion was starting to turn into panic that he'd fallen, hit his head and couldn't hear her, when she noticed what was in front of her all the time. A huge box, exquisitely wrapped in violets, with a matching envelope on top.

She pounced on it, taking longer than her nerves could stand, preserving the wrapping. Then she snatched open the lid.

Inside was a folded lavender paper. He had everything in her favorite colors.

She unfolded it. His handwriting. She felt as if he was whispering the words in her ear.

"I'm resurrecting the Castaldinian ancient custom of *prima notte di nozze nascondino.* But this wedding night hide-and-seek has a twist to it. Instead of the groom pursuing the bride, you, *leonessa,* champion runner bride of mine, will pursue me. I've done my share of the running for six years, after all."

"Did you think I was going to let you off the hook?"

She could almost hear his teasing, feel his hands and lips trailing a path of sensual torment all over her secrets and hungers, before he stepped away, left her gasping for more.

"But since I'm not a merciless, shameless siren, I'll give you clues, so you can catch me."

"My first clue is: Where did I first claim you?"

She was zooming up the stairs to his bedroom, when she faltered. He'd really claimed her with that first kiss.

She could be wrong, but what was the worst thing that could happen? She'd return to his bedroom to find her clue.

But she believed she was right.

She took off her high-heeled sandals, hooked them in one hand, gathered the layers of her skirt in the other and ran out, following the same route he'd taken her on that first night.

She again reveled in the feel of sand below her naked soles, wished he was there running with her.

She arrived at the spot of their waveside dinner, found the circle of brass poles blazing. In its middle, instead of their table, she found a huge mother-of-pearl sea snail shell.

She snapped it up, found her next clue.

"How did you know where I was the night I made you mine?"

The answer came to her at once this time. She'd headed west.

She headed west now.

The more distant she was from the mansion and the fire and the darker it got, the more the gibbous moon blazed to illuminate the night. Then she saw it in the distance. A path of flame-lit lanterns. She gathered her skirt higher and ran.

The trail ended at stone steps winding around the foot of the mountain she'd seen from the mansion. She'd run that far? Good thing she was in shape.

She scaled the wide steps, knowing now why he'd said no parachutes. Wearing one of those inflated skirts, she could have launched off the mountain with the strong gusts of breeze. There was also no way she could have climbed them in a permanent train.

Then she reached the top of the winding steps and finally saw her destination. An observatory-like building.

The huge edifice stood framed against the rising moon, making her feel as if she'd stumbled into a scene from a Gothic romance.

Which wasn't far from the truth. She was rushing to her tormented, tormenting, irresistible, all-powerful lover.

She ran to the door, found it ajar. She entered, adrenaline rushing through her blood. She'd never felt so excited. So alive. One more unprecedented experience he'd given her.

And it was only beginning.

She put her sandals on again and followed the light.

With every step she felt she was wading deeper into another waking dream, as she reached the beginning of a path cleared between the candles he had crowding every surface imaginable.

Then the candles ended abruptly, and she found her next clue on top of a big brass lantern in the middle of the next dark hall.

"Now, follow what is your name."

Her name. Clarissa meant bright or brilliant. But there was only darkness from here on. What else emitted light?

The moon. But how did she follow it inside here?

It came to her. She had to find windows. As long as she saw the moon from them, she was on the right track.

She found the windows, followed the moon. That led her to another chamber filled with candles, almost surrounded by open, floor-to-ceiling windows letting in the night breeze that kept the hundreds of tiny flames flickering. A huge bed spread in dark satin that she was sure was violet was at the far end by the western windows. By the eastern ones, there was a dinner set up like the one they'd had by the sea.

He walked in from the verandah. Her Roman god come to life.

"I knew you were brilliant, in every way."

His voice cascaded over her, intertwining with the composite music of the night. The sea's rushing and receding tempo, the wind's whistling sighs, tranquility's still song.

He prowled toward her slowly, so slowly across the expansive space, giving her a hormone-roaring show of contained power and inbred poise in his king's regalia. She couldn't bear it, started to run to him. He raised a hand, stopped. She stopped, too, starting to shake with the pressure of craving.

"Take that work-of-art wrapping off for me, *regina mia*. It's done its purpose, tantalized and maddened me all day by how it worships your beauty, caresses and kisses and clings to your flesh when I couldn't. It has overstayed its welcome."

"Don't—don't you want to take it off me?"

"Undressing you is now my main mission in life, along with possessing and pleasuring you, but I'm feeling almost hostile toward the thing. I might not be considerate of the imbalance of power between us if I wrestle it off."

"There'll be no wrestling. It's easy to take off. That *was* one of your demands." Excitement and the blaze of appreciation and lust in his eyes made her brazen. She twisted around, leaned to make her hair spill forward, presenting him with a clear shot of her back, widening her stance and thrusting her hips at him slightly in provocation. "Down the zipper goes, and the dress follows."

His rumble harmonized with that of the sea. "Or I can just

flip up that skirt, bend you over and give you what you're asking for." She almost fell to her knees begging him for it. "And I will. Sometime during the night, I'll put you back into that virginal torture device and ride you like that until you faint with pleasure again. All in good time. The best."

The fire in her loins was spreading, consuming her. Gush after gush of readiness was now flooding down her thighs. And all he'd done was expose her to his visual and verbal desire. He could talk about torture. He was a connoisseur at it, after all.

"Now show me the miracle of you."

She opened her mouth to ask him for help. The back zipper had needed an extra pair of hands to do it up. She clamped her lips. He wanted her to undress for him on her own. And she was doing it.

She reached back and managed to yank the zipper down in a feat of agility she hadn't known she was capable of. Unbearable hunger was an unstoppable motivator, a miracle worker. The dress spilled off her arms. She caught it before it pooled to the ground.

"Let it go, Clarissa. Let me see what ingenious lingerie you've got underneath."

She let it go.

Ferruccio stared. And stared.

He'd told her to be creative. He hadn't imagined anything like that.

"This was the most creative thing I could come up with."

He shuddered at the mixture of uncertainty and brazenness in her voice. Why uncertain? She wasn't sure how this affected him? She didn't know he'd never again open his eyes or close them and see anything but the sight before him now?

Her. Standing tall and proud and annihilating in her transparent high heels and the jewels he'd had made for her, in the middle of a dream of glittering white. Totally naked.

He wanted to hurtle to her, slam into her, squeeze and

devour every inch of her. He rocked on his heels under the force of the compulsion. But he wanted to savor the sight of her more, her counterattack on his reason, see her coming to him, bent on pulverizing it, on beating him at his game of seduction.

"An ingenious choice of…*un-wear, regina mia.*" He beckoned to her. She stepped out of her pooled dress, prowled toward him, her beauty intensifying with every step. He licked his tingling lips, almost feeling them on her shiny lips, on her other now equally smooth ones. "Unique and unrepeatable."

"Glad you approve." She entered the circle of moonlight, stopped. He rumbled, prodding. She was half-a-dozen steps away.

She stood her ground. "Show *me* your magnificence, *re mio.*"

His first impulse was to tear at his clothes like a demented man. He called on the remnants of a control he'd once thought unassailable and unhooked his cape. He swung it over his shoulders like a matador, before giving it a swirl and tug, bringing it spooling around his forearm.

She whooped, clapped. "Do it again!"

His lips spread in delight at seeing hers. "Glad you approve. But there will be only one thing I do again—and again—tonight."

Her pose grew languid, seductive and shy all at once.

He took off his sash and sword, undid his jacket a button a second, dropped it to the floor. His dress shirt followed. The moment his hands went to his pants she ran to him.

She grabbed his hands, stopping them. "My turn."

His eyes glazed over her as she dropped to a crouch before him. The sight of the ripe swell of her buttocks, the graceful curve of back, her gleaming skin and sparkling hair almost drove him over the edge. She pulled his pants down, causing his engorged manhood to rebound against his belly, throbbing, straining.

She tried to touch him, but he stepped away and out of his pants, kicked away his shoes and got rid of his socks. Then he did what he'd wanted to do ever since he'd first seen her.

He bent and hauled her over his shoulders.

She gasped as he swept her across the chamber, crossed into the wide circle of candles and lanterns around the bed that he'd placed by the open windows overlooking the sheer side of the mountain and the sea. Her panting became moans, then he felt her lips latching on to his shoulder blade, her teeth sinking there. He roared, ran the last steps, flipped her over onto the bed, watched her bounce on the dark violet sheets, a goddess of sensual decadence and dementia, bidding him come lose his mind.

He obeyed, came down over her, filling her outstretched arms.

She grabbed his head as his lips branded their way from her neck to her nipples. "Sorry I couldn't layer more clothes."

He raised his head. "Sorry I couldn't grow my hair faster."

She buried her nose in his chest, inhaled his unadorned scent. "But you followed my other instructions. I say we call it even."

"I say we call it even better. Than our first night."

"There could be nothing better. I just want encores."

"Ah, Clarissa, you force me to sound condescending, but you have no idea. The pleasure I gave you was only an appetizer. Now I will give you a…full meal."

"Oh? And how are you sure of that?"

"I'm going by the fact that you were in a measure of pain then. Now, it will all be pleasure."

"Show me."

"I will. Always." He rose, bent to run his lips and tongue over her breasts, her abdomen, lower, bringing her to the edge before retreating, until she was begging for his invasion. He held back, came up, captured one nipple after the other, drawing soft, then hard, had her thrashing with each pull.

She sabotaged his reason, surging into him, bringing him full over her, taking his weight, containing him in hunger-driven limbs that clamped him, body and will. Her fingers caressed his flesh, unraveled his control, her lips, full and fragrant, pressed against his, her tongue invading his mouth, flooding him with her taste and her passion, turning the kiss into a full rehearsal of the mating they'd soon lose themselves in.

He tore his lips from hers, growled at the separation, at the convulsion that went through her, saw his insanity reflected in the depths of eyes gone purple. He shuddered in unison with her as arousal turned into agony.

"I can't bear it…just thrust inside me."

He had to face it. He couldn't wait. Not this first time. And she couldn't either. He'd give them this, the first explosive release that would free them to explore the fathomless depths of their passion with the leisure it deserved.

He reached for the side table and grabbed one of the foil packets he'd placed in a bowl, which sat among the colorful array of wine, brandy and water bottles and crystal glasses.

"Don't." She stayed his hand as he began to open the condom.

His eyes clung to hers, as if he could read her mind if he looked into them intensely enough. Had she installed her own protection?

Whatever the reason, she wanted to feel him without barriers again. Wanted to feel him pour his seed inside her. And that was the biggest gift, the only real one he felt he'd ever received.

He threw the condom away and crashed his lips on hers.

She jerked, wailed into his mouth, "Just fill me."

He rose between her splayed thighs, probed her with a finger, then two. She was flowing for him. He soothed her frenzy, trying to rein in his own, took her buttocks in one hand, tilted her to him as his other hand roamed her, in wonder, in ownership. He brought his shaft to her scorching entrance, rested there, struggling with the elemental need to plunge hard, seek her depths, go home. There would be no rush this time. No pain.

"Take your fill of me, *regina mia*." Gritting his teeth, he began to invade her, the beauty open before him, her constant pleas a current fusing his insides.

He went blind with the burst of pleasure, at the heat and slickness and tightness of the velvet vise enveloping him. He stilled in her depths as she arched off the bed at his invasion.

"Perdonami, amore mio," he rasped in his agitation.

She panted. "Forgive you? For what?"

"For not taking you with more restraint the first time."

She thrust her hips up. "I didn't want you to be restrained. That's why it didn't occur to me to tell you you were my first."

"And *only*." He thrust, stamping his claim deeper. She swooned beneath him, opening wider, accepting anything he'd do to her. "You're mine and mine alone. But it didn't matter that you didn't tell me. I should have noticed, should have felt your pain. Damn me, I thought it was extreme pleasure."

"It was. The pain merged into pleasure and was…incredible."

"Whatever pain I caused you, I'll make it up to you, in a lifetime of pure and intensifying pleasures."

"I don't know if I can survive more pleasure than that." Her fingers dug into his chest, his shoulders, bringing him down to her, forcing him to stroke deeper into her. She cried out, a hot sharp sound of exultation that tore a growl of pride out of him.

She thrashed her head, never taking her eyes off his, letting him see every sensation rip through her, the thousand shades of gold in her hair, her golden paleness brightening with her rising pleasure, burning up the darkness she lay on, an image the old masters would have paid in blood to capture unto eternity.

"You feel…magnificent…inside me…" Her voice was smoky, exhilaration thickening it, sending another tidal wave of arousal crashing through him. "I never imagined so much pleasure existed. Give me all of you, as you promised, *amore,* take all of me."

The word *amore* gasped with such conviction, burst in his mind, in his heart, with such acute surprise, such pleasure that he almost keeled over.

He rose on extended arms, surveyed her feverishly. She looked every inch a woman in a tumult of…love? Or had it just been an endearment fueled by pleasure and the maddening need for release?

He'd take anything. Need could become love.

He fed her hunger for more of him, struggling as the slide inside her gripping heat sliced through him. He wanted this to last.

He watched in awe as she accepted all of him, wild, abandoned. Then she was weeping as she sought his lips, her core throbbing around him, demanding him harder, faster. He had to obey her.

His plunging rhythm became pounding, until her cries rose to a shriek that ripped through him. She arched up, convulsed in a full-body fit that shredded her cries, wrenched at his shaft. The knowledge that he was fulfilling her tore his own climax from depths he'd never known existed.

With a prayer that his seed would take root in her womb, he jetted inside her, causing her paroxysm to spike. Detonations of ecstasy rocked him, and her, locked them in a closed circuit of overstimulation, dissolved them into each other.

When it felt his heart would never restart, the tumult gave way to the warmth and weakness of satiation. He felt her melt beneath him, awe and fulfillment glowing on her face.

"Moglie mia, regina mia," he rumbled against her lips as he twisted, bringing her on top of him, maintaining their connection.

She pressed her lips to his heart. *"Marito mio, re mio."*

Her answering proclamation confirming him her husband and king, roared through his blood with pride and relief. Resurging desire, too, since she spoke in that new voice of hers, the one she now used only with him, awareness-laden, smug, overcome.

She raised her head, her hair draping over his chest. She gave him such a smile, no inhibitions, awakened, gaining in confidence. She would be annihilating when she realized her full power. He couldn't wait to be devastated. "You're always right, aren't you? I thought our first time was magic. Now I've given up trying to come up with descriptions. No language can do justice to what you do to me, what you give me."

He stroked her, moved, grateful, bursting with pride and joy. "It's the same with me."

Her gaze faltered. "You don't have to say that. Your experience—"

He cut her off, needing her to know, to never doubt. "Is obscenely overrated. And irrelevant. You would understand, if you had any. You would realize that what you knew as sex is nothing when you can experience *this*." He crushed her whole length to him. "Raging, blinding, transfiguring passion."

She cried out at his intensity, her face blazing with emotion at his confession, her body blossoming under his hunger, undulating in a renewed dance of sinuous demand and submission.

He rose, swung her up in his arms. She clung to him as if she was a part of him as he took her to the next phase he had prepared in her seduction and sensual enslavement. And his.

He'd given her that ride he'd promised her, under a canopy by the lapping waves. Then he'd stripped her of her torture device of a dress and taken her into the warm waters, driven her over many edges there. *Then* he'd wrapped her in silk and carried her back to their mansion. He'd taken her again in the swimming pool. Then she'd taken him, dissolved him in her hands and mouth. It had been another first for him, surrendering control to that extent.

Now she was curled into him, replete and depleted, a smile painting her face even in sleep, taking her beauty to a new level.

If their first night had been earthshaking, their wedding night had been life-changing.

She had changed his life in the past ten days. Changed *him*. Beyond recognition. And he liked the man she'd changed him into. He could finally be at peace with that man.

And that man couldn't wait to experience every second of their deepening passion, to surrender to the magic that bound them.

Clarissa watched Ferruccio answer one phone call and put two on hold as he signed the papers that Alfredo flipped over for him.

It was a financial treaty with a neighboring kingdom. He

hadn't had time to read the fine print, and she'd stepped in, in her role as financial advisor and analyst, gone over it with a fine-toothed comb and recommended that he sign. He refused the very idea of her double-checking her verdict. She'd fallen in love with him a bit more over that. If that was humanly possible.

For the past six weeks Ferruccio had been embroiled in the duties of his new status, putting right so many things that had gone wrong long before her father had fallen ill. He'd told her he'd been able to do so much in that time frame because he'd had her help and counsel. He seemed to revel in their interaction as much as she did, their synergy, in matters of state. And on every other level.

He now gestured for her that he'd take the phone calls and catch up with her, and she walked out to their apartments.

As she entered the place that had previously been an unused wing in the palace, which he'd transformed into their own world of ecstasy and intimacy, she found herself holding her breath.

She was almost always holding her breath, with dread that something might happen to shatter the perfection.

Ferruccio had turned out to be far more than she'd ever dreamed. He was a better king than her father had been, and she didn't feel disloyal thinking that. It was simply the truth.

He was the right man at the right time, giving Castaldini the stability it needed, introducing innovations with utmost care, while making certain to maintain its uniqueness and traditions, and to protect it from the infringement of harmful outside influences.

The one thing she'd thought marred his character, the chunk of steel he had for a heart, was nowhere to be found. As a liege he was approachable and just, as a new member of an extensive family where many had accepted him only as a dire fate, he was tolerant, patient, even amused. As a lover and husband he was…indescribable.

She kept wondering, could this be real? Or was he only

making the best of it, as he'd told her during their wedding? To keep the future mother of his children happy to stay in the marriage? But if he kept on being this incredible to her, should she even care about his motives or his true emotions?

She hadn't done anything about protection, for fear of harming the baby that could have been forming inside her. She'd also wanted to have full intimacy with him, and wanted all this pleasure to bear fruit.

It hadn't. She'd had a period.

He hadn't said anything, but she felt his disappointment. He really wanted a child. Probably more.

What if she couldn't give him one? What would happen if, after the time he'd specified had elapsed, she still hadn't? Would he decide their marriage wasn't a "viable endeavor" and cast her out of his life? Could she survive if he did?

She felt sick with uncertainty.

She sat down, leaned over until her head was almost between her knees. The world spun in a purple vortex.

"Clarissa!"

She jerked up, but her blood didn't follow. Everything blinked out.

It blinked back again. Ferruccio was kneeling before her, propping her up. She'd fainted. She didn't know how he'd reached her in time to prevent her collapse to the ground. Her superhero.

"Clarissa, *amore,* you're sick!"

She waved away his diagnosis. "I'm just missing a few hours of sleep. You know, those I regularly forgo to feast on Your Mouthwatering Majesty."

His lips compressed. "I'm calling in a doctor."

Her objections that she was fine fell on perfectly formed, selectively deaf ears.

Twenty minutes later, she was in bed being prodded by five royal physicians. She was sure there was nothing wrong with her. But it *was* bliss to be fussed over by Ferruccio like this.

Even if he was only concerned about the health of the potential mother of his child?

She sighed again as she lay back for the exam.

Yes, even then.

Ferruccio sank his fingers in his newly grown hair, almost pulling it out.

He'd been constantly wondering whether Clarissa really no longer considered him beneath her. If she really didn't think him a marauder, a usurper. If she'd truly forgotten their original deal, wanted to continue their marriage because it was all working so spectacularly.

Everything had been flowing so much like a dream that he'd been constantly dreading some rude awakening. But all his anxieties paled into nothing compared to the dread that ate at him now. He would welcome anything now, would be willing to lose her in any way but something happening to her. He'd give up everything, his very life, to make her whole.

"King Ferruccio."

He turned around, looking at the five men as if they were monsters he would take apart at the slightest wrong move. *That* move would be to tell him anything was wrong with Clarissa.

"King Ferruccio, are you all right?"

"Shut up," he snarled. "Talk."

The men looked more confused and more than a little alarmed, until one seemed to understand, came forward, his expression that of someone bearing news he knew he'd be obscenely rewarded for. "Congratulations, Your Majesty. The queen is pregnant."

Ferruccio stared at the man as if he'd just told him the queen was really a man. Then he growled, "What are you talking about? She's just had a period!"

This time none of the men were fazed. Another doctor ventured to approach. "That does sometimes happen during the first couple of months of pregnancy. But it means nothing, and it doesn't affect the pregnancy in the least."

Ferruccio's world emptied. His mind. His heart. And then, one thing filled them all. Clarissa. Everything to him. And now, impossibly, more than everything. She'd already given him everything. Now she'd give him more. *Pregnant.*

"By our calculations, the queen must have conceived on your wedding night."

Ferruccio's gaze swam around, registering the men with the last working faculty in his mind, seeing the male kudos in their eyes at the proof of his virility.

Then he no longer saw them. Everything disappeared from his awareness except one thing. A conviction. He *knew* Clarissa had conceived that first time they'd claimed each other.

Then he was hurtling through their apartments on a tidal wave of joy, sending a pile of paper scattering as if zapped by a whirlwind. He was. A whirlwind of boundless bliss and eternal gratitude.

His Clarissa would give him a miniature of her to adore.

He slowed down as he entered their room. She might not be sick, but she wasn't feeling well. How thoughtless would it be to explode into the room like a delirious dog, oblivious of her state and bound only on slurping her up in his hyperexcitement?

Good thing she hadn't seen him yet. She lay on the bed facing away from the door. She hadn't heard him, either, not with the ultrathick carpets he'd strewn the place with so they could make love anywhere and everywhere. *Grazie a Dio.* Outside, he'd sounded—and must have looked—like a one-man riot.

He started crossing the room and…stopped. Froze. Impaled on the spear that had stabbed him through the heart.

Dio santo…Clarissa…she…looked bereft.

She didn't want the baby? Because it was his?

Basta! Stop it…you fool. *Dio solo sa*—God only knew what she was feeling now, physically. A woman pregnant for the first time, in that delicate first trimester, with all its physiological adjustments, when she'd had to deal with so much during the past weeks. The wedding and coronation, the enormous workload she'd imposed on herself. But the real tests had been the emotional upheavals he'd put her through, the unrelenting physical demands he made on her, as she'd told him just an hour ago. He was the cause of her distress the way he'd been... *Dio*, he hadn't even asked those doctors if he should...

Her sob fractured his thoughts. His world.

Clarissa...no...*prego*...please...don't...

She didn't hear his mental pleading. She started sobbing as if her heart had splintered, was tearing the rest of her apart.

She hated it, the child that was growing inside her. Couldn't bear to have it invading her flesh, drawing from her life. Just because it was his child, too. Because she hated him.

He staggered. Nothing...*nothing* in his miserable, violent life had hit anywhere near this hard. Every injury he'd sustained had made him stronger. This...this finished him.

Something agonizing forged like white-hot skewers through his brain, poured like molten lead down his face, scorching his flesh and soul. He didn't know what it was. Didn't care.

Time distorted into a monstrous dimension more hideous than his worst nightmare.

Then it ceased. He didn't know when or where he was. Just that he was leaning against a wall, feeling like a building about to collapse, and his eyes were burning and wet. Tears?

But he'd never shed them. After all he'd been through, he'd believed he wasn't equipped with that most basic of human outlets. Now he knew. Among all the horrors he'd survived, *nothing* had hurt enough, mattered enough, to wring tears from his soul.

Her rejection far more than hurt. She far more than mattered.

He'd opened himself to her, let her in all the way. He'd let go of his safeguards, his anger, his pride. He'd believed in what he thought they shared. He'd deluded himself that she must have come to feel the same for him, to be that magnificent to him.

She felt nothing but abhorrence. She'd been forced into this marriage, hated bowing to the dictates of desire and the demands of patriotism. She despised him and loathed the idea of carrying his child.

He pushed away from the wall, slowly, methodically wiped away the unknown weakness, the manifestation of his surrender, his dependence. Then he headed back to Clarissa.

What she felt changed nothing. She was his wife. His queen. The mother of his child. What *he* felt didn't matter.

He'd lived without a heart until he'd seen her. He'd grown one to love her with. It had been quivering and dancing in hope within him since their first night together. And she'd stilled it forever in one annihilating blow. Now it was as good as nonexistent again. And he'd just have to learn to live without it again.

The first crushing wave of misery receded.

Clarissa knew it would only crash over her with more brutal force when it gathered momentum. For now, she was floating within the calm between devastating hurricanes. Now she could analyze her misery, not just come apart under its onslaught.

So she was pregnant. According to the doctors, she'd been pregnant for a while. Now that they'd explained the mystery of the period she'd had, she knew. She'd gotten pregnant that first night. As Ferruccio, in his endless insight, had foreseen she would. It was the best thing that had ever happened to her. It was by far the worst, too.

Now she'd never know if Ferruccio would remain married to her to have *her,* or to have his child. She'd been fooling herself, telling herself it wouldn't matter as long as he remained this wonderful to her. She *couldn't* live her life beside him, not knowing if he reciprocated her feelings, or knowing he couldn't. That day he'd struck his bargain, he'd said that if either of them wanted to be with someone else, they'd find a civil solution.

What if that bargain wasn't erased, and his heart was untouched? What if, one day, he found the woman to touch it?

She finally understood the depths of misery and desperation that had eaten through her mother's psyche, that had driven her, as they all suspected, to end her own life, when she'd come to believe that the husband she'd worshipped hadn't just never loved her, but had given his heart to another.

"Clarissa."

Ferruccio's whisper hit her all the way from the door, clanged inside her as if he'd shouted her name.

She jerked around, thanked God her tears had dried. Her lips trembled into a smile of dread and longing. What was he thinking?

His tranquil steps brought him to her side in what seemed like an eternity. Why was he so calm? So...opaque?

He sat down beside her on the bed, reached out a gentle hand and stroked away tendrils of hair from her face. The tenderness of his touch didn't match his guarded look. *Dio...Dio...*he wasn't happy about this. She knew it. Just before he'd been told the news, he'd been passionate, impatient, eager...open. Now it seemed that he'd retreated where she couldn't see him, let alone reach him.

Basta, you idiot! This was as life-changing to him as it was to her. He'd just been told he'd become a father for the first time. And to him, of all people, having a child within a solid, happy marriage, giving it what he'd never had, raising it between two loving parents, must be his foremost priority in life.

If their marriage was solid and happy.

"Congratulazioni, futura mamma." She tried to sit up, throw herself in his arms. He stopped her. She almost started weeping again, at his care. That he didn't take her in his arms. "No, don't move. No more bouncing around, and no more work until the doctors say it's one thousand percent safe."

"As long as it's not no more you, I'm fine with it." She tried to quip, knew he must see the turmoil in her eyes. She saw nothing in his as he brushed her quivering lips with his own.

"We'll see about that. Now rest, Clarissa." He withdrew, and she felt as if he would never come back. He looked down at her for a long moment. Then he exhaled. "I have to get back to work, but anything you need, *amore,* just summon me. I'll bring the whole world to you."

But I just want you.

The cry congealed in her throat as he turned and walked away.

He'd said all the right things, was fussing over her health and comfort. But he hadn't said how he felt about this. Not that he needed to. She'd never seen him look despondent. Now she had.

So he didn't want a child that would tie him to her forever? But if he hadn't wanted it, why hadn't he used protection? Did he just want the baby to cement his claim to the D'Agostino family name, but would rather she didn't come attached to it?

Was this how her mother had gone mad, destroyed her life and attempted to destroy the child of the man who couldn't love her?

But no. She wasn't her mother. She was herself, and no matter that she felt she was dying inside, she'd live for her child, love it more because it was his, too.

Even if he never loved her, she would always love him.

Clarissa finished watering her plants, then sat down to leaf through the baby magazines Ferruccio had deluged her with.

She looked at all the dimpled, smiling babies and felt she was sinking soundlessly in quicksand. The more she struggled with the determination to make the best of it, the faster she sank.

"Clarissa."

The lethal growl jammed her heart into her throat. *Durante.*

She swung around, suddenly seething with anger. *"Maledizione,* Durante, why did you bark at me like that—?"

The words froze on her lips, followed by the blood in her arteries. He…he looked…rabid.

Had something happened? To their father? To Gabrielle and their baby? But no…he didn't look agitated, he looked incensed, murderous.

Suspicion bludgeoned her heart.

Ferruccio and Gabrielle…?

His next words confirmed her most insane paranoia. "I had to see you, tell you, before I killed them both."

She flew to him, threw herself at him. "Durante, *no.*"

"Those two bastards deserve to die."

Two *bastards?* He was talking about two men? Ferruccio must be one of them. Who was the second? Gabrielle had more than one lover?

Could this get more insane?

Durante grabbed her arms. "You have to know how this happened. Before I married Gabrielle, I confronted our father, and he confessed he'd had a mistress for a very long time. I wanted to know the rest of the truth, but he wouldn't tell me, so I made investigations, found out his mistress was Gabrielle's mother. I went mad, drove Gabrielle away. *Grazie a Dio,* she took me back when I came to my senses and realized she had nothing to do with our parents' affair. But I forgot to call off my investigators. A few days ago their boss called with evidence that Gabrielle's mother had thirty-eight years ago given birth in Napoli to a son, then given him up for adoption. Along with the other evidence, the suspicion was too much. So I had DNA tests done. And redone. The results are conclusive. That son was Ferruccio. He is our father's son."

Eleven

How many times since Ferruccio had entered her life had he caused the world stop for her? Now it had stopped making sense, devolved into absolute chaos and madness.

Durante had said…had said…

Her mind shut down. Then Ferruccio walked in.

He stood at the door, his eyes moving from Durante to her in a slow sweep. Then they closed. He understood what this was all about. And since he did, then he'd…he'd known he was…was…

Ferruccio rushed to her, urgency blazing on his face, vibrating in his voice. "*Amore,* it is *not* what you think."

Durante slammed into him, aborting his momentum, wrestled him by the lapels, roared. "You don't talk to her, you bastard. Say whatever it is you want to say to me, before I kill you."

Clarissa noted, with the detachment of total breakdown, Ferruccio breaking Durante's hold with the explosive economy only a vicious, expert streetfighter could employ.

He staggered away, the turmoil on his face that of a man about to amputate his own arm. "I wanted to take this to my grave, but you've cornered me, Durante. I can't let either of you suspect what you do for one more second. I have to tell you the truth."

The truth. From the agony in his pleading eyes, it was something worse than anything that had come before. When there could be nothing worse. Yet it seemed there was. And he would finally tell her. Would she survive it? Would she want to?

Ferruccio knew the secrecy was over. He had to confess. It still felt like he was tearing out his own heart. Because he'd tear out Clarissa's with his confession. He would have given his heart for hers if it would have resolved this, protected her. But it wouldn't. There was no way out.

"Yes, I am the king's son." He panted with the effort of having to deal Clarissa such irreparable damage. Then he did. "It's you, Clarissa, who is not his daughter."

Clarissa collapsed.

His heart and skull felt as if they'd exploded.

He was beside her, catching her before she finished her plummet, frantically begging her to come back to him. He barely felt the vise that sank in his shoulder. Durante's grip.

"Is that the truth?"

He glared up at his half brother. "You think I'd lie about something like this? If you do, why don't you take a hair from her, too, and run more 'conclusive tests'?"

Durante seemed about to collapse himself. "*Dio*…what kind of parents did we have?"

"We still have one around. At least, you and I do. Both of Clarissa's are dead." Ferruccio carried Clarissa as if she were made of fragile glass, took her to their bedroom. She was breathing easy. Her nervous system must have shut down to protect her from any real damage. He still called his air ambulance and her doctors, told them to stand by.

He sat down beside her on their bed, which they hadn't shared for the past week. He'd been dying to have her, and he'd felt her equal need for him, but he hadn't been able to initiate intimacies. He'd done her enough damage, had wanted her to be the one to seek physical pleasure from him, at her own pace, of her own unpressured volition.

Now all he wanted was to curve himself around her and protect her from her pain and shock, beg her to take of him all she needed to heal herself.

"So you're my half brother. Why did you never tell me?"

Durante. He was still here.

Ferruccio turned to him, feeling worse than he had after a gang had broken almost every bone in his body.

"For her." Durante answered his own question. "You never wanted the truth about her parentage to become known, or for this terrible suspicion to stand in the way of your courting her."

"I've always wanted to tell you, but I loved her more. I was content that you thought of me as a friend."

"*Best* friend, Ferruccio. And now, brother."

"Yes. But, my best friend and brother, for now, please leave me alone with my wife."

Durante pressed his shoulder once, his eyes glittering with emotion, then he turned around.

When he was at the door, Ferruccio called out after him. "And leave King Benedetto alone."

Durante shook his head, gave a mirthless, ragged laugh. "Now, how did you know confronting him would be the first thing I'd do?"

"I'm serious, Durante. This must stay between us. I don't want King Benedetto learning that Clarissa has found out the truth. He spent his life protecting her from it. It would serve nothing but to make him desolate."

Durante closed his eyes on a grudging nod. "We have a lifetime and six years of acquaintance to rewrite."

"Actually, many lifetimes, Durante. Mine, your mother's, my mother's, Clarissa's father's. When and if I'm able to resolve this mess with my wife, if anything good comes of this, it will be that we finally forge a deeper relationship as siblings.

In secret. This *isn't* going public under any conditions. You'd better have been careful in your investigations."

"My investigator only came up with circumstantial evidence, he couldn't learn your identity. It's me who worked that out. I kept the medical evidence anonymous, the samples unnamed. Only I knew who they belonged to."

"Good. Now please, get out of here. Let me tend to my wife."

"You love her the way I love Gabrielle, don't you?" Durante's eyes filled with wonder, relief. "You would die for her."

"To start with. Now, get."

This time when he turned away, Durante did leave, still clearly in turmoil, but with a smile on his face.

Ferruccio forgot him the moment he exited his field of vision. He forgot that a world beyond the woman filling his arms existed. And he did what he'd longed to do for the past week.

He curved himself around her, contained her, whispered against her velvet cheek, "I'm here, *amore*. I'll always be here."

Clarissa surfaced from the nightmare, struggling to reach for the soothing lure reiterating, "I'm here. I'll always be here."

"I'm not who I thought I was."

Her own voice finally dragged her out of the vortex.

She'd passed out. To escape the medley of living nightmares she'd been living through. Living without Ferruccio's love, the horrible suspicion, then the terrible truth.

It had to be the truth. A DNA test like the one Durante had done would prove it. But she didn't need a test. She knew Ferruccio had told the truth. And he'd known it all this time.

He gathered her tighter to him. She didn't know if the tremors originated from her body or his arms.

"It doesn't matter. You remain the same, your life does, past and future. Your father…"

She whimpered.

"He *is* your father. He never cared that you aren't his biologically."

"He knew...all along?" Could this get worse? And she wailed, "How did this happen? Ferruccio, *please,* tell me the whole truth."

Every muscle in his face worked. Then he at last nodded.

"My mother's name was Clarisse LeFehr." At her gasp, he took her lips in a compulsive kiss. "Yes. *He* named you, Clarissa. He loved you from the moment you were born, and he named you for the love of his life. She was a ballerina with an Italian ballet company that performed in Castaldini. He was the new king, and they fell madly in love. Then she betrayed him, or so he believed. He cast her out of his life, immediately took a 'suitable' wife, your mother, Angelina. Their marriage was arranged, with no passion on either side. Even so, they had Durante, then Paolo. King Benedetto said he cared for her, but could never love her, not when he still loved his ex-lover, my mother. Then *your* mother's old lover—Pierro Bartolli, the man her father must have 'disciplined' her over—resurfaced, and she resumed their affair. When she got pregnant with you, she told him she would leave your father. But he convinced her not to, said that they would remain lovers. So she confessed to the king.

"At the same time, the king had long discovered that my mother hadn't betrayed him. Knowing how much he'd wronged her, and having never stopped loving her, he'd been searching for her, intent on resuming their relationship. So he felt as responsible as your mother for the situation. He told her they'd continue to project a façade of a solid marriage for their children's and their kingdom's sake, that he'd love her daughter as the daughter he'd longed to have.

"Your mother probably didn't believe him, and that may be why she overprotected you when you were young. But your biological father—according to King Benedetto—was only using her to live way beyond his means. When she'd expended all her personal fortune on him, Pierro tried to pressure her into asking the king for money, or even to steal it for him. He verbally abused her. She started pawning her jewelry for him, and Antonia told the king, who got it back and basically put your mother under house arrest. She considered him a jailer, escaped and went to her lover. She found him with another woman. When he was certain she couldn't get him more funds, he told her she was worth nothing without the money she'd provided him with from the first day, that he'd spent all her money on his lover, a woman she wasn't fit to be a servant to. I think that's when she began to abuse you."

"She wrote all that in her diaries. Durante thought she'd meant our...*his* father." She struggled to hold back sobs. Then she choked, "What happened to my...my biological father? Pierro? What about his...my...family."

Ferruccio's face became impassive. She guessed he was trying to withhold his opinion of the man who'd abused her mother and denied her, his flesh and blood. He didn't want to add to her turmoil. She felt rage and affront blasting off him. But when he spoke, he sounded controlled, neutral. "Pierro died five years ago, just before your mother did. In a boating accident. As far as I know, he had no living relatives. He came from a background much like my own."

"And his death...that was why she..." Her words choked off again, her tears now a stream.

But they weren't tears of pain or shock anymore. They were tears of pity. For the pettiness of it all, the waste. And of relief. The release of finally knowing how and why. Of closure.

Through her tears, she saw something she'd never thought to see. Tears in Ferruccio's eyes. *Those* hurt.

She surged up, clutched his face. "No, Ferruccio, no... please, don't cry. Not you."

"You suffered so much, *amore*. And now..."

"Now I'm just relieved I know at last." A tear escaped down his cheek and she cried out, caught it with her lips. "Don't make me hate myself for daring to feel devastated for a second, when I had the loving father—*your* father and the privileged up-bringing, while you had *nothing*."

He wiped at his tears, his smile coming out a grimace that severed more of her heart's tethers. "I have everything now."

"That doesn't make it any better."

"It more than does. It erases it."

She felt she'd have a seizure from the pressure of her emotions. She wanted to scream and say that nothing would ever erase his suffering. That not even her and her father's lives would be enough to repay what they owed him. "Tell me the rest, Ferruccio. Your story. Did my…your father know about you, too?"

He looked away. She guessed that he didn't want to add to her pain. *Her* pain. Hatred, for herself, for her father, for the world, shot to a new height. She grabbed his face, forced him to look at her.

At last he muttered. "He found out when I was fifteen."

"And he left you on the streets? *Oh, Dio…Dio…*"

He sat up, taking her with him, cradling her in the curve of his body. "*Amore,* it doesn't matter."

"*Doesn't matter?* That is the worst thing yet. It's unbearable. Unimaginable. It's an unforgivable crime!"

"It didn't happen like you think."

"Then tell me how it did happen before my head bursts!"

He exhaled his surrender to her need to know. "When King Benedetto sought out my mother, she was married, and she'd already had Gabrielle."

It clicked in her mind. "Gabrielle is your sister! *That's* why you look at her that way!"

"Yes. I thought I'd never be able to approach her, since the price was telling her the truth. Even with Durante's prior investigations and the subsequent revelations before she married him, she remained ignorant she had a brother."

"But even without knowing, she…recognized the bond between you. I can swear she did."

"It was fun to see you act jealous, though. It gave me hope."

She wasn't in a condition to understand what that meant.

"And you were willing to live your whole life not telling her that you are brother and sister, to protect me from the truth?"

"Considering I have her in my life anyway, that isn't such a huge sacrifice."

"*Dio,* Ferruccio, shut up. And *talk.*"

He huffed a distressed laugh. "I said exactly that to your doctors a week ago. And if you're in half as appalling a state as I was then, I'd better talk fast. Just promise me, no more tears."

Her eyes gushed again. "No can do. Please, Ferruccio. You were saying your mother was married, had Gabrielle…?"

He kept wiping her tears with his fingers, his lips. "When King Benedetto reappeared in her life, she told him about me, how in her worst moments after she'd given birth, she'd weakened and put me up for adoption. She tried to look for me later, to take me back, but she'd been denied information. All she could find out was that I was never adopted, that I ended up in the foster system. They searched for me, but didn't find me until two years after I left my last foster home. They were heartbroken to find their son a hardened survivor on the streets."

"*They* were heartbroken? The nerve!"

"There was no villain here, *amore,* it was all a series of horrible miscommunications and terrible decisions."

"Which *are* crimes, and makes them villains, especially since there was only one victim. You!"

"Are you defending me again, *leonessa mia?* Against the pain of the past and the mistakes of my parents?"

"If that pain and those mistakes were flesh and blood now, I'd tear them apart with my teeth and nails!"

His laugh was delighted this time, as he hugged her. "You see? Hearing you say that erases it all." An impatient, indignant sound rolled from her throat. He raised a placating hand. "Don't growl, *leonessa mia.* I'll go on peacefully."

He adjusted their position to place her on his lap, where she could feel every rock-hard inch of him thrusting between her legs. Even through the upheaval, her body blossomed and melted into instant readiness. How she'd starved for him.

"My parents were justifiably shocked. I was a hulking, surly, violent teenager they had every reason to suspect would become, or already was, a hardened criminal."

"Thanks to them!"

"Actually, I don't believe there is any excuse for turning to crime. Not neglect, not hardships, not abuse. I never considered my ordeals a reason to take the easy way out."

"I did tell you before, Ferruccio. You are a miracle."

"Look who's talking." He hugged her again, pressed his forehead to hers in a gesture that melted all her heart valves. "But I did look scary. And as much as they were shocked to see me, I was shocked to see them, to discover that I wasn't just any bastard, but a royal one. The king pledged to support me, but he told me, for the sake of his family and kingdom, he wouldn't be able to acknowledge me. I told him what to do with his support. The only thing I'd ever accept from him was his name."

"He's the man who raised me, and I love him. But I also hate him now. How could he think his other children more important than you? How could he deny you what he gave them?"

"It was all for you, *mia bella unica*. He might have lost you completely if a chain reaction of revelations was started."

To that she could only sob and bury her face in his chest. She tugged at him to go on.

"The king kept putting money for me in the bank, enough to have seen me through a luxurious life and the best education."

She glanced up. "But you never touched it."

His chuckle rumbled beneath her ear. "You know me well. That money in the bank was like a tormenting imp, lashing me to succeed, to reach ever higher on my own. I was bent on showing him I didn't need him in any way. So, I guess I should thank him for that. And because I became who I am, I can now do all I'm doing for Castaldini. So in a roundabout way, all of Castaldini is in your father's debt, too."

"In his debt for not acknowledging his son?" she seethed. "Excuse me as I puke! And bull to this owing your success to your ordeals or to anyone. You would have suceeded no matter what!"

"But maybe I wouldn't have become the same man."

The man I worship? she almost blurted out.

She didn't. It was time she asked the question that really mattered to her. "T-tell me about the first time you came to Castaldini."

"Ah, that first time. Even with my very…eventful life, that was the day its course changed forever." The look he gave her told her she'd been the reason.

How?

"With my success established and the fire in my heart banked, I felt the need to establish some sort of relationship with the king. So I came here on the pretext of doing business. The king was ecstatic that I'd decided to come to him at last. I even felt that he'd finally acknowledge me, that everything was going right. Then I saw you."

She clutched at his shirt, which she'd soaked in tears. She sensed that she'd now hear what would explain the past—and unravel the future.

"I'd never wanted anyone on sight like that. And I thought I saw the same recognition, the same instant hunger in your eyes. But before I could walk up to you and claim you, the king joined me and something he said made me realize that you were his daughter. I was so appalled that I walked away without looking at him. I think I would have decked him if I hadn't."

That was it. The mystery behind the misery that had ruled her for the past six years. Everything fell into place like a hail of bombs. "And you reached for the first woman—or two—to drown your sorrow."

His gaze stilled before he threw his head back and barked a stunned laugh. "*Maledizione,* you're uncanny, *mia bella.* I was out to prove to myself there were plenty of other fish in the sea." His lips twisted wryly. "And the moment I felt my sinker bob,

I tossed the whole fishing rod into the water and ran away. And that was when the king found me again, dragged me away. The minute we were alone, I turned on him, ranting that I hated him, that he was the reason for every horrible thing that had ever happened to me and that I'd never come back.

"But he understood the reason behind my turmoil. He'd seen the hunger in my eyes as I looked at you, said he was stunned at the clarity of instinct that had told me I could covet you. And he told me the secret he'd intended to take to his grave—that you weren't his biological child. He'd decided by then to make my parentage known, to let you and the world believe that I was your half brother. I refused point-blank, and he said that meant he'd have to let the truth about *your* parentage be known.

"And I made my decision. I would remain the illegitimate one among us. I was used to it, and it meant nothing to me anymore. While you—I couldn't bear to think of your devastation if you found out the king wasn't your father."

She heaved a huge sob and burst out weeping again. He stroked and soothed her. "It was in my best interests. As a stranger, I was free to pursue you. When I said that, the king was alarmed, said he wouldn't let me toy with you. I said he had no say in the matter, but should put his mind to rest, anyway. That clarity of instinct he'd talked about had always made me sure of what I wanted, what would work, and work spectacularly. And I'd never been surer about anything. I wanted you. And I was getting you. And it would be beyond spectacular."

Her tears stopped, foreboding squeezing her heart. He'd come to the part when she'd smacked his advances back in his face.

"But I shouldn't have been so sure. I went after you, and you turned me down, so disdainfully. Kept on doing it for six years. It took a crisis in your kingdom and some convoluted black-mail to make you accept me."

Suddenly his body stiffened beneath her, his jaw muscles

bunched as if in excruciating pain. Then he carefully set her away from him, rose to his feet, a defeated slump to his shoulders. "Not that you have accepted me."

Clarissa lay on the bed where he left her, pinned under a mountain of humility and gratitude and love and awe.

Then her mind caught on this last comment, and she was on her feet, across the room and grabbing him by the arms. "I work with you by day and make delirious love with you every night—at least, before you suddenly seemed to stop wanting me after you found out I was carrying your child. What do you *mean* I haven't accepted you?"

Ferruccio looked down at her, his reason and reasons made flesh and bone, his soul made woman. And he let his anguish out. "I mean you're trapped in our marriage. You don't want my child, you've always believed I'm beneath you. That was always the reason, from that first night, that you rejected me, wasn't it?"

She gaped at him. Then she started shaking him with all her strength. "Are you *really* insane? *Beneath* me? You thought my rejection all these years was rooted in snobbery? How dare you think me that stupid and vicious and shallow. How dare you want me when you thought that of me."

"I didn't…" He stopped, swallowed the knot of confusion that had never let him finish a coherent thought in this matter. "I did think that. But then I was with you, and everything you said and did told me you were everything I could admire and love. Then you rejected me *again,* and I could find no other explanation. I was going around and around in my mind, on an endless spin cycle of belief and doubt, hope and despair."

"*Dio,* this is beyond ridiculous. It seems you're not all-seeing, after all. Not with a blind spot the size of Africa."

"So, why did you keep rejecting me?" he groaned.

And she yelled at him, at the top of her voice, telling him exactly why she'd been scared to give in to him, to her feelings.

He was shaking with relief and elation when she finished.

But she wasn't finished. "And just what were *you* feeling all the time, as you thought that of me? Were you internally gloating at the stupid snob who was herself illegitimate? If so, I wonder at your willpower that you haven't smeared my face in it. But then, you should have. Maybe then you would have gotten your facts straight, and all this could have been resolved earlier."

He opened his mouth to protest and she bulldozed on. "And don't you dare turn this on me. It's you who seem to be trapped in our marriage, you who are unhappy that I'm carrying your baby. The day you found out, you looked as if you'd been told you had a chronic, debilitating disease."

He was shaking as hard as she was now, finally seeing it all. "I saw you crying. I went back to thinking you hated me, couldn't stand having my baby. *Dio santo,* Clarissa, we've both been so afraid to believe all this magic was for real that we kept tormenting ourselves with worst-case scenarios."

Her violet eyes turned purple with the enormity of emotion igniting them, the silvery tears magnifying their beauty, reflecting shards of pure, agonizing ecstasy into his soul.

"So do you want my baby? And…me?" Then he added the word he'd held back during their marriage ceremony. "Forever?"

She dove into his arms, felt as if she surged into his being, as she had—lived there now, ruled supreme. "Since I love you endlessly, you'd better make it at least that long."

He held her tight, then tighter, and they exchanged confessions and pledges and he soothed her turmoil over her discoveries, wallowed in the still wary, yet deepening certainty of their mutual devotion.

When it all threatened to overwhelm them again, and fearing for her health, both emotional and physical, he suddenly tickled her.

"Now I am the king's bastard and the bastard king. While you are the queen's bastard and the bastard queen. How's that for proof we're made for each other?"

She kissed him, sobbed and giggled. "*Uomo cattivo,* you wicked man, how dare you make it funny when it isn't?"

"No, it isn't. But it's destiny. Ours."

"Show me."

He swept her into his arms and showed her. And with every word and touch, he wrote with her another page in what he was now certain was a destiny that would leave its mark on the world.

Epilogue

Ferrucio looked around the room where his family had gathered.

He still couldn't believe it. He still woke up suffocating, fearing that the last twenty-one months hadn't happened. That he was alone, with only work for company and comfort.

Each time, he'd woken up in Clarissa's arms. Which made him fear even more that he was dreaming.

But he couldn't have dreamed her. His wildest imaginings wouldn't have created her, his wife and best friend and ally, his queen and lover. And as if she wasn't beyond what any mortal deserved, she'd gifted him with more.

Their son.

His heart almost burst yet again, as he watched their determined tyke trying in vain to catch Clarissa's disdainful—and he suspected, intentionally taunting—cat, Figaro. Love and pride and fear and hope reduced his insides to the consistency of jelly.

It was a whole year today, since their perfect Massimo was

born. And the months before he was born had all flowered in escalating harmony and pleasure and joy.

It wasn't just his and Clarissa's tiny family that was flourishing. The king—or the ex-king, as he insisted on being called, an insistence which no one heeded—was in the best condition he'd been in since his stroke. Julia, Phoebe's sister, was in the best state she'd ever been in since her affliction with a rare partial paralysis. Gabrielle and Durante, after their initial confusion, were delighted to share Ferruccio as a sibling, Gabrielle on her mother's side, Durante on his father's. While Durante's and Paolo's relationship with Clarissa seemed only to deepen, now that the real cause behind their mother's depression had come to light.

"Admiring the view?"

Ferruccio turned to see Leandro. Durante was a step behind. He greeted his two friends, whom he'd finally been able to tell they were more than that and whom it had taken minimal groveling to get to become his main men on the new Council they'd forged, the one Castaldini needed now.

"What's not to admire?" Ferruccio said. "Look at her. Have you ever seen anything more miraculous?"

"Uh, actually, yes." Leandro smirked. "Take a look around."

Ferruccio did, this time attempting to focus on anyone besides Clarissa and Massimo. Phoebe was at her most radiant, talking animatedly to Julia and Gabrielle and the king. Her and Leandro's little girl, Joia, now twenty months old, was fast asleep on Phoebe's round-again tummy. Gabrielle and Durante's fourteen-month-old boy, Alessandro, was playing with the fifth—and they swore last—addition to Paolo and Julia's family, with their older kids all over the place yet managing not to be noisy or disruptive, mostly babysitting the younger ones to give adults space to talk.

Durante nodded. "We're all lucky bastards."

"Since I'm the literal lucky bastard among you," Ferruccio said, "I reserve my place as the luckiest among us."

"Let him have first place, Durante." Leandro smirked. "He just can't live if he isn't the first in everything."

Ferruccio started to protest, then shook his head and laughed.
He *was* the luckiest. No need to rub their noses in it.
The other two men joined him in laughter.

Clarissa scooped Massimo off the ground before he grabbed
Figaro's tail. Figaro knew he was a kid, treated him with the
condescending tolerance the status deserved. But the imperious tomcat had his limits. His tail was foremost among them.

She turned around at the sound of three men's laughter, her
heart twisting with love as she watched her *amore,* her king and
husband. She hadn't thought she could possibly love him more,
but she did, every day. For who he was, what he did, not only
for her, but for all of Castaldini, the kingdom that was once
again a haven of peace and prosperity. But one thing made her
so grateful to him, so proud of him, she sometimes couldn't
breathe, thinking of it.

The incredible sacrifice he'd so selflessly insisted on, to
remain the "bastard king," as he called himself, to protect his
father and her. They'd never let King Benedetto suspect that
she knew the truth. She loved him now even more, for being
her father when he wasn't her real father. She felt his eyes
on her now.

She walked up to him and whispered in his ear. He nodded.
"Hey, everyone!" she called out, and everyone turned to her,
a hush falling over the huge chamber. "King Benedetto—hush,
Father—" she shushed him when he protested to being called
king now, as he never failed to "—has some news for you!"

As everyone turned to him, all attention, he stood up and
took his first steps since Ferruccio's and Clarissa's wedding.
Strong steps, almost with no visible limp. He'd been practic-
ing, exercising, but hadn't wanted anyone to know until he was
able to walk without his cane. He'd told only her.

The chamber echoed with sounds of delight as everyone
surged to congratulate him.

Ferruccio was the last to approach.

Clarissa's heart ached. Ferruccio still considered King Benedetto her father, not his, and the tension in their relationship was not completely gone. He said he loved the king for being her father, for protecting her as a child, for loving her as she deserved to be loved. She still prayed for the day he'd come to love him for himself, to forgive him his trespasses and guilt.

Now the considering look Ferruccio gave her father rattled her with anxiety. He'd never say anything cutting to him, not anymore, especially not now. But what did that look mean?

Ferruccio stood before her father, seemed to be examining him. Then he said, "Seems to me you're back in tip-top shape. Does this mean you want the crown back?"

She exhaled her immense relief at his obvious teasing, as King Benedetto embraced him.

Ferruccio stepped back from his father's embrace, doing a double take. What was that he saw on the old jackal's face? That smug, got-you-where-I-want-you look?

He didn't have time to interrogate him, as the women and children swept the king away. Ferruccio turned to Leandro and Durante, saw the same puzzled look on their faces.

"Tell me you saw that," Durante exclaimed.

"I saw it." Leandro nodded. "I think he meant for us to see it."

"*Dio,*" Ferruccio groaned. "I feel likc the biggest sucker in the known universe."

"Oh no you don't." Duranted echoed his groan. "That is one status you'll have to share with us."

"This was all a plan. A master plan by your canny old man." Leandro shook his head in wonder, admiration tingeing his gaze as he looked at King Benedetto.

"Everything falls into place, doesn't it? We're all exactly where he wanted us to be all along," Ferruccio said.

The three of them exchanged looks, suspicion becoming conviction in a heartbeat.

They all burst out laughing at the same moment.

"For the first time in my life," Ferruccio guffawed, "I want to kiss the man. I want to smother him in kisses."

"You'll have to wait in line." Durante wiped away tears of hilarity.

Leandro still shook his head, the look of admiration on his face deepening. "Between our hugs and kisses of overwhelming gratitude, we might even make him sorry for manipulating us so unrepentantly."

"And considering what we all ended up having," Ferruccio said fervently, "*grazie a Dio* a billion times that he did."

"Amen, *fratello*, amen." Durante echoed his passion.

At that moment Clarissa walked up to Ferruccio.

He scooped her off the ground into a convulsive hug. She giggled and hugged him back, whispered in his ear.

He froze before he whooped and swung her into the air.

As everyone gaped at them, he clutched her in his arms and rushed out on a beeline to their apartments.

He couldn't have waited to make an announcement out of her news.

Having a second baby on the way was something he needed to celebrate in private first, and urgently.

* * * * *

FRIDAY NIGHT
MISTRESS

BY
JAN COLLEY

Dear Reader,

Feuding fathers are great catalysts for romance stories. I don't recall my father ever feuding with anyone, but I think most feuds involve great wealth and I could never accuse my dad of that! What I can accuse him of is imbuing me with a love of stories. He used to tell wonderful tales of his life in the British and Australian armies in India and Korea. (I suspect he still does, but sadly, the pace of life and my inability to sit still long enough means that he doesn't get the chance very often.) As an aside, my dad is one of the few people in the world who could say he has met Mahatma Gandhi, Marilyn Monroe and Nelson Mandela.

But back to feuding fathers: historical conflict between families gives a writer rich pickings to inflict suffering on the new generation. The hero and heroine of this book struggle with the sins of their fathers and events not of their making. But in my mind, two cranky old men will one day sit on the couch together, dangling the grandkids on their knees and telling them about the time they...

Hope you enjoy Nick and Jordan's story.

Best wishes,

Jan Colley

Jan Colley lives in Christchurch, New Zealand, with Les and a couple of cats. She has travelled extensively, is jack of all trades and master of none and still doesn't know what she wants to be when she grows up – as long as it's a writer. She loves rugby, family and friends, writing, sunshine, talking about writing and cats, although not necessarily in that order. E-mail her at vagabond232@ yahoo.com or check out her website at www.jancolley. com.

Thanks for all the stories, Dad!
And thanks to Stephen Bray, our friendly family
lawyer, who let me pester him about courtroom
legalese and only charged me a chocolate fish.
And to Maureen Coffey of Havelock Sea Charters, who
answered my questions about chartering a boat in
the Marlborough Sounds of New Zealand.

One

"All rise."

Spectators and participants in the Wellington High Court rose as one. Day one of the defamation case brought by Randall Thorne, founder of Thorne Financial Enterprises, against Syrius Lake had begun.

Seated behind his father in the front row of the gallery, Nick Thorne frowned as his younger brother slipped into the empty seat beside him. "You're late," Nick muttered without heat. Adam was always late, even while on holiday.

The judge bustled in and motioned for everyone to take their seats.

"Would you look at that?" Adam whispered, nudging

Nick. "Little Jordan Lake, all grown up and pretty as a picture."

Nick tilted his head and flicked a glance to his right. He'd noticed her earlier, surprised at how demure she looked with her hair tied back, wearing a white blouse and a knee-length black skirt. Everyone here would be more used to seeing her in the tabloids, partying it up with some rock star or other, her golden hair flowing and plenty of long, smooth leg on display. She was every inch the heiress, daughter of one of the richest and most flamboyant men in New Zealand.

Adam leaned in close. "I'm surprised you've never considered hooking up with her. An alliance with the Lake princess would be one way to bury this stupid hatchet that's been the bane of our lives forever."

"She's more your type than mine," Nick murmured, settling back in his seat as his father turned his head and sent him a disapproving look.

It was true. Jordan and Adam were rebels, whereas Nick was duty-driven and responsible. The brothers could almost pass as twins with their olive coloring, dark hair and brows and their father's tall, broad frame. But Adam, with his designer stubble, flashy suits and bad boy demeanor, was far removed from the quieter, more conservative Nick.

"True," Adam whispered, rubbing his chin thoughtfully, "but I live in London."

The infamous feud between Randall Thorne and Syrius Lake had tainted their whole lives, especially their late mother's, a former close friend of Syrius's wife, Elanor. Nick felt a pang of compassion for the woman sitting at the end of the row in the aisle to his right. Elanor had spent thirty years in a wheelchair because of Nick's father, all the more galling because she and his mother were once national ballroom dancing competitors and partners in their own dance studio.

"You can't help your looks, big brother," Adam went on, "but you're still not a bad catch. CEO of the biggest privately-owned finance company in New Zealand…"

"Not yet," Nick said tersely.

"Soon." His brother waved a nonchalant hand toward Jordan Lake. "Cultivate something with her. It's a dirty job, but somebody's gotta do it."

Their father turned again, this time with a stern look at Adam.

The respective counsels droned on. Nick shifted impatiently. He'd felt duty-bound to stand by his father today on the first day of the trial, but there was no way he could afford to be here all day, every day for the next week or however long the trial lasted. That would fall to Adam, who'd come home for a few weeks' holiday and to support his father through the trial.

To his right, Nick caught a flash of tanned leg as Jordan shifted. His eyes lingered on her black pump-clad foot as it bounced up and down. Was she as bored and impatient as he was? Hell, she had nowhere else to be. She didn't work, unless you counted the pursuit of a good time work.

The hair on the back of his neck prickled and Nick looked up. The heiress was watching him, her mouth slanted in a cool smirk. Then she tilted her head toward her mother and whispered in her ear.

Adam cast him an amused glance, seeing the direction of his gaze. "You know you want to," he murmured.

Nick gave his brother a wry smile. It was great having him around. Nick missed him, even though their father constantly played them off against each other, unheeding of Adam's wish to have nothing to do with the family business.

Randall raised them with an abiding fascination for money, but Adam preferred to be at the cutting edge while Nick liked to have his finger on the pulse, maintaining and building strength. Adam departed four years ago to live his dream as a trader in London's stock exchange.

At the break, his father and lawyer seemed supremely confident, Randall declaring none too softly that he intended to annihilate Syrius Lake, whatever it took. With a sinking heart, Nick realized that if it wasn't this case, it would be something else. Without his mother's tempering influence, Randall would stop at nothing to get his revenge—and that directly impacted on Nick's future. He intended to be named successor of Thorne Financial Enterprises when his father retired in a few weeks. *If* his father retired…

Adam's words played over in his mind. Could he honestly consider cultivating something with Jordan Lake? Putting an end to the bitterness their fathers had supped on for three decades? The more he thought about it, the more he agreed with Adam. His eyes followed the swing of her ponytail as she walked ahead of him back into the courtroom and a smile tugged at the corners of his mouth. Jordan Lake would be the ultimate takeover.

Days later, Nick stirred as the mattress shifted and the woman next to him rose and walked into the bathroom. Sated, a little sleepy from the late nights he'd been keeping since his brother hit town, he wondered idly if he'd drifted off.

In a few short weeks, Adam would be gone, back to the high-velocity stock exchange world he ruled. Privately, Nick worried how long his brother could handle the pressure. He might be flavor of the month now, lauded by all and making an absolute fortune. But that was the thing about the share market. There was a never-ending supply of hungry young sharks circling, just waiting until someone made a mistake. Adam had been one of them not so long ago.

Nick stretched and plumped up his pillows, resting one arm behind his head. The bathroom door opened and a tall, slender blonde walked into the room. She moved to the dresser mirror, her arms raised as she fiddled with her long, tawny hair. Nick's eyes feasted on the long line of her spine, the curvaceous swell of her hips, and her skin, which had a luster to it even with the heavy drapes drawn against the afternoon sun. He liked how at ease she seemed about her nudity.

"Got time for a drink or are you rushing off?" he asked, aware that his question would surprise her. They didn't make a habit of small talk after their lovemaking sessions.

She flicked him a curious look in the mirror and continued twisting her hair expertly into a knot that looked at once messy but sophisticated.

"Let me guess." Nick clicked his tongue. "Cocktails. The Zeus Bar."

Again, he felt the wash of cool blue in her glance as she turned. "A little early for me." She bent and plucked something from the floor.

Clothing would be scattered all over, he thought. It was always like that. The moment they were inside the room, there was no decorum, no neatly undressing and folding and hanging. Sometimes they were lucky to get out of here without ripped garments.

Today she'd worn a short fuchsia shift dress, with a strap over one shoulder tied in a big extravagant bow. Easy to get in—and out—of, and entirely suitable for cocktails in any of the bars she was frequently photographed at, although never with him.

Despite her accessible outfit, it had still seemed to take an age to get his hands on her today. Time moved like a slow-motion movie clip when he entered this suite at the five-star hotel every Friday. Each image burned into his brain: the silkiness and fragrance of her creamy skin, the tumble of her hair as he tugged it into disarray, her sighs as he bared her to his hungry mouth and hands. As if she, too, had pictured this moment, his kisses and touch, the way he tore at her clothing. As if she, too, had longed for it every day between. Each set of images stayed with him, replayed over and over in his mind throughout the week until he could have her again.

Once a week for four months, and Nick knew nothing personal about her, except for what she brought to his bed.

"I saw you on TV last night," he commented as she untwisted her panties from her dress. "A short, puffy black skirt." He paused. "And a tall puffy pale man."

The woman daintily stepped into her underwear. "Not me. I stayed home last night."

Nick's mouth went dry at the little shimmy her hips did to facilitate the placement of her underwear. "I'd know those legs anywhere," he countered mildly. "I could sculpt them."

She blinked, shaking out her dress. Probably wondering what on earth did it have to do with him, he thought.

"I do have a short black puffy skirt, and—" a breathy huff of amusement burst from her lips "—a tall puffy man or two, but it wasn't last night."

She raised her arms fluidly and the dress floated down like a pink cloud, veiling her body.

Nick gazed at her, desire curling its claws into him again. Even after two tumultuous orgasms in less than two hours, he wanted her again, quite savagely. "Where do you go, Jordan Lake, when you leave my bed?"

Jordan had managed to lower her brows and close her gaping mouth by the time the dress passed over her head. She wasn't bothered that he didn't believe her about last night—she owed him no explanations. It often happened that on a slow news day, the press or TV used file pictures of her on a night out. It had been a couple of weeks since she had worn that skirt.

What surprised her was that he'd asked. They had been meeting here every Friday for four months and Nick Thorne never once expressed an interest in her activities outside of this suite.

She turned her back, arching a brow at him in the mirror. "Jealous, Nick?" she asked, deliberately imparting an edge of sarcasm.

She recalled blushing the color of this dress after their very first time together. She'd lain in bed, covers drawn up to her chin, waiting for him to return from the bathroom. What next? she'd wondered. Would they talk? Cuddle?

But Nick made it painfully obvious that this was merely a sexual arrangement. He had quickly dressed, commanded her to be here the same time next week, pressed her hand to his mouth and was out of there in five minutes flat. No backward glance, no promise to call. Nothing.

Jordan had been shocked, a little hurt and felt foolish. He thought she knew the game but she wasn't nearly as sexually experienced as the media portrayed her to be. Of her four previous lovers, two of those were fairly serious relationships. It was just that her taste in men ran to playboys, pro athletes and musicians. But her wild days were definitely behind her by the time she met Nick.

Holding his gaze, she carefully tied the bow on her shoulder and then reached behind her to tug at the zipper of her dress.

Nick threw back the covers and in a second, stood behind her, his knuckles pressing purposefully into every nub of her spine as he worked the zipper slowly up.

He took her breath away, even after all this time. His shoulders seemed an aircraft wing-span across compared to her narrow frame. He was a full head taller than her, his short, dark hair a little disheveled. In the dimly-lit room, he looked almost Latin with his thick dark brows, dusky skin and full, sensuous lips.

Lips that brushed her ear, generating a flutter of excitement deep in her belly.

Bad sign. She should definitely go. Her mother was expecting her for dinner, anyway.

But then his eyes locked on to hers in the reflection and he bent his head to nuzzle at the top of her shoulder. "No hurry, is there?"

Jordan leaned her head back to nestle in his throat, watching him with half-closed eyes. Behind her, his hand continued its slow progress, now in between her shoulder blades, each centimeter a wand of heat that caused her back to arch. She sent a silent apology to her mother for her anticipated lateness.

Nick Thorne was irresistible to her. It had been that way since the first clash of their eyes in an elevator in this very hotel. She was leaving an aunt's eightieth birthday afternoon tea party. Nick was leaving a banking conference. A chance meeting so powerful, she couldn't believe they'd even made it out of the elevator without her skin blistering. The intense attraction led to an indecently quick drink at the bar and an even more indecent mutual decision to take a room, there and then. The thrill of it all was intensified by how forbidden it was because of the hatred between their fathers for the last thirty years.

The zipper was fully up but Nick's green-gold gaze was not that of someone who wanted her dressed. He caressed the back of her neck close to her hairline, an exquisite touch that made her breath catch. The heat of him behind her, naked and masculine, bathed her skin. He slowly moved his hand to the bow on her shoulder, watching her as if challenging her to stop him. The ribbon had as much resistance as her mind, and the front panel of the dress collapsed in front but was supported by the zipper at back. Not supported enough for the weight of her breasts, which spilled out, taut and aroused.

"Now look what I've done," Nick murmured in her ear. "And I was only trying to get to know you better."

Jordan swallowed and raised her hands, cupping her breasts. "You know me," she said breathlessly, playing the game. "You know these."

"Yes, I know these." His big hands relieved hers of their burden, kneading and squeezing just the way she liked. Jordan welcomed the onslaught of sensations that had become familiar yet never failed to render her boneless. Even as she wondered vaguely why the sudden interest, it was beyond her to resist his touch. She swirled in a hazy pool of delight at his breath on her neck, his hands on her flesh, the hot, hard wall of him pressed up against her back.

He used his hands unhurriedly, feathering down her sides to her buttocks, pausing to caress them in a circular motion that made her shiver.

"I know these..." he murmured as his hands slid over the sensitive backs of her thighs, down to her knees and up again, the fabric of the dress slipping and sliding over her smooth skin, higher and higher until it was bunched around her hips.

Her breath came in shallow gasps now as he held her captive in front of him. She ought to feel wanton and ashamed, watching them in the mirror, observing her total submission to his hands, his mouth as he nibbled and licked her neck and the top of her shoulder. This was, after all, what everyone expected of her. A spoiled, rich, man-eating socialite who spent her entire life in the pursuit of pleasure.

She was on her way to perdition and pleased about it, she thought, feeling the scrape of her panties down her legs. When Nick Thorne touched her, she felt beautiful and proud that he wanted her. He was a man of substance, successful and wealthy in his own right, not some flighty playboy. Their relationship may be based on the most primitive of urges, but his desire for her, the passion he evoked from her, made her feel his equal. Love didn't come into it, but Friday afternoons were the best thing in Jordan's life and she wouldn't give them up.

She brought her fingertips down to the dresser to steady herself, just as his thigh wedged between her trembling legs, nudging them apart. His breath skittered up the length of her back, making every downy hair stand to quivering attention. Anticipation backed up in her throat.

"I know this," he insisted, his fingers lightly probing while she moaned softly, her eyes closing to contain the most sublime pleasure.

He shifted closer. A red-hot streak of sensation ripped through her and she realized it wasn't his fingers probing and gliding now, sliding in between her legs. The weight of him leaning over her back forced her forward and she pressed her palms down on the dresser, bracing herself.

"Open your eyes, Jordan," he instructed, sliding one arm around her waist.

Her head lolled heavily back and hit his chest. She pried her eyes open and found his, fierce and compelling, staring back at her through the mirror.

"Does it bother you," he asked roughly, "this secret of ours? This thing between us?"

Jordan was past reason. She wanted much more of "this thing" between them, and she wanted it now. She stared at him, pushing back into his body, squeezing her thighs together to trap him.

With an effort almost too much to bear, she forced her mouth to open, to speak. "I know the score, Nick," she told him tightly. "I'm playing the game."

Sex.

Simple. Sensational. Secret.

It was what she wanted. What she lived for. Her Friday afternoon delight.

Two

"It's all right for you," the stooped man with the trembling hands told her belligerently. "You get paid to sit around all day. I had to take the morning off work and now it looks like I won't get seen at all."

"I'm sorry, Mr. Hansen. It's been very busy this morning." Jordan tried to warm him up with a sympathetic smile but the man sighed loudly and stomped back to his seat in the crowded waiting room.

She exhaled slowly. Not even lunchtime and already a tension headache throbbed dully in her temples.

It was her turn on the voluntary roster to work two full days in Reception at the Elpis Free Clinic, and just occasionally, uncharitable though it was, she found it a little overwhelming dealing with unwell people. Thinking she was unobserved, she dropped her head down onto her arms for a second.

Behind her, Reverend Russ Parsons put his hand on her shoulder and she jerked up.

"You should have told him that no one gets paid around here. Not the doctors, cleaners, admin staff or our beautiful receptionist."

Jordan laughed ruefully. "Some receptionist! Some days I just don't seem to have the knack with people."

"You'll never get it right all of the time, but what's important is that you try so hard." He took some leaflets from the counter in front of them and handed them to her. "Why don't you give him some info on our natural healing classes?"

She took them, silently berating herself for not thinking of it.

In addition to the free clinic, the Elpis Foundation she'd set up a year ago helped Russ's parish to identify at-risk families who were stretched financially. They also provided a raft of self-help courses. Jordan was incredibly proud of the strides they'd made in a short time, but her lack of work experience spoke volumes about how she had chosen to spend her time up until recently.

"Are we still on for the Working Bee this weekend?" Russ had turned to go but stopped at the door.

Jordan nodded enthusiastically. She had recently purchased an old backpackers hostel in the beautiful Marlborough Sounds at the top of the South Island. The hostel had gone out of business years ago and was rundown and neglected, but with the volunteers from Russ's parish, she hoped to develop it into a retreat for the families in the program who never got to have a holiday. "How many are coming? I'll book the ferry tickets."

"Ten. Is Friday afternoon all right? I'll have to get the late ferry back on Saturday for services on Sunday."

Friday afternoon? Jordan's heart lurched. She shook her head and lowered her eyes, feeling the onset of an embarrassed blush. "Sorry. You guys could go but I won't be able to until Saturday morning." Philanthropy was one thing; denying herself Nick Thorne's body quite another—especially on her birthday. "My parents are putting on a thing for my birthday."

A "thing" by her father's standards would probably cost the annual wage of four or five of the people in the waiting room combined. This year, her twenty-sixth, she had prevailed upon Syrius not to go too over-the-top. "You're welcome to come," she added lamely, hoping Russ would decline. Her father didn't approve of the way she spent her time and money and she was afraid his infamous lack of tact would offend the gentle reverend.

Syrius Lake was a man of unfashionable and inflexible opinions, especially to do with women. They were to be protected and indulged but not to be taken seriously in the workforce. "I didn't work my fingers to the bone so that my princess would have to," he was fond of saying.

That made her cringe these days but Jordan had made

the most of her privileged upbringing for a long time—
way too long—before coming to the realization that
being a princess was a fairly boring existence.

"Speaking of invitations," Russ said as she rounded
the reception counter, leaflets in hand and Mr. Hansen
in her sights, "this charity ball and auction you're organizing…shouldn't we be promoting it? It's only a
couple of weeks away."

Jordan paused, aware that this project departed
somewhat from the more conventional fund-raising activities of the church, but the Elpis Foundation, though
closely affiliated, was not a religious organization. "It's
not that sort of auction, Russ. It's more of—" she
searched for the right word. If there was one thing
Jordan Lake knew, it was rich people and parties "—an
event. It's invite only and no press."

She knew how to put on a classy yet original
function, and she'd managed this one on the cheap. She
would pay the orchestra herself but the ballroom was
gratis, courtesy of her mother's old dancing contacts.
Friends in a local venue management company had
agreed to take care of the lighting and decorating for
nothing. She had plenty of "volunteers" as wait staff
since she'd promised an amazing after-party. The champagne hadn't been confirmed yet but the *coup-de-
gras*—the catering—was coming together nicely. A
truckload of fish and chips would be delivered on the
night to astound the ballgown-and-tuxedo-wearing
guests, courtesy of an old beau whose family owned a
chain of fast-food restaurant outlets. Jordan was noto-

rious enough to be able to pull off such a cheeky gesture. "It's all in hand," she assured Russ. "At this stage we have about a hundred people coming, but I have a bit more time."

Russ pursed his lips. "I'm sure if we advertise, we can do better than that."

"Russ, that's a hundred extremely wealthy people, the movers and shakers of the country. Trust me, the really rich want discretion with their philanthropy."

He smiled wryly. "Is that why you're so reluctant to put your name on all the good work you do?"

Jordan shot him a warning look. "No one takes me seriously. The kind of publicity people associate with me is not the kind of publicity I want for the Elpis Foundation. That was the condition of me setting it up. It's better that way, believe me."

Famous for being famous… She walked into the waiting room, determined to make Mr. Hansen like her. Forever the focus of the newspapers and TV cameras but for all the wrong reasons, even though she had toned it down over the last year. Reporters didn't care a jot if most of what they wrote was wrong. Philanthropy was a serious business and she needed to protect the Elpis Foundation. It was her one redeeming feature.

On Friday morning, Jordan passed Nick in the corridor of the High Court. He paused as they drew level, looking straight ahead. Since court was in session, there were few people around.

"See you at three?" he asked in a low voice.

Her pulse skittered as it always did when she looked at him. His presence in the courtroom for most of this week had underlined her desire for him and the forbidden thrill she got from knowing that he wanted her.

But they had to take care. It wasn't just the stress her father was under. Nick was different. Somehow, she wanted to keep him to herself.

She hadn't expected the amount of public interest there was in the case—every day she ran the gauntlet of photographers and reporters, all of whom seemed more interested in what she was wearing and how her love life was than the actual semantics of the trial.

"Nick, there are so many reporters," she whispered back. "Don't you think we should cool it, just till this trial is over?"

He turned his head and met her eyes and Jordan's heartbeat went wild. If eyes were the windows to hell, then Nick was on fire—for her. Right now, this moment.

Her knees turned to water.

Nick nudged her toward the stairwell a few steps away. She kept her head down, aware that if anyone looked at her face, they'd know exactly what she was thinking—that she wanted his hands, his mouth on her. Preferably both and *now* would be good.

He pushed through the door, her hot on his heels, then turned and crowded her against the wall, his arms resting on the wall above her head. The rest of his body did not touch her at all.

The sweep of his eyes over her face, down her body

and back again, was a tangible caress. Thankful for the support of the wall at her back, Jordan pressed into it, squirming with a restless heat.

His face was close—not close enough, but close.

"You want to 'cool it?'" Nick demanded in a hot whisper.

"I don't *want* to," she whispered back. "Your reputation as a steady, conservative banker will suffer a lot more than mine if we're caught."

"It's driving me mad, seeing you in there," he growled. "So close, not able to touch."

She reeled with the need to touch him, and with her own panic. Nick had never done anything so reckless before. "Oh, Nick, this is dangerous."

"I haven't touched you," he murmured, his eyes burning. "Yet."

He knew, as Jordan did, that if he touched her, she'd offer no resistance, despite the fear of discovery.

"Someone is going to walk through that door any minute," she cautioned him.

His eyes tracked a heated path, lingering on her lips, then in slow, hot increments down her body. "All part of the fun, isn't it?"

Their eyes met. Clearly, steady and conservative Nick Thorne was as hooked on the danger of the situation as she was.

She shifted again, craving his touch, knowing she shouldn't. It was torture being this close, seeing him this excited, yet denying her.

His hand landed in her hair, then moved around to

cup her chin. Despite her alarm, her lips parted in anticipation.

Nick stared down, his thumb moving softly over her cheek. "You are seriously beautiful."

Her eyes flew wide. That was new, too. Nick preferred a more earthy flavor to his compliments, more show, don't tell. The daily exposure in the courtroom must be having an effect on him as well.

Meantime, his gaze moved down to her mouth, stayed, heated. His thumb circled down and laid on her bottom lip. His face bent, inched closer. He was, quite simply, driving her mad. Who cared if anyone saw? She clamped her lips around his thumb, drawing it slowly into her mouth. Nick's eyes widened, and then some more when she swirled her tongue around the tip. Two could play at that, she thought triumphantly, watching the torture darken his eyes.

But then he slid his thumb slowly out of her mouth. "Cool it? I don't think so. I'll see you at three o clock."

He stepped back and Jordan ducked smartly out from under him. She looked back as she passed through the heavy door. He still leaned on the wall, his head raised, looking after her.

The cooler air of the corridor was a welcome relief. Away from Nick's potent presence, she pressed her hand on her stomach, aflutter with nerves. Even if he was willing to take the risk, she couldn't embarrass her father while he was under so much stress.

Still, her mind and body hummed with anticipation. Instinctively, she knew that their afternoon rendezvous would have more bite to it than usual.

* * *

Spending every morning in court was impacting his work, so Nick sighed when the intercom buzzed and his personal assistant's voice informed him that his brother was here. The door opened and Adam appeared, looking relaxed in jeans and a leather jacket. He turned side-on to Nick's desk and approximated a smooth golf swing. "It's a beautiful day, big brother. What say you play hooky for the afternoon and we hit the golf course for a quick nine?"

Nick shook his head. In little under an hour, he would be at the hotel, relieving a certain heiress of her clothes. And for that reward, he didn't care if he had to work all weekend to catch up. "I have an appointment."

Adam frowned and flopped down in a chair facing Nick. "Cancel it."

"If I get this backlog cleared tonight, I might be free tomorrow," Nick said with a pointed look at the stack of papers in front of him.

Jasmine, his personal assistant, appeared at the door. "Would you like coffee?"

Adam spun around in his chair. "I would, thank you, Jas*mina*."

The beautiful brunette blushed and turned away.

Nick frowned. Adam had a hide like a rhino. No way could he have missed Nick's "I'm busy" hint. And the last thing he needed was his Casanova brother upsetting his workplace. "Stop flirting with my personal assistant."

Adam turned back to him. "Why? Something going on with you two?"

"Adam, she works for me."

"So? If she worked for me, I'd add to her job description."

Nick sighed and made a show of checking his watch.

"I thought you should know," Adam began, "Dad's been ear-bashing me over lunch again about staying on and giving you a hand."

The real reason for his visit… "I don't need a hand," Nick said in a long-suffering tone.

"I know that, Nick. You have more than earned your place at the helm of this ship. I have no intention of muscling in on your territory."

Nick's jaw tightened. "There's the rub. It isn't my territory, is it?"

It was Randall Thorne's greatest wish that both sons run his empire after he retired. No matter how often Adam resisted, his father never stopped trying to lure him back from London. The disbursement of their mother's will last year had shocked the brothers and delighted their father. Instead of a sizeable chunk of the company shares going to Nick, as everyone expected, he got baubles and a beach house and Adam got the shares. Whether his mother intended it or not, she had handed his father a lofty weapon to pit brother against brother. To delay, yet again, announcing his retirement and naming Nick as his successor.

"Dad was nearly resigned to the fact that you didn't want it," Nick said moodily. "But now—he'll do anything to have both of us on board."

"The will stated that I can't sell my shares to you, but

I can vote with you, Nick. Tell me how you want to play it. And remember, the old man can't put off retiring forever—he's seventy next month."

"Since Mom died, there is no reining him in." Nick scowled at the newspaper on his desk. "Her past friendship with Elanor Lake was the only thing that stopped him from going after Syrius years ago. He's using the court case as another tactic to postpone announcing his retirement." He reached out and turned the paper toward Adam. A good portion of the front page covered the court case—and Jordan Lake's wardrobe. "If it's not one thing, it's another." His mother's illness and subsequent death, Adam's presence or absence—his father threw excuse after excuse into the pot to put off the inevitable.

Adam nodded thoughtfully. "I'm pretty sure he's got something else up his sleeve to get at Syrius. He was being very cagey at lunch, always a sign that he's plotting something."

Nick tugged on his earlobe, a wry grin on his face. "I've tried telling him that once he's retired, he can spend twenty-three hours a day going after Syrius Lake if he wants to, but he's adamant he wants to bury him before he retires."

Nick wasn't alone in thinking his father would win the defamation case, but had a nasty feeling that the small victory wouldn't appease him for long.

Adam cast an interested eye over the newspaper. There was a footnote to the court case: Jordan Lake's birthday bash tonight, organized by her father. The paper called it an "ostentatious display of wealth." He tapped the paper idly. "I told you. The best way to stop this stupid feud is to get Jordan Lake to fall for you. That man cannot, it seems, deny his little girl anything."

Before Nick could respond, Jasmine entered with a tray. She set it down on Nick's desk and lifted the coffeepot. Adam leaned in closer than he had to, Nick noticed, and held up a cup, smiling into her face. "How long have you worked for my brother, Jasmine? Must be nearly five years."

Jasmine blushed to the roots of her severely pulled back auburn hair. "Yes, I—ah—think so. Nick?" She raised her eyes to him.

Nick nodded, mildly surprised by her discomfort. He'd known English-born Jasmine for years. Her composure was legendary. "Have I told you, Jasmine, that my younger brother is nothing but a flirt and not to be taken seriously?"

He noticed the slight tremble in her hand as she poured the coffee, and how resolutely she kept her eyes on the task at hand and nowhere near Adam's face. Could his calm, efficient, very proper personal assistant have a thing for Adam?

Adam raised the full cup and saluted her. "Why don't you give all this up and come work for me? London's where it's at."

Jasmine kept her eyes averted and poured Nick's coffee, apologizing when she slopped a little in the saucer.

"Thanks," Nick said drily as she finished and left the room.

He glanced at his brother and warned, "Don't even think about it. She is much too good for you."

Adam turned his palms up innocently, then glanced toward the door. "You work too hard if you haven't noticed how very lovely she is, in a quiet sort of way."

"I don't want you messing with her," Nick told him shortly. "Good staff are hard to find, and you're leaving soon." His brother's trail of broken hearts stretched a million miles.

Adam shook his head, amused. "You're too good, Nicky. You wouldn't dream of tupping your personal assistant, just as you wouldn't dream of going after Jordan Lake and risking Dad's wrath. Mom was right, you need to live a little."

That was a low and quite unnecessary dig. His brother referred to the letter Melanie Thorne had left with her lawyer to give to Nick at the will reading. "You're a good son, Nick, strong, ambitious and loyal." Christ, he sounded like a golden retriever! "But it's time you learned to live. Want something you shouldn't. Take something you have no right to. Fight the good fight and have some fun."

He didn't know what the hell his mother was on about, but she was right in that he always did the expected thing.

After Adam had gone, Nick got up and opened his office safe. Inside were three jewelry boxes, his bequest from his mother, gifts from his father over the years. There was a blue diamond cluster ring, a necklace with a centerpiece of a four carat blue diamond and a pair of blue diamond earrings.

Nick had the relevant documents from the IGI, the

world's largest gem certification and appraisal institute. He knew the worth of the stones. He also knew that his mother would expect him to present these priceless gifts to his bride one day. And Nick always did what was expected of him, didn't he?

He glanced at the newspaper on his desk. She wouldn't expect him to give blue diamonds to Jordan Lake, he was sure of that. Neither would his brother, and his father would probably disown him if he found out.

Nick closed the ring box and returned it to the safe, wondering what Jordan herself would think if her Friday lover gave her diamonds. He lost himself for a long moment, imagining the incredulity in her blue eyes.

He closed the necklace box, berating himself for even considering changing the dynamic of a relationship—a good relationship—based on sex.

His hand reached toward the box containing the earrings, and at that point, he fully intended closing it and replacing it in the safe with the others. But something made him pause and lift the box toward the light above. Would she wear them? She might if she recognized that the jewel's electric blue were very similar to her own eyes, especially when she was helpless with lust—like earlier in the stairwell.

He closed the box and put it in his pocket. Nick was going to do something irresponsible for once. Not for her or for anyone else. Just for himself.

Three

Later that day, as the first mad rush of desire ebbed away, Nick rolled out of bed and picked up his suit jacket from the floor. "I have something for you."

Jordan lay in the middle of the big bed with the sheet pulled up around her middle, a sharp contrast between the pristine white sheet and her lightly-tanned body. The slight flush on her skin was fading, her breathing more steady than a minute ago. She lifted her chin, watching him curiously.

"But first…" Nick grabbed the edge of the sheet and tugged it away, leaving her naked.

She maneuvered herself into a sitting position and crossed her long legs at the ankles, but made no effort to clutch at the sheet or cover herself. He liked that she was totally without guile or vanity in this room. It occurred to him that he also felt comfortable standing, walking around in front of her naked. Had he ever felt this level of ease with a casual girlfriend before?

Unable to recall, he offered her the jewelry box.

Jordan hesitated before taking it, her eyes on his face. "A birthday gift?" Her voice was low and puzzled.

Nick perched on the edge of the bed. "If you like."

She dragged her eyes off his face and opened the box. Her mouth moved in surprise, a soundless question. She tilted the box this way and that and finally spoke, still looking at the earrings. "Nick, a man gives me diamonds. What am I supposed to think about that?"

He shrugged. "Don't think about it at all."

She looked up at him, a crease of perplexity between her eyes that he'd never seen before. He silently cursed himself for confusing her. What was he thinking, messing with the natural order of things? "Don't read anything into it," he said a little roughly. "I believe I thought more of my own pleasure than yours."

The little frown deepened, as if she couldn't make sense of it.

Damn Adam and his crazy notions. Nick exhaled loudly and leaned toward her. He picked up one of the precious, glinting jewels, brushed her hair behind her ears and went about fitting it. "They matched your eyes. I wanted to see you naked, wearing only these. That's it."

That wasn't it. Hadn't he done it because he was sick of being labeled the good son, the one who never rocked the boat?

Her face cleared, as if she'd solved a riddle. "They're a gift for your mistress."

Nick's lip curled in distaste. He hated that word. "I don't think of you as my mistress. Neither of us is married. We're free to indulge ourselves."

She gazed at him solemnly. Nick picked up the other earring, pried the butterfly clip off and indicated that she turn her head.

She obeyed. "What *do* you think of me as then?"

"If we have to put a label on it, I'd call you my luxury," he said as he pushed the other earring through the piercing in her lobe. He secured the post and drew back, looking at her face.

"Your luxury." She nodded and her smile was without reproach. "I'll save them just for this room. They'll be our secret."

Nick sat back, admiring his handiwork, thinking she did indeed look spellbindingly luxurious. Her golden hair, a mass of loose curls today, cascaded over her shoulders like the caps of a choppy sea captured and molded in gold. Yesterday, in court she'd worn it straight and smooth.

And then her words hit him, or more, her tone. Had he imagined a slightly sarcastic edge to her voice?

Nick dropped his hands to his bare knees. "I'm not ashamed." Not of her. Maybe of himself for confusing her. "Hell, Jordan! They're yours. Do what you want with them. Sell them, if it pleases you."

Hurt showed in the little press of her lips and the way she suddenly looked away from him. "I don't need any *more* money from a Thorne," she said quietly.

Nick had made a real pig's ear of this. An off-the-cuff gesture and he'd ended up bringing the past into this room. He should have remembered that whatever this madness was between them, the past would always be a barrier.

Thirty years ago, Nick's father was driving the two couples home from a night out when a tragic accident nearly claimed the life of Syrius Lake's pregnant wife. The injuries she had suffered put her in a wheelchair for life and killed her unborn son, but five years later she endured a difficult pregnancy and gave birth to Jordan. Lake never forgave Randall Thorne and when his financial situation worsened because of high medical costs, he demanded assistance. Randall signed over a huge valuable block of real estate in Wellington's CBD, with the understanding that when Syrius was able, he would repay the loan. But on the day of Jordan's birth, the bitter ex-friend transferred the property to his daughter's name.

Prevailed upon by guilt and his own wife, Randall Thorne let it ride, but it rankled. Both men went on to become business icons in New Zealand's capital city and the bad blood simmered away, helped along by repeated sniping from both camps.

So technically, Jordan was rich on Thorne money, but Nick didn't care about that. It wasn't her fault or his. It just was.

He put his index finger under her chin and turned her face to look at him. "I'm sorry. I didn't intend to hurt you…"

Her smile, when it came, was more rueful than hurt.

"You haven't." She lifted her hands and touched her new adornments. "I'll wear them with pride."

Nick's instincts were right on the nail about how perfectly the blue diamonds matched her eye color. They gazed at each other, gratitude and regret gradually giving way to an acute awareness of where they were, what they were to each other. The urgency escalated, the air between them smoldered with its hot breath.

They moved toward each other in a rush, their hands reaching greedily. She was fine, they were fine, nothing had changed. He'd done the right thing, giving her blue diamonds that twinkled and trembled with desire and anticipation when he pushed her down on the bed, ravaging her mouth. That warmed with sultry promise as he drew her arms up over her head and moved into position. That exploded with blue sparks when he filled her, an inexorable upward motion into infinite pleasure…and crackled with the fury of reaching for, overtaking, plunging into blissful release.

He'd done the right thing giving her the earrings and who cared if was for her or for him? They'd both enjoy them.

But somehow, he left the hotel feeling he'd missed an opportunity of some kind, or they both had. If Jordan Lake was his luxury, could he pay the price?

Jordan was late for her own birthday party. She rushed up the stairs of the up-market club, apologizing loudly, knowing her parents expected her half an hour ago.

She needn't have worried. Everything was under

control and most of the guests hadn't arrived yet. The champagne was chilled and delicious, the lighting perfect, security on the door. Of the expected one hundred and fifty guests, twenty or so would be friends of hers, the rest would be her parents' friends, business colleagues, local celebrities in the arts, politics and sports and a smattering of reporters and photographers. Jordan would pose with all the usual suspects, regulars of the It crowd. And then she would go home alone, as she had for most of the last year. Even her father would yawn at her lifestyle these days—except for her Friday afternoons.

She bent to kiss her mother, knowing this was the last real kiss she'd get all night. As she drew back, her mother's hands firmed on her cheeks for a few seconds, holding her. Elanor Lake frowned at the earrings. "They're lovely, darling. Where did you get them?"

She hadn't been able to resist wearing them no matter how often she told herself to lock them away. But, oh, they were so beautiful, and Nick hadn't said not to wear them. He hadn't even stipulated that she wasn't to tell who gave them to her.

Vanity won. The earrings were perfect with the pale yellow dress she wore, lending it a hint of boldness.

Jordan straightened and flicked her hand in the air. "Just one of my many admirers."

Her mother gave her a measured look. "Which admirer is giving you blue diamonds?"

Her father snorted. "Anything less than diamonds, then he isn't worth his salt, princess," he declared.

One by one, the beautiful people arrived and she laughed and kissed air so many times, her lips were bruised. But often, she touched the earrings and her thoughts turned to the confusing man who'd given them to her.

The extravagant gift had blown her away. Up to now, Nick was the only man she'd met who'd been completely straight about what he wanted from her—her body. There were no expectations past that, on either side. Their weekly meetings in the luxury Presidential Suite were all about an extraordinary attraction and nothing else.

She couldn't put her finger on when things had started to feel different, but it was recent. He'd changed. Suddenly he was asking questions, taking risks, talking to her. He'd watched her today as if trying to divine her thoughts. Hurt her a little by admitting he'd thought more of his own pleasure in giving her the gift. Then again, that admission spoke volumes for a man who was so spare with words: he saw something beautiful; he thought of her.

But it hurt her more when he reminded her of the origins of her trust fund, and the reason they could never have more than they had right now.

Her oldest friend, Julie, dragged her onto the dance floor and she happily acquiesced. But her mind strayed often to Nick. Jordan looked around at the glitzy lights and gay smiles, wondering if he'd like this sort of place? Would her friends like him, and vice versa? Was he a dancer? When it came down to it, she knew so little about him, just that they fit together perfectly in the bedroom.

"Oh, my God! Look-it!" Julie pointed through the throng to a tall, handsome man leaning on the bar, looking their way. "Isn't that…?"

Jordan looked over and her heart did a weird slide. "John West," she said in dismay.

Jordan's first heartbreak. She'd been in her first year at high school, he in his last. His interest in her caused a ripple of excitement through all her friends; someone of his stature expressing interest in a first year was unheard of.

Alas, the romance floundered quickly.

"Let's see if we can pick who he's here with," her friend said.

Jordan wondered if it was the same girlfriend he'd dumped her for two days after he'd first crooked his brow at her, commanding her to parade around the school quadrant with him like his queen.

She shrugged and turned away. Although it was a minor blip on her heartstrings that she hadn't thought of in years, the one thing that stuck was the crushing realization that despite her money and social standing, she wasn't smart enough, pretty enough, interesting enough to hold his attention, not even for a week! Her father's shameless indulgence reminded her that the world saw her as a bubble-headed trophy with only her wealth to offer. She knew better. She was different now, more than that.

Nick Thorne was the real deal—respected, smart, ambitious and successful. Whatever he called it, she was his mistress. She'd live up to his expectations in that regard, but she'd do her best to protect her heart.

* * *

On Monday, the court clerk announced the lunch break to sighs of relief. The morning had dragged. Nick looked forward to getting back to his office, if only for a break from the steel thread of sexual tension that came with sitting ten feet away from the object of his desire, and the knowledge that it would be four torturous days before he could have her again.

Suddenly the wiry figure of Syrius Lake bounded across the aisle. His face was an interesting shade of plum. He sidestepped Randall's counsel and stood defiantly in front of the complainant's bench.

"Randall Thorne," he rumbled, his deep voice belying his rather slight frame. "Keep your pup away from my daughter."

Nick's heart stopped and he involuntarily flicked a glance at Jordan. She had jumped to her feet, and stood with one leg in front of the other, ready for flight, the line of her body taut with tension. Her eyes were huge but they were on her father, not him.

Randall rose, towering over Syrius, the table in between them. Nick rose, too, and brushed past Adam to stand by his father's side.

"Nick's got too much sense…" Randall began.

"Not him." Syrius pointed a long, bony finger at Adam, still seated in the row behind.

Adam! Nick turned his head slowly, and in those few seconds, everything inside him went cold, and his throat closed as if gripped by a vise.

His brother raised his brows in studied nonchalance

and shrugged. "I hooked up with a couple of lovelies at a bar, tagged along to a party. How was I supposed to know it was Jordan's birthday bash?"

Through the ice-cold rage bathing his belly, Nick barely noted that Adam directed his explanation—and a quizzical look—at him, rather than Syrius.

All around people had stopped, enthralled by the drama. And then his father gave the crowd what they wanted.

"If he's a pup," he suggested, "perhaps she's a bitch in heat."

Nick tore his eyes off his brother's and glanced at Jordan's white, shocked face. He gripped his father's arm firmly. "You'll apologize for that."

"The hell I will!" Randall blustered.

The two Lake women reached Syrius. Elanor spoke in urgent whispers while Jordan grasped the sleeve of her father's suit, tugging at it ineffectually.

Randall lifted his arm in a half hearted attempt to remove it from Nick's grip.

Nick only gripped harder. "*Now*, Dad."

Accepting defeat, Randall launched a scathing glance at his enemy, cleared his throat and nodded vaguely in Jordan's direction. "I beg your pardon, Jordan." Turning back to Syrius, he raised his chin, "When I've finished mopping the floor with you here, Lake, I'm going to start all over again. I wouldn't let your lawyer take a holiday anytime soon if I were you."

"Bring it on, Thorne," Syrius snarled. He shot one last look of loathing that encompassed all three Thornes, then he stomped off with his counsel in tow, making no effort to assist Jordan with her mother's wheelchair.

Mortified, Nick couldn't look at Jordan, but as she pushed her mother's chair past him, Elanor met his eyes and gave him a distant but not unfriendly nod. Despite the ridiculous circumstances, Nick found himself admiring her for her fortitude and grace when she had more reason to hate his family than anyone. He watched until they disappeared out of the courtroom, then turned back to find his father glaring down at Adam.

"Well? What have you got to say for yourself?"

Nick's jealousy returned full force, crushing his chest and throat again. The thought of his playboy brother anywhere near Jordan incensed him. "Did you—" *touch, dance, kiss* "—speak to her at the party?" He could barcly get the words past his clenched teeth.

Adam's glance was sharp as a tack. "Nick, I didn't get a toe in the door before Syrius was bleating at security to have me removed. Why?"

Intense relief laced Nick's exhalation. He unclenched his palms and they were damp. Ignoring Adam's question, he turned abruptly and reached for his jacket. The act of putting it on, gathering up his phone and briefcase, gave him a few seconds to think about that relief. *Okay, we've ascertained that I'm not fond of the thought of anyone else's hands on her. Fine. We can work this out.*

Now composed, he gave his father a stern look. "I have to get back to the office, but try and behave yourself this afternoon." He frowned at Randall. "Insult Syrius all you like, but leave his family out of it."

He strode away, allowing himself a small smile when he heard his father say to Adam, "Why can't you be more like your brother?"

Four

Nick pressed the doorbell, glowering at the peephole when he heard her ask who it was. "It's Nick. Open up, Jordan."

He still waited half a minute, tapping his thigh impatiently, until she opened the door. She peeked around the corner of the door, one hand covering her lower face. Her hesitation became immediately clear; a pale green chalky substance covered most of her face. Her hair was loose but held back from her face by a headband. She wore silky light blue pajamas, a less than welcoming expression, and her feet were bare.

That didn't mean she was off the hook. "Are you ill?"

"No." Frowning, she looked over his shoulder into

the empty corridor of her apartment building and then stepped back.

"Expecting someone?" he asked, giving her a thorough inspection.

"Do I look like I'm expecting someone?" She lifted her hand from her face and gestured him forward impatiently. "Come in before someone sees you."

Nick stepped inside and then turned and waited while she closed the door.

Jordan leaned her back against the door her skin flushing pink beneath the green facial mask. "How did you get up here?"

He shrugged. "Someone was coming up, I followed."

"Nick, you shouldn't be here."

His temper bridled. He'd been on a slow burn for about twenty-four hours now. He'd had a huge row with his father last night after confirming his plans to hire a P.I. to investigate one of Syrius's directors for corruption. It became more and more obvious that the old man had no intention of retiring any time soon, not while Syrius Lake was around to take potshots at.

Reading the papers today had turned the heat up. Nick's frustration had about hit boiling. "We had an arrangement."

"I sent you a text."

Nick swore under his breath. A text that said nothing. *Sorry, something's come up.*

He would have accepted her canceling their regular appointment if she hadn't been photographed eating a late Friday afternoon lunch with Jason Cook, the most worthless playboy on the planet. An ex-pro rugby player who destroyed hotel rooms, threw things at bartenders and went through money like water. And who'd reportedly had a steamy romance with Jordan a year ago.

His father's next potential campaign against Syrius made Nick's decision to ally himself with her all the more attractive, but the lady herself seemed comfortable with the status quo. Somehow he had to persuade her that she wanted more, knock her off balance enough to start thinking of him in a different light.

Hence the unannounced visit. It didn't hurt that the thought of Cook's hands on her infuriated him. He reached out, hooking his finger into the V of her pajama top, and pulled her into him. "You and Jason in the newspaper this morning… You want him, Jordan?"

As her unresisting body bumped against his, the impact caused the top button to slip through the hole. The material gaped as she inhaled in surprise. The creamy swell of a luscious, unfettered breast taunted him.

How many men did she share her body with? The question had tormented him for hours. How many men savored that perfect mouth, nuzzled her impossibly soft and fragrant skin.

Under his glare, her eyes sparked with annoyance and her pink cheeks burned through the green streaks. She laid her hands flat against his chest and braced against him. "I didn't realize that giving me a gift branded me as your exclusive property."

"It doesn't, but your Friday afternoons are mine, not bloody Jason Cook's."

"Jason is only a friend these days. Not—" she lifted her chin defiantly "—that it's any of your business."

"Some friend. I thought you were satisfied with our arrangement."

"I was." Her eyes flickered away and back. "I am. But I think we're being watched."

Nick raised his brows, waiting.

Sighing, she clasped the edges of her pajama top closed and pushed past him, padding down the short hallway through a stylish kitchen and to a side table in the lounge. Nick followed, his eyes closely monitoring the sensual slide of blue silk-clad hips.

Jordan picked up an envelope from the table and turned to him. "These came yesterday."

Nick took the envelope and pulled out two enlarged photographs of Jordan entering and leaving their Friday hotel, wearing a little black dress with a wide belt. He remembered it because the belt had an unusual clasp and his eager fingers had wasted at least three seconds fumbling with the damn thing. The photo was dated last Friday, their last meeting. "You're always being watched and photographed." He handed the photos back. "What of it?"

"These were couriered to me here, yesterday morning. No note. No sender details."

Nick pursed his lips. "And that was enough to send you rushing into Jason Cook's arms."

She gazed at him steadily. "Why do you suppose we went to the Backbencher's Bar, Nick?"

"Probably the only place in town he hasn't been thrown out of."

"Because it's the press's watering hole, where most of them spend their Friday afternoons. I did it to throw whoever might be watching us off the scent."

Nick processed her tone and earnest expression and battled down the jealousy bubbling in his blood. Considering the publicity surrounding the court case, she would have known her presence at that bar, especially with a man of Jason Cook's reputation, would end up in the next day's papers.

Not to make him jealous. Not to patch things up with a past lover. The relief surprised Nick with its intensity. He had to remember his purpose here tonight—keep her guessing, spike her interest. His very real jealousy was an added bonus.

Jordan shifted under his gaze as if uncomfortably aware that her face was covered in green goop. "Get yourself a drink," she told him, pointing at the small bar in the corner of the room. "I'll go and clean up."

Nick's eyes stayed with her until she turned into the first door down the hall. Her bedroom, he presumed, relieved to be left alone momentarily. It gave him a chance to explore, try to get a handle on her.

He moved fully into the lounge, his eyes busy.

Her apartment was modern, minimalist, but surprisingly homely and welcoming. One of the two black leather sofas was scattered with papers. There were more papers on the coffee table and a mug of something in the middle with steam coming off it. The expansive drapes were drawn but he'd bet there was an amazing view of the city and harbor beyond from her thirteenth story apartment. The walls were bare except in the dining nook where two large, striking sketches faced each other above her elegant dining table. One depicted a 1920s couple sitting at a table, the woman looking coyly away as the man held her arm by the wrist and above the elbow, kissing his way up her arm. The other was a couple dancing, maybe the tango, he decided.

The bar had everything he could want but Nick wasn't in the mood for alcohol. He walked to the sofa, sweeping the papers into a pile and setting them on the coffee table.

There was a property listing on top, torn from a real estate magazine. It depicted an old villa in the Marlborough Sounds at the top of the South Island. Not the sort of place Jordan would be interested in, surely. The lady could afford to buy the entire South Island. She was luxury all the way. What use would she have for a broken-down old villa?

Then again, what did he know of her likes and dislikes outside of the bedroom?

While waiting for her return, he glanced at the next item on the pile and saw a newsletter headed The Elpis Foundation. He only took note because the author was Reverend Russ Parsons, an old family friend.

Before he could read the contents, Jordan returned, her face clean and her hair released from the headband. Nick nearly smiled when he saw she'd changed. A cream sweater and soft black pants were probably safer than the lovely but flimsy pajamas. She obviously didn't trust him to keep his hands to himself.

Jordan perched on the arm of the couch, her hands restless. Her feet were still bare, toenails pearly-pink and gleaming. Nick swallowed the remnants of his unwarranted anger and jealousy, thinking that this was how she looked alone in the evenings. Freshly bathed, by the clean scent of her. Her hair brushed out and gleaming. Skin scrubbed and glowing.

She fidgeted under his scrutiny, her mouth a little sullen.

"Nice apartment," he commented pleasantly.

She glanced at his empty hands. "Did you not want a drink?"

He wasn't bothered but then again, he liked the idea of her waiting on him. It would also serve to prolong his visit, break the ice, open the way for him to try out a little charm.

"A Scotch would be good."

She hadn't expected him to say yes, he knew by the little twist of her mouth. He settled back while she prepared his drink with a kind of polite displeasure. No smile when she handed it to him, either.

Nick reached for the mug on the coffee table. The liquid inside was cooling by the pinched look of the surface. He handed it to her, thinking how improbable this was. Jordan Lake home alone on a Saturday night with only a face mask and mug of chocolate for company.

She took the mug. An awkward silence descended.

"Looking to invest in some property?" he asked, picking up the leaflet. It would be a good investment. Marlborough Sounds boasted some of the most desirable real estate in the country.

"I already bought it."

Nick looked up in surprise. "Can't see you in the DIY store, somehow."

Her mouth twitched but the smile didn't reach her eyes. "You'd be surprised."

He leaned back, spreading his arm along the back of the couch. Their eyes met and held for long seconds and that old familiar awareness arced between them. She was so naturally beautiful, larger than life beautiful, even with little or no makeup on. Nick's chest swelled when her eyes widened and then hazed over with her own recognition of the incredible desire between them. She felt it, too, he exulted, this pull that gripped his throat and stole his breath. Every time was like their first meeting in a sterile elevator. An unquenchable desire that hit him like a bullet between the eyes.

Just like now.

Jordan broke the spell and looked down into her drink. "You're—different," she said. "What's changed?"

She shifted one foot to rest on top of the other, her restlessness showing insecurities he didn't know she had.

Nick faced her fully. "I want you, Jordan," he answered truthfully. "That hasn't changed."

She looked up under her lashes. "And you can have me. On Fridays. At the hotel."

It didn't surprise him that she'd picked up on his recent change of behavior toward her. In their brief conversations to date, she'd shown a perceptive intuitiveness, eroding his assumptions that she was nothing more than a spoiled heiress who liked making an exhibition of herself.

Damn his brother for putting the thought in his head. Damn his mother for the will and her belief that he was the perennial dutiful son, and his father, too, for being such a vindictive, intransigent bastard. But for their interference, Nick would be perfectly happy with the prior arrangement. The thrill of a forbidden pleasure. A once-weekly event that, while momentous at the time, belonged in a compartment of his brain that had no bearing on how he lived his life or the decisions he made.

"Perhaps it's seeing you in court every day," he suggested. It was as good a lie as any, he supposed.

She nodded. Her feet were still playing with each other, he noticed. "By the way, I'm sorry about my father's behavior the other day."

Jordan shrugged, drawing his attention to her front, his interest quickening when he saw she wasn't wearing a bra under the soft wool.

"They're as bad as each other," she responded.

"What would Syrius do if he found out about us?" Nick probed.

She rolled her eyes. "I don't even want to think about it."

Nick knew that was his major stumbling block. He had to get her so interested, so wound up in him that she'd forget about her father's wrath.

"And yours?" she inquired politely.

He sipped his drink, wondering how truthful to be. Lies had a way of tripping you up, so it was best to keep things simple. "He wouldn't like it," he said slowly, "but it's not up to him, is it?"

Jordan sighed and looked away. "Maybe we should…"

Nick's whole being jolted in rebellion. He knew what she was going to say. Stop? No way! He was already on edge after only a week's abstinence. It was torture sitting in that courtroom day after day, watching her every move out of the corner of his eyes. Her mile-long legs crossing and uncrossing, the drift of her expensive scent, an occasional hot-blooded glance in his direction. Nick was at the end of his tether. He shook his head adamantly. "I'm not ready to give it up just yet."

Jordan pursed her lips. "And the photos?"

Nick had had enough. The desire he felt for her was too close to the surface. Besides, it wouldn't hurt to allow her to see that she affected him. Intensity so often created the same interest in the recipient.

He stood abruptly, looming over her. She raised her head just as his hands dived her hair, lifting her face to his. "You think I want this? Need this?"

Her eyes were wide with surprise. She gasped in a quick breath.

"You're like a drug to me," he gritted, glowering down. "An addiction. Every Friday, I leave that hotel and think, yes. This time, I've got her out of my system. This time…"

Despite this being about knocking her off-kilter, his own body was primed like a detonator. He exhaled, fighting for control, searching for the innate good manners and responsible behavior that had shaped his life. He was a businessman, dammit, not one of her playboys.

He gentled his hands, stroking her hair. Soothed by the silky soft strands running through his fingers. "But then I change my mind, start thinking about next Friday."

He caressed her cheek and her eyelids fluttered as he knew they would.

"It's just sex, Nick," she whispered, turning her face to press a kiss in his palm, that one small act softening her cavalier words.

In her hurry to wash, she'd missed a tiny patch of green by her earlobe and he rubbed his finger over it, his own excitement rocketing when her lips parted involuntarily on a sigh.

"Yes it is," he murmured. He stroked one finger down her throat, felt her pulse leap. She ghosted a fraction closer while keeping her backside in contact with the arm of the sofa. Her head fell back even more in invitation and he bent to nuzzle the fragrant skin under her earlobe. Soft and smooth, her skin was still slightly damp from being freshly washed. Whatever she'd used in her face mask smelled good enough to eat, to taste, again and again.

She strained up, her face turned to his. Darned if he could remember what they were talking about when her mouth bumped against his cheek. It was too much of a temptation, even though he was pretty sure he'd started the body contact not intending to kiss her, only to tease a little. To make the point that she wanted him as much as he wanted her.

Just before his lips met hers, he touched his index finger to the corner of her mouth and frowned down into eyes that smoldered with electric blue desire. "I won't give it up just yet."

Her expression softened. Dipping his head, he took her mouth, filled her mouth, sank in welcome relief. His desire flowed from him into her and back again in a heady rush. She moaned low in her throat, trying to rise, pressing up into him. Happy to help, he slid one arm down her back and brought her hard up against him. The kiss deepened, she opened for him, hungry, appealing for more, her tongue eagerly seeking his.

With one arm supporting her back, he slid the other hand under the sweater, needing the silky slide of her skin. Always when he touched her, some part of his mind registered the softness of her skin. Never had he felt such soft skin; his fingers rejoiced in it. He palmed her torso; she felt hot, so hot. She swayed, her hands clutching at the backs of his arms. Nick slid his hand up, climbing the taut slope of her breast. He heard her breath catch, felt his, when she twisted and pushed her nipple, tight and hard, into his palm. He held her like this, almost horizontal, one arm supporting her back, the other playing with her breasts, exulting in the response he knew he could elicit in her.

But then she sucked in air and shrank away, her mouth stilling under his. When she opened her eyes he could see the battle she waged, need versus denial. Self-denial.

Jordan swallowed audibly. "Not here."

"Are you sure, Jordan?" He ran his thumb over her nipple again, loving it's proud texture.

Jordan closed her eyes and her mouth fell open on a

gush of air. "You can't…" She arched her back to press against his hand once more.

Nick bent his head and sucked at the pebbled peak through her sweater, hearing her whimper. He doubled his efforts when he felt her knee nudge in between his legs, stop, and rub again.

"I can," he whispered, raising his head. Still supporting her, he took his hand from under her sweater and placed it between her thighs.

She tensed and squeezed, her body stiffening.

Nick cupped her, feeling her damp heat. "We both know I can."

He took her mouth again, recognized her capitulation in the way she strained against him, the insistent push of her knee into his aching groin. He'd held this woman in his arms, practiced his seduction on her enough times to know she was fast reaching the point of no return.

To know he was, too.

But even as her arms came around his neck, as she sagged back onto the arm of the couch, her weight dragging him down with her, his brain kicked into a higher gear, sending messages he didn't want to hear right now. He tensed, listening to her breath come in gasps, feeling her fingers tugging at his shirt buttons.

Yes, he could take her right now, right here. He'd proved it. But that made it just another coupling that underlined the shallowness of this affair. He needed her to believe he felt more for her than just a quickie once a week, to wonder if he had real feelings for her. If that was his goal, he had to stop.

Now.

Groaning, Nick pulled back, tearing his mouth away. She stilled, clutching a handful of shirt and confusion and desire smoking up her eyes. He pulled her upright and removed his hand from between her legs. "You're right." His thought processes might be on target but his hands were unsteady and awkward as he tugged the hem of her top down. "Not here. Not now."

Jordan sank back onto the arm of the sofa, her breathing still labored. As she fussed with her clothes and hair, a deep blush crawled up her throat and face.

Nick sighed. He hadn't meant to embarrass her. "I didn't come here tonight to take you to bed."

Her eyes slid over him briefly, then she leaned forward and rested her elbows on her knees, studying her feet. Her hair gleamed, a sparkling curtain in the dim light. Nick reached out and stroked it, feeling ridiculously tender.

"Come out for a drink with me." He tugged on a long lock of silky hair. "Who cares what anyone thinks?"

She shook her head, not looking at him. "I can't go out for a drink with you."

"Because of our fathers? How long are we going to let two old men dictate our lives?"

"It's just not worth the hassle, Nick." For a moment there, he almost thought she sounded sad.

"I think it is," he argued, surprised at how stubborn he felt.

"Let's just stick to Fridays for now." She reached out and covered his hand with hers, looking at him beseechingly.

If she didn't care a little, wasn't secure in the knowledge that he cared a little, she wouldn't have looked at him like that.

Mission accomplished. At least, he'd given her something to think about. He couldn't afford to push too hard or force her to choose between family loyalty or him until he was assured of success.

His breath returned, along with the blood to the rest of his body. He checked his buttons—often an occupational hazard with Jordan's impatient fingers. "Next Friday?"

Jordan rose to show him out. "Shouldn't we at least change the time or place?"

She was obviously still wary about the photos she'd received but Nick wasn't worried. "It's just some eagle-eyed reporter sniffing around. If he'd meant business, there would be a photo of me leaving the hotel, too, or a blackmail note."

Besides, he paid the hotel handsomely for their discretion. Why improve the odds of discovery by going somewhere else? "Make it earlier, then. Two p.m."

Five

To heck with chocolate! Jordan took her mug into the kitchen and tipped the cold contents down the sink, then poured herself a glass of pinot noir. Frustration, confusion—she paced the floor restlessly, going over every minute of the last half hour.

The whole episode was an embarrassment, starting with him catching her in a stupid avocado, cucumber and milk-powder face mask—oh, very elegant! Her humiliation was complete once he touched her, kissed her. He'd said *she* was like a drug, but he'd lit her up so quickly.

Thank goodness he'd had the sense to stop. Nick Thorne was already commanding way too much of her mind lately. Not that she'd ever tell him, but she thought about him plenty outside the hotel room. Several times a week at least, and always with a shiver of erotic anticipation. And when she did, suddenly the days of the week until Friday were an interminable bore.

The last thing she needed was the memory of him here in her lounge, naked, making love to her.

She flicked through the TV channels in an attempt to banish that enticing vision. Although—Jordan turned off the TV—thinking about sex with him was safer than thinking about anything else with him. Confident she could hold him enthralled in the bedroom for a while longer, she determinedly crushed the hope that, someday, Nick might see her as more. Starting a relationship with sex gave her no room to maneuver. He would never take her seriously—no one did. Even her father, her biggest fan, considered her an ornament. Despite her best efforts to change her lifestyle and prove everyone wrong, it really was easier to accept the cynicism and get on with the job. But she had the right to protect her heart along the way.

Even so, she hugged the memory of his jealous face tightly to her all night long.

On Tuesday, she was nearly involved in an accident when a car pulled out behind her into the path of an oncoming car. Jordan thought little of it until she noticed the same gray car behind her ten minutes later. It followed her to the supermarket and then to her parents house. Bemused, she drove around the block a couple of times. The car followed. Jordan pulled up and opened her door. The gray car slowed and then sped up and turned the corner. As it streaked past, she saw a bullet-shaped dark head in dark glasses atop a pair of burly shoulders.

She tried to shrug it off. Like Nick said, probably just a nosy photographer.

But the strange feeling stayed with her. The next day, as she waited for the lift in her building, a giant of a man stepped out. He wore a black suit and dark glasses. His head was close-shaven. She couldn't see his eyes but something about his expression, the look he gave her, made her shiver. He turned as she passed him and did not take his eyes off her until the doors closed.

The hairs rose on the back of her neck at the intensity of the look he gave her. Even once inside her apartment, she couldn't shake the feeling. She drew the drapes, poured herself a soda, started on dinner, all the while berating her vivid imagination.

She was being silly. Was it the photos, or her fear that if she and Nick were found out, she'd have to give him up?

She'd always felt perfectly safe here. There was no designated doorman manning the entrance, although there was a building supervisor. The residents used a swipe card to get in, which, as Nick had proved with his unannounced visit on the weekend, wasn't foolproof.

On her way to the court next morning, she asked the building super if he'd noticed a big man in the building yesterday.

"Big man, suit, dark glasses?" Robert said, and she nodded, her stomach doing a weird slide.

"Not in the building but there was a bloke across the street for most of yesterday, either sitting in his car or leaning against it. Seemed like he was watching the building. I thought it might be a cop."

"What kind of car?"

"Mercedes. Silver."

Jordan had no idea what type of car had followed her yesterday but the difference between gray and silver was open to interpretation.

Grow up in a fishbowl and you get suspicious.

But later, she thought she spied the same car following her home. Quickly pulling into a space on the street, she went into the nearest coffee bar and ordered a drink. Sure enough, a couple of minutes later, the big man in the glasses entered. He ordered from the counter and sat down by the door, facing her. She stared over the rim of her cup, her heart thudding, watching as he opened the newspaper he'd brought with him and raised it to conceal his face.

Despite herself, she smiled, looking for peepholes in the paper. What did he want? Feeling like a regular Nancy Drew, Jordan decided to have it out with him. Anything was better than wondering and at least there were people around.

Draining her cup, she stood and marched over to his table, flicking the newspaper smartly. "Is this it?" she demanded in a loud voice. "The rag you work for?"

The paper lowered and the man stared up at her, ridiculously still wearing his dark glasses. "Sorry?"

"I want to know who you work for," Jordan repeated.

The man picked up the cup in his dinner-plate-size hands and sipped before lowering it again. "I'm just hanging, reading the paper," he said.

Jordan frowned. Why wouldn't he tell her? It would come out anyway. "Do you deny you have been following me all over town, watching my building, every move I make?"

The woman at the next table stared intently with that gleam of sly recognition Jordan was only too familiar with.

The big man leered at her, leaving her in no doubt that he was enjoying the altercation. "I have no idea what you're talking about, Miss Lake," he said insolently.

Jordan sighed. She was getting nowhere, except making a spectacle of herself. At least the guy knew he was rumbled and when his story—whatever it was—hit the headlines, she'd have her father roast the editor.

She shook her head in disgust. "Just leave me alone," she muttered and stalked out the door.

He must be a reporter, she reasoned as she got into the car. The only other possibility was an investigator and why would someone want to investigate her?

Nick's thunderous face when he'd turned up at her apartment entered her mind. Jealousy, unwarranted as it turned out, but what if he hadn't believed her about Jason?

Jordan laughed out loud at the thought he would go to any trouble to keep an eye on her. Ridiculous! They each had their own lives and there was no tie between them. Sparked by the delivery of the photos, her imagination had spiraled into paranoia, just another example of her attention-seeking personality.

Nothing further happened that week and by Friday, she'd forgotten it and arrived at the hotel at the new time of two p.m., very much looking forward to seeing him.

Usually Nick checked in and waited for her in the

room. She headed for the elevators but happened to glance at Reception where two men stood with their backs to her. A thrill of excitement jetted through her when she recognized one as Nick. Jordan hesitated by a tall potted plant and decided to wait until he'd gone up, just in case she was recognized.

She thrummed with anticipation. Maybe he was right about their increased exposure to each other in court. She'd felt his eyes on her several times today, like a hot caress, making her tingle, building her excitement.

As she watched, Nick turned away from the reception clerk and spoke to the man beside him. A big man, with shaven head, a prizefighter's body and dark glasses.

Jordan froze. It was him—coffee bar man! She was sure of it.

She barely noticed as Nick walked on toward the elevators. Her eyes remained glued to the man, who just stared after Nick until he disappeared behind the elevator doors.

She moved right behind the plant now, shaking her head to clear it. Stay calm…she needed to think this through. The sequence of events was only seconds and she went over each one in slow motion. Nick reaching for the keycard, talking to the smiling receptionist, turning away from the counter, pausing to talk to the big man beside him. And then walking to the lift.

The man now had his back to her and Jordan took the opportunity to escape. She drove home in a daze and let herself into her apartment. And then she began to tremble.

Could it be true? Was Nick behind a sinister campaign to unsettle her? Was he having her followed because he thought she was sleeping with Jason? She sat there for nearly an hour but peace of mind eluded her. When her phone rang, she answered it with a sense of ominous fatalism, remembering his face on Saturday night, the hard tone of his voice that she'd never heard before. *"You want him, Jordan?"*

But it was her mother to say Syrius had suffered a heart attack and was being rushed to hospital. Jordan ran, forgetting all about Nick Thorne. Just as she reversed out of her space, she noticed Robert, the building supervisor, waving out to her. Next thing, there was a huge bang and sickening crunch, so loud, she thought there had been an explosion.

Her heart racing in fear and shock, she checked the rearview mirror to see a gray car at the back of hers, its front passenger door crumpled. A gray car—it filtered through the funk in her mind and she looked wildly about for Robert. Her panic eased slightly when she saw him crossing the car park toward her. She pushed open her door, her veins flooded with adrenalin.

And just as she did, Nick Thorne alighted hurriedly from his dented car. His gray Mercedes.

She froze, her mouth dropping open, keyed so tight, she thought she might scream.

"Are you all right?" In two steps, he was beside her, his face full of concern.

"Just *what* do you think you're doing?" she demanded, curling her hands into fists by her side.

"Are you all right, Miss Lake?" Robert approached, his eyes wide.

She ignored him and stared at Nick's face, catching the tension that rolled off him in waves.

"Why don't you look where you're going?" he demanded. "You could have been hurt…"

"You hemmed me in on purpose," she fumed. "Why are you following me?"

"I came to see where you were. I waited for nearly an hour."

"You had your stooge to keep you company. Get this—" she flicked her hand disdainfully toward his car, "—out of my way. I'm in a hurry." Turning, she stalked back to her car and yanked the door open.

"Oh, no, you don't!" Nick skirted around the car and grabbed her arm.

Vaguely she heard Robert offer a protest but all she could see was Nick's furious tight-lipped face.

"I'm not hanging around waiting for you, Jordan. That's the second time you've stood me up. You'd better have a damned good reason."

She tugged her arm from his grasp, desperate to get away and be with her father. "You're following me, stalking me," she said loudly for Robert's benefit. "And I want it to stop."

She slid into her car but he barred her door from closing. "What are you talking about?"

"Keep away from me, Nick!" Her demand was almost a yell. She glanced at the doorman. "I have a witness and he'll back me up. You're stalking me and I want you to leave me alone."

She gave a mighty pull on the door but he held it firm. "Request granted, and gladly." His eyes glittered like the ice in his voice. "You have much too high an opinion of yourself, Jordan Lake."

With that, he slammed her door and swiftly made his way to his car, flinging a sour look at Robert, who backed off quickly. Then he gunned the engine and sped from the car park, leaving only the tinkle and crunch of glass.

The aftershocks hit Jordan in a series of hot waves. She laid her forehead on the steering wheel, trembling with emotion. Incredibly, her anger had vanished along with Nick, and although he hadn't denied following her, the confusion in his face confused her. But she didn't have time to worry about that now. She had to get to the hospital.

Robert tapped on her window. "Your taillight's broken, Miss Lake. It'll need seeing to."

She grimaced. "Later. Robert, was that the car you saw outside the building this week, the one with the big man in dark glasses?"

Robert shook his head. "No, ma'am. It was a Mercedes, but silver, not gray."

Six

At eight-thirty on Monday morning, Nick exited his office elevator to find his brother sitting on his assistant's desk. His black mood darkened even more. "What do you want at this time of the morning?"

Noting Jasmine's flushed and suddenly busy demeanor, it occurred to him that maybe Adam wasn't here to see him at all. Scowling, he strode on into his office.

He'd spent the whole weekend stewing about the fight with Jordan—not that he had any idea what it was all about. One minute he was eagerly anticipating their lovemaking after a week's abstinence. The next, spun into a rage when she didn't turn up. Her accusations in the car park outside her building floored him and he could still hear the anger in her voice when she demanded he stay away from her.

Well, she'd got her wish. He flung his briefcase onto the desk, glad he was finished with it. Now, at least, he wouldn't have to lie about being booked up every Friday afternoon.

He hadn't even taken off his jacket when he heard Jasmine's startled "Wait!" and looked up to see the subject of his thoughts stalking in through his door. She marched straight in and flung the newspaper in her hand onto his desk.

Nick froze, his jacket half on, eyes leaping eagerly to her face. Jasmine appeared behind Jordan. "Nick, I'm sorry."

"Excuse us, please."

Jordan stood tall, her cheeks pink, eyes blazing. "What the hell are you playing at?"

With effort, Nick tore his eyes off her face and glanced down at the "Stepping Out" page of the local daily, picturing Jordan leaving the hotel. A brief caption read "Jordan Lake takes a break from the court case between her father and Randall Thorne looking glam as always in her little black dress." It was the same photo as the one that had been sent to her home. So it was a newshound after all.

But what did that have to do with him? He looked up into her face. "What am I supposed to have done now?"

"Don't give me that," she fumed. "Having me followed, watched—badly, I may say. Your goon didn't even care that I caught him."

Nick stared at her, uncomprehending.

She huffed out an agitated sigh. "The same gorilla I saw you with on Friday?"

Shaking his head, Nick finished removing his jacket and draped it over the back of his chair. "Gorilla?"

"At the hotel reception."

He eyed her while unbuttoning his cuffs and rolling his sleeves up. He'd never seen her angry before last Friday. Two minutes ago, he hadn't cared if he'd never seen or spoken to her again. Now, treacherously, his whole being warmed at the sight of her, sparks spitting from her eyes, her haughty chin raised high and mouth plump with a sullen moue. Nick was dangerously close to enjoying himself. "Jordan, what possible reason would I have to follow you?"

"I want it to stop, Nick." She leaned forward and rapped on the newspaper. "Now even my mother is asking questions, thanks to this."

She thought *he'd* sent the photo to the papers? Completely bamboozled—and worryingly exhilarated with it—he bit back a smile. The clouds that had darkened his weekend vanished in her presence, but he was astute enough to discern that if he smiled, she would probably deck him.

So he looked her straight in the eye. "Why don't you sit down and tell me about it," he suggested, doing his best not to sound patronizing. "I'll order some coffee and we'll…"

"I don't want coffee," she blurted, "and I don't want

to talk. I just want you to leave me alone." She stabbed the air between them with her index finger.

Nick started, filled with concern. There was something very wrong here. She was close to tears, more upset than he'd realized. Glistening eyes, the tremble in her voice… "Jordan…" He stepped around the desk but she whirled and made for the door.

He saw red. She couldn't just leave without giving him the chance to defend himself. He strode after her, his fingers grabbing her arm as she yanked the doorknob. "Don't you walk away from…"

"Keep away from me!" She lifted her arm to shake him. The door flew open and there was Adam, standing close, blatantly eavesdropping. Several heartbeats went by while both of them glared at him. At least he had the grace to step to the side and look contrite.

With a little huff of disgust in Adam's direction, Jordan turned her head to Nick. "In fact, keep your whole family away from mine."

Randall Thorne chose that moment to walk out of his office, stopping dead when he saw Jordan.

Jordan's eyes narrowed, all trace of her heated passionate plea lost in cool disdain. "You'll be pleased to know," she addressed the room in general, "that you won't be required in court this morning. The case has been adjourned."

Nick shot a warning look in Randall's direction in case the old man smart-mouthed her again.

"My father had a heart attack on Friday," Jordan continued. "He had an angioplasty and is still in the hospital."

Nick exhaled and took a step toward her. "Jordan…"

"Don't you dare say you're sorry," she snapped and gave each of the men in turn a bitter, recriminatory look. "Just keep away from us."

She stalked to the elevator, pressed the button and left.

No one spoke for a long moment, all eyes on the elevator. Even Jasmine looked stunned. Nick turned and walked stiffly to his desk, trying to assimilate what just happened. She thought he was stalking her, trying to blackmail her? And her father—sympathy welled up. God in heaven, what more damage could his family inflict on hers?

Adam and his father walked in. "What was *she* doing here?" Randall Thorne demanded.

Nick gave him a narrow glance. "Her father? What do you think?"

Adam cleared his throat and sat. Nick decided not to look at him, guessing his brother had heard a little more than he was entitled to.

He sat and rubbed his face briskly. "Christ, a heart attack." He felt somehow responsible and he could see on Randall's face that he felt the same. "This has got to stop, Dad."

"What did I…?"

"This bickering and fighting between you and Syrius. I don't care if you never shake hands and make up, but no more, do you understand?"

"He started this…"

"No, you started the latest outbreak by taking that award off him. He just carried it on."

"I've been insulted and slandered for years by that man. I've been the soul of patience and tolerance because your mother begged me…"

Nick raised his hand sharply and his father's voice trailed off. Come to think of it, he was just in the mood for a family conference. His blood was pumping—frustration, indignation at Jordan's wild accusations and shock about her father. And, if he was honest, the zing he got every time he looked at her…

It was time he got a few things sorted out around here. "Dad, I want you to announce your retirement at the birthday party."

His father looked up in astonishment. "Next month!"

"You'll be seventy. It's time to go."

"I'm in good health—" Randall harrumphed "—and things aren't settled yet." He cast a sideways look at Adam.

Both brothers raised their brows at their father.

"Adam hasn't decided—"

"Yes, I have, Dad," Adam cut in quickly. "And I've told you repeatedly."

"You're not on the plane yet, my boy," his father rumbled. "I want both my boys here."

"It's not going to happen," Adam stated.

Nick studied his hands. At thirty-four, the managing director of this place in all but name, he was tired of being fed crumbs and kept hanging. Of his father constantly playing him off against his brother. Nick had to show he was strong and worthy of the position. Randall valued strength above all else.

"Let's have this out right now," Nick said, leaning

back in his seat. "Face it, Dad. Adam is not coming back to Thorne's."

His father's eyes bored into him. "He would if you needed him, if you asked him."

Nick inclined his head. "Maybe. But I don't and I won't."

A sly light leapt in Randall's pale green eyes. "You jealous of your brother, Nick?"

Nick clasped his hands together, a small smile tugging at his lips. "Not at all." He flicked a glance at Adam who had the same thoughtful expression he'd worn since walking in here. "He knows that. But if you keep pushing, you'll lose him to London for good."

Nick hoped not. Adam had always said he'd settle in New Zealand eventually but for now, the lure of the world financial markets was too strong.

His father turned to Adam.

"Nick has it in one," Adam said, preempting the next salvo. "I'm doing what I want to do."

Randall's thick silvery brows knitted together. "This company is my legacy to you both…"

Nick sighed. He'd heard it all before, many times. "Are you unhappy with my performance?" he demanded, leaning forward intently.

His father blinked. "Of course not. You're doing a fine job."

"Then step aside," Nick said quietly. "Give me the recognition I deserve for running this place in all but name for the last five years."

Randall got heavily to his feet. "And do I interfere?

No! Why can't you be happy with that until Adam comes to his senses, dammit?"

Nick eyed him steadily. "Would you be?"

He knew the answer to that. Randall was a pioneer of his time. The empire he'd started was now one of the top three financial lending companies in the country, with a triple-A international credit rating and branches in all the main centers. Randall Thorne had never played second fiddle in his life.

"Not even to fulfill your mother's last wishes?" Randall had turned to glare at Adam's dark head.

Oh, he was good, Nick thought with a grudging admiration. He'd used every excuse in the book over the last couple of years. The truth was, he liked to keep an edge. Didn't want anyone getting too comfortable, too secure in their positions. Randall liked nothing better than having everyone scurrying around currying favor, vying to please him.

The old man left the office with a heavy step.

Adam stirred only when the door had closed behind him. "Good performance," he said quietly. "You weren't bad, either."

Nick leaned back, exhaling. "Am I being unreasonable?"

"Not at all. It's not like he does anything around here anymore."

"And I don't have a problem with him dropping in as often as he likes. But this is my domain now, and he's encouraged me every step of the way. He can damn well follow through."

Adam nodded. "You'll get there. But," he stood and moved to the window, "you have options, Nick."

Nick joined his brother at the window, glancing at him curiously. They were very alike, same height and coloring, although Nick was broader. He took after his father in physicality while Adam had a touch more of Melanie, slightly finer of bone, sharper facial features and fuller lips. Nick used to call him a pretty boy when they were young. He absently rubbed his nose, remembering some epic fights. Pretty Boy could pack an impressive punch, even if he was smaller.

"Maybe I'm tiring of the traveling, the women, the excitement—or it's tiring of me." Adam grinned. "I'm setting up an entrepreneurial start-up company. Savvy people with big ideas apply for funding and mentorship, but it's not just another angel investment company. I'm thinking big—global—and with some big names behind me."

"You've been watching too much reality TV," Nick said drily, but it was an interesting notion and one he'd like to hear more about. "Who are your investors?"

Adam named several captains of industry and IT. "I have my eye on a couple of big names, investors who will bring expertise and notoriety, not just money. If all goes to plan, I'll be ready to roll in the new year. But I could use a good man here. New Zealand is ripe for this type of opportunity." Adam turned to him with a glint in his eye. "It's not that different to what you do here, except that most of your clients are retirees and farmers." He approximated a yawn. "Be in on the ground floor, new innovative ideas, the future of the country."

Nick smiled, welcoming an old memory. "Remember when Dad used to bring us here on Saturday mornings before rugby? I'd watch him, listen to him talking to clients, working them. For all he's a bit rough around the edges, he knew how to treat people."

"So do you." Adam shoved his hands in his pockets. "You're just more refined."

Nick returned to his desk and sat. "Thanks, Adam. I appreciate the offer, but like you, I'm doing what I want to do."

Adam nodded. "I know. I'm just saying, you have options." He started for the door, then turned back. "Are you going to tell me what is going on between you and the Lake girl?"

Nick involuntarily glanced at the photo in the paper. His assault on Jordan's affections had hit a temporary snag with her father's heart attack. She wasn't likely to view his advances with a friendly eye while Syrius was in any danger of leaving this mortal coil.

But it was still the best option open to him, especially in light of his father's intransigence. And she was more than just a roll in the high thread-count linen of a five-star hotel. Nick hadn't even started showing her how much more.

But she would be the first to know. Meeting his brother's curious gaze, he smiled. "Nothing," he said firmly. "Nothing at all."

"Yeah, right," Adam muttered skeptically and sauntered to the door. "See you later, big brother."

Seven

"This beautiful Marlborough Sounds property for three million dollars, going once."

Nick scanned the crowd for the flash of blue silk that would give her away. He'd caught glimpses only, which probably meant she was avoiding him. It was nearly the end of the evening and he had only just arrived in time for the big item being auctioned tonight. He'd planned it that way.

"Three million dollars going twice."

A few faces close to him turned and nodded, their expressions curious and friendly. This was a media-free event, in as much as a hundred or so of New Zealand's high society could be secret. The organizer had wanted it that way. If Reverend Parsons hadn't filled him in on

Jordan's full involvement in the charitable Elpis Foundation, he'd be pretty miffed at throwing away a king's ransom just to impress a woman.

"Sold to the highest bidder."

Strangely, Nick felt little emotion for the huge outlay. No doubt his conscience would prick him tomorrow, especially when Adam or his father found out, but it was his own money he was using.

The auctioneer appeared and led him to a discreet table upfront, but to the side of the sumptuous ballroom to allow the dancing to resume. A couple of acquaintances patted his shoulder or winked as they passed but he invited no further conversation. His goal was to see Jordan.

"Please sit, Mr. Thorne," the auctioneer invited. "Can I get you some champagne?"

"No, thank you. Could you fetch Jordan Lake for me, please?"

The older man's face leaped with surprise and anticipation, but he immediately bowed his head. "Certainly. Feel free to look over the sale documents."

For the last three days, Jordan had refused to return his calls and after her performance in the car park, he was reluctant to go to her address. This morning, a wealthy client let slip that she was attending a charity auction for the Elpis Foundation. Nick recalled seeing the name in Jordan's apartment and that Russ Parsons was involved.

While he waited, he flipped through the pages of the Purchase agreement and assorted documents. Even with the real estate photographer's skill, the property looked shabby. The ad said the lodge was built at the turn of the century and still retained its "old-world charm"—another way of saying dilapidated. For one brief second, he wondered what the heck he was thinking.

But then he smelled her perfume, heard the swish of silk and the uncertainty of her voice when she spoke his name.

Nick got to his feet and stared at her for so long that the auctioneer who'd accompanied her backed off quickly. Jordan sat down stiffly.

She looked absolutely incredible. If he could recapture this moment in his mind forever and a day, he would recall every detail: the shade of her dress that matched her eyes—and the blue diamonds at her ears, he thought with a stab of triumph. Her glorious golden hair piled high with ringlets coiled around her face. The exact shade of pale pink lipstick as that which graced her fingernails, and her toenails, if he remembered correctly. The dress was a dramatic sheath of crisp silk, strapless, with a split bodice that emphasized her bust and cinched in her waistline. She was every inch the princess.

"You look lovely, Jordan," he said simply.

"Thank you. I'm—surprised to see you."

"Didn't Russ tell you? I asked him for an invitation, since mine obviously got lost in the mail."

"I didn't realize you knew him," Jordan said, smoothly ignoring his dig.

"My mother has always attended his church. He was a regular visitor to my parents' house during her illness."

Russ couldn't have been more enthusiastic with his endorsement of Jordan's many virtues. Tonight's glittering shindig she'd organized on the smell of an oily rag, begging favors all over town. Nick learned that she'd set up the Elpis Foundation with her own money a year ago. He heard all about her volunteer work at a free medical clinic and numerous other projects she had initiated.

And about her refusal to have her name associated with any of it. That interested him most of all.

He realized he was still gazing at her face when she shifted and cleared her throat.

"If you'd like to sign the contract…" she said with a pointed look at the papers on the table.

Nick sat down, giving her a smile that didn't quite reach his eyes. "Just as soon as you have the last dance with me."

She shook her head, confirming that she didn't trust him an inch—or was she worried about being seen with him? He observed that no one was paying them any attention. The orchestra was two minutes into the feisty *Die Fledermaus* and they were mostly obscured by the throng of dancers moving around the floor.

He faced her and leaned forward. "Come on, Jordan, do all your stalkers throw away a couple of mil just to impress you?"

She gave him a guarded look. "Some of my father's closest friends are here."

"I've just topped your sales for the evening. He'll understand."

"He's not well," she retorted. "And anyway, this isn't the last dance."

"Good, then you have a few minutes to explain why you think I've been stalking you."

Jordan sighed, staring moodily into the dance crowd. "You know why. The silver car. The big burly man with dark glasses, watching my building and following me everywhere." She picked up the pen, turning it over in her hands. "He gave me the creeps, staring at me all the time."

Nick decided not to point out that any red-blooded male in the world would have to be blind not to stare at Jordan Lake, especially tonight. "For someone who's made a career out of spicing up the gossip pages, you seem a little tense about some old photographer."

Her brows knitted in irritation. "It wasn't a photographer. I confronted him when he followed me into a coffee shop and he denied it—why would a newsman do that if his paper is about to run a story?"

Nick shrugged, skeptical. "What made you think I had anything to do with it?"

Jordan hesitated. "I—I remembered how you looked when you came around that night, when you thought I'd been with Jason."

"How I looked?"

She flushed prettily. "Angry. Jealous."

Nick leaned back in his seat. "And I don't have the right to be jealous, do I?" He knew he didn't. He'd given nothing of himself to this relationship, such as it was.

She looked down at the pen in her hands.

"I swear to you, Jordan, I had nothing to do with anyone following you. I was as invested as you were to keeping our meetings under wraps, especially with the court case going on. What possible reason…?"

Jordan took a deep breath. "Okay, I might have been

prepared to admit I was wrong about your involvement. And five minutes before I hit you in the car park…"

"Rammed me," he injected drily.

"You hemmed me in," she retorted. "I'd just been told of my father's heart attack. But it was seeing you with the man in the hotel that really spooked me."

"Back up. You went to the hotel on Friday?" He cast his mind back to Friday, a roaring of anticipation in his ears, fading with each passing minute, then an hour. The black rage of frustration that had him speeding over to her apartment building to have it out with her.

"Of course." She sounded surprised he would even doubt that. "I wouldn't let you down without calling."

He shook his head, confused. "I wasn't with anyone at the hotel."

The arch of one perfectly sculpted brow confirmed her skepticism. "I'd just walked into the lobby when I saw you talking to a man. You were both standing at Reception."

Nick started to deny it but her raised hand stopped him. "It was the same man, Nick. I got a great look at him in the coffee bar."

"I just picked up the key card…" Nick began, and then a memory kicked his indignation into touch.

"You were talking to him," Jordan insisted, "and then you walked to the elevators and he just stayed there, staring at you."

Nick remembered an insignificant detail. "Someone asked me the time." His mind had been so full of Jordan, he'd barely noticed the man who stood at the reception desk while he checked in. He hadn't given it another thought but in hindsight, it was a strange request considering the hotel wall behind reception had about a dozen clocks, all displaying time zones from around the world. "That was it. I told him the time and walked away."

Maybe this was something to be uneasy about after all. "Are you sure it was the same man, Jordan?"

"Yes."

"Perhaps you should call the police," he told her. "It's probably nothing, just a photographer hoping for a story, but just to be on the safe side…" He didn't want to spook her but she'd described quite a catalog of incidents. Some of it could be imagination, some less likely.

"The photo in Monday's paper was the last straw," she said gravely. "I thought you were playing some sick game."

"So you stormed into my office." No wonder she was rattled, and with her father's heart attack coming on top… He leaned forward again, resting his arms on the table. "Jordan, do you believe I had nothing to do with any of that?"

Jordan gazed at him for a long moment. She wouldn't describe herself as a great judge of character but she could see only concern and sincerity in his face— exactly what she wanted most to see. The past few days, she'd been miserable, hoping against hope there might be an alternative explanation.

His eyes reassured, soothed, seemed to see deeper into her than anyone had before. She nodded. "Yes. I'm sorry. It was just a weird couple of days."

The master of ceremonies announced that Strauss's *Wine, Women and Song* was the last dance of the evening. Nick stood and extended his hand. She rose, looking around nervously, but when he enfolded her hand in his and gave a reassuring squeeze, her reservations about her father finding out seemed trite. The man had made an enormous boost to the fund-raising coffers tonight. It would be surly to refuse him a dance.

She wanted to trust him. She'd trusted him with her body for months, and now her fears seemed silly. That aside, he was still the son of her sick father's oldest enemy. And she was afraid of risking her heart to someone who would tire of her soon enough.

They joined the other dancers on the floor and as the first notes rang out with military drama, the men bowed low to their partners. There was a lengthy introduction but at least this waltz was one of the shorter selections tonight. Jordan stood stiffly, waiting for the waltz steps to start and Nick moved close and put one big warm hand on her back.

And then she forgot everything, lost in the music she loved, the million double-quick turns and jaunty steps that he seemed to know as well as she. Jordan was a student of waltz for many years and liked to think she had inherited some of her mother's grace and ability. Nick moved well, full of confidence and purpose. Like he did everything, she thought wryly. But of course, his mother had been an outstanding dancer and teacher, too.

The music swirled, lifting her spirits, and she followed his commanding lead in perfect synchronicity, thrilled to find such a capable partner. Nothing beat the rapture of a fast Viennese waltz when two capable participants clicked on the floor.

Well, almost nothing…Nick rarely took his eyes from hers and she could see he, too, enjoyed the self-imposed discipline of being this close and yet perfectly proper. The teasing brush of his thighs, the masculine pressure of his hand at her lower back, the flat of his palm upon which her fingers rested, it all merged into a dance of restraint. How she knew was a mystery but she sensed how much he wanted to pull her close, mold her body to his. His hand wanted to close around her fingers, his other, to stroke up her back. That he managed to convey all this without a word was testament to their undeniable physical connection.

She sighed and tore her eyes from his. If the last week had shown her anything, it was that she'd become too vulnerable where he was concerned. It seemed Nick could elicit all sorts of wants and needs that she had no idea she was missing.

"Whoops, did I miss a step?"

He'd misinterpreted her sigh. She shook her head. "You dance well," she told him as the dance concluded and everyone ringed the floor and clapped the orchestra.

"My mother was determined that Adam and I could hold our own on the dance floor." He put a hand under her elbow and led her back to the table, his eyes suddenly troubled. "I'm sorry. It can't have been easy with your mother in a wheelchair."

Jordan was touched that he'd remembered, that he

cared enough, felt bad enough on his father's behalf, to mention it. "She supervised. We often watched videos together of her and your mother, the competitions."

"They were quite something," Nick agreed, pulling out her chair. But Jordan remained standing, somehow feeling she had more power that way.

How charming he could be. How strange that in nearly half a year's acquaintance, she was only just finding that out now. Not that he'd ever treated her with anything but respect, but what was his game now? What did he want from her?

The more she saw of this new Nick, the more she was being drawn in, but it couldn't be. Not now, not ever. He would find her out, find her wanting if he dug beneath the surface. And by then, she would be hopelessly in love.

And her father was ill, seriously ill. She couldn't add to that. She raised her chin. "Thank you, Nick." Picking up the pen, she held it out to him.

Nick glanced at it and then back to her face. "Am I being dismissed?"

"I have things to see to." She had to be strong, had to resist him.

He took the pen but made no attempt to use it. "You do believe that I had nothing to do with any of that last week?"

She held his gaze. "Yes. I believe you." Silently, she implored him to sign the paper. Leave while she still had a hope of saying no.

Nick's eyes bored into her, glinting with comprehension and disappointment. "This isn't over, Jordan. I want more."

Maintaining eye contact and a casual tone when every cell in her body clamored to know how much more wasn't easy. "It was fun, but it's over."

He didn't move one facial muscle but his flinty expression warned her it wasn't over, not yet. "That's it? One dance for three million dollars?"

It was like a slap with a cold fish. Charming when things were going his way, but ultimately, out for what he could get. She summoned an icy look of her own. "Why, no. You get this lovely property in a beautiful part of the country. It's an excellent investment."

The corner of his mouth lifted but his eyes were cool. "There is a condition of sale. I want you to show me the property."

Her eyes widened. "An auction is unconditional…"

"You want it sold or not?"

Damn, damn, she'd made a huge tactical error, shot her bullets too soon. "Nick, you can't go back on your word. This is for charity."

He scowled. "Are you willing to risk a bird in the hand?" He turned his head, gesturing at the queue of people lining up for their coats, the catering staff clearing empty tables, the orchestra packing up. "The evening is over. I'm your only buyer—*potential* buyer."

Her heart sank. How could she refuse with three million dollars at stake? How could she ever explain the collapse of the deal to Russ? They were counting on this money. "Why are you doing this?"

He picked up the contract and folded it. "I'm waiting."

He had manipulated her with cold, calculating

finesse. That was bad enough but how would she handle going off into the middle of nowhere alone with him?

Was it him or herself she didn't trust?

She had no choice. "If you think we're just going to pick up where we left off…" she muttered furiously. "Your three million bought this—" her fingers flicked the folded contract in his hand "—not me!"

He raised his hands. "That's your choice. Nothing will happen that you don't want."

That was cold comfort. They both knew she was incapable of resisting him once he started touching her.

"Be at Aotea Marina at eight a.m. on Saturday."

Great. She'd have to spend the three-hour ferry trip pretending she didn't know him—not that she would be talking to him. "The ferries don't leave from Aotea Marina," she said testily.

"Aotea Marina. Eight a.m sharp," Nick said firmly and tucked the contract into his jacket pocket.

Eight

"Something wrong?" Nick asked from the wheel of the Liberte 1V luxury cruiser.

Jordan closed her cell phone, frowning. They were an hour out from Wellington and her phone had just died in the middle of a text. She normally got reception most of the way across the Strait on the big public ferries.

She looked up into his questioning gaze. "One of the girls in our Outreach program has gone missing. Russ wants us to keep an eye out for her."

Letitia was fourteen. She came from a large family who'd hit hard times. They were loving and kind people who qualified for the support the church and the Elpis Foundation offered—and they gave much.

But two nights ago after a fight with her parents over

a cell phone—Letitia wanted one and they couldn't afford it—she'd left home and hadn't been heard from since.

Nick grunted. "Probably just hanging with her friends."

Jordan hoped so. In fact she could remember running away to friends to cool off herself at fourteen. But there was little comparison between the places she'd hung out and the options open to a young girl alone on the streets of Wellington.

"She came out here a couple of weeks ago. We had a Working Bee."

"At the lodge?"

Jordan broke off a little of the fluffy croissant on the plate in front of her. Nick had promised her a decent lunch on the floating palace, but for now, she was making do with coffee and still-warm croissants. "We've had a couple. Mostly picking up rubbish around the place and pulling up old carpet. Letitia had a ball and hasn't stopped talking about it, according to her parents."

"And Russ thinks she might have come back?"

Jordan sipped her coffee. "I don't see how. She has no money for the ferry, or the water taxi from Picton."

Talk of the Working Bee reminded her… "Do you mind if I bring back some stuff that we left last time? Some tools and food we were keeping for the next Working Bee. I'll bring it back today and get it out of your way."

He nodded briefly, but if he'd noticed the reference to coming back today, he didn't say anything.

Jordan had arrived at Aotea Square as instructed at eight sharp. Nick helped her aboard and then immersed himself in skippering the cruiser out of the harbor and into Cook Strait, that turbulent stretch of water linking the North and South Islands of New Zealand. He estimated the trip to their destination to be under four hours, plenty of time to make it back today.

And that was the only option, as far as Jordan was concerned. She was still miffed at his strong-arm tactics to get her here but she would play along—for now.

"Why were you holding Working Bees there when you intended to auction it off?"

"I hadn't intended to sell it at that stage. I'd planned to develop a retreat for families who never seem to have enough money to take a holiday." She felt her cheeks color. The idea seemed to have merit at the time she'd purchased the lodge, but in the cold light of day... "It was a pipe dream." She lifted her shoulders carelessly.

"Why?"

Jordan glanced at him. Nick looked like he was born on a boat. He wore tan chinos, moccasins without socks and a casual white shirt that he'd left untucked. A world removed from his suits and crisp business shirts. The breeze ruffled his dark hair, spinning it with dark gold tips. With the backdrop of the sparkling sea, his hands strong and capable on the wheel, he was master of his destiny.

And she'd do well to stop admiring his physical attributes and remember that she was here under duress. "I hadn't thought it through. Needy people don't want a holiday, they want tangible support, support they can see in their wallets and on their table. I meant well, but..." Jordan had no idea, really. How could she with her upbringing?

Nick frowned. "Doesn't sound like such a bad idea to me. Is it only the well-heeled who deserve holidays?"

"No, of course not." She lapsed into silence, feeling foolish.

"Why did you change your mind?"

"The big boy toys were a bit light."

He raised his brows.

"The auction," she qualified. "We expected a few more high-value items to put up for the charity auction. When they didn't eventuate, I thought the property might provide a draw card and fetch a good price for the coffers."

"Did you get what you hoped for?"

More time with you? The thought popped into her brain with the speed of light. That was how it had turned out but Jordan knew that wasn't what she needed. She merely nodded.

"Why all the secrecy, Jordan? Most women in your position can't wait to let the world know about the good works they do."

She knew that, but she'd also had a lifetime of people looking down on her because she was rich. "It's better that way. No one takes me seriously but this—the Foundation—is a serious business. The minute people realize that I'm involved, a lot of the support would dry up." She looked at him candidly. "For example, did you see an amusing headline about me three weeks ago? The Penny-Pinching Million-Hair-ess!"

Nick nodded. "Something to do with buying up shampoo on special."

"A woman took a picture of me with half a dozen

bottles of cut-price hair products in the supermarket. Neither she nor the rag she gave the photo to bothered to find out that I'd bought them for one of Russ's jumble sales. I often do things like that, but maybe I should cover myself in sackcloth and ashes."

"That would be a crime," he quipped, but there was genuine sympathy in his face.

She turned away from it. "I brought it on myself, the way I behaved—used to. People don't want to see me as anything other than a rich bitch."

"You're being too hard on yourself," Nick commented. "It's a lot more than most people are doing."

He was right, she supposed. Pity it had taken her so long to get a conscience.

"Tell me about Elpis. It means hope, doesn't it? Something to do with Pandora's box?"

"Technically, it was a jar," Jordan murmured, surprised at his interest. "A curse given by Zeus to punish mankind. It was entrusted to Pandora and when she opened it, all the good spirits were lost to mankind, except for hope." She shrugged self-consciously. "Something like that, anyway." Russ's interest in Greek mythology had inspired the name.

"And you set up the Foundation, financed the lot?"

Jordan nodded. There were no prizes for guessing what was going through his mind, that it was Thorne commercial real estate her trust fund was built on. Paid for by his father, so ultimately him. "Yes, it was from the trust fund that came from your father's land. But I think you know that."

"Do you think I'm after reclaiming that money, Jordan?" His tone was casual, his long considering look anything but.

She searched his face for hidden meaning, liking his directness. "No."

"Do you feel guilty about it? Is that why you give it away?"

That had occurred to her before. She had plenty of money apart from this particular trust fund. What had spurred her into suddenly developing a philanthropic streak a year ago, when this fund matured? "Do *you* think I'm guilty?"

It took a while but when it came, his smile was warm and melted her insides. "Guilty of being too good and too hard on yourself, maybe."

Too good? She wondered if anyone, especially her father, would see it that way if her torrid affair with Nick Thorne was discovered. "I'm no angel. I just have too much time on my hands."

"Did you never have any plans or ambitions of your own?" he asked.

Jordan liked art, which played right into her indulgent father's hands. A hobby rather than a career choice. "Daddy didn't exactly imbue me with a good work ethic." The sad thing was that Jordan had let him get away with that for so long. Taking his handouts, indulging in every pleasure, pleasing herself.

"Surely he could have set you up in one of his businesses somewhere."

She laughed out loud. "He doesn't believe in women

working. How he gets away without sexual discrimination charges for the lack of female employees—especially in the corporate sector—is beyond me." She glanced at him sideways. "And you are the very last person I should have shared that with."

Nick gave her another of his long, assessing looks. "I'm on your side, Jordan."

Her heart sank because something in her knew he spoke the truth. Suddenly his words at the ball the other night—I want more—took on ominous meaning. This wasn't just about sex or resuming their previous relationship. Somehow, for whatever reason, Nick Thorne wanted something more from her. And that was going to cause her heart all sorts of problems.

Jordan stayed silent, pretending he hadn't said that.

"You never wanted to get away, strike out on your own?"

"I'd miss Mom too much." That was a little twist on the truth. Syrius was a social animal whereas Elanor preferred home life. It was common knowledge he'd had a mistress for several years, but his wife and daughter always came first. The fact was, her mother would be more alone than ever if Jordan left Wellington.

It was a beautiful day with none of the bad weather and big seas that Cook Strait was famous for. Jordan asked Nick how long he'd had the big boat. He told her this was a charter.

"I had something similar but sold it three years ago. I never seem to find the time these days."

"Will you take over from your father when he

retires?" She knew her father and Randall Thorne were similar in age. Her mother made noises about Syrius retiring but Jordan privately thought they'd haul him out of his office in a body bag. That he had no son to take over from him was a source of great sorrow for her father, and something he constantly alluded to as proof of Randall Thorne's sins.

"That's what I'm working on."

She wondered why he sounded so grim, but he didn't elaborate.

After awhile, Jordan explored the plush vessel, surprised at the level of luxury on board. The stateroom was lavishly furnished, the kitchen nearly as good as hers at home, the bathrooms and hot tub inviting. To her surprise, she found two big cabins, both with beautifully decked out queen-size beds.

Jordan fully intended to ensure they got back to Wellington today but it was comforting to know she had a choice.

They weighed anchor in an inlet at the very tip of the Marlborough Sounds with the lovely name of Curious Cove. True to his word, Nick provided a fantastic picnic of chewy focaccia bread, tedaggio cheese, cold meats and crayfish. For dessert, there was a warm blackberry tart. There was wine, too, but Jordan declined, feeling she needed a clear head about her with Nick around, especially when he wasn't drinking.

After lunch, they made their way through the beautiful bays leading to the famous Queen Charlotte Sound, and finally they arrived at the jetty that led to the lodge.

"Don't expect too much," Jordan warned as she packed away the food while he prepared to tie up the boat. "No one has lived here since it went out of business seven years ago. The owner died, someone in the family contested the will and it's been tied up in an estate wrangle till I bought it two months ago."

The jetty was quaint but serviceable, but Nick's smile faded fast when confronted with the deteriorating facade of the house. Weatherboards missing or rotting away, crying out for a lick of paint, broken windows…

She quickly drew him away from the spot where the veranda sagged alarmingly, handing him the keys before he bolted.

"How often have you been here?" he asked dazedly.

"Three or four times, twice with the Working Bee." There was a tense moment when she wondered if he'd actually rip up the contract before setting a foot over the threshold. The old house was in terrible condition, but there were some lovely features inside and the setting made up for it.

They spent the first hour on the upper level and discovered the three bathrooms needed serious remodeling and plumbing. The seven bedrooms were dated but dry and she noted a little more enthusiasm from Nick when he saw the views they had to offer. From every window, hills toasted by the sun gave way to slopes of dense dark green forest, rising out of the network of sparkling waterways.

Then it was downstairs to the three living areas. There was a huge room that could almost have been a ballroom, complete with some lovely leadlight windows, all of which seemed to be intact. A smaller room with a conservatory boasted wonderful water views. Finally, the large open dining room with built-in rimu wood benches and tables, leading into the kitchen. The wall-paper was peeling, the paint on the kitchen cupboards too, but it was big and bright and airy.

Jordan moved into the kitchen, hoping their efforts last trip had eliminated the rodent problem. The large sports bag she'd left on the kitchen bench last time was open, a box of teabags sitting beside it with some of the contents spilling out onto the bench.

Funny, she could swear she'd packed everything away before leaving.

"I've seen something like this before," Nick called from the dining room.

Jordan looked up to see him gazing at the large bold mural on the wall.

She zipped up the bag, wondering which of the kids had nicked her large Tupperware container filled with biscuits.

"Something similar, anyway," Nick said, peering closely at the mural. "No signature."

Jordan felt no need to volunteer the fact that she was the artist. Drawing was just a hobby, not something she took seriously. She had been rained in on her second trip here, alone without the group. Sketching seemed a great way to pass the time, although she fully expected the wall to be painted over sometime soon.

Nick turned around. "This was in your apartment. Not this exact one," he gestured at the mural "but something similar. Same tone, a couple dancing." His face suddenly cleared. "*You* did this."

Jordan hoisted the bag. "Uh-huh." She wondered where to look for the other tools and paraphernalia the Working Bee had left.

"These are good," Nick enthused. "Do you sell them?"

"No. It's just a hobby." Jordan frowned at the sight of the old black kettle sitting on the bench. She thought she'd emptied it and set it on the gas cooker. She reached out to touch the kettle.

"How do you expect anyone to take you seriously if you don't yourself?"

Jordan didn't answer him because she was distracted by the warmth of the kettle. She spread her fingers on the belly of the vessel, frowning. "It's hot," she said, more to herself than him.

Nick came over to lean on the bench. "It's sitting in direct sunlight."

Right, and it shouldn't be. There were matches on the bench by the gas cooker. "I wonder…I could swear I packed everything in that bag before we left last time and zipped it up. And there's a big box of biscuits missing."

Nick shrugged, his interest waning. He wandered over to the huge open pantry, his nose wrinkling in distaste.

Jordan nearly smiled. Rodent droppings, perhaps, or a corpse in one of the many mousetraps she'd set.

There were no cups in the sink. If there was an intruder, they were house proud. "I'm thinking of Letitia, the missing girl."

"More likely to be a hunter or tramper. This is on the Queen Charlotte Track, isn't it?"

The Queen Charlotte Track was one of New Zealand's most popular tourist destinations, a seventy kilometer walk through lush subtropical native bush, showcasing the tranquil and stunning scenery of the Marlborough Sounds. Many thousands took to the track all year around.

"The door was locked," Jordan pointed out, unconvinced. The house seemed secure downstairs, but perhaps someone could access one of the broken windows upstairs from the crumbling exterior fire escape. She tried to call Russ to see if the girl had returned home but there was still no cell phone reception, even on Nick's phone.

"Atmospheric conditions." He shrugged.

They decided to explore the grounds. After all, that's what they were there for. But now they had an additional purpose: looking for Letitia.

They wandered the expansive and overgrown grounds for the next few hours. Nick wasn't much of a gardener but even he could see that under the neglect, this was a pearl of a property. There were treasures everywhere. Human faces carved into punga fern trunks, hammocks entwined with ivy, perishing between their supports, stone seats set in the most glorious positions to catch the late sun over the web of waterways and forested cliffs.

Jordan spotted a plastic wrapper; the brand of biscuits that were supposed to be in the Tupperware container in the kitchen. "It could have been there for ages," Nick cautioned, not wanting to get her hopes up.

"Our Working Bee went through here with forks and bags, picking up all the rubbish."

Perched on the hill behind the lodge was an old rickety chicken coop, the straw molding and smelly. And there was the empty Tupperware container, sitting in the corner.

"It *must* be Letitia."

Although Nick was skeptical, he accompanied her, clambering around the steep slopes and thick scrub high above the house, calling the girl's name.

No one answered their calls. Finally, Jordan looked at her watch and gasped with dismay. "Are we going to get home before dark?" He'd told her it was a condition of the charter that the boat be moored after dark.

"If you really think she's around here somewhere, then we'd best stay and have another look in the morning," Nick said casually as they started down the hill. "Besides, I hired the boat for two days."

Jordan stopped abruptly and turned her head. "Two days?"

Nick gazed at her unrepentant. Surely she didn't think this was just about sex, did she? His plan was to get her to himself for a while, away from the hotel room and the constant worry of discovery. He wanted to see if they clicked outside of the bedroom as well as they did in.

Anyway, this wasn't his fault. If she hadn't been adamant her runaway was here, they could have started for home two hours ago.

Jordan turned fully to face him, something close to

a pout on her lovely mouth. "And if I have plans for the evening?"

"Then he's going to be disappointed," he said evenly, absorbing the jolt he always got when she looked at him face on and close. The shape of her brows provided a perfect frame for those gorgeous almond-shaped blue eyes. Her luscious mouth with the prominent bow in the center just begged to be kissed. Beauty was in the eye of the beholder, he knew, and for Nick, he could never tire of looking at her face.

His body, too, rarely escaped the knowledge without a reaction of some kind. His mouth dried, his stomach muscles tensed. Every nerve ending sent an "I want" message to his brain.

"I didn't bring anything with me," she said curtly. "Clothes. Toothbrush."

"There are spare toiletries on board. As for clothes…" His gaze swept over her white top and long white shorts and sneakers. It was too late for them, streaked with dirt and plant matter. His own weren't much better. "I think there are robes in the bathrooms," he said innocently. Clothes were optional for what he had in mind…

Her eyes narrowed as if she read the path of his thoughts. "Well, that's worked out nicely for you, hasn't it?"

She was right, it had all worked out perfectly. The missing girl situation was an unexpected stroke of luck.

Still, he didn't want her sulking all night. "We'd have finished exploring the gardens two hours ago—plenty of time to make it home before dark—if we weren't looking for your friend," he reminded her. "Jordan, you have options. There's enough food and wine for dinner, I think. And there are two cabins on board, as I'm sure you noticed."

Nick wanted this chance for her to get to know him. It would take a major leap of trust for her to consider a public relationship with him while her father was ill. But if she thought he was really into her…Randall and Syrius had to be persuaded that further offenses would hurt their children.

As he watched her struggle with the desire to keep a cool distance between them, Nick knew he was getting under her skin. She could dictate the time frame and boundaries—to a point—but he would use the irresistible sexual connection between them to achieve his goal.

Nine

They searched the house once more, then locked up and walked back down the jetty to the boat. Jordan rubbed her arms briskly. "I hate to think about her all alone out here."

"If she's here, she'll know we're looking for her," Nick reassured her. They'd yelled themselves hoarse. "She'll come down to the boat when she gets cold or hungry."

Together they prepared a salad and the leftovers of their lunch. Nick had brought pre-baked rolls which they warmed up in the small oven in the galley. He opened the wine, his eyes following Jordan as she moved around setting utensils and crockery on the table, lighting candles. He wanted her more with each passing second, but tonight was going to be her call all the way.

The meal was simple, enhanced by the wine and the candles she'd lit. The reheated blackberry tart tasted even better than at lunch. They got through it all with an easy rapport, the wine mellowing her initial reticence.

"This is a novel experience," he commented as they finished. "Sitting across a table from you, eating and talking."

"We did that at lunchtime," she reminded him.

Nick pushed his dessert plate aside. "Will your father be in court on Monday?"

"If the doctor is happy." Jordan paused then rolled her eyes resignedly. "I spoke to him yesterday and he was looking forward to it."

"You know he's going to lose, don't you?" He wasn't being confrontational. There was little doubt about it.

Jordan nodded. "We've all told him but he's too stubborn to accept it."

"What's he like?"

She smiled fondly. "Impossible. Everything is black or white with him. He has an opinion on everything and I don't think he has ever been persuaded to change it, even in the face of irrefutable evidence."

"And you're crazy about him." Nick wondered if one day her eyes would mist with emotion for him.

"There's being crazy about him and there's driving me crazy."

Their eyes and smiles met and tangled but curiously, every time they did, Jordan would take a sip of wine. Her nervousness was unexpected.

She sat across from him in a decidedly grubby top,

her ponytail slipping and a twig in her hair. Used to seeing her light up the tabloids in designer clothing that flattered her magnificent body—or alternatively, naked on Fridays—Nick warmed at the sight of her. The sparkle in her eyes could be put down to the wine or candlelight, but he hoped he may have contributed there in some small way.

Operation Jordan was under way. "It must have been unreal growing up in that mansion as an only child." The Lake mansion in Kelburn was infamous for its grandeur.

Jordan relaxed back into her seat. "I think there was a friend roster. I don't recall being lonely at all."

"Spoiled rotten," Nick grinned. "The biggest and best birthday parties…" The ostentatious celebrations were legendary in Wellington society.

"They were insane! Clowns, animals, costumes, so much cake and sweet stuff that we'd all get hyper…the tantrums when it was all over!" She gave a mock shudder. "My poor mother. I'd make myself physically sick with the excitement of it all!"

Jordan picked up her glass again. He was going to have to carry her to bed at this rate.

He stood, picked up the bottle and topped her glass off, smiling at her. While he was there, he pulled gently at the twig tangled in her hair, handed it to her and then went back to his seat.

"It's interesting," he said as he sat. "You have the whole world at your beck and call and yet you hide behind some foundation, too scared to show yourself.

You don't want anyone to know that you have values and talent."

"I know I have those," she said, lifting her shoulders in a careless shrug, "but it's the money that makes the difference, that differentiates me from anyone else."

Nick laughed. "I must be wearing rose-colored glasses then because from where I sit, I see something else entirely."

Jordan didn't respond, toying with the twig he'd handed her.

But Nick was interested. She seemed to have everything a young woman could want. What was she afraid of? "Gorgeous," he began, smiling again when she frowned, "Talented as I can attest to, having seen some of your art…"

"Drawings," she interjected.

"Art," Nick went on, heedless. "Proactive—you're doing something that makes a difference to a lot of people."

"Lots of people do that…" She snapped the twig in half and laid it on the table, looking at it as if it personally offended her.

"Probably, but they don't hide it. Did I mention creative? That ball the other night was a work of art, if I'm any judge of things."

"You think putting on a party makes you an artist?" she asked innocently, but sarcasm laced her tone.

"Don't knock it. People go to college to learn that stuff. The skills required get you a diploma. You just get on with it and make it happen."

"Because of my money." She insisted, nodding vigor-

ously. "Do you honestly think I would have put together
that ball without my father's influence and contacts?"

She sat back as if she'd won the argument.

"The difference, Jordan, between you and most rich
people is that you use your money, you do something
useful with it."

"Oh, I've frittered away a lifetime of money,
believe me."

"I believe you," he said, grining, "but take some
credit for making up for it now."

"What was your childhood like?" she asked, twisting
the stem of her glass, moving the focus from her.

"Pretty normal. School. Rugby. Sailing. A few
family holidays."

"Were you close?"

Nick had no complaints about his upbringing. "Adam
and I were—are—I suppose. Mom and Dad—we got on
all right. They weren't very demonstrative and they
were always so busy with their respective careers. Dad
liked to pit me and Adam against each other all the
time. Everything was always a competition." He rolled
his eyes. "Still is, far as Dad's concerned."

"Who won?"

"It was about sixty-forty. I was bigger but preferred
negotiation. Adam liked to pretend he was David to
my Goliath."

Her smile faded as she gazed into his eyes over the
candlelight. Nick nearly groaned aloud. She was killing
him here, so damn beautiful, so desirable. The sexual
chemistry between them was a palpable pull, one he

wasn't used to tamping down. That was the main dis-
advantage of starting as they had started—having to
exercise self-control.

But he had to, just for a while longer. Until she
accepted that what they shared was worth the fire and
brimstone their fathers would rain down on them.

The moment lay between them like a suffocating cloud
of fizz-edged awareness, stretching for long seconds.

Finally she looked away, frowning. "I was trying to
imagine you as a boy."

Yeah, right, Nick thought. She was wondering why
he hadn't moved, leaped across the table, pushing and
demanding as he usually did when she looked as him
with naked desire in her eyes.

Your move, baby.

The silence lengthened as they stared at each other,
rocking gently in the swell of the waves lapping the jetty.

What was the deal? Jordan wondered. Didn't he want
her anymore?

Nick's smile was strained at the edges, his eyes
feverish with want. She recognized that because she
saw it every Friday when he opened the hotel door to her.

Yet he sat there, one hand spread on his thigh as he
lounged in his seat, the other on the table. Looking at
ease and yet ready to pounce.

Why wasn't he pouncing? He always made the
moves. In the time it took for them tonight to prepare
dinner, eat and then have a nice little chat, they would
normally have made love two or three times.

Was it a test of some kind? Jordan shifted in her chair, a meter away from a man bristling with sexual tension and yet concealing it—not even that. Accepting it.

What was his game?

She stood abruptly, needing some space. "Do you mind if I take a shower?"

He moved his head from side to side, his eyes hooded.

Jordan made her way to the small bathroom off the second cabin. True to his word, there were unopened toiletries, toothbrushes in their wrappers and a stack of soft white towels on the vanity. She turned the shower on and scrutinized her grubby clothes. After clambering around a dusty house and up cliff and vale, the white lacy top was a shambles and the cutoffs weren't much better. She stripped and took the top and her panties into the steaming shower with her; the cutoffs wouldn't dry before morning.

The hot blast of water was bliss after a long day. She'd drunk too fast. Nervous. He made her nervous because he was different. Holding back, even though every look told her he wanted her. The only conclusion she could make was that he wanted her to make the moves. But why?

She turned and let the water pummel her back while squeezing shower soap through her clothing. It was all so confusing. At the ball, she'd told him it was over. Now she wished they could return to sex on Fridays, where they both knew where they stood. Two unattached people sharing an amazing attraction.

That reminded her of what he'd said at the ball. *"I want more."*

She turned off the shower and grabbed a towel. Did she want more? Of course she wanted more. The idea grew and grew until it pushed everything else out of her head. More with Nick than Friday afternoons. Dating Nick. Making love with him in her apartment, his house. Talking about their day. Making plans.

She had drunk too much to be thinking along these lines. The prudent thing to do in the circumstances was to poke her head back into the saloon, wish him good-night and go to bed—alone—in the second cabin.

She rubbed the steamed mirror with a corner of the towel. Looking at herself, her naked body, reminded her of when he'd made love to her in front of the mirror at the hotel. She could see him behind her, his dark hands on her white breasts, his face above hers, eyes holding hers fiercely, compelling her to watch...unmentionable pleasure coiling through her body as he moved inside her, came with her.

Jordan flushed bright red. God, she was hot for him. He was addictive. She craved him. And trying to deny the craving, she began to justify herself. It was she who'd said they weren't going to pick up where they left off. Her rules, she could break them. Going meekly off to bed alone was going along with him, changing the direction of what was a great sexual relationship.

The best solution was to go out there and seduce him. Remind him that they were about sex. Remind him how good they were at it. Keep things on the only level she was prepared to contemplate. Because she didn't want to risk her heart, which she feared was already attached.

She dried herself, brushed her teeth and her hair, and hung her panties and top over the towel rail to dry. Then she went out to seduce Nick Thorne before he turned her head with his charm and his patience and his tests.

Jordan walked out into the stateroom wearing only a towel. He lifted his head and watched her approach, his eyes gleaming. She tried to pretend this was the Presidential Suite at the hotel on a Friday afternoon. She'd done this a dozen times…

He'd cleared the table and now sat on the sofa, holding his glass. "Shall I find you a robe?"

Jordan shook her head, confusion welling up again. Why wouldn't he just stand and take charge? Tear the towel off, put his hands on her…

"Would you like coffee?" His voice was so soft that she strained to hear him.

"Maybe later," she said huskily, moving closer. Her bare legs were just inches from where his stretched out in front of him.

"You want me, Nick?"

He moistened his lips. "You've never asked me that before."

"I've never had to."

He laid his head back on the back of the couch, watching her inscrutably. Never had she known him to exhibit so much restraint. Admirable restraint, considering the impressive bulge at the apex of his trousers.

Goose bumps rose on her arms and she shivered, the tension coiling up her insides.

"Remember our first time?" he asked suddenly, his

voice low and hard. "You trembled then, too, just like now. Were you nervous?"

She exhaled in a rush. "Just like now."

She hadn't meant to admit that.

She took a tentative step closer.

"Why?"

There was nothing in his upturned face she could read, no clue as to what he was thinking. "Because I was overwhelmed."

The back of her neck—her whole back prickled like freezer burn.

"And now?"

"Because I don't know what you want anymore." Jordan hadn't intended to say that either. But she couldn't think with his impenetrable eyes boring into her.

"I told you the other night," Nick said quietly. "I. Want. More."

Someone had switched scripts. She suddenly felt all at sea again—she nearly snorted but it wasn't funny. Desperate to regain the lead—wasn't that what he wanted?—she slipped her fingers between the folds of the towel, under the knot, peeling the sides back a little, slowly revealing what was underneath. "You can have everything."

Nick smiled then, as if to himself. "Oh, I intend to."

It sounded like a threat.

Firmly pushing her worries aside, she stepped inside his legs and sank down onto her knees before him. That got a result. Quickening breath, eyes widening and alert. The column of his throat bobbed in a hard swallow. *Got your attention now,* she thought.

She reached out and spread her hand on his groin, soaking up the heat that radiated out. The answering surge of welcome under her palm made her smile and she pressed down gently. "You want this?"

His chin dropped down to his chest. Nick always liked to watch.

"You know what I want."

She bent to her task, brushing off the niggling unease about his unaccustomed passivity, the way he answered her every question with a variation of "I want more." His arms were still, hands on his thighs, when usually he moved, directed, arranged her to his satisfaction.

Thankfully as she unzipped him, her natural instincts took over. Jordan was enthralled, turned on beyond belief. She didn't need to ask again. She knew by the fire in his eyes. The way the veins on his hands stood out, even though they appeared to be relaxed. The muscles in his upper thighs tightened with each swirl of her tongue around his swollen flesh.

She knew exactly what he wanted when she felt his hands in her hair, firmly holding her in place while he moved under her.

But then someone changed the script again. His hands tightened in her hair and he lifted her head and pulled her up over him.

Nick had never stopped her before.

It cost him. The strain on his face, a single bead of sweat crawling down his temple, told of the cost. He framed her face with his hands and kissed her, deeper and deeper, and it was somehow more intimate than her ministrations a minute ago. She felt heavy, dragged down by desire.

They kissed and kissed, cupping each other's faces, learning the shapes of their cheekbones and skulls, fingers lacing through hair. There seemed to be no urgency and neither of them closed their eyes. To Jordan, the sight of him was just so good.

His hands slid inside the still-knotted towel, stroked slowly down her body, massaging gently while they kissed. Lying on top of him, feeling him hard and wanting underneath her, she drowned in pleasure.

Maybe she'd begun by seducing him, showing him how sexy he made her feel, teasing him until he begged. But he was involved now, involving her completely, taking her under. She needed skin and squirmed to get her arms down, trying to get to his buttons. There was too much between them. She fumbled and tugged and got his shirt undone so at least she could feel his warm skin on her front, the hairs on his chest causing fantastic friction on her breasts.

Under her towel, he stroked and stroked, his hands questing and probing. She lay across him, lifting her hips. His fingers played her like music, inside and out, and she flowed into orgasm with blinding ignorance, not even realizing she was close. Her hands fisted, her knuckles pressing into his chest and for the first time since she'd walked out from the bathroom, she broke eye contact and sank into deep and shuddering satisfaction.

Soon, he slid out from under her, sitting her up, pulling her forward—this was more like it, she thought, taking charge, directing operations. All thought fled when he knelt in front of her and made love to her with his mouth.

Too sensitive to bear, she had nowhere to hide. Her hands plunged into his hair. She arched her back, fighting for breath that refused to come and then roller-coasted over her with a low keening sound that went on and on.

When it was over, she attempted to relax her stiff fingers from his hair, but it wasn't easy. "Yes," she said and her voice sounded a million miles away. The boat rocked gently on its mooring. "This. This is what I want."

Nick sat back and pulled his shirt over his head. Sated yet burning for more, she watched him strip and take care of protection. Then he pushed her down on the couch, moving purposefully over her and looked into her eyes.

"No," he said, matter-of-factly. "It's not all you want." He nuzzled her lips before raising his head again, his gaze triumphant.

She felt his tip nudge her, realized he was right.

"You just don't know it yet," he said in a voice that told her with certainty that the lesson was about to begin.

Her eyes flew wide as his hands moved up her forearms, pushing her arms above her head, lacing their fingers together.

She was tired of wondering and wanting. She just wanted him inside her. "Nick…"

He obliged. The blistering invasion, slow and strong, deep and relentless, filled her so utterly it forced the air from her lungs. He stilled, tense as a board, his hands pressing hers down into the sofa, forcing her to look at him. They gazed at each other for long seconds while he pulsed inside her, and Jordan understood. Never again could she not take this seriously. Never again could she think it was just sex.

Not just sex. Sex of the mind and body and soul. As he moved, slowly withdrawing and then sliding home again, imprisoning her eyes, she forgot everything but the wonderful warm rush of emotion that accompanied this act, this time.

Countless Fridays, countless orgasms, but never a bond so deep before. It shone from his eyes, so strong she turned her head but he wouldn't let her. It pumped through his body till she felt it in her womb and in the pulse beating through his fingers as they gripped hers. *I want more,* his eyes said as he moved, each deep thrust shattering her fears. "More," she answered him, exhilaration bursting through when he smiled down, warming her heart.

Drunk on it, she wrapped her legs around his waist as he plunged with consuming intent. The pace and intensity got crazy, the flashpoint poised, hissing, and then boiled over in a rush. He choked out her name once as she moaned her satisfaction. And she knew nothing could ever be desired again. The rush slowly ebbed. The thud of their calming breath and the occasional sound of small waves lapping the hull was all she could hear.

Still looking into her eyes, Nick slid his arms around her and held her, for the first time ever.

Ten

Jordan awoke slowly, in her customary manner. It took a few seconds to realize she wasn't alone, quite a few more to replay the night's events in her mind and think about how she felt, waking next to Nick.

They'd enjoyed many sexual adventures in the past, but last night easily qualified as the best night of her life. It was almost like a real date, spending the day together, making dinner together, talking. And then, the most emotionally-charged lovemaking she'd ever experienced. How could she even think of holding anything back? He wouldn't let her.

Nick stirred behind her with a contented growl. Jordan sighed, her erotic memories scattering. Moving an inch at a time, she began to edge toward the side of the bed but hadn't gotten far when his warm arm clamped around her middle.

"Morning," he mumbled.

Jordan mumbled a similar response.

"Where do you think you're going?" He shifted closer, his big warm body enfolding her back like a heated cloak.

She half-turned, craning her neck to see him. "Bathroom. I need to clean my teeth."

Nick lifted up on one elbow, blinking owlishly.

She squeezed her eyes shut. "You're not allowed to look at me until I've got my face on."

He tapped her on the nose until she looked at him. "I've seen you with the green goop, remember?"

Oh, God, how could she forget?

"You, Jordan Lake," he said gallantly, "don't need makeup to look beautiful."

She smiled into his eyes, thinking she could get used to waking up next to a sleepy, unshaven, tousled man whispering sweet nothings in her ear. But within seconds, his gaze sharpened and flared with heat. He shifted his body, imprisoning her under him and she felt his arousal, thick and hot against her thigh. The messages to her brain had nothing to do with vanity now.

How long before this wanes? she wondered, running her hands over his long, broad back and thickly-muscled arms? With one look, like the flick of a switch, he turned her on instantly. Her body responded, quickening, moistening. Would the time come soon when they could look at each other and resist succumbing to the most urgent and primitive desire?

Nick's hand slid under the small of her back, lifting and angling her hips, then bent and sipped at the corners of her mouth. She kissed back and decided to enjoy it while it lasted. "While we can both still walk," she murmured against his chin. He pulled back an inch, his eyes questioning. In response, she hugged him tighter, welcoming his advance, his slow, slick invasion. Welcoming him home.

An hour later, she was in the galley making coffee when she heard strange noises outside. Peeking out the porthole window, she saw her runaway sitting on the wooden jetty, hugging her knees to her chest and sniffing loudly.

"Letitia!" Jordan rushed out and sank down beside her. The poor girl sobbed with relief, nearly hysterical with nerves and cold. She wore scruffy dungarees, sneakers with no socks and only a thin hoodie.

Nick responded to her calls and they helped the teen aboard and wrapped her up in a duvet. It may have been late spring, but the sun hadn't made it over the valley yet and the air was crisp and cool. Nick set about making breakfast while Jordan sat with the girl, rubbing her frozen hands between hers.

Letitia had sneaked under the tarpaulin of a utility as it boarded the inter-island ferry in Wellington. She then walked from Picton to Anakiwa and linked up with the Queen Charlotte Track to get here, which had taken "at least a whole day." She'd eaten the biscuits and made cups of black tea from the provisions the Working Bee left in the old lodge kitchen. But the cold was her enemy.

"There was nothing to sleep in, not even any old curtains."

The Working Bee had disposed of all the moldy old drapes that had hung in the lodge for decades.

When Nick and Jordan docked, the girl hid, determined not to be discovered, but another night alone in the cold had changed her mind.

"Why didn't you answer our calls? You must have heard us." It occurred to Jordan that while she and Nick were making love here on the boat last night, this poor girl was frozen and alone. "You should have come to the jetty and called me."

Letitia wolfed down eggs and toast like she hadn't eaten in a week. Then Jordan tucked her up in the bed in the second cabin. "Poor kid," she said to Nick as they prepared to set off back to Wellington. "She just wants some attention. She's the youngest of six. Her older brothers are in and out of jail and her sister has leukemia. Her parents spend all their time either at the hospital or bailing the boys out. No one has time for Letitia."

Jordan couldn't comprehend that, coming from a one-child family, the apple of her parents' eye. She resolved to keep a much closer eye on the girl from now on.

"Told you so," Nick said lightly.

"What?"

"Sounds to me like that family needs a decent holiday, spend some quality time with their kids…somewhere nice and remote with fishing and tramping…"

Jordan felt her face color in pleased embarrassment.

He liked her idea after all. That meant a lot, even though it was no longer hers to develop.

They made good time on another amazingly calm day. After a couple of hours, Letitia appeared and helped Jordan cobble together enough leftovers to make some sandwiches. Then they sat out of the sun in the state-room, leaving Nick on deck. Since neither had gotten much sleep the night before, it wasn't long before they stretched out on the sofas and their chatting dwindled to sleepy sighs.

Jordan awoke an hour later and the city of Wellington sprawled on the horizon. Letitia was on deck, steering the powerful boat, supervised by Nick. Jordan smiled at the nice picture the two of them made. It was kind of Nick to spend time connecting with the troubled teen.

"Letitia is going to talk to Russ about letting me join the Outreach team," Nick told her, as if it was something he'd always wanted to do. Jordan grinned, thinking if only he knew what he was getting himself into.

"Nick knows some people at the Marina," Letitia enthused, "and he's going to speak to them about teaching us water sports."

"I believe I said water safety," Nick cut in, reaching across her to nudge the wheel slightly.

Jordan had never seen him so relaxed and at ease. His teeth gleamed in his tanned face and his eyes shone when they looked at her. He was so breathtakingly handsome. She imagined drawing a frame around him, depicting with fine detail everything a man should look like, should be.

As she watched him smile and tease, and the young girl's shining face as she bantered with her new hero, something warm and heady washed over Jordan, through her. The cautionary walls she'd erected to protect herself melted and seeped away. Her heart began to beat, slow and strong, so strong she could feel it in her fingertips. A giddy feeling made her wobble on her seat and grab the side.

She loved him. It was as clear and shining and joyful as Christmas. She loved him and wanted him, and all the problems that would entail were as far away as the shoreline. Still there, still beckoning, but with a lower level of importance.

Nick said something to her and she was so distracted with her newfound knowledge, she had to ask him to repeat it. He reached out and ruffled her hair and she felt his hand there for long seconds after he'd taken it away, caressing, caring, branding her as his.

Once ashore, they reunited Letitia with her grateful parents and then Nick drove Jordan home. Her stomach growled as they entered her apartment, reminding her that the meager sandwich she'd had at lunch was many hours ago. "Would you like to stay for…"

"I thought you'd never ask," Nick growled, pushing her up against the wall in the passageway. Her bag hit the deck, her clothes were roughly pushed aside. He ravaged her mouth and she soared so high, so quickly as he took her against the wall. They didn't even make the bedroom.

Nick stayed the night, waking her early to make love once more before he had to go to the office. Jordan linked her arms around his neck as he kissed her goodbye. "Aren't you forgetting something?"

He smiled and leaned forward to sear her with another kiss.

"The sales agreement?" she laughed.

"Ah." He nodded. "I'll have my lawyer witness it."

"What are you going to do with it?" Jordan asked, leaning back on her pillows, looking like Aphrodite.

"I haven't decided yet," he told her. "Maybe I'll turn it into an exclusive art gallery and exhibit some starving but brilliant artist who's got a bunch of insecurities about her work."

Her eyes shone with amusement.

"And people will come from miles around," he continued, enjoying himself, "and she'll be famous the world over."

Jordan chuckled. "Except that no one will ever know because the gallery is so exclusive, no one can find it."

"Which will add greatly to her fame, in turn, making her forever grateful to me."

Nick found he liked this, waking with someone, sex, chatter and banter before getting on with the day. The prospect of making it a permanent arrangement entered his mind. It was a win-win, as far as he was concerned. He enjoyed her company, and the sex was beyond incredible.

"Did you get around to having plans drawn up for the refurbishment?"

"As a matter of fact, I did," she said, her eyes shining.

"Give me a look at them sometime."

Jordan kissed him fervently and asked if she'd see him Friday.

Nick groaned. "Friday is eons away. I have to go to Sydney on Wednesday for a meeting, but I'll be back late Thursday." He lifted a strand of her hair, ran it slowly through his fingers. "You'll be in court today, right?"

Jordan inhaled, her expression becoming cautious. "Nick…"

He knew what she was going to say: Don't let anyone know that they were together. Not that they'd articulated anything yet… "Don't worry," he reassured her, bending for one last taste of her lips. "We'll talk about it later."

He drove to his apartment, struggling to keep the smile off his face, an alien concept to his facial muscles, he was sure. This was a watershed weekend, one which had gone exactly to plan. She was crazy about him, he saw it in her face every time she looked at him. And that was just fine by Nick. Things were moving along smoothly and he was enjoying the ride.

He showered, changed and headed in to the office, looking forward to seeing her in court in an hour or so. He wondered if anyone would guess they'd spent the weekend together, if something would show in the way he looked at her.

"I'll be back after lunch—probably," Nick told Jasmine as he left for court. Adam and Randall had gone on ahead after the court clerk had called to confirm that Syrius was fit to attend.

Leaving the office building, he noticed an eye-catching pale blue limousine parked outside. He noticed it because he'd seen it before somewhere. The driver leaned against the car but straightened when he saw him and tapped on the back window, then gestured for Nick to approach. He did so, frowning.

The back window slid down. "Hello Nick," Elanor Lake said pleasantly. "May I have a few minutes of your time?"

After a moment's hesitation, Nick got into the limo and sat opposite her, his mind racing.

Jordan definitely got her looks from her mother. Soft golden hair clouded around Elanor's face. Her skin was creamy and smooth, her clothes elegant. She regarded him in a friendly, frank manner. The driver remained outside and Elanor pressed the window control closed.

"What can I do for you, Mrs. Lake?"

"It's Elanor," she said. "And I want you to stop seeing my daughter."

He saw from her demeanor that there was no point denying it. "I would gladly do almost anything you asked of me," he said sincerely, a slight inflection on the word you; his father's guilt ran deep. "But not that."

Her facial muscles tightened and she studied him at length. "This has gone further than I thought," she said finally.

Nick wondered if it was she monitoring her daughter's movements.

"I've always liked you, Nick. I've watched you grow, followed your career. You're well known for being straight. Responsible."

He inclined his head. Her approval of him could be

helpful in the bun fight that would ensue when Syrius found out.

Elanor sat back clasping her hands in her lap. "My husband has heart disease. It's quite serious. If he finds out about this—affair—it will possibly kill him. If it doesn't kill him straight off, then he will take a gun and shoot you."

Nick pretended to give it due consideration, allowing three heartbeats to go by. "I'll take my chances, but thank you for the warning."

"You're not listening. I believe you are an honorable man. Your mother was my best friend for many years. We resumed our friendship in secret a couple of years before she died."

Nick remembered then that's where he'd seen the limo. At the cemetery on the day of his mother's funeral. The windows were tinted and he couldn't identify the occupant. The car left before the end of the interment.

"Your mother was incredibly proud of you. She said you were honest and fair-minded. Very strong without the headstrong traits of your brother. She said you could always be relied upon to do exactly the right thing."

It seemed to Nick she enunciated every syllable with great care—*do exactly the right thing*. He continued watching her steadily, waiting for her to get to the point. His family owed her a hearing.

"Nick, I've watched my husband struggle over the years to try to modify his personality, and fail to do so. I've watched him have affairs and that's all right because I can't give him what he needs, and he always comes home to me. He treats me with the utmost care and allows me my dignity by being discreet. He loves me." Elanor leaned forward, watching his face intently. "But that love pales in comparison to what he feels for his daughter. Syrius loves Jordan more than his own life."

Nick grappled with some residual familial guilt that had unfairly passed down from his father. He and Jordan should never have started…it was self-indulgent and irresponsible. But it was too late now. "Elanor, I am sorry for what my father did to you. He is sorry for what he did to you. But it's unfair to expect Jordan and me to take the rap for past mistakes."

Her eyes were bright with sharp emotion. "I lost everything in that accident. My unborn son, only three weeks from birth. The use of my legs when my greatest passion—and my career—was dancing."

Nick flinched and swallowed to clear the ball of sympathy that had closed his throat.

Elanor saw it and her mouth thinned. "Syrius will never accept this relationship, do you understand?" She raised her hand, pointing at him. "Your father took his son. He would die rather than let a Thorne have his daughter."

Nick felt the blood drain from his face. He wanted to look away but a twisted respect forced him to keep eye contact.

Elanor wasn't finished. "I will lose everything. Again. Jordan will never be able to look at you without seeing the tragedy of what will confront her beloved father, who will be either dead or in prison. Your own father will probably cut you off."

He could only stare at her. For the first time, he began to truly understand the magnitude of the battle ahead.

"And all for a sordid turn between the sheets once a week. Something you could get from anyone."

Nick inhaled. He wasn't having that. "I care for her. I believe she cares for me." He knew she did.

A ghost of a smile softened her lips for a second. "Jordan falls in and out of love every other week."

He wouldn't dignify that with a response.

Now her eyes implored him. "I beg you, Nick, on your mother's love for me, do the right thing."

He knew his facial expression hadn't changed, outwardly resolute, but it was a different story inside. Emotions that he wasn't accustomed to slammed him, one after the other. Pity for the woman in front of him. Injustice that he and Jordan should pay the price for their fathers' sins. And anger that Elanor obviously had no intention of broaching the subject with her daughter. That meant it was up to him. If he agreed to her demands, if he agreed to finish it, he was the bad guy.

He couldn't give her what she wanted. Not yet, not without a fight. Hadn't his mother been on the mark? Want something you shouldn't. Take something you have no right to. He raised his chin. "I'll talk to Jordan. *We'll* decide."

He reached for the door handle but she laid her hand flat on his arm. When he looked back, the respectful demeanor of a minute ago had lapsed into ominous regret.

"Then you leave me no choice but to take this information to your father."

Nick settled back in the seat, rallying for another blow. Randall would hate it, there was no doubt about that. He needed to prepare the ground first.

"Nick," Elanor said quietly, "you've worked hard to get where you are, yet still your father stalls about naming you as his successor." She paused, building the tension. "You being involved with the daughter of his most bitter enemy would be a big strike against you, wouldn't it? He'd wonder about your loyalty."

Nick said nothing but silently agreed. Loyalty was a favorite catch phrase of Randall's.

"One strike against you in this situation is bad enough. Two might just tip the balance."

Nick frowned. What did she mean? A fatalistic sense of foreboding stabbed him at the sympathy in Elanor Lake's eyes.

"What's the other?"

"You're not his natural son, Nick," she said quietly. "You're not even legally adopted."

Eleven

Nick drove straight home after leaving Elanor's car and took his birth certificate from the safe. His mind soared with relief. She was lying. It was a bare-faced lie by a bitter woman intent on having her own way. Obviously Syrius didn't hold all the vindictive cards in his family.

But still, something inside him continued to niggle. He drove to his parents' house and asked the house-keeper where the family photos were stored. It was a standing family joke that if it moved, his mother pho-tographed it. Nick spent hours poring through boxes and albums, searching out familial similarities. Nothing con-clusive came of it. He was bigger, broader than his brother. His facial features were thicker than either of his parents, while Adam bore a striking resemblance to his mother. Coloring and eyes were similar enough to all members of the family to reassure him.

His scant relief receded when he opened a pack marked Pregnancy and flicked through tens of snaps of his mother during pregnancy but they were all dated 1979. Adam's year of birth, not his. Feverishly, Nick went through the rest of the box but was unable to find one picture of his mother pregnant in 1975.

He drove back to the office, told Jasmine he was not to be disturbed and sat there for the rest of the day, building up a good head of steam.

Had they treated him differently? He racked his brain for childhood memories. Nick was the eldest, mature beyond his years so he got lumbered with most of the chores and was expected to keep an eye on his younger brother. Elder kids always thought their younger siblings were spoiled and he was no exception. But one thing about Adam, he followed Nick around everywhere, "helping" him, he'd say.

The bond was real between the brothers, but he wondered about his parents. They weren't the hands-on parents of modern times because they'd always put career first. Randall worked tirelessly building up his financial business while Melanie ran her dance studio six days a week. Public—or even private—displays of affection were rare.

He checked his watch for the umpteenth time. This rated as the longest day of his life. No matter how often he cautioned himself not to jump to conclusions, something told him Elanor had spoken the truth. Recent events backed it up. His mother leaving the share package to Adam, her *natural born son*. His father wanting Adam, his *natural born son*, to run the company.

The moment Randall returned from the court, Nick marched into his office, threw the birth certificate on his desk and demanded the truth. Randall insisted on knowing who he'd been talking to; when Nick told him, he blanched and did not deny it. And Nick faced the fact that up until now, his whole life had been a sham.

Two years after their marriage, the Thornes were told that they could never have children. Coming on the heels of the accident and Syrius's decree that banned Melanie from seeing his wife, Nick's mother fell into a state of deep depression. Randall, acutely aware of his business reputation, ensconced her in a luxury villa in one of Sydney's beach suburbs and commuted between Wellington and Sydney every other week.

Deeply depressed and lonely, his wife befriended a pregnant and unmarried housemaid. The next thing Randall knew, they had arranged an illegal adoption. Much money passed hands. Melanie even procured a forged birth certificate naming the Thornes as parents. Nearly a year after she'd left, Melanie returned to New Zealand with Nick in her arms. The couple maintained that he was their own miracle child. Four years later, against all odds, Melanie became pregnant with Adam.

"Did you know about this?" Nick asked Adam, who'd unwittingly walked into the tense confrontation.

"God's truth, I didn't," Adam assured him. "But it doesn't make a scrap of difference. You're my brother, Nick."

"Nor to me," his father said shakily. "Blood or not, you're my son."

"I want details," Nick declared. "Names, dates…"

"What's the point, Nick? We raised you as a Thorne, loved you from day one. Why rake it all up again?"

"Afraid you'll go to prison for fraud, not to mention buying a baby?" Nick looked at him scathingly, then immediately felt wretched. He softened his tone. "I'm going to Sydney tonight rather than Wednesday. I don't know when I'll be back. I need the address of the villa, her name, her lover—my father's—name, the dates she worked there…"

He wondered if his birth parents had ever contacted the Thornes again. Had they ever wanted to see him, or was it all about the money? Nick wondered what he was worth. "I see now why you want Adam to run the company, not me."

He heard Adam's sharp, indrawn breath, but his eyes were on his father's pale face.

"That's not true," Randall's voice implored him. "Not just Adam, not just you. Both of you."

Nick saw a world of fear in Randall's eyes. How long had he worried over this day?

Even so, he couldn't bring himself to say "Dad." Not yet.

"Nick, my feelings remain the same in regard to the company—and you." Adam lounged in his chair, seemingly relaxed but his expression was bleak, his face as pale as his father's.

Nick stood abruptly, knowing he had to get home and pack for the flight he'd booked earlier. "I'll be leaving for the airport in about two hours. Call me with those details."

"I'll come with you," Adam said quickly, rising.

Nick stopped and turned to face his brother.

Not his brother. Not even his legal adoptive brother… "This is something you can't help me with…"

"But…" Adam looked as stunned as Nick felt and it hit him a vicious blow. They were close, always had been. They even looked like each other. God's little joke… All these years, they'd believed in that blood bond, enjoyed each other's company, missed each other when they were apart. Would this revelation dent or change their relationship? How could it not?

Nick reached out and patted Adam awkwardly on the arm. "Thanks anyway, but I'd prefer to do this on my own."

Jordan left the courtroom on Monday, disconcerted about Nick's absence. When he didn't show up for the rest of the week, she began to worry. Which days had he said he'd be away? She'd been half asleep when he'd kissed her goodbye.

Calling his office was out and he didn't answer his cell phone. Not wanting to be labeled a nag, she decided against leaving a message but her unease grew with each passing day.

When he stood her up at the hotel on Friday, her

miserable confusion gave way to anger. Was he just playing with her? Surely she wasn't alone in thinking they'd forged new ground last weekend in the Sounds.

Heedless of being recognized, she inquired about the booking. "I'm sorry, the booking we have for Room 812 was cancelled on Monday," the receptionist said and looked at her with such pity that Jordan hurried out without another word, feeling quite ill.

Come to think of it, she'd felt unwell yesterday, too, but passed it off as nerves. A fleeting thought that she might be pregnant crossed her mind but she dismissed that. Nick always used protection, even though she was on the pill.

That day, she felt entitled to leave a message on his voicemail and his house phone, which also went unanswered. And even though she felt nauseous and lonely, she forced herself to go out that night to a film premiere with two friends. They bumped into Jason Cook and went clubbing. When Nick didn't call over the rest of the weekend, even after she'd left several more messages, she went out both nights and made sure she was photographed.

The trial entered its expected last week, but still Nick didn't show and her phone remained silent. Oh, why had she allowed herself to hope, to believe that she was enough for him? She would have been happy, she *was* happy knowing it was just sex, until he made her fall in love with him.

Forget him! She called Jason and a few of the party hounds she used to spend time with. It was easy to slip right back into party mode, like the Jordan of old. Club openings, premieres, she attended every glitzy occasion she could think of to court the press. Even the tummy bug that lingered didn't stop her, although she was unable to stomach alcohol. Nick Thorne had blown it, she thought angrily. No one rejected Jordan Lake! She intended to make him so jealous he'd come crawling and then, she'd kick him aside like a dog.

Only he didn't come crawling. Jordan played at being the life of the party because she dreaded going to bed. The only way she could contain the pain slicing her up inside was to curl into a ball, rocking and hugging herself hard enough to bruise her flesh. In this bed, he had made love to her, had kissed her goodbye for the last time. Unshed tears dogged her day and night, making her eyes and throat ache. What was so wrong with her that he didn't want her anymore?

One night in a crowded club, someone tapped her on the shoulder and she turned to find Adam Thorne smiling down at her.

"Are you going to have me thrown out of here as well?" he asked jovially.

Jordan responded to his friendly manner like a lifeline. They'd never had an official introduction so they remedied that now. Her friends raised their brows and whispered about how hot he was. Adam was considered one of the most eligible bachelors in the city. But she could see little of Nick in his face. There was no magic there.

She longed to ask about him but knew the hurt was

too close. Her heart may just break and bleed all over the floor. No one must see how empty and sad and hurt she was.

Adam stood behind her chair, bending his head to hear over the music. They chatted for some time about the case and their impossible fathers. "You know, I told Nick the best way to end this stupid feud is to hook up with you."

The knife in her heart twisted painfully but she managed to keep some semblance of a smile, she hoped. "Really? When?"

"When the trial started." Adam sent a huge smile of welcome to a pretty woman who'd just entered the club. Jordan recognized her as Nick's secretary.

"Nick wants to run Thorne's," Adam said distractedly. "He can't do that while the old man is around, and the old man is so busy chasing your old man around a courtroom, he won't retire."

"And what did Nick say?" she asked faintly, chewing on the straw of her drink.

Adam straightened, still looking at the woman. "Oh, Nick's way too clever to take my advice. It was nice meeting you at last, Jordan Lake. See you in court." He paused and winked at her. "I've always wanted to say that."

Jordan sat for at least a minute with the same stupid, dazed smile on her mouth, trying to make sense of it. He had a plan? A sick dread blanketed down over the misery of unrequited love in her heart.

Was it right from the start? she thought dazedly—no, Adam had said the start of the trial. That was about the time things changed between them. He'd started bringing gifts and acting jealous.

She tried to breathe but the ache inside constricted her chest. Dear God, he'd planned it all along. He didn't want her. This wasn't about them. It was a cold, calculated plan to get her to fall in love with him and realize his ambitions.

The reality twisted the knife some more, causing bile to rush to her throat. She rushed to the bathroom where she was violently sick. Someone helped her out of the club and into a cab. And the tabloids faithfully reported her incapacity the next day.

"You're certainly burning the candle at both ends, dear," her mother commented. "What on earth were you drinking?"

"I hadn't had anything," Jordan said defensively. Her mother had a knack of drawing her secrets to the fore. Her broken heart was one secret she wouldn't discuss, not with her mother or anyone else. She couldn't bear the humiliation. "I have a bug, that's all."

By day, she sat in court, staring stiffly ahead, acutely aware of the empty space across the aisle. After her fifth consecutive night out, she was exhausted and low as she could ever remember feeling. The lack of sleep and this interminable tummy bug had her head spinning, so on Wednesday night, she bought a home pregnancy test. It was just a precaution. She was ninety-nine percent certain she wasn't pregnant; surely she'd feel something—a bond, a connection—instead of just miserable and confused and god-awful sick.

The digital display on the stick flashed *Pregnant.*

No, no, no. This couldn't be happening.

When was her last period? Things had been so up in the air lately. Working bees, nosy newspapers, charity balls. Nick. Taking a deep breath, churning up with nerves, she took the second stick from the box.

She was late to court on Thursday. Her heels seemed inordinately loud on the wooden floor as she entered. Heads turned in the gallery and the judge gave her a baleful look. "Sorry," she whispered loudly.

And then she saw. He turned his head and looked straight at her, his expression cold. Scathing.

Jordan sat shakily, absorbing the rush of elation that always came with seeing his face. The emptiness inside her began to fill…but then his icy expression filtered through her joy.

Her stomach churned. What gave him the right to look at her like that? It was she who should feel aggrieved. He'd used and discarded her without so much as a word.

You have to tell him.

"Not yet," she whispered. Her mother turned and looked at her, eyes full of concern. Jordan could only shake her head mutely.

Not yet. Home pregnancy tests were not foolproof. She would say nothing until she had seen a doctor. Which doctor? She couldn't rely on the discretion of the Elpis Clinic doctors—they were all volunteers.

He'd think she'd trapped him. Worse, he'd question

whether he was the father. So many morbid thoughts surged through her brain, even as common sense told her Nick was a decent, responsible man. He'd do the right thing by her.

It was the longest morning of her life. She made it until lunchtime, then bolted for the bathroom, throwing up for the third time that week.

When she came out, Nick was about to descend the steps outside, alone. Jordan felt like death but she couldn't cope with the misery any longer. Forcing herself to stop shaking, she filled her heart with steely determination.

He'd shoved his hands in his pockets and his head was bowed. For a brief moment, as she approached, she thought he looked unhappy. But then all the tortured hours of the last week or so swamped her. He'd made her feel a failure as a woman, a lover, a friend. She wasn't about to let him off scot free. She strode up behind him, grasping his arm firmly. "I want to talk to you."

As he swung around to face her, just for a second, she saw something so uplifting, so eager in his face, as if he was glad to see her. But then the shutters came down like the night. His cold, closed expression slayed her.

This wasn't the man she knew—*thought* she knew. This was someone else entirely. She almost quailed before him and if she hadn't just lost her breakfast, that would have been a real possibility.

Nick glanced around quickly. "This isn't the time or…"

"Well, if you'd returned my calls…" Jordan felt like she was swimming in treacle. But then he grasped her arm and pulled her around the side of the building, out of sight of the trickle of people emerging from the court.

"I'm surprised you could drag yourself out of bed this morning—whose bed was it today? Do you even remember?"

Oh, that was a slap in the face. Okay, she had played the party girl this week but that was down to him.

She pried her arm out of his grasp. "What *is* it with you?" she demanded. "All over me one minute, then nothing?" Her voice rose high and shrill and she sucked in a furious breath. She didn't know him. His tight, hard face mocked her. A nasty, bilious taste rose from her chest, burning her throat.

She swayed, fear flooding her. Fear that she'd throw up right here. Fear that the next words said would be their final words ever. "I thought we had—" her voice cracked and broke "—something special."

His expression did not change. She hadn't reached him, only given him another chance to kick her. A hard little knot of anger formed. That was a mistake she wouldn't make again.

"Looks like you've been enjoying a lot of something special with a lot of men," he muttered, not looking at her as if the sight of her made him sick. "How's *Jason?*"

"Jason's just fine," she retorted. Apart from a dose of frustration, since she'd spurned his advances all week. Nick had no reason to be jealous.

"How many men, Jordan?" he asked in a deadly low voice. "How many does it take to satisfy you?"

This was too much. She had done nothing wrong!

She was the one who'd been wronged. "You have no right to ask me that," she told him angrily. "Not when it was all a lie. You used me. It was all about the job, wasn't it? Getting a promotion?"

Nick flinched and she saw she'd hit the mark. She wanted to howl with rage. "You wanted the feud finished and thought being with me would do it. All you had to do was lay on the charm and you knew I'd take it seriously, poor, gullible fool I am."

He recovered fast. "Let me tell you something, no one takes you seriously, Jordan Lake. You're just a spoiled little rich girl who dabbles in charity work with about as much feeling as you dabble in men."

Jordan saw red, buckets of it. Her gut churned with injustice. The hurt and anger rolled through her with impetus. She straightened her spine and fixed him with as imperious a look as she could muster. "Well, you better start taking me seriously, since I'm carrying your baby!"

Nick jerked back as if she'd slapped him. The blood drained from his face so quickly, a tangible dragging that left him lightheaded. He thought he heard his stomach gurgle.

Pregnant? His whole world crashed around him. On top of the week he'd just endured, this was too much. He stared at her face, her deathly pale face. Pregnant? His lips moved soundlessly, shaping the word.

"You can't be," he managed in a strangled whisper. "I always protected you."

He had. Who knew about Jason Cook? "You're on the Pill."

She stared back, eyes wide open and shocked, her lips firmly pressed together.

Nick took a step back, fighting for control. So many revelations, so many life-altering shocks, one on top of the other. But this…this was the last thing he expected.

Jordan was never far from his mind over the ten days he'd been away but between business, meeting his mother and trying to ascertain his father's whereabouts, he couldn't bring himself to call her. He was picking through an emotional minefield. With Elanor's demands that he finish it still ringing in his ears, his pedigree—or lack of—added another dimension, another burden to bear. These were things best said in person, not over the phone.

But he didn't expect to have to read about her in the newspapers and woman's magazines. Headlines leapt out at him, everywhere he went, at his mother's house, walking past bookstores in Sydney's business district, the plane on the way home. A quick trip to the Internet got him hundreds of hits on Jordan Lake's antics since he'd been away. Everyone seemed very excited about her reconciliation with Jason Cook, although apparently she wasn't limiting herself and had been seen with others. Being snapped drunk and sick with alcohol poisoning just capped it all off perfectly. She was weak, he realized, weak and self-indulgent. Not what he needed right now.

As far as Nick was concerned, Elanor Lake had done him a huge favor.

Now she stood in front of him, pale and weary from her hectic social life, telling him she was pregnant. To him?

Glancing around quickly—the ramifications if this little tidbit got out did not bear thinking about—he swung back to her, glowering.

"I want the truth right now," he gritted. "Are you pregnant—by me—or not?"

A sheen of perspiration glowed on her upper lip, lips that had drained of color. Her normally vibrant skin looked thin as tissue, but Nick clamped down on a spurt of unwelcome worry. Get the truth—and the proof—and decide what to do about it then.

She blinked quickly, opened her mouth. God help him, she looked as shocked as he felt. Even her anger would be better than this frozen-in-the-headlights look. "Well, you can't blame me for asking," he said roughly.

Her trembling mouth firmed. "You stood me up, you bastard. Not so much as a phone call. Just how long did you expect me to sit around waiting?"

The bleak wind of betrayal went through him, spreading its poison. "Poor little Jordan," he said wearily, feeling like he'd gone ten rounds with Mike Tyson. "You've just got to be the center of attention, haven't you?"

She backed off, swallowing, her eyes sliding all the way to his shoes. Her head was down, and for the first time, he noticed that her hair, her beautiful golden hair, looked lank and lifeless. A hank of it fell forward over her face. And then she looked up at him, and he reeled at the disappointment in her eyes.

"You're just like everyone else, aren't you?" Her voice held an element of surprise.

Nick wanted to rage, to put his hands on her and shake the disappointment out of her. But somehow he couldn't do anything other than glower down at this woman, this addiction he had, this spoiled, self-indulgent woman who'd filled a hole inside of him that he hadn't even known was there.

Pregnant! How ironic. Someone had gotten pregnant thirty-four years ago, but had decided money was more important than raising a child. Illegitimate, disenfranchised—he wasn't even adopted.

"Nick!" Adam called from the top of the steps. "The judge is coming back."

The verdict was expected today. Jordan hadn't even glanced up when Adam had spoken. Nick exhaled loudly. "I can't deal with this right now."

She raised her head slowly, met his eyes. He didn't want to read what was in hers.

"You don't have to *deal* with anything," she said curtly, then spun on her heel and walked away.

Nick's head rolled back and he looked skyward, feeling the anger ebb away. Now he just ached with wretched need and disappointment. She was like a drug to him, and despite everything, the withdrawal symptoms were powerful. But a drug was a drug. It pulled you down and sucked you dry. You had to kick it to survive.

Twelve

The judge gave his decision, awarding damages of five hundred thousand dollars to Randall Thorne. Everyone agreed it was a predictable outcome. Nick declined the celebratory drinks mooted and returned to the office, aware of Randall staring sadly after him.

He let Jasmine go early and poured himself a Scotch, trying to obliterate the memory of Jordan's face, twisted with anger and fear and—disappointment. In him.

Nick hated disappointing anybody. But Jordan— Jordan with the big blue eyes that reached in and touched him, connected with him on some level that no one else ever had. No matter how many times he told himself it was just an overpowering sexual attraction, he knew deep down it was real.

Having his baby…

Nick had decided weeks ago to go after her, forge a future with her to force an end to their father's feud. But this…this was definitely not what he envisaged. Not when he was only just getting his head around being illegitimate himself.

Did he believe her? Yes. She might cheat, she might make the wrong choices sometimes—Nick scowled, wanting to smash Jason Cook's face—but if she said the baby was his, it was his. She was too good a person to let him take the rap for someone else.

The Scotch slid down his throat smoothly. He listened to the sounds of the office packing up, the noises of the city down below. It rarely happened that Nick searched for answers in the bottom of a bottle. The foundations of his life had been swept away, but he was who he was. He would do the right thing by Jordan.

After all, that's what he'd wanted, eventually. Did it matter that the schedule had changed? Feud or no feud, his baby would not be born illegitimate, like him.

Randall knocked and poked his head around the door. "Son, we need to talk. There are things I should have said a long time ago."

Nick nodded toward the bottle and glasses. They hadn't spoken about their situation since his return from Australia. Now was as good a time as any.

"Nicky." His father brought his drink to the desk and sat, looking very ill at ease. Nick knew talking from the heart wasn't the old man's strong point; it never had been.

"If I've made you feel less important to me than

Adam, then I'm very sorry. It was unwittingly done. You mean just as much to me—did to your mother, too. I couldn't be more proud of you."

"I know that," Nick said gravely. "Which is why you'll cooperate when I get my lawyer to apply for a new birth certificate showing my birth parents' names." He watched Randall's cheeks hollow. "Did you know that I cannot be legally adopted in this country after the age of twenty?"

"I didn't know that."

"I doubt there will be consequences, after all this time," Nick continued, pursing his lips.

"I'll take the damn consequences," Randall interjected. "And while we're crossing the T's and dotting the i's, I'll make a new will naming you as an elected beneficiary, or whatever they want to call it."

Nick settled back in his chair.

"It's the least I can do," his father finished bleakly.

Nick studied the older man's face. It was time to press his case, once and for all. Perhaps he'd lose, perhaps he had underestimated Randall's feelings for him, but at least he'd go out trying. "It's taken me a while to figure out why you're reluctant to name me as managing director but I think I'm getting there."

His father started to interrupt but Nick stopped him. "You're afraid of being left alone. Mom's gone. Adam's in London. With this illegal adoption…hanging over your head all these years…so many years building a business that you want to live on after you're gone."

He sipped his Scotch, his gaze steady. "I may not be

your blood, Randall but I'm in this for the long haul. You've taught me—us—well. You need to have faith that you've done your job. Have I ever let you down?"

Randall shook his head at the quick question, subdued. "You never have."

"I won't leave you," Nick said firmly. "Nor will Adam. That's a promise. It's time you stopped worrying about this."

Randall was old school, brought up to keep his emotions carefully hidden. But Nick saw the love and support—for him—on his father's aged face and knew he was on the mark. "I may not be your blood, Randall," he repeated, "but I'm your best—no, I'm your *only*— option to take this place, keeping all your values and integrity intact, and grow it to pass on to my kids one day."

The old man's eyes gleamed and he suddenly found something very interesting in the bottom of his glass.

"And you'll be around to see it," Nick finished.

Randall sat for a minute, swallowing several times, his aged throat bobbing. Then he slowly got to his feet and came around to Nick's side of the desk. "Nick. Son." He extended his hand. Nick rose and they clasped hands. "I couldn't bear to lose you," his father mumbled, clapping him hard on the back in a semblance of an embrace.

Nick thought that might be the only time in his life his father had hugged him and he knew playing hardball and declaring his loyalty had been the right thing to do.

"Right, then," Randall huffed, drawing back, patting pockets, buttoning his jacket and generally doing a good impression of businesslike busyness. "You'd better start packing in here in preparation for your move to the corner office." He stepped back and raised his glass. "I'll announce it at the birthday party next week. Get yourself a new suit and bring a date."

Nick nodded. A date…since it was a day for revelations, he could do better than that, couldn't he? "Sit down, Dad. I have something else to say."

Jordan sat on the couch, leaning on Elanor's shoulder. "Do you think he'll be all right?"

Elanor nodded. "He'll appeal, just to be bloody-minded, but deep down he knew he'd lose. Even the lawyers warned him this was the likely outcome." She slipped her hand through her daughter's arm. "I'm more worried about you, rushing off like that."

Jordan heaved a heavy sigh. "I'm sorry. I just felt so ill." She hadn't been able to face going back into the courtroom after Nick's cold, hard put-down. His words his face—her throat closed and she was overwhelmed at last by the tears that had backed up for days, threatening to choke her.

She threw herself into her mother's lap and sobbed out the whole story, while Elanor stroked her hair and murmured comforting platitudes. Then, with typical pragmatism, she phoned her specialist and got Jordan an appointment immediately. "Home pregnancy kits aren't always accurate. We have to be sure."

Jordan washed her face and helped her mother into the car.

"Do you love him?" Elanor asked quietly.

That started a fresh round of crying. "With all my heart."

Mopping her face with tissues, she heard her mother sigh, and looked up. Elanor's yes were very troubled. "Oh, Jordan."

"I know. I'm spoiled and selfish, just like he said. He's the son of Dad's worst enemy, but did I let that stop me?" She shook her head miserably.

"Darling, it's not that. We can't always control these things." She took Jordan's hand. "I have a confession to make. I warned Nick off last week, insisted he stop seeing you."

Jordan's head jerked up. "How did you…?"

"I had you investigated," her mother said quietly.

Speechless, Jordan could only stare, wondering if she'd heard correctly.

"I'm sorry. Your social life until a few months ago was well documented. At least I had an idea of what was going on. But there has been no one for months, nearly a year. I just wanted to make sure you were all right. And when I found out who it was, I tried to scare him off."

"I can't believe you'd…" Jordan reeled with the revelation that her kind, sweet mother would go to these lengths. That sounded like something Syrius might do, but…another thought twisted through her over-loaded brain. "What—what did he say? Nick?"

Her mother bit her lip. "That he cared for you."

That should have elated her. It didn't. After the altercation earlier, it only intensified the ache.

"I didn't realize the extent of your feelings," Elanor

continued. "With the court case going on, your father would have exploded if he'd found out. But if I'd known how you felt about him, I would never have spoken to him...told him..." Her voice trailed off.

"Told him what?"

Her mother hesitated. "That's better coming from him. You need to talk to him."

"Except he doesn't want anything to do with me," Jordan said, sniffing. "Apart from your interference, I've spent the last week childishly trying to make him jealous. He thinks I'm sleeping with every man and his dog."

"I'm sure once he calms down and gets over the shock, he won't believe that."

The car turned into the consultant's car park. Jordan took out her compact and checked her face. "You sound almost hopeful." She grimaced at her red, swollen eyes and blotchy cheeks. If she was seen going into a private ob-gyn clinic looking like this, the press would have a field day. She tied her hair back hurriedly and slid her sunglasses on. "But the fact remains that Dad will never accept it."

"Let me deal with Syrius," her mother said grimly.

As they waited to be seen, Jordan tried to make sense of it all. If Nick had refused her mother's demands, what had happened between then and now, when he could barely look at her without disgust?

She had happened. Hurt by his silence, she had lived up to his expectations of her, as she so often did. What had he said? That she always had to be the center of attention.

The consultant took a blood test, which their on-site

lab rushed through. Less than two hours later, they returned to the car. Exhausted after the stress of the day—and of the last week or so—Jordan leaned back in the seat and turned her tear-streaked face to her mother. "Oh, Mom, it just hurts so much."

Elanor stroked Jordan's hair and wiped away her tears, her own eyes glistening.

"Can I stay with you tonight?" Jordan felt so helpless, so out of control. She needed the comfort of her old room, familiar surroundings, the arms and love and sympathy only a mother could provide.

"Of course you can," her mother murmured. "For as long as you like."

Nick tossed and turned all night, despite the whiskey sedative that should have ensured sleep. What was the matter with him? He'd achieved his goal. He would be named as the managing director of Thorne Enterprises the following week. He'd made peace with his father over his parentage and gotten to know his mother a little. Surely he had everything he wanted.

Except…the woman carrying his baby thought he wanted nothing to do with her. The pain in her eyes as he'd heaped insults and scorn upon her haunted him. He tried to justify his behavior by remembering the publicity of her partying up with her new/old lover. And she hadn't denied it—not that he'd given her much of a chance.

He should have called her; he knew that now. With her insecurities and mystifying low self-esteem, his lack of communication must have hurt. She wasn't responsible for what his personal life had served up to him. All she knew was that he'd stayed away.

The sunrise began to streak the sky with gold. Nick gave up on sleep, pulled on some track pants and sat on the step of his large, modern town house, cradling a mug of black coffee. Looking out over the easy-care garden, across the busy road that ran alongside the bay, he suddenly wondered if this house would be suitable for a child. Built on three levels, not fenced in—Lord, it was a death trap!

A baby. He allowed his mind to process the word, but found he couldn't assimilate it quite yet, couldn't conjure up a picture in his mind. But Jordan pregnant— now that was easier. She would make a beautiful mother-to-be. His mind wandered back to waking snuggled up behind her on the boat, and then he imagined his arms around her swelling middle, feeling the baby move, sharing the appointments, buying…whatever prospective parents bought in preparation for the event.

A ripple of exhilaration swept him from head to toe, and he threw his head back at the lightening sky. A baby. A chance to right the wrongs of the past. To stamp his identify on another human and show him or her that they were precious, wanted, loved.

Suddenly he could hardly wait to start sharing the experience. He had to wait, thought, since it was only five-thirty. He dragged on a T-shirt and some trainers and set off for a run along the stony beach, needing physical exertion to curb his growing elation at the thought of becoming a father.

And what of Jordan herself? He'd changed their intense and forbidden affair into another step on the ladder of his ambition. Technically, now that he had what he wanted, she was surplus to requirements. Pounding along the long stretch of beach, sweat dripping into his eyes, he asked himself the question: *if* he hadn't gone away and *if* she hadn't fallen pregnant and *if* she hadn't taken up with her former lover, would they have continued their affair, even after he'd been made managing director?

Yes. They would have. Other than their fathers' prejudices, he and Jordan were great together. The time, effort and resources she put into trying to make a difference suggested she would work hard to support his career and make their marriage and family succeed. He could help her grow in confidence and develop her foundation. Even now, as his lungs screamed, the incredible sexual pull that they shared had him wanting her more than his next breath. She was fun, kind and sexy. He felt comfortable with her and yet fiercely passionate about her.

And insanely jealous…. The storm clouds gathered in his mind as he turned for home, his steps accelerating. Nick would fight to the death to keep her. No one, neither Jason Cook nor her sanctimonious father, would keep him away from the woman he loved.

Nick rang the doorbell at the Lake mansion, filled with grim determination. Walking into the lion's den on the day after the verdict was not the most sensible thing he'd ever done, but he'd had no luck tracking Jordan at her apartment.

The Lake's housekeeper opened the door just as Elanor wheeled herself into the impressive entrance. "Thank you, Helen," she said, then dismissed the housekeeper, keeping her eyes on Nick. It may have been the early hour, but she looked strained, as if she hadn't slept.

Nick girded himself for battle. "Is she here?"

"She's upstairs. Nick…"

He hesitated, awash with relief. If she were here, her mother must know about the pregnancy. "What about Syrius? I'll need to talk to him."

"He left early to catch up now that the case is over."

Nick gave a brief nod and turned his eyes on the stairs. "Which room?"

"Second on the right. Nick…"

He paused, his jaw set with impatience.

Elanor sighed heavily, her face lined with sadness. "She's— fragile right now. Go easy on her."

Thirteen

Nick's eyes narrowed with concern. What was that supposed to mean? Morning sickness or something more sinister? He remembered her words in the car—Jordan falls in and out of love very other week. What if Elanor was trying to tell him that her daughter was in love with someone else or, worse, pregnant to someone else?

Elanor fidgeted under his gaze.

Nick needed to get those answers from Jordan herself, no one else. He knew her. She wouldn't lie about him being the father of the baby. He'd do whatever he had to, but he wasn't going to allow her to throw her life, her talent, her goodness away on a loser like Jason Cook.

He snapped off a brief nod and headed for the stairs.

As he reached the top, aware of Elanor's anxious eyes following his every step, a door opened and Jordan appeared in the hallway. They both stopped dead, staring. She wore a bright orange floral robe tied at the waist. She seemed to have lost weight. The robe clung to her as she stood, the sharp angle of her hip clearly showing through the flimsy fabric. Her hair was loose and brushed behind her ears.

She looked done in. Her eyes were pink and puffy, her lips paler than lilac. Nick stroke forward, filled with an irrational worry that she might fall if he didn't catch her, hold her up. "What is it? Are you sick?"

Her eyes widened as he approached, and she opened her mouth, but nothing came out. He reached out and ran his hand down her arm, needing to touch her, to make sure she wouldn't disappear into thin air.

Jordan shrank away, a tiny shift back that sliced at him. "What do you want, Nick? If my father…"

He shook his head, stung by her disapproving tone. "I went to your place," he began curtly.

"And naturally you assumed I was with someone else." Her surprise had cooled into sullen weariness.

"Whatever happened in the past week," Nick ground out, "we have to put it behind us."

Jordan swallowed and looked away. He imagined it was guilt making her chew her bottom lip, but then reminded himself of his purpose. The baby came first. Whatever mistakes she'd made—they'd both made— they could work on forgiving each other after he had an assurance from her that they had a future together. "I'm not blaming you, but I won't let you throw your life away on that loser."

She blinked. "You won't let me…who?"

"Jason!" he snarled, his jealousy perilously close to the surface. "Your ex—and soon-to-be ex again."

She huffed out a weary breath, shaking her head slightly. "You really believe I've been sleeping around?"

Yes. No. Hell, all he wanted was her denial.

"Haven't you noticed," she said with exaggerated patience, "that the papers don't care about true or false? If I trip over, it's because I'm drunk or on drugs. If I say hello to someone on the street, I'm engaged."

"You said yesterday—you intimated…"

"Oh, Nick." She sighed. "Can't you recognize when a woman is in love with you?"

Nick stared at her, the wind knocked completely out of his sails. She loved him. There was no one else.

Jordan stood in front of him, rocking on her heels a little. But at least some of the color was returning to her cheeks. She was still the most beautiful woman he had ever seen. Relief and elation threatened to overwhelm him.

"I didn't deny your accusations," she continued, "because you hurt me so much. You just disappeared off the face of the earth. I didn't know what I'd done. And when you looked at me like that yesterday…" Her voice broke. "Why, Nick? Why did you brush me off like I was something on your shoe?"

Nick closed his eyes against the pain darkening hers. Unfamiliar emotions slammed him. Elation that she loved him, relief that she wanted no one else, guilt for putting that pain on her lovely face. Moving purely on instinct, he reached out and took both her hands in his. "Didn't your mother tell you what was going on?"

Her hands lay limply in his. "She told me she warned you off. And that she'd had me investigated." Her voice was listless, as if declaring her love had drained her of energy.

She really looked done in. Nick pointed his chin at the door behind her. "Can we sit down?"

Jordan led him into a large, feminine bedroom. The colors were peach and sage green. The windows overlooked the rhododendron garden that the Lake mansion was quite famous for. His eyes darted to the sports and dancing trophies lining one massive bookcase, and to a clutch of photos of her at a young age, wearing ballet costumes or a net-ball skirt or a school uniform. He wanted to inspect them more closely, but she had sunk down onto an unmade queen-sized bed. As he joined her, she grabbed a pillow, hugging it to her stomach.

"I was away," he began, wary of implicating her mother in this part of it.

"Sydney." She nodded.

"I found out I wasn't Randall's son, or my mother's. I was—purchased."

Nick still couldn't believe it himself. He knew Randall and Melanie loved him, as did Adam. As for his birth mother, he'd made a start, and was grateful she'd given him up to the best possible family.

But he needed to be with Jordan. He needed her love

to make him whole. She was home to him in a way he'd never felt before.

He felt the pressure of her hand on his shoulder, warming him, as welcome as the comfort, acceptance and empathy that showed in her eyes.

"I spent ten days in Australia, tracking my birth parents. I thought of you—often—but it was just so complicated. I didn't want to get into it on the phone."

"Did you find them?" she asked after a few seconds.

"My mother, yes. Not my father, though I've got some leads I'll probably check out."

"Did you like her?"

He nodded. "She's nice, has her own family. She'd like to keep in touch." At least he'd gotten one thing clear in his mind. "She may have given birth to me but Melanie was my mother."

Jordan's hand slid off his shoulder. He missed it immediately.

"How did Randall take all this?"

"I think he's been expecting it—dreading it—for years. It's probably a relief."

Jordan looked down at her feet, swallowing. "That's huge, Nick. I wish you would have told me."

He should have, he knew that now. Maybe he was afraid that with all the barriers to them being together, his illegitimacy might be the last straw. Jordan wasn't the only one capable of holding things back.

"Nick, I need to know if you planned this whole thing so you could get a promotion."

He'd wondered when she'd get around to this. "We

met, fell into bed, kept meeting. Jordan, I lived for our Fridays. When the case started, Adam made a lighthearted suggestion that a union between us might persuade our fathers to cool it, stop with the fighting and the legal battles. That comment fell on fertile ground because I was already halfway there. It wasn't exactly a hardship," he said earnestly, taking her hands in his. "We're good together. Everything that grew out of that was real."

Her thoughtful expression gave no clue as to whether she believed him.

"Anyway, it's a moot point now. Dad's going to announce it next week. You're looking at the new managing director of Thorne Enterprises."

She smiled faintly, "Congrats."

Nick hadn't expected much enthusiasm under the circumstances, but still, he squeezed her fingers and ducked his head to peer into her eyes quizzically. "Jordan, I'm so sorry about yesterday, and the lack of communication. I never meant to hurt you."

She looked down at their joined hands. "I can't remember ever feeling so—" her shoulders rose and fell "—low."

"Hormones, I suppose," he said, thinking of the pregnancy. "This puts everything in a new light. Jordan," he said, reaching out to smooth a rogue strand of hair behind her ears. "I want our baby to be born legitimate, not like me. I want us to make a good home for him or her, a great family home...why are you crying?"

Tears began to slide down her face, and his heart did an ominous slide in his chest.

"I should never have said anything," she blurted. "Not until I was sure, but I've been sick, and the home test was positive—twice—and you got me so riled…" She tugged her hands away from his and covered her face.

He sat there stupidly, wondering what she meant, helpless in the face of her distress.

"I'm not pregnant, Nick," she said sadly from behind her hands. "I never was."

Jordan couldn't look at him, but felt his eyes on her. The sadness pressed down, making her neck ache. "Mom took me to a specialist yesterday for a blood test, and it came back negative." A shuddering sigh caught her unawares and she pressed the pillow into her stomach. "I'm supposed to go back in a couple of days for anther test, but I probably won't bother since I got my period in the night."

"But you were sick."

She shrugged, still not looking at him. "Nerves. Stress. A bug…"

They sat there for a minute in silence. She didn't want to see his relief. In reality, she should be relieved herself, having no desire to raise a baby on her own. But all she felt was a dragging grief, as if someone close had died and nothing would ever be the same again.

Nick cleared his throat. "No baby," he said, as if he still couldn't believe it. She braved a look at his face. Incredibly, he looked dazed and terribly disappointed.

Disappointed? He was off the hook. "You must be relieved."

She immediately wished the words back when he swallowed and looked away. "Relieved?" His eyes tracked slowly around each wall of the big room, an excruciatingly slow inspection, before finally coming full circle to her face again. "I don't know," he said slowly. "It's amazing how quickly I got used to the idea, even embraced the idea, of having a baby with you."

That was unexpected, although finding out recently that he wasn't who he thought he was probably had something to do with it. While she mulled that over, Nick reached out and lifted her chin, his eyes full of concern.

"How do you feel about it?"

"Sad," she whispered. She'd already told him she loved him. She didn't have to hide anything now. "It was something of you, and the most worthwhile and important part of me." She shrugged again. "So I thought, for a few hours, anyway."

Nick slid his hands up her arms and around her back to draw her close. It was a relief to hide her face in his chest, to rest against all that clean warmth and solid support. She closed her eyes.

"There'll be other babies," Nick muttered into her hair. "It doesn't change how I feel about you."

She smiled gently, remembering. "Your luxury." But she knew she couldn't go back to what they were. Everything had changed. She wanted to be worth something now. "Our Fridays are in the past," she said firmly, as if to convince herself. Would she ever feel the same burning need for anyone else? Perhaps companionship and common goals might be a safer gamble next time.

"I agree." His arms tightened around her. "But I still want to marry you."

Jordan snuggled in close, mentally saying goodbye to their Friday afternoons. Nick's words took an age to filter into her woolly brain. Lack of sleep, of food, of anything resembling sunshine since their weekend away on the boat had withered her comprehension.

Had he just said he wanted to marry her?

She leaned back a little, squinting over the crisp collar and blue silk tie, past the strong, square chin and into his piercing eyes. Her heart gave a healthy kick.

No trace of amusement sullied Nick's serious contemplation of her. Instead, he reached down and curled his fingers around her hand, squeezing gently. "I love you, Jordan, and I still want to marry you, baby or not."

Her eyes filled, and a lump the size of Gibraltar invaded her throat. She shook her head impatiently. Why cry when she'd just heard the words she wanted to hear more than anything in the world? When she lay encircled in the arms of the man she loved more than anything in the world? When the sincerity and love shone from his eyes, soothing the hurt of the past few days, giving her hope for the future? "Really?" she asked, aware of how inadequate the question was. But her mind hadn't yet cleared for takeoff.

Nick laced their fingers together and raised her hand to his mouth. "Really," he murmured. "I *really* love you, Jordan."

She shivered—delayed reaction. She could listen to those words all day.

"It was inevitable," he continued, "once I got to know you, saw how hard you tried, how generous and giving you were. So sexy, you should be illegal." He kissed her knuckles one by one. "You accepted me, although I gave you little enough. And I hate that it took me so long, and all this upset, to realize how I feel."

A bit, fat tear escaped and slid slowly down her cheek. "Oh, Nick, I love you so much, it hurts."

"Perhaps this will ease your pain." He wrapped her up in his arms and bent his head to kiss her. At the first touch of his lips on hers, she tensed, waiting for the irresistible thrill that never failed to suck the breath from her lungs and sent her heart galloping. But this was a healing kiss, a kiss to say sorry, a tender, nourishing lifeline that she never wanted to let go of. She relaxed into contentment, trying to burrow closer, loving his clean, warm scent and the strength of his arms around her.

"There is still," he told her a minute later, when he'd stopped kissing her into next week, "the matter of how your father is going to take this."

She blinked slowly, still dazed by that kiss. "Mom likes you. She's an amazing woman, my mother." Jordan couldn't quite believe Elanor had spied on her. "I'm only starting to realize *how* amazing—and exactly who wears the pants around here." She smiled up into Nick's eyes, feeling quite light-headed with happiness. Her stomach rumbled. It could be hunger. "What about your father?"

"He'll do anything to stay in my good books at the moment," he said, planting a kiss on each corner of her mouth. "I told him I was crazy about the devil's daughter. He said bring the little hussy to his retirement party next week."

"Will you protect me?" Her smile faded into pensiveness. "Wouldn't it be great if they could be friends one day?"

"They started that way," Nick said, nibbling his way around her jawline to her earlobe. "You'd be surprised at the impact a grandkid or two might have. It's our duty to work on improving relations between the two most stubborn old goats in New Zealand." He leaned back, his hands sliding from around her back to rest at the tops of her arms, holding her up. "To that end, Jordan Lake, would you marry me in the not-too-distant future? Any Friday will do."

Jordan caged his face with both hands, unable to stop a huge smile stretching her mouth wide. "Friday works for me." She leaned in and they touched foreheads, and stayed like that, smiling at each other, basking in a love that was sure to survive.

"Me, too," Nick murmured. "As long as I can have you every day in between."

Epilogue

The retirement party stepped up a notch once the formalities were dispensed with. It took Nick an age to get to the bar since everyone wanted to congratulate the new managing director along the way. He looked about for Jordan, thinking he'd barely seen her since the speeches. Randall had taken her under his wing and seemed determined to introduce her to every one of his cronies. With her tucked closely into his side, the old man practically dwarfed her slender form, in her striking, siren-red cocktail dress. He paraded her about proudly, as if she were *his* escort for the evening.

"Scotch, rocks," Nick said to the barman, and helped himself to an hors d'oeuvre from the platter on the bar. Jasmine had done an amazing job of organizing the re-

tirement-cum-birthday-cum-promotion party on such
short notice. Stunning floral arrangements and clusters
of cheery balloons lifted the small former ballroom at
the top of the Thorne building into an elegant venue, far
removed from its normal function as a conference
facility. The food and drink were top-notch, and the two
hundred guests seemed to be enjoying themselves. Nick
reminded himself to give his trusted personal assistant
a decent bonus for her efforts.

"Well, big brother, it's your night, and not before time."
Adam appeared out of the throng of people and saluted
him with his glass. Nick reciprocated, and the brothers
leaned with their backs to the bar, surveying the party.

"They look cozy," Adam commented, indicating their
father and Jordan. "When are you going to let the best-
kept secret out of the bag?"

Nick and Jordan's public relationship had sent the
press into a frenzy, coming on the heels of the court
case. Their expected engagement even had punters at the
betting agency jostling for odds. "Soon," Nick replied.
"I didn't want to steal Dad's thunder tonight."

"I suppose I'll have to come home for the wedding."

The happy couple wanted to get married as soon as
possible, but Elenor confirmed that, even though he
technically wasn't talking to them, her husband would
expect the biggest and most flamboyant wedding ever
staged in Wellington. They were doing their bit for
family relations. It just wasn't possible to organize such
a huge event before Adam left for England.

"You'll be back in the next few months, anyway."

Nick turned to Adam, but his brother wasn't listening. He was watching something or someone in the crowd. Nick followed his gaze and, sure enough, it was his personal assistant who held Adam's rapt attention.

Nick sighed. His brother hadn't taken his eyes off Jasmine all afternoon. Jordan had even commented on it. Hell, if he honestly thought Adam would ever settle down and take a woman seriously, Nick would be delighted in his choice. But Jasmine was too nice a person, and too valuable an employee, to have her heart broken by her boss's careless brother.

He took Adam's arm and turned him slightly. "I'd like to introduce you to a couple of our new corporate executives, Sandra and Melanie." He indicated two extremely attractive women in their twenties, deep in conversation by the punch bowl.

Adam didn't even look over. Jasmine had retreated to the corner of the room and slid her jacket off the back of a chair.

"I think I'll hit the road," Adam said, and drained his glass.

Nick laid a hand on his brother's arm. "Adam, you'll be gone in a day or so. Don't start anything with her."

Adam turned his light brown eyes on him. "I can give a woman a good time without breaking her heart, you know."

Nick knew there was little use in arguing once Adam's mind was made up. He was devilishly stubborn. Nonchalance might be a better weapon. "I'm only trying to keep you from making a fool of yourself. A woman like Jasmine wouldn't even give you the time of day. You're just not her type."

His brother only smiled, and giving him a look that clearly said, "Wanna bet?" Then he hightailed it toward the exit after the departing Jasmine.

Nick smelled Jordan's perfume and turned his head as a vision in red walked up to him. "I think your brother has just broken the hearts of every single female here by leaving," she quipped.

Nick gave her a rueful smile. "I should know by now that saying 'no can do' is like a red rag to a bull where Adam's concerned."

Jordan raised her brows.

Nick put his arms around her waist and pulled her in close. "Never mind. I have much more important things to think about. Such as—" he nuzzled her ear "—when can we leave?"

"Where are we going?" Jordan picked up his glass and stuck her nose into it, inhaling.

"I have a private function to attend at a certain hotel." Nick bumped their lower bodies together suggestively.

Grimacing at the smell of his Scotch, Jordan raised her eyes to his innocently. "I thought we were giving up the hotel on Fridays."

"Now why would we want to do that?"

"Because it's environmentally unfriendly, all that cleaning and polishing and lighting and so on."

Nick looked down into her shining eyes and beautiful smile, and silently thanked the Lord for cantankerous old men.

"And anyway," Jordan continued, "I spend half the week at your place and you spend the rest at mine."

"We're not married yet," Nick told his secret fiancée, "and until we are, you're my Friday mistress."

* * * * *

Turn the page for a sneak preview of

Royal Seducer
by Michelle Celmer.

*Available from Mills & Boon® Desire™
in July 2010.*

Royal Seducer
by
Michelle Celmer

Melissa Thornsby never got nervous.

She'd been raised in the pretentious and oftentimes eccentric New Orleans high society, where it wasn't all that uncommon to check one's back and occasionally find a knife or two sticking out. But that was par for the course.

After Katrina, she'd started a foundation to rebuild the city, and when she met presidents, past and present, actors, musicians and other celebrities eager to "do the right thing," it was just another day at the office.

Even when she'd learned she was the illegitimate princess of the country of Morgan Isle and made the decision to move there permanently to be with a family that was, to put it mildly, suspicious of her motives, she barely broke a sweat. She took her late mother's advice and viewed it as an adventure.

So, visiting Thomas Isle, the former rival of her native country, and meeting the royal family, really wasn't a big deal.

Until she saw *him*.

He stood on the tarmac of the small private airstrip in the bright afternoon sunshine, flanked by two very frightening-looking bodyguards and a polished black Bentley at the ready. And he was, for lack of a better word, *beautiful*. Tall, fit and well put together in a tailored, charcoal-gray pinstriped suit.

Prince Christian James Ernst Alexander, next in line to the throne of Thomas Isle. Confirmed bachelor and shameless playboy. His photos didn't do him justice.

She descended the steps of the Learjet and the prince approached, flashing her a million-watt stunner of a smile. Her heart leapt up into her throat and a curious tickle of nerves coiled in her belly. Was it too much to hope that he was to be her guide for the duration of her two-week stay? Although in her experience that task was typically left up to the princess since the crown prince was usually busy with slightly more significant tasks, such as preparing to run the entire country.

Flanked by her own equally threatening entourage— the security detail her half brother, King Phillip, insisted she have accompany her—she stepped forward to meet him halfway.

When they were face to face, he nodded his head in

greeting and said, in a voice as rich and as smooth as her favorite gourmet dark chocolate, "Welcome to Thomas Isle, Your Highness."

"Your Highness." She dipped into a curtsey, turning on the Southern-belle charm. "It's an honor to be here."

"The honor is all ours," he said with a lethal smile. Lethal because she could feel it, like a buzz of pure energy, from the roots of her hair to the balls of her feet.

He watched her intently with eyes a striking shade of green, and behind them she could see very clearly a hint of mischief and sly determination. She couldn't help wondering if he'd spent his previous life as a cat.

He noted her security detail and with one brow slightly raised, asked, "Expecting a revolution, Your Highness?"

Nodding to his own "muscle," she answered, "I was going to ask you the same thing."

If the question had been some sort of test, she could see that she'd passed. He grinned, playful and sexy, and the coil of nerves in her gut twisted into a hopeless knot. This really wasn't like her at all. Heaven knows, she was used to men flirting with her. Young and old, rich and poor, and all of them after the ludicrous trust her great-aunt and uncle had left her. But somehow, she didn't think the prince had money on his mind. He was one of the few men she'd met whose wealth exceeded her own. At least, she was assuming it did.

"The bodyguards were King Phillip's idea," she told him.

"Of course, you're welcome to keep them with you," he said, "but it's certainly not necessary."

Phillip had insisted she take the bodyguards with her, but he never said she had to *keep* them there. And call her optimistic, but entrusting her welfare to Prince Christian's staff seemed to her a valuable gesture of good faith. In the vast, stormy history of their two countries, the peace they had adopted was for all practical purposes still in its infancy. And her duty, the way she saw it, was to build on that.

"You'll see that they're flown back safely?" she asked.

He nodded. "Of course, Your Highness."

She cringed inwardly. She still hadn't grown used to the royal title. "Please, call me Melissa."

"Melissa," he said, with that sexy British accent. "I like that."

And she liked the way he said it.

"You can call me Chris. I imagine it best we drop the formalities, seeing as we will be spending a considerable amount of time together the next two weeks."

Would they? Another jolt of nerves sizzled inside her stomach. "Are you to be my guide?" she asked.

"If you're agreeable," he said.

As though she would say *no* to two weeks with a gorgeous and charming prince. She smiled and said, "I look forward to it."

He gestured to the waiting car. "Shall we go?"

She turned to her bodyguards, dismissing them with a simple, "Thank you, gentlemen."

They exchanged an uneasy glance, but remained silent. They knew as well as she did that Phillip would not be happy she'd sent them home.

Oh, well. If there was one thing her new family had learned, it was that she had a mind of her own. As deeply as she longed to be accepted as one of them, to have a real family for the first time since losing her parents, there was only so much of herself she was willing to sacrifice. At thirty-three, in many respects she was too set in her ways to change.

The prince touched her elbow to lead her to the car, and despite the layers of silk and linen of her suit jacket, her skin simmered with warmth. When was the last time she'd felt such a sizzling connection to a man? Or perhaps the better question was, when was the last time she'd let herself? This was as much vacation as business, and it wouldn't hurt to let her hair down and have some fun.

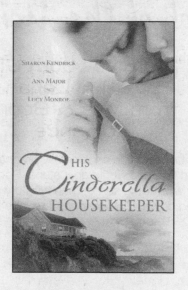

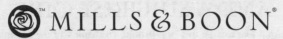

2 FREE BOOKS
AND A SURPRISE GIFT

We would like to take this opportunity to thank you for reading this Mills & Boon® book by offering you the chance to take TWO more specially selected books from the Desire™ 2-in-1 series absolutely FREE! We're also making this offer to introduce you to the benefits of the Mills & Boon® Book Club™—

- **FREE home delivery**
- **FREE gifts and competitions**
- **FREE monthly Newsletter**
- **Exclusive Mills & Boon Book Club offers**
- **Books available before they're in the shops**

Accepting these FREE books and gift places you under no obligation to buy, you may cancel at any time, even after receiving your free books. Simply complete your details below and return the entire page to the address below. You don't even need a stamp!

YES Please send me 2 free Desire stories in a 2-in-1 volume and a surprise gift. I understand that unless you hear from me, I will receive 2 superb new 2-in-1 books every month for just £5.25 each, postage and packing free. I am under no obligation to purchase any books and may cancel my subscription at any time. The free books and gift will be mine to keep in any case.

Ms/Mrs/Miss/Mr _____ Initials _____

Surname _____

Address _____

_____

_____ Postcode _____

E-mail _____

Send this whole page to: Mills & Boon Book Club, Free Book Offer, FREEPOST NAT 10298, Richmond, TW9 1BR

Offer valid in UK only and is not available to current Mills & Boon Book Club subscribers to this series. Overseas and Eire please write for details.. We reserve the right to refuse an application and applicants must be aged 18 years or over. Only one application per household. Terms and prices subject to change without notice. Offer expires 31st August 2010. As a result of this application, you may receive offers from Harlequin Mills & Boon and other carefully selected companies. If you would prefer not to share in this opportunity please write to The Data Manager, PO Box 676, Richmond, TW9 1WU.

Mills & Boon® is a registered trademark owned by Harlequin Mills & Boon Limited. Desire™ is being used as a trademark. The Mills & Boon® Book Club™ is being used as a trademark.